For Lindsay –
my sister, my supporter, my friend

ANCIENT ROYAL LINES

DAL RIATAN ROYAL LINE

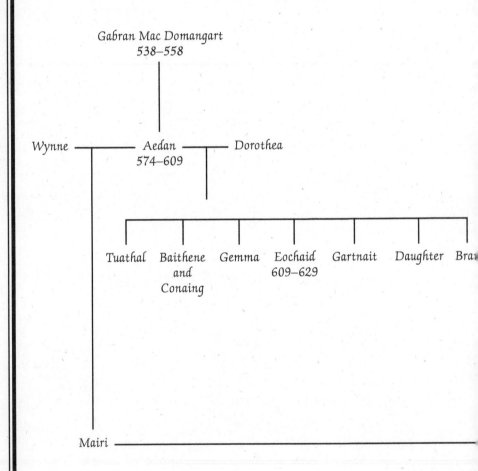

Gabran Mac Domangart
538–558

Wynne —— Aedan —— Dorothea
574–609

Tuathal Baithene Gemma Eochaid Gartnait Daughter Bra
and   609–629
Conaing

Mairi

(Dates given are dates of rule in respective kingdoms.)

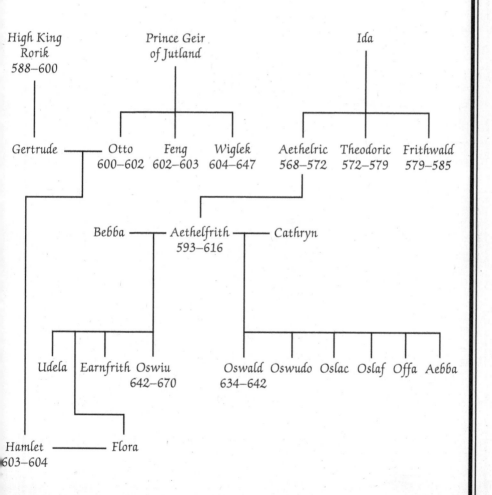

High King
Rorik
588–600

Prince Geir
of Jutland

Ida

Gertrude ——— Otto   Feng   Wiglek   Aethelric   Theodoric   Frithwald
                 600–602   602–603   604–647   568–572   572–579   579–585

Bebba ——— Aethelfrith ——— Cathryn
              593–616

Udela   Earnfrith Oswiu   Oswald   Oswudo   Oslac   Oslaf   Offa   Aebba
                   642–670   634–642

Hamlet ——— Flora
603–604

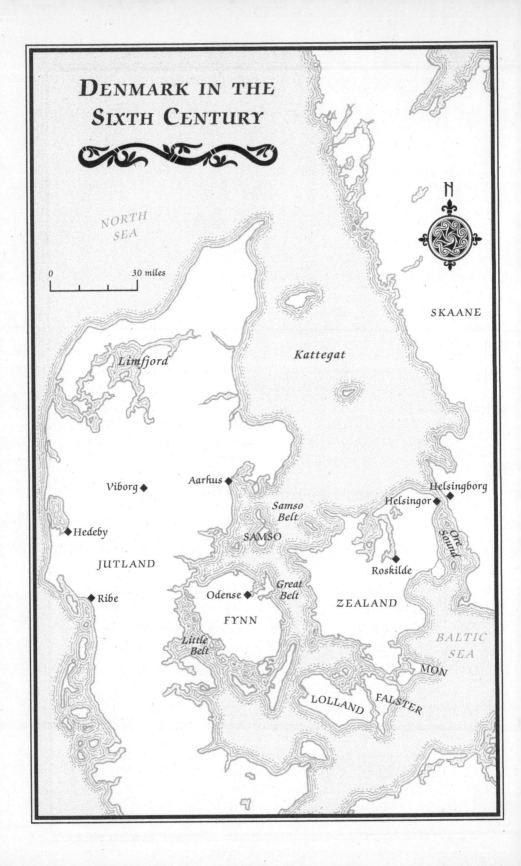

DENMARK IN THE SIXTH CENTURY

N

NORTH SEA

0   30 miles

SKAANE

Limfjord

Kattegat

Viborg ◆   Aarhus ◆

Helsingborg ◆
Helsingor ◆

Samso
Belt

◆ Hedeby

SAMSO

Ore
Sound

JUTLAND

Roskilde ◆

◆ Ribe   Odense ◆

Great
Belt

ZEALAND

FYNN

BALTIC
SEA

Little
Belt

MON

LOLLAND   FALSTER

Prologue

Aarhus, 592

It's the scream that always comes for her. It finds her in the thin time between night and day when it is too early to rise and too late to recover sleep, and it is fire-licked and blood-streaked so that all her dawns are coloured in vivid oranges and reds. They are colours she finds both exquisitely beautiful and searingly painful – just like the scream.

It is merciless. Hard as a spear-tip to pierce her heart and then soft and sinuous as a thousand serpents to chase down her blood until her body is burning with it, as her mother's body burned. And every time it comes, she can see it all again. She can picture the ship, its prow curving high into the darkening skies as it was prepared for its last noble journey to the otherworld. She can hear the crowds cheering to the gods and smell the burning brand as the druid lifts it high above her father's corpse, making the gold trim on his great cloak glitter as if beckoning the flames close.

Then she can see her mother, two steps in front of her, and it is as if she is there again. She is touching Lady Sigrid's skirt, white as the moon, and finding the rich fabric reassuringly cool as the air fills with fire. She is using her mother's body as a shield to stop her streaming eyes from drying instantly in the funeral

I

pyre's merciless heat, letting them flow freely down her cheeks instead, to soothe her grief for her father.

And then the shield is gone.

Sigrid moved so fast, as if the gods themselves had whisked her up, though Ofelia clearly saw her feet on the burning planks, saw the hem of her moon-white dress catch as she scrambled upward, and then her golden hair catch alight as she flung herself into the very centre of the inferno and onto her husband's body. And she heard the scream her mother gave, sharp as a fox's cry – agony and ecstasy – carrying up into the night, cutting through the swirling threads of smoke with its bitter glory.

The crowd gasped and the gasp gave way to a sigh at the glorious sacrifice but all Ofelia heard was the scream and all she felt was the double-heat scorching the sweet tears from her face and Lars' hand sneaking into hers as the scent of their parents' roasting flesh wafted around them.

'Is she gone?' Lars whispered.

'She's gone.'

'Who will look after me now?'

Ofelia looked for a moment to their uncle Peder, the wifeless chamberlain of Jutland who saw the precious province as his only true care, then back to her brother.

'I will, Titch.'

'And who will look after you?'

'I will do that too.'

She held his hand tighter and forced herself to stare deep into the flames as they devoured her known world. She knew then that any hope of cool, calm refuge was gone from her life and she was consigned to the heat forever. And she knew, too, that she would never subjugate herself to a man enough to cast her life away upon him like a fool. Her own shadow, unlike her mother's, would stand alone – alone and strong.

Part One

Chapter One

'May the gods take our blessed prince unto themselves!'

The priest flung his scrawny arms high to the darkening skies, silhouetting himself carefully against the flaring pyre like Odin's own raven. His insistent voice seemed to rattle at the purple clouds massing low above the funeral gathering, demanding entrance for the soul of Prince Geir, currently wreathing its way upwards on the dark curls of smoke from the furious blaze.

'May he feast with Odin in Valhalla for all eternity!' the priest exhorted, rapping his long stave one, two, three times against the hard earth, to set it quivering beneath the feet of the many gathered to see their longstanding Prince of Jutland sent to the gods.

Ofelia, watching from as far back as she could get, hoped Geir was indeed feasting with Odin and his warriors for he had been a good ruler and he deserved a merry rest, but the thought of it sent cold tendrils through her stomach despite the scorching heat of the pyre. Was Geir clinking cups with her father? Was he, even now, kissing her mother on both pretty cheeks, Lady Sigrid

5

flushed eternally pink from her final act of sacrifice at that other great funeral nine years before? And if so, where, in this land studded with endless memorials to the dead, were they actually to be found?

Ofelia shivered and looked around, hoping to escape, but all Denmark's finest were packed onto the low-lying peninsula at Aarhus to celebrate Geir's journey to the afterlife and there was no retreat open to her. The doors to the great hall stood wide open and there were as many people within as without. Most of the farm buildings were over on the mainland but guards stood on the three bridges over the river that divided off the inner sanctum to keep the mass of rapt commoners away and though they would not stop her leaving she could not face their curiosity. These were men she trained with, day in, day out. At least two of them she'd sported with when she'd ached for something harder than swordplay and she did not want their pity.

'Meat for Odin's table!' the priest shrieked suddenly, lifting a hare high in the air with one hand and drawing a thin knife with the other.

It was a fine blade, carved with elaborate whorls that caught in the firelight as if it were twitching in anticipation of the kill. The hare kicked its back legs ferociously against the old man's arm but there was god-given strength in his scrawny frame and he did not seem to notice the scratches the creature's claws carved into his flesh. He cut the hare's throat in one swift movement and held it even higher so its blood poured down, mingling with his own. The crowd gasped and then roared approval as the now limp creature was flung into the flames, landing with a wet splat on the fast-disappearing remains of Prince Geir.

Ofelia closed her eyes against the sudden image of her mother dashing into the flames nine long years ago. Sigrid had gone so lightly, as if she were simply scrambling up a hill to picnic or giggling her way into a dance. She had not looked back, not once. The hem of her dress had slipped through Ofelia's fingers as easily as her soul had slid after her husband's into the otherworld. Only that one piercing scream had told of the suffering she'd so keenly embraced.

Ofelia screwed up her eyes against the memory that tortured her but with the sickeningly tasty smell of roasting flesh on her tongue, the heat of the flames against her skin and the hiss of the crowd's disgusted delight in her ears, it would not be banished and she could only pray to the gods for this all to be over. There was, however, small chance of that.

As the flames began to drop, the mood on the island rose. The druid, his drama done, retreated to a small podium where he began beating out a fierce pulsing rhythm on a large drum. Musicians were appearing at his side as if rising up from between the mourners, their lutes and flutes drawn like weapons against grief, and a tune lifted on the air, mournful at first but gathering pace and quickening into trills and runs of joy. Prince Geir was in Valhalla and they must not grieve but celebrate.

Sol was tugging the sun down below the sea like a kind parent leaving her sons to revel unnoticed and the dancing began. Ofelia's feet, however, stayed locked against the earth as she looked for somewhere to hide. Hamlet would find her soon. He would want her to dance and she would upset him by refusing and she would rather not do that for he deserved to dance. Had he not, this very afternoon, before the as-yet-unlit pyre, been pronounced Prince of Jutland and heir to the High Kingship of all Denmark? What man would not want to dance after receiving such an honour?

And what man, she reminded herself, would lack for partners? Every eligible girl in Denmark would be pressed forward by eager mothers and fathers. Hamlet's strong arms would be full to bursting with ripe, biddable flesh so he had no need of her. He'd still come looking though.

'You will be there at the ceremony?' he'd demanded after training this morning as they'd both bent, panting, over their practice swords. 'I want you there, Lia.'

'And what of what *I* want?' she'd shot back, bracing herself for dispute.

Hamlet, however, had simply absorbed her words in his usual calm way and then asked: 'What *do* you want?'

A fool's question; though one she'd deserved.

'I want to fight.'

'Again?'

'Again.'

But he'd shaken his head.

'I cannot. Father has commanded my presence in the hall before the ceremony and I can hardly appear before the High King in a sweaty leather practice jerkin.'

'You would rather bathe than fight?'

He'd refused to rise to her jibe, as he so often, so infuriatingly, did.

'I would *rather* fight, but I *must* bathe. And you know it.'

She'd sheathed her sword, tilting the blunted blade so that it rasped loudly in the scabbard, and then bowed low.

'Well then, pretty prince, I shall not stand in your way.'

He'd rolled his eyes and grabbed her hands.

'You will be there, Ofelia?'

She'd tried to pull away but he'd held on tight. He was stronger than she was these days. The tide had turned somewhere around his fifteenth birthday when he'd suddenly shot up like a sapling in the spring sun. For a pleasing month or two more he'd struggled to control his long limbs and she'd continued to hold an advantage over him in swordplay but once he'd mastered his new height she'd struggled. She could still sometimes beat him with her speed, agility and skill but increasingly less often.

'I know funerals are hard for you,' he'd said this afternoon as she'd squirmed in his grasp.

'They are not.'

'But this is a new start for me. I will rule Jutland and you will stand at my right hand. I must have you there.'

'I am yours to command, lord prince.'

He'd groaned at her mockery.

'Would that you were. Please, Ofelia.'

The sudden catch in his voice had disarmed her far more than his grand words and she'd sighed her assent.

'I will be there, Hamlet. Of course I will be there.'

'I am glad of it.'

He'd held her for too many heartbeats longer and then let her go and she'd run from him, making for the stables and her horse, Ansgar. The stallion had needed exercise and so had she and she'd taken him far out over the moors while Hamlet had been primped and preened and dressed in the brightest Danish wool ready to be proclaimed High Prince. But she'd been at his shoulder as the slim diadem had been placed on his head and in truth she'd been glad to be a part of it. Now though, with his duties done and the dancing upon them, he was better off with a pretty girl in a gown.

Ofelia felt an ache deep inside and looked again to the guards. She'd sported with the nearest lad, Eric, a few times. He was good – hard and fast and silent, the way she liked it. She might have sworn not to give herself to any man but she'd learned early on that taking what she needed from them could help pound the screams of the dead out of her foolish brain and with Geir's damned pyre still burning high she needed that more than ever. Surely Eric's fellow guard could hold a little footbridge against a handful of gawping peasants on his own? It would not take long and perhaps, afterwards, she would be in a better mood. She might even dance.

She sidled through the crowd, taking her time as she moved past the front of the great hall towards her target, relishing the prospect of losing herself in someone else for a little while. But as she drew close, a disturbance broke out on the far side of the bridge. Two wrestling lads had knocked into a barrel of ale and it was pouring wastefully onto the dry ground. People rushed to right it whilst others turned on the lads and in an instant Eric was off across the bridge to impose his bulk on the situation.

Ofelia sighed and leaned back against one of the few trees on the peninsula. She glanced up. A low branch extended invitingly at shoulder level and in an instant she had grabbed it and heaved herself up into the V it formed with the trunk. She nestled back, feeling the bark pleasingly rough against her hot skin, and looked out over the scene.

At the far edge of the peninsula the pyre was caving in on itself as Prince Geir's ship burned through in the middle and the two high ends rolled into the heart of the flames. Sparks flew up and children chased them to the ground, stamping on them in delight, the sombre corpse already forgotten in the joy of ongoing life. Ofelia looked up to the sky and saw the prince's ashes whirling with the sparks and wondered where the gods were carrying him. The dead were all around, she knew. Their cries still pierced the air if you listened hard enough, or even if you tried not to listen at all, and sometimes she itched to track them down and silence them once and for all. But not tonight.

The druid, old and wearied by his theatricals (and no doubt uncomfortably sticky with hare's blood), had retreated with his drum but the other musicians would play all night to dance Geir firmly into Valhalla. Myriad ale barrels stood on wooden frames to one side to slake the thirst of the exuberant mourners and next to them long trestles groaned with food to help them keep up their strength.

Opposite the musicians, on a dais erected this morning by some of the younger soldiers, sat King Otto, Hamlet's father, with Queen Gertrude at his side. Hamlet's mother, an exceedingly elegant woman who was forever trying to persuade Ofelia to wear a gown and loosen her dark-blond hair from its tight braids, looked poised and at ease. Otto, in contrast, was jumping up and down to greet people, yanking them onto the dais to chat like hearth mates.

Otto was Prince Geir's younger brother but had made such a name for himself fighting in High King Rorik's army against the Norwegians that he had been granted Rorik's daughter as reward. It had been a fine honour but none had foreseen that over the next years, as the couple quietly brought up young Hamlet in the relative obscurity of Jutland, all three of Rorik's sons would be killed in battle, leaving Otto, his son-by-marriage, as his unexpected heir. When Rorik had died last year Otto had duly been raised up to the High Kingship and it was testament to his reputation and popularity at court that none had contested the appointment. He had ruled wisely ever since. Prince Geir's funeral was the first time he'd been back in his own Jutish homeland and it was clear he was delighted to be amongst old friends.

'He likes Zealand well,' Hamlet had assured Ofelia earlier, 'but Jutland is home to him.'

'And Jutland is *better*,' she'd countered, for everyone knew the Zealanders were soft, concerned more with fashions and ornamentation than with the realities of farming and fighting.

'How do you know?' Hamlet had demanded.

'I've been there too many times.'

'But only for festivals – for Walpurgis and Eostre and Yule. Everyone is a little bit mad at festival times; they are not a true reflection of life.'

'So will you go to live in Zealand once you are heir apparent?' she'd demanded, trying not to panic at the thought.

Hamlet had been her friend for as long as she could remember and her sparring partner for not much less. It was Hamlet who had been there to hold her back when her mother had dived for the flames and Hamlet who had sat stolidly at her side through the bitter months afterwards, refusing to be driven away by her snaps and hits and endless flares of temper. Aside from her little brother Lars, Hamlet was the only one in Denmark who knew and accepted her as the miserable, spiky sow she was. Life would be very dull for Ofelia if he went away.

'I will go for some of the time,' he'd agreed easily. 'And to Fyn and Lolland and Skane too, to meet their people and learn their ways. And you will come along.'

'I will?' She'd tried to disguise the hope with disapproval but her voice had just come out sounding squeaky.

'Of course. You will be my constable so I will need you with me.'

'Constable?'

'Absolutely. Lady Ofelia, Count of the Stables.'

'Cannot I be a lord instead?'

But at that Hamlet had shaken his head.

'Even you, Ofelia, cannot defy the gods. You have the body of a woman.'

There'd been a pause then, a catch even. For a moment he'd looked at her as if he was all too aware of her woman's body and she'd felt a mad impulse to gift it to him but she'd recovered swiftly and said, 'But I have the heart of a man,' and he'd bowed and reached for his sword and the crazy moment had passed. Now, however, as Ofelia saw him leap up off the dance floor to talk to his royal father on the dais, she felt her loins lurch dangerously. Why could Hamlet not be ugly? Why could he not have a twisted limb or a stooped spine or a hideous scar across his handsome face?

She forced her eyes away from him to Eric, now resuming his position on her side of the footbridge, and thought how clumsy and thickset the big man looked compared to Hamlet's lithe form. Her body ached, not just with the usual itch of dissatisfaction with the troublesome world she lived in but with a fierce, almost painful need.

'Ridiculous,' she chided herself and dug her fingers into the tree's coarse bark so as to stay rooted up there, out of harm's way.

Why not? said an unexpected voice, so loudly that she looked around for a tree sprite perched in the branches with her, but if there was such a creature nearby it lurked under a cloak of invisibility. It was persistent though: *Why not bed him? What difference would it make? It's just swordplay in another guise.* Ofelia's eyes shifted back to Hamlet, bowing low over the hand of a high-breasted young girl, and she felt a knife-prick of jealousy.

'No,' she told herself sternly.

She had vowed on her mother's ashes that she would make

herself a slave to no man and that included Hamlet, however fine his limbs.

But you've sported with plenty of others in the barracks, said the bothersome tree sprite. Ofelia hit out at the branch, hoping to knock it away, but it didn't work. *What's so different about Hamlet?*

'Nothing,' Ofelia snapped out loud. 'He's just a man.'

So treat him like one – have what you want from him and move on. Why not?

Why not? Why not? The question seemed to bounce off the now dark sky and Ofelia rubbed her back viciously against the bark. Hamlet was dancing with the girl, his eyes locked onto the inviting swell of her breasts beneath the pretty dress, and Ofelia twitched crossly at her own high-necked tunic and leather jerkin.

She looked to the sky again, searching for feisty Freya, the goddess to whom she had long since pledged her allegiance. The scudding clouds were lit from beneath by the still rampant flames and would make the perfect chariot for a goddess but she did not appear. Not that it mattered. Ofelia knew exactly what Freya would advise, for she herself lay with whomever she chose, whenever she chose, and did not trouble herself with consequences. But then, she was a goddess, not a flesh and blood woman.

Ofelia turned her eyes determinedly to Eric. He was free now the peasant folk were dispersing and he had little left to do. He could easily spare some time to rut the restless desires out of her and she knew from experience that he would not be slow to seize the chance. Men never were. She sighed. Eric wasn't exactly setting her on fire but the haunting scream was threading its way out of the land of the dead, wherever that might be, and deep into her flesh so he would have to do for now. She reached along the branch, seeking a firm grip to swing herself down, but voices from below stopped her.

'Look at them all – sycophants!'

Ofelia froze and peered down to see Hamlet's two uncles, Lords Feng and Wiglek, lurking in the shadows just a few paces away. Wiglek was gesturing disgustedly to the dais where King Otto, their elder brother, was laughing heartily at a tumbling fool some-one had brought forward.

'Can you blame them?' Feng asked. 'He's the king, Wiglek.'

'Don't we know it? He's a lucky bastard, always has been. Who'd have guessed all three of Rorik's sons would die before him?'

'Wouldn't surprise me if Otto didn't have a hand in that.'

'Me neither. Devious bastard. Remember when we were young – he always had to win, no matter what it cost.'

Both men grunted crossly and, unseen above them, Ofelia shook her head in disbelief for it was this sharp-faced pair who liked to win. She often trained alongside them in the yard and they had all the most devious tricks. Feng thought nothing of tripping a man up, or of bribing stable boys to create distractions during a competitive bout, and there were more than a few soldiers in the barracks with the mark of Wiglek's teeth in their skin. She kept herself as still as possible as they huddled tighter in against the side wall of the hall.

'And now bloody Hamlet is Prince of Jutland,' she heard Feng grumble, 'set above us both, though he is still but a boy.'

'He's not fit to step into Geir's shoes,' Wiglek snorted. 'What does he know of ruling? What about us? We've lived in Jutland nigh on forty years.'

'And been crucial to its governance for twenty.' Feng set his stocky legs a little further apart and planted his hands on his broad hips. 'I've all but ruled for the last two, with Geir fading and ...'

'*You* have?' Wiglek demanded.

'Yes, *I* have.'

Wiglek snorted.

'I'm here too, brother. And besides, everyone knows Chamberlain Peder runs Jutland.'

Feng spat into the dust.

'Peder orders the supplies and counts the beans and makes sure the cobwebs are swept away. Any fool can do that.'

Ofelia bristled at this sweeping dismissal of her hard-working uncle. She wasn't close to Peder but after their parents' deaths he had given her and Lars a home and had seen them warm and fed and trained in warfare, for which she was eternally grateful. She ground her teeth and gripped the branch tighter.

'Chamberlain Peder is just a petty lord,' Feng went on. '*I* am of the royal line.'

'As am I.'

Feng waved this away.

'You're younger than me, Wiglek. Remember that.' Ofelia squinted down to see Feng ramming a fat finger into his brother's furious face. 'If anyone deserves this throne I do, and if you had any sense you'd support me and gain yourself high office in return.'

Wiglek knocked the finger aside.

'I don't see why I should defer to you because you're one measly year older. And, besides, Hamlet has a greater claim than either of us for his mother is of the high line.'

Feng stamped his foot.

'So what's your plan then, little brother?'

Wiglek flinched.

'I don't have a "plan", Feng.'

'Which is precisely why you don't deserve any sort of advancement in life.'

'And you have a plan then, do you?'

Feng sighed in the darkness, a sound half of amusement, half dark triumph.

'Of course I have a plan.'

'What? What plan, Feng?'

Feng drew the moment out, needling his brother until his own impatience drove him to speak again.

'Remember King Aethelfrith who was in exile here some years back and married Lady Bebba of Viborg?'

'The lady you wanted for yourself?'

'I did not.'

'You did, you ... '

'Listen, Wiglek! You have to stay focused or you'll get nowhere in life. I've been in contact with Aethelfrith. He grows in power. After reclaiming his own kingdom of Bernicia he's taken the neighbouring one of Deira. He has great lands, Wiglek – great power. And he has daughters besides, daughters who are half-Dane and I warrant would like a bit more inside them!' He gave a low grunt and kicked suddenly against the wall. 'Gods, I'm always horny at wakes. It's death, Wiglek – it makes you itch to *live*.'

Up in her tree Ofelia nodded at this, the first sane thing either of Hamlet's uncles had said. The rest had been dangerous; treasonous almost. She'd have to warn Hamlet. She caught sight of him at the edge of the dancing and, as if he felt her eyes upon him, he turned and stared straight at her in the flickering firelight. With a wink, he lifted his arms towards her and instantly her body was aflame.

She glanced down. Wiglek was gone and Feng had collared a slave girl and was fumbling roughly at her skirts as he pushed her up against the hall. Ofelia swung down unnoticed and pushed through the crowds to Hamlet.

'At last,' he said, grabbing both her arms, his touch searing her skin. 'Can we dance now, Lia?'

She looked up at him, his eyes bright, his lean body close against hers. It was too much.

'We can dance,' she agreed. 'We can dance all night. But not like this, not here.'

'Do you mean . . . ?'

His eyes darkened but still he looked unsure. She took a step closer and smiled wickedly up at him.

'That's exactly what I mean.'

He hesitated just an instant longer then spun her round and dragged her, at a half run, out of the crowd.

'Then let's go. Let's go now!'

Chapter Two

They passed Eric so quickly he barely had time to raise his eyebrows.

'Where are we going?' Ofelia gasped.

She wanted to get on with it fast, before dawn brought sense crashing back in and robbed her of the glorious foolishness of whatever they were about to do.

'Somewhere quiet.'

'Why?'

Ofelia pulled Hamlet sideways, pushing him up against the wall at the back of the stables, but he held her off.

'Because I'm prince here now.'

'And that makes you too grand to sport in the woods like everyone else?'

'Nope, it just makes me foolish to put myself in a vulnerable situation. You, beautiful Ofelia, are quite distracting enough to take a man's mind off even the most obvious of sword-wielding enemies.'

Ofelia was momentarily caught off guard by the word 'beautiful' but mention of enemies drew Feng and Wiglek back to mind. It was almost a relief to have something else to think about. Almost.

'Hamlet, I have to talk to you about your uncles.'

'Now?'

His dismay was so comical she smiled.

'No. Not now.'

She reached for his trews but he surprised her by spinning her round and pinning her tight against the wall.

'Not so fast. This is too good to rush.'

'But I might change my mind.'

'You won't.'

He leaned in and covered her mouth with his own and she knew, with shuddering certainty, that he was right. No one had truly kissed her before, not as Hamlet was kissing her, and his lingering intent disarmed her.

'Take me,' she whispered when he finally pulled back.

'Oh, I will, but I told you: not here.'

He took her hand and pulled and she felt herself following blindly like some fool girl.

'Hamlet . . .'

'In here.' He shoved open the door to the stables and tugged her inside. 'There's a stall free at the end now that Geir's horse has ridden into the afterlife beneath him.'

Ofelia shuddered at the memory. The horse had had its throat slit long before the hare. It had been done with more dignity but its blood had poured out every bit as fast as it had sunk to its knees, eyes staring wildly into the afterlife, and died. It had taken six men to lay the beast beside Geir's body in the ship to accompany him to Valhalla but no one could go into death alone – though they could, it seemed, be left so in life. Images of her mother's last moments flickered at the edges of Ofelia's mind and she made a grab for Hamlet, thrusting him into the little stall and down on his back in the straw as she straddled him.

'Where do you think the dead go, Hamlet?'

'What?'

He blinked up at her, his hands frozen at her waist.

'Where do they go? Where is Valhalla?'

'In Asgard, of course, the land of the gods.'

He tried to pull her towards him, but she resisted.

'But where is Asgard? Is it below the earth, think you? Are there gateways to it from all the barrow graves? And if so, why do we burn people? How will they find joy in the insubstantial air if the gods are feasting below ground?'

Hamlet groaned.

'I know not, Ofelia, truly, and care less. Why worry where the dead are when we are here, together?'

He pulled harder and she fell against him, his hands running up and down her back, sending her mother, thank the gods, dancing away. She cried out with the pleasure of his touch and he responded with a groan of his own that pulsed through her body. She scrambled to her feet to remove her breeches but now he was sitting up and his hands were on her bare thighs as he held her still.

'Take your time.'

'Why?'

'I want to see you.'

'You see me all the time.'

'Not like this.'

He rose, stepping unselfconsciously out of his trews and reaching for her tunic.

'Too slow,' she moaned.

'No rush,' he countered, lifting the fine fabric over her head and dipping his mouth to her breasts – and, oh, gods, it felt so good.

She arched, willing him to get on and pound away the perpetual itch inside her, but instead he stepped back and let his fingers trail over her stomach, across her hips and on down her legs before he stood back to take her in. She was naked before him, the dying light of the prince's pyre playing across her body through the window, and she instinctively put up her hands. But then, despising herself for her timidity, she whipped them away, dropped her weight onto one hip and set her back straight so that her breasts jutted out. She was rewarded by a low groan of appreciation.

'Like what you see, Prince?'

'It's all I have dreamed of . . . and more.'

The answer set an alarum buzzing inside her but not loud enough to drown the roar of her own need.

'Then take it, man, before I find someone swifter to the quarry.'

Hamlet gave her a slow smile and licked his lips. Then he ran the lightest of fingers down her cheek and removed his own tunic so that they stood naked together.

'Beautiful Ofelia,' he whispered again, and then, at last, he was upon her, drawing her tight against him and running his hands all over her as if he were a blind man feeling his way and they were falling into the straw, rolling over and over until finally, in a tumble of limbs and kisses, they came together. Then all thoughts of her mother, or of pyres or horses or hares, were gone and there was just him; just Hamlet.

Afterwards they lay beneath his princely tunic, now creased and threaded with straw, his freshly bathed skin slicked with sweat. Ofelia felt light enough to soar across the skies behind Sol and heavy enough to lie, for once, completely still, her head on Hamlet's chest and his heart thumping a rhythm louder than any druid's drum into her ear.

'That wasn't your first time then?' she murmured sleepily against him.

He stiffened.

'Course not.'

'Sorry, I forgot – you're a desirable prince.'

'A desirable *man*,' he corrected her, giving her rump a friendly slap.

The easy familiarity of the gesture jolted her and she sat up a little.

'Who?'

'Who what?'

'Who else have you rutted with?'

'Does it matter?'

'I'll tell you who I've been with.'

'I haven't got all night!'

'Oi! It's my body and I'll do what I want with it.'

'As you should. It's a beautiful body.'

'Will you stop saying that?'

'What – beautiful?'

'Yes. Stop it. I'm not beautiful. I'm too thin and muscled and my breasts are too small and my hips too narrow and my hair not soft and golden enough ... '

Hamlet looked at her curiously.

'Who's told you that?'

'I have. And I never lie.'

'You misjudge yourself though. You are not thin, but lean; your breasts are as ripe as figs; and your hips are wide enough to straddle mine, which seems perfect to me. And as for your hair ... ' He took up one of her many braids and twisted it, playing with the amber bead securing the base. 'Your hair is glorious because when you bounce up and down on top of me these beads clack together as if cheering me on.'

'Hamlet!'

It was so foolish she could only laugh and now he was grabbing her and twisting her so that she was on her back and he over her, his face just a finger's breadth from her own.

'If you must know, nosey, I was very well initiated into the loving arts ... '

'The *what*?'

'Hush! I was very well initiated into the *loving arts* by an older woman gifted to me by my royal father on my sixteenth birthday.'

'How thoughtful of him. Who was she?'

'Not someone you know. It was in Zealand.'

'Of course it was!' She grabbed his bottom lip between her own and sucked, feeling him harden gratifyingly fast against her. 'She taught you well,' she allowed.

'Oh, I was a willing pupil and it was fun. But not like this.'

'This is not fun?'

She pouted but he just stared intently back at her.

'Oh yes, but it is so much more too because I did not care for her. It was nothing with her, whereas with you it is everything.'

'Shhh.' Panic screamed through Ofelia and she wriggled furiously beneath him. 'Don't say that. Don't talk of this as if it is something meaningful.'

'But . . .'

'It is sex, Hamlet – nothing more. Fun. Pleasure. Lust. A tangle of bodies. Swordplay, if you will.'

'It is nothing like swordplay, Ofelia.'

He looked cross. No, worse – he looked sad. She forced him away and wormed free.

'You know I will not give myself to a man, Hamlet. You of all people know that. Have we not spoken of it a hundred times?'

'Yes. Yes, of course. But we spoke, did we not, of other men?'

Ofelia shook her head.

'We spoke of *all* men.'

He sat up, frowned at her.

'So we cannot do this again?'

Her stomach lurched.

'Oh no! That is, yes – we can do it again, if we both want to. Think of it, Hamlet, as scratching an itch.'

'I am your itch?'

'No! Life is the itch.'

'And I am the scratching post?'

'Exactly.'

He considered this.

'It is not the most flattering thing I've been called all day.'

'I'll make up for it.'

'Now?'

'Now,' she confirmed, and drew his mouth to hers, and then they were kissing again and the only image in her mind was of his hungry eyes upon her as he took in her naked form and called her beautiful. He was deluded, of course, but as he entered her again and his blood seemed to course around hers, as if they were not just joined but inextricably linked, it was hard to care.

Chapter Three

Fyn, Yule 601–2

Ofelia looked at the upturned faces of the court children as they sat in a tight circle around the fire, their eyes fixed intently on the skald as he moved between them weaving his tale.

'Have we not all heard the Wild Hunt riding the skies this dark winter?' he demanded and the children nodded keenly.

The adults nodded too, for the gods had hunted close to the earth these last months, chasing down the evil spirits who had felt too unnervingly close to their doors for people ever truly to rest.

'Have we not felt the rush of the gods' horses pulling the air apart, night after long night? Have we not heard the moans of their trumpet calls in the skies? And the clap of Thor's hammer more times than ever before as he has laboured to keep us safe? Has not his lightning bolt struck fire time and again at enemies unseen? Every one of us could have been taken by the restless dead in these dark days if not for the gods driving on their heavenly steeds to hunt them down. Odin be praised!'

'Odin be praised!' all cried back, Ofelia as loud as any for it had indeed been a fearful winter.

The skies and the earth had been shaken by the forces of darkness until it had felt as if they might crack apart and swallow them all. She had sat awake too many nights, hearing the dead tearing up the skies and wondering if her father rode with them and if that were a pleasure or a torture. Sometimes, if the hunt chased sleep right out of her, she would ride out to one of the myriad ancient barrows that pushed out of the Danish earth, pulsing with spirits, and lie across the top, arms and legs splayed so that she might absorb a little of their energy.

One day, she swore, she would open up a grave and search for the entranceway to Valhalla. She would seek out her mother, confront her as she had been unable to do on the day Lady Sigrid ran into death's embrace. For now, though, it was easier to face a thousand sword-wielding warriors than one selfish ghost and as the winter had battered on she had sought sleep more and more often in Hamlet's arms, praying that from their easy comfort she would somehow find the courage to face the dead before her time on this uncertain earth was over.

'Oh, we have suffered,' the skald said, his voice low now and quivering with emotion. 'We have suffered and we near have perished, for the dread wolf Skoll hunted the blessed Mother Sun hard this year. He hounded Sol mercilessly, stalking her on his powerful haunches, slaver dripping from his great jaws in anticipation of his feast and his eyes so yellow with menace that she had to hide away and looked like to be devoured before she could birth her daughter and bring new light to us all.'

He paused. No one spoke. All knew it had been close run this winter. For days the sun had barely been seen and all had feared Skoll had hunted down the sun goddess and triumphed over her, and her light would be gone forever. The trip here to Fyn, where Otto had chosen to celebrate the twelve days of Yule at his new estate of Odense – named after the great Odin – had been one of the most terrifying Ofelia had ever taken.

The land had been so sodden with water and so strewn with broken branches that they had chosen to spare the horses and take the longer sail from Aarhus. Barely had they got a turn of the hourglass from land, however, than the waves had gathered, building in size and strength until finally they had risen above the height of the mast, higher than anyone had ever seen in the normally tame Samso belt. Every moment they had dreaded spotting the scales of a sea-beast cresting the next sickening rise and when they'd finally been tossed up on the Fynnish sands they'd all fallen to their knees to thank the gods for their deliverance.

And still the storms had raged. Otto had called in druids from all over Denmark and its neighbouring lands. King Aethelfrith of Bernicia, far over the Northern Seas in the Angles' land, had sent two men who had been punctilious in their observances to Odin and even more so in their attentions to Lord Feng. Ofelia had often noted them talking with him and Wiglek and feared their intentions, but surviving the battle of the gods had prevented her from worrying overmuch about the machinations of mere men.

And then somehow, Odin – perhaps pleased with Otto's new hall, named for him with great ceremony by a huge gathering of druids – had led bold Frey and the other gods across the skies to save Sol.

'Frey be praised!' the skald cried now, drawing all eyes back to him as his voice rose in calculated gradations of joy. 'For it was Frey who scented the evil wolf Skoll at last and Frey who rode forth on Gullinbursti, urging the great boar to speed across the skies in frantic pursuit of their enemy. It was Frey who held his gold-tipped spear aloft and Frey who hurled it with all of his great might straight down the jaws of the ravening wolf, piercing his throat and stoppering his teeth before they could clamp around blessed Sol and sink us into darkness forever. It was Frey who saved the light!'

And it did seem that he had. The last twelve days of Yule, as the young sun been nursed into strength with all the incantations of the many druids, had been a tense time but, gods be praised, the skies grew daily lighter and the nights were being slowly beaten back. It seemed, now, that the New Year would indeed come and all were giddy with the relief of it.

'Frey be praised!' the skald exhorted, and the chant came back over and over: 'Frey be praised! Frey be praised indeed!'

The skald paced, his eyes red in the firelight, and the children huddled tighter against one another, shifting their little bottoms nervously on the soft furs beneath them and looking to the hall doors, bolted tight shut against the forces of evil. He spotted it immediately.

'You fear still, little ones?' One or two of them nodded; most just stared at him, round-eyed. He paced around them. 'You are right to be scared. You are *wise* to be scared for the Wild Hunt is not yet over. The greatest victory is won but Odin must battle for our souls for long nights yet. He must ride Sleipnir high; he must drive the great horse on with all the power in every one of his eight strong legs, to lead the gods in their pursuit of darkness.'

He dropped suddenly to his haunches amongst the children and his voice softened.

'Sleipnir is tired, children.'

Ofelia saw them all lean towards him. The older ones glanced at each other and sat up a little straighter – they knew what came next.

'Sleipnir is hungry.'

One or two of the children nudged each other. A few smiles crept onto faces and the adults standing behind their offspring relaxed perceptibly. It *had* been a fierce battle but the new light had come and all would, surely, be well again.

'What shall we feed Sleipnir, children?'

One boy's hand shot beamwards.

'Hay!' he cried.

'Hay,' the skald agreed. 'And ... ?'

'And honey-balls,' another burst out, jiggling with the excitement of it.

The children began to look keenly around for their parents.

Earlier they had lined their best boots up in careful pairs either side of the great hall doors, ready to be stuffed with hay brought in from the stables and the tiny honey-balls they had been eagerly frying with their nursemaids at first light. These treats would feed Sleipnir over the remaining days of the Wild Hunt and in return he would leave a gift for every child. That would not come until the morning but for now there was treat enough.

No one had been allowed – on pain of being handed to the wicked god Loki as a toy – to eat any honey-balls earlier but as soon as two had been placed in every boot for Odin's hungry horse, those that remained were there for all to enjoy. It took time to collect honey so such sweetness was rare to their tongues and now the long-awaited time was upon them the children's fear was rapidly dissolving into giddy anticipation.

The adults stepped hastily back as maids claimed their charges and led the scramble to fill the boots. Ofelia knew – for she had seen them in the kitchens when begging food after training this morning – that there were many honey-balls spare for those smaller children less able to scrap for the first batch, but the children did not and the race was on.

'I remember this so well,' a voice said softly in her ear and she turned to see Hamlet, standing uncomfortably close. Her body reacted immediately and she tutted under her breath.

It had been a little awkward for the first few days after Geir's funeral. Ofelia had been torn between avoiding Hamlet altogether and jumping him again and again. Avoiding him had not been possible, however, as she'd had to train with him every morning, so for a little time she'd indulged herself. That could not, she'd known, be sustained without tipping unfortunately from indulgence to habit and she had forced herself finally to pull back.

Hamlet had objected but had let her lead and she was both grateful for his respect and furious at the way it forced her to make hard decisions again and again. Gradually, though, they had found a balance and now she leaned easily back against him.

'I remember it too,' she agreed, looking again towards the bright-eyed children.

'I still feel this knot of excitement in my stomach just looking at them stuffing the boots. I remember feeling as if I would never sleep as I lay listening for Sleipnir's hooves with the glorious taste of honey in my mouth. And then suddenly it was morning and we were rushing to look for presents.'

Ofelia smiled.

'Mainly I remember getting cross at having to put scratchy hay and sticky honey in my boots, especially the year when Father had had a pair dyed bright red for me. Freya knows, I loved those boots and no petty present was ever going to make up for ruining them.'

Hamlet laughed.

'You're a funny one, Ofelia.'

'She is that,' Lars agreed, stepping up beside them and dodging a small child as it darted between his long legs.

At nearly sixteen, Ofelia's brother had been growing as fast as Hamlet and was now, she noticed, taller than him. Hamlet noticed it too.

'And you, Lars, are a man indeed.'

Lars grinned and raked a hand through the blond curls he wore vainly long.

'But with a girl's hair,' Ofelia teased.

'One of us has to have it,' he shot back, tugging on one of her braids like a sail-rope.

Ofelia yanked indignantly away. She considered challenging him to a fight but she was far too likely to lose with her brother grown so strong. It wasn't fair. As Lars and Hamlet became men, it forced her, by sheer dint of the contrast, into being more of a woman. And the differences between them seemed to be permeating not just her body but her mind too.

'Would you like to see me in a gown?' she'd asked Hamlet one time as they'd panted together after a particularly energetic afternoon in a shepherd's hut on the moors.

'No.'

'Oh. Why not?'

'Because I like to see you with nothing on at all.'

'Hamlet!'

'It's true. If you must wear clothing – and I suppose sometimes you must – then I care little what sort it is.'

She'd considered this.

'But would not a gown remind you more of what is beneath?'

He'd smiled at this suggestion.

'Oh, Ofelia, beautiful Ofelia, I need no reminding for it is clear in my mind's eye at all times.'

'All times?'

'Yes – *all*.'

He spoke that way often, making no secret of his feelings for her and seemingly not caring that she refused to pledge him the same devotion. It made her angry. If he thought he would somehow grind her down into the pattern of a meek, submissive woman, he was very much mistaken. Ofelia was made of steel, tempered and hardened in her parents' funeral pyre, and no one, not even Hamlet, would grind or bend or shape her to their own ends. For now, though, Lars was awaiting her riposte and she fought to think of one.

'I am told,' she said eventually, careful not to catch Hamlet's eye, 'that my beads clatter most erotically against one another with the right movement.'

Lars chuckled.

'What crap! Have you been riding a skald, sister?'

She grinned.

'Something like that.'

'Well, I wish him well for he must be a brave man indeed to risk tangling with you.'

'Beads are hardly dangerous, Lars.'

'I did not mean the beads.' She frowned and he flung a muscular arm around her shoulders. 'Oh, come, let's not fight. See – the children are off to bed and the feast can begin. The boar smells divine. Did you swear an oath to him?'

As Lars led her and Hamlet easily up the hall towards the table at the top, Ofelia thought back to the oath-swearing. As the children had fried honey-balls earlier, the adults had gathered on the frost-bright grass to dedicate a fattened boar to Frey in thanks for his defeat of Skoll. The beast had been chained in a golden pen, lit at its four corners with tall torches, so that men – and women if they so chose – could see the boar clearly while they swore an oath upon it for the year ahead. Words spoken to the boar were held inside it and released direct to Frey when it was sacrificed by the druid.

When Ofelia's turn had come she'd knelt before the boar, so close she'd felt its sour breath against her face, and looked it straight in its pinprick eyes.

'I swear my loyal sword to Hamlet, Prince of Jutland.' The boar had seemed to look right into her, the light from the two torches at her back flaring in the very centre of its dark eyes, and she had hastily added, 'My sword only,' and retreated from the pen to make way for the next devotee.

The boar had been run through not long afterwards and now it was roasting on the spit, its soul gone to Frey along with their hard-sworn oaths and just its flesh left behind for the faithful to feast upon. She had promised Frey now: Hamlet had her sword and only her sword. She might gift him her body from time to time but her allegiance to him was as his constable. Nothing more.

Mind you, she feared he would soon have need of her in that capacity. The mood on Jutland had been uneasy since Geir's funeral. Feng had been throwing his not inconsiderable weight around and these last twelve days in Odense Ofelia had seen him endlessly sidling up to people, whispering to them. It worried her and she looked around now to see him escorting Queen Gertrude to her seat with ostentatious solicitude.

'I don't like the look of Feng,' she said, low-voiced, to Hamlet.

31

'No one likes the look of him; he's a wart of a man. Why do you think he has no wife?'

'Oh, he has money enough to attract a wife even if he were a dwarf. And your mother seems to like him well enough.'

She pointed to where Gertrude was bending back to hear something Feng was saying close to her ear, laughing and batting flirtatiously at his arm.

'Oh, Lia, that's just courtliness. They're all like that on Zealand.'

'It looks more like danger to me. I told you, Hamlet – Feng's plotting.'

'Of course he is! He's always plotting, be it his next cheat at knucklebones or the next poor slave girl he'll impregnate with his seemingly endless seed. I tell you, that man has bastards all over Denmark.'

'An *army* of them perhaps?'

'What? Oh, come, Ofelia, you worry too much. Feng is a nuisance, no more. I have suggested to Father that he be given Fyn to rule, to keep him quiet.'

'You have?'

She stopped dead, surprised, and Hamlet ran into the back of her. His hand gave her bum a quick squeeze and she jumped and turned to glare at him but he stared placidly back.

'I have. You're not the only one with sharp eyes, constable. I know he is restless. Wiglek too.'

'Feng talks of England.'

'So you said. Well, why not? It could be a useful alliance for us.'

'For *him*. He seeks power, Hamlet.'

'Which is why he should have Fyn. And it will keep him separate from his damned brother too. Wiglek's resentment burns slower but, perhaps, more steadily, and it would be best if he did not have Feng constantly fuelling it.'

Ofelia nodded. It was a good idea, that much she could see, but as she watched Feng murmuring the gods knew what into Gertrude's ear, she feared it would not be enough.

'You think he will accept the offer?'

'I hope so. But dinner awaits and my father is beckoning us over. Come.'

'Not me, Hamlet.'

But he was tugging her after him as Otto called: 'Hamlet! Here, boy – sit by my side.'

The king was dressed in flowing white robes with his fine beard made white with chalk so that he could preside over the festivities as Old Man Winter. He was in fine spirits and Hamlet hurried to join him, pulling Ofelia into the next seat on the top bench. With the king waving a welcome to her she hardly dared protest. Then, as she looked self-consciously around, she saw several prominent lords eyeing her furiously from the benches below and decided she rather liked her seat of honour.

She beamed openly at them all as she made a show of settling herself just two seats from the High King then watched, amused, as everyone else jostled for positions. Otto kept an easy court, preferring open hospitality to strict order. Ofelia knew some of the older, more formal members – her uncle Peder included – did not approve but she liked the king's ways and she was not alone for Otto was proving to be a much-loved ruler.

'So, Lady Ofelia, what think you of my new hall?' he asked her, gesturing expansively around.

'It's wonderful,' she told him without reservation for she loved the beautiful building.

At nearly sixty paces end to end, it was the longest she had ever seen. It had needed huge supporting pillars to keep the long roof beams locked in place but Otto had ordered sculptors from all across Denmark to put their own special stamp on each one and now the carved golden oak flourished with all manner of plants, vines and creatures. Ofelia swore you could spend days in here and still find new things to please the eye.

'You should build something like this on Jutland,' she told Hamlet.

'He should,' Otto agreed, delighted. 'You are right, Lady

Ofelia – he should. And if he gets on with it perhaps we could celebrate a very special occasion there? This summer perhaps?'

'Lithasblot?' Ofelia asked, puzzled.

The harvest festival was important but not usually considered "special".

'No! Not Lithasblot, my lady. I am thinking of a more *personal* celebration.'

His words pierced her as if a sea-beast had at last risen up above the waves and she shied back so fast she almost fell off the bench.

'You mean Hamlet's marriage, my lord king?'

'What else?'

She had not known it was planned. Hamlet had not spoken to her of any discussion with his father though she supposed, with an heir to secure, it was important to proceed as quickly as possible. She swallowed hard.

'And who is he to marry?'

Otto looked from her to his son and back again.

'Isn't that obvious? It is unusual, I grant you, for a prince to wed his constable but you are an unusual woman, Ofelia.'

'Me?'

She didn't know if this was better or worse than Hamlet marrying another woman. She looked to him for help but he seemed as stunned as she.

'You wish me to marry Lia — the Lady Ofelia, Father?'

'I think you wish it yourself, Prince Hamlet.' Otto beamed benignly at him. 'Do you not?'

Ofelia felt the glorious new oak beams closing in on her as if leaves and vines were twisting out of the knotted wood and the creatures carved there were shaking themselves free. She swallowed again and again but a lump of something – fear, horror, hope? – had lodged in her throat and there was no shaking it. She looked desperately to Hamlet but his eyes were fixed on the king.

'I do wish it, Father.'

'Then ...'

'But *I* do not!' Ofelia's words came out like a whiplash and Otto jumped.

'Sorry?'

'I beg your pardon, my lord king, and thank you greatly for the honour you have done me in considering me, but I do not wish to wed. Not Hamlet, nor any other man.'

Otto looked at her long and hard.

'Marriage can be a great blessing, you know, my dear.'

He did not seem offended by her refusal and she was emboldened to reply frankly.

'For men perhaps but for women it brings only servitude.'

Otto blinked.

'That is a little extreme.' He glanced towards Gertrude seated on his other side. 'I do not see my wife as a servant.'

Ofelia blushed.

'Of course not. I apologise.' She looked to Hamlet but he was refusing to meet her eye. 'It was a poor choice of words. I mean, rather, that in a marriage a woman must always take second place.'

Otto thought about this then gave a slow nod.

'I suppose that is true in theory but in practice, you know – and certainly in private – the woman always rules.'

'See!' Hamlet said suddenly, the first word he had spoken since Ofelia had made her objection, though it was not clear to whom he addressed it.

Ofelia felt the lump in her throat swell until it was so tight it almost brought tears to her eyes. First gowns, then marriage talk and now tears. It was too much. She squared her shoulders and faced Otto.

'Hamlet is the dearest man on this earth to me, save perhaps for my brother Lars, and I have sworn my sword to him forever. Indeed, I swore it to Frey's boar this very morning.'

'You did?' Hamlet asked, and at last he looked at her.

'Of course I did, Hamlet. I would die for you as my prince and as my friend – but I will not live with you as your wife.'

'But ...'

Ofelia saw Otto put a hand on his son's knee and was grateful for his intervention.

'If I were to wed any man it would be you, but I will not.'

'Only because of ...'

Otto's hand tightened on Hamlet's knee and, thankfully, he ceased talking.

'It matters not what the reason is,' Ofelia told him tightly. 'It matters only that it *is*.' She waited for another objection but none came so she steeled herself. 'But your father speaks true on one thing, prince – you must marry. You are Denmark's heir and it is your duty to breed and keep her secure. We should find you a bride.'

'Ofelia ...' His voice was dark with warning but she ignored it.

'What of her?' she demanded, pointing wildly down the tables to the girl she'd seen Hamlet dancing with at Geir's funeral before she had seized him for a jig of her own making. Theirs had been a fine dance but foolish. Now it was time to call the music to a halt.

'Lady Agnete?' Otto asked, easily enough, though his voice was strained and his hand still tight on his son's leg. 'She is of good blood, Hamlet, and comely, is she not?'

Hamlet said nothing.

'Very comely,' Ofelia agreed for him, her voice sounding ridiculously shrill even in her own ears. 'Luscious breasts.'

'Ofelia!' Otto gasped.

She flushed.

'I apologise. Again. I am used to barracks-chatter.'

Otto sighed.

'I suppose you are. Perhaps you are right not to wed.'

'I *am* right, my lord,' she agreed solemnly, but with Hamlet glowering between them her privileged position on the top table suddenly did not seem so covetable and already she longed for the meal to end.

'So that's it then?' Hamlet's words slammed into Ofelia as hard as his sudden grip on her wrist.

She struggled but he'd picked his moment well, waiting until she made her way back from the latrines to pounce, and no one noticed as he pulled her round the side of the hall. A short distance away a couple were gasping warm air into the cold night and Ofelia instantly envied them their simple release. Sadly, it wasn't always that easy.

'If you mean my refusal to marry you – or any man – then, yes, that's it.'

'Why?'

'You know why.'

'Because your mother sacrificed herself to your father and you don't want to have to do that?'

'No, I . . . It's not that simple.'

'It can be. I don't want you to sacrifice yourself to me, Lia. I don't want your bloody servility. I won't ever ask you to be "second best" and it offends me that you think I would. Don't you know me at all?'

She heard the hurt in his voice and hated it.

'It's not you, Hamlet; it's everyone else.'

'You don't care what they think.'

That much was true and yet . . .

'You are Prince of Jutland. One day you will be High King of Denmark. You need a wife to sit at your side and bear your children and grace your ceremonies in fine gowns.'

'Always with the gowns! It's foolish. A gown is just a long tunic.'

'That you cannot walk in and certainly cannot fight in. Gowns are fit only for those who sit weaving and sewing and simpering.'

'So don't wear a gown. I told you, I don't care.'

'You say that now when it doesn't matter, when you are just a prince and can indulge yourself. But you will change.'

'I don't have to.'

'But you *will*.'

'Oh, I see, you know more of me than I do of myself?'

She shrugged.

'Yes.'

He banged one hand suddenly against the wooden wall.

'Then marry me! Help me. Stand always at my side.'

'I will, Hamlet. I will stand at your side but as your constable, not your wife.'

'That's it then?'

'As I said, yes.'

'And if I don't want you as my constable?'

She sucked in her breath.

'Don't you?'

'No.'

His eyes bored into hers, challenging her. It was a look she'd seen in them a thousand times on the training yard and always there she rose to it. But it was easy to fight with swords; words were far trickier.

'Then I must respect that decision, Hamlet, as you should respect mine.'

His hand went up and she braced herself for him to hit her – willed him to do so. It would be a release of sorts, if not the one she craved.

'Go on,' she goaded him. 'Hit me. Beat me into submission. I am but a woman after all, but a servant to your desires.'

He dropped his hand, let go of her wrist and stepped back, his eyes cold now.

'I have never treated you like that, Ofelia. I have offered you nothing but my time and care and love. Yes, love. I love you and you love me too, yet you will spoil it for both of us with your petty stubbornness.'

She shook her head.

'And so it begins . . . '

'Aaargh!'

He banged his hand so hard against the wall that she feared the bones might crack. Further up, the amorous couple fell still then looked over at them. Ofelia heard the girl giggle and the man whisper something low and urgent and then they were off again, lost in their own joy.

'You are infuriating, Ofelia.'

'I know it. You are best rid of me. Find a biddable wife.'

'I don't *want* a biddable wife. The gods help me, I want you.'

'But I am not yours to want.'

Hamlet's eyes narrowed and his shoulders stiffened.

'Very well then. Safe trip back to Jutland, Lady Ofelia. May your sword bring you joy for I know not what else will.'

And with that he gave a tight little bow and was gone, back into the giddy Yule crowds, leaving Ofelia to feel for the dint in the wooden wall where he'd lashed out and to bang her own forehead against the imprint of his fury.

The next morning the royal boats sailed for Zealand. Ofelia dared not go down to the jetties but stayed wrapped tight in her cloak amongst the stand of trees on a barrow grave above the shore. She had sat there all night, hoping that the frost seeping up from the dead men below might numb her pain but it seemed it had not done so for it still hurt like a thousand knife pricks when she saw Hamlet step out behind his father, ready to sail away from her.

She watched him look around, his eyes scanning the sparse crowd of those who had raised themselves after last night's revels to see their king on his way. Was he seeking her? Almost she rose, cried out to him, but it seemed the frost had worked its icy charms on her limbs if not her mind for they were stiff and disobedient and before she could uncurl them he had gone aboard and turned his head firmly seawards.

Well, good, she thought. *Let him go.* It was for the best. He would be angry for a while but he would recover. She knew him. He could never hold a grudge for longer than it took the next meal to arrive. He was too warm and kind and open-hearted and . . . Ofelia closed her eyes, dug her fingers into the hard soil of the barrow, and willed up the picture of her mother scrambling into the flames but for the first time in nine painful years it would not come and when she finally opened her eyes again Hamlet was sailing away.

Chapter Four

Roskilde, Walpurgis (May Day) 602

Ofelia lifted her face to the deliciously warm spring breeze and willed herself to enjoy the sensation but it was impossible. Why did the wind not blow faster? Every day of the drawn-out last months of the winter Wild Hunt she had longed to see Hamlet and at last she was close – though not close enough.

So many long nights she had lain awake, cursing herself for her hot-headed handling of his marriage proposal. Almost she had wished the terrors of the Wild Hunt back and several times she had set herself against the stones of barrow graves in the hope of opening up something dangerous enough to take her mind off the ridiculous emotions coiling around her heart. In the end, though, she'd realised that even if she unleashed all the forces of the under-world, she would still have to face Hamlet and had forced herself to find a more practical solution.

She had to apologise to him, that was all. She had to set things straight – or at least as straight as possible since she'd brought about this painful estrangement – and so she'd been delighted to step aboard ship to sail to Roskilde to join the court for Walpurgis. The great festival celebrated the end of the Wild Hunt and the coming of Trimilchi, the summertime, and so represented a period of new beginnings that Ofelia was determined to make the most of. Just as their ship had rounded the top of Zealand, however, the winds had dropped right away, leaving the sail flapping uselessly. There had been little choice but to lower the mast and draw out the oars and their progress down the long Roskilde Fjord had been, as a result, agonisingly slow.

'Why can't they go any faster?' she moaned to Lars who was standing at her side in the prow of Peder's ship.

'Go easy on them, Lia. They've been rowing all morning and they are fasting like the rest of us.'

Ofelia's belly rumbled obligingly. The nine days before Walpurgis were honoured with fasting in the daylight hours and as it was now the last day everyone was feeling the pinch of hunger. But that was no excuse.

'Let me take an oar,' she said, 'and I'll show them speed.'

Lars looked at her curiously.

'Do you know how to do it?'

She shrugged.

'How hard can it be? It's just in–out, in–out.'

'And you are good at that, sister.'

'Lars!'

She flushed. In truth she had been useless at "in–out" since Hamlet had left. She'd had a couple of half-hearted encounters with Eric but they'd left her somehow itchier than before and she'd given up and taken to riding Ansgar further and further across the Jutish moors instead. The horse looked lean and fit on it but it had done little to benefit her. Ofelia leaned impatiently against the masthead, as if she could physically impel the boat to travel faster.

'You are eager to see someone, sister?' Lars asked, turning his head to the all-too-gentle breeze to let it lift his curls.

'Just eager to attend our High King at court, brother.'

'I see. So no particular lord draws your attention? Or prince perhaps?'

Ofelia shoved at him so that for a moment he lost his balance and nearly toppled into the fjord. Sadly though he caught at the side in time to steady himself and his pretty curls stayed dry.

'What about you, Titch?' she countered. 'Any maidens caught your eye?'

'No *maidens*,' he replied pointedly.

She glanced at him askance. Was her little brother already sporting with girls? She supposed he must be for he was decent enough looking if you hadn't known him as a little brat, but the thought of it caught at her all the same. They were neither of them children anymore. That time was past and they had survived it. Thrived on it even. Their father would be proud to see them here now; their mother too, perhaps, though she had not cared enough to stay.

Ofelia shook the bitter mood away. The sun was shining, the breeze was soft – too soft – and she had Lars. It was enough.

'Someone in particular?' she asked him.

'Nope.'

'Just slave girls then?'

'No! I like my girls willing, thank you very much. I'm no Feng.'

Ofelia shuddered as if a cloud had passed over the sun and glanced to the boat ahead of their own. She could see Feng and Wiglek at the prow, urging on the clutch of burly men at the oars. These were not the usual Jutland hearth soldiers but warriors from afar who had been arriving in Jutland in twos and threes for the last month. Some were hardened young Danes, living from harbour to harbour on the strength of their swords, but others were from Norway, Sweden, and even the lands of the Franks and the Angles. Their tongues chattered in mismatched variants of Norse but these men had two key things in common: all of them were big and all of them fought hard. And dirty.

Feng had turned down the governorship of Fyn, saying he was

needed on Jutland to prepare for an attack from Norway that his spies had assured him was imminent. He and Wiglek had been amassing men ever since, drawing considerable sums from Peder's precious treasury to pay for their keep.

'But you have Norwegians in your band,' Peder had protested when Wiglek had come knocking for yet more gold a week or two back.

Ofelia had been in the hall, teaching a handful of children how to sharpen arrow-heads for it had been a rainy day fit for little else. She had listened in shamelessly.

'Which is how we can be so sure of the threat,' Wiglek had replied smoothly. 'Our Norwegians are disaffected from their homeland and seek a better leader.'

'In you, Lord Feng?'

'And myself,' Wiglek had snapped, before swiftly composing himself. 'But we are training these men for my brother, High King Otto. Would you rather we left Jutland exposed? Would you rather keep your paltry treasures locked away in caskets so that they are easily to hand when the enemy comes rampaging onto our shores with no soldiers to stop him?

Peder had put a protective hand on the nearest casket almost as if it were a child.

'We *have* soldiers, Wiglek, a whole household troop of them.'

'And they are fine men – and women.' Ofelia could swear Wiglek had looked her way then and had kept her head low over the arrow-heads. 'But we need more.' He had brought his fist down heavily on Peder's accounting table, making him bounce back like a startled flea. 'The threat is very real, Peder – why will you not see it?'

The chamberlain had gathered himself with care and said, 'Very well, but I will need the prince's permission to release further funds.'

It had been the worst possible answer. Ofelia had seen the back of Wiglek's thick neck turn purple with rage before he'd shot out one of his meaty hands and grasped Peder around his bony wrist.

Ofelia had been on her feet instantly and had her sword against Wiglek's back before he'd even heard her move. She might not be as big as his new troops but she would always be more agile.

'Let him go, Wiglek.'

'Oh, look, Peder, your pet girlie threatens me.'

'I'm no pet, Wiglek.'

'True – more of a wildcat.' He'd let go of Peder and spun around to face her. She'd kept her sword high, pointed at his throat, but he'd looked scornfully at her over the top of it. 'You've got spirit, I'll give you that, but cats shouldn't play with swords.'

She'd looked at him scornfully.

'I'm not playing, Wiglek. I'm constable here, appointed by Prince Hamlet himself.'

'Are you sure about that, cat? He's not here after all. He's gone and left you. Why's that? Weren't you good enough for him?'

It had been pathetically unsubtle but she'd felt herself rising to his taunting all the same and had had to force herself to breathe slowly and deliberately to stay calm. She'd sensed the children gathering curiously behind her and seen Peder watching with obvious concern and had mustered all her scant dignity.

'Hamlet is absent on royal duties, Lord Wiglek, as well you know. He appreciates your care of Jutland in his absence but you should consult me, as *constable*, on all matters of soldiery.'

She was painfully aware of Hamlet saying he no longer wanted her in that role but until he appointed someone else she would hold onto it.

'Constable,' Wiglek sneered. 'Such a sweet title for a mistress.'

'I am not . . .'

'But even so, I outrank you, Lady Ofelia. You too, Lord Peder. Jutland is in the care of myself and my brother and we will see her safe. Open the caskets!'

There had been little more to say for Wiglek, as brother to the High King, was indeed the senior lord present and Peder had had little choice but to hand over his carefully husbanded funds

44

to provide more and more meat for their hand-picked war band. Ofelia had sent urgent messages to both Hamlet and Otto but word had come back that the threat from Norway was real and Otto's brothers had been given royal approval for their scheme to bolster the household troop.

They'd both been almost unbearable since. Feng was forever strutting around like a cockerel, with his men scurrying in his wake like burly chicks. She swore they must even watch when he rutted with slave girls, as he did so often that Ofelia had seen the poor wretches going ridiculously long routes around the compound to stay out of his sight. Wiglek contented himself with prowling after Ofelia. So far he had not dared actually to assault her but she had taken to wearing a sharp knife in her belt and would not scruple to use it against him if he put a finger out of place.

It was not, however, for herself that she truly feared but for Hamlet and she watched his uncles' meaty warriors power them up the fjord towards Otto's court with cold foreboding. Hamlet might think Feng capable only of plotting petty cheats but Ofelia feared he had a grander design and wished she had been able to discover the details of it. The brothers kept their men separate from hers in the training yard and they sat tight around their own hearths of an evening so it had been impossible to strike up so much as a passing friendship with any of them.

'I do not trust Feng,' she said in a low voice to Lars.

'And you are right not to. But at least once we are at court it will be King Otto's problem rather than ours.'

Ofelia looked at her brother and had to smile. He always saw the best in every situation.

'You are right, Titch. The only question, then, is when will we actually get to the damned court? We go so slow!'

She peered up the fjord, desperately seeking a view of the royal estate. They must be deep inland for the fjord was narrowing and she could see the rough paths to either side and spot fishermen throwing lines and nets into the water's edge, but they were not there yet. She pictured Hamlet at court, waiting, and it was all she could do not to jump up and down on deck. She had never before been parted from him for this long and it had been agony for her. She just hoped it had been so for him too.

Her heart lurched. What if he'd been glad to be free from her grumbling and bossing and teasing? What if he'd done as she'd suggested and found himself a biddable princess and forgotten all about his rough-edged constable? Ofelia had a hundred apologies ready for him and had spent sleepless hours thinking up answers to all possible arguments but what if he simply didn't care? What if he greeted her with formal politeness and suggested they were "friends" in the way that people who thought little of you did?

It would be no less than you deserve, she told herself, but that was no comfort and she clutched nervously at the masthead as, at last, the ship splashed round a bend in the fjord and she saw Roskilde.

'Look, horses!'

Lars pointed down the left-hand bank and, sure enough, a small band of mounted men was visible, riding at a smart pace along the bridle path. Ofelia reached instinctively for her sword and glanced to Feng's boat but the men there were pointing too, seemingly as surprised. The horses drew closer so that Ofelia could hear the beat of their hooves echoing off the low hills to either side and she strained forward, trying to see the riders.

The front man was drawing away from the others, urging his horse on, and she saw him wave towards the boats and then, finally, caught his cry on the warm air: 'Ofelia! Ofelia!'

'Hamlet?' she whispered. She could feel Lars grinning down at her but she didn't care. 'Hamlet!'

He was there, on the bank before her. The slow pace of the damned boats had got to him too and he had ridden out to find her.

'Hamlet! Hie!'

'Ofelia!'

He stood up in his stirrups, waving like a child. He was close enough for her to see the lines of his lithe body and the shape of his handsome face and even the light in his eyes as he called her name. It was too much.

Unsheathing her sword and thrusting it at Lars, Ofelia stepped up onto the gunwale, took a breath, and dived. The waters of the fjord were cold but they caressed her skin like a lover as she struck out for the shore. She could hear Peder calling frantically and Lars laughing and hushing him, but her eyes were fixed on the water's edge where Hamlet flung the reins of his horse to one of his fellows and came running into the shallows to haul her out.

'Ofelia – you're mad!'

'Impatient.'

'For what?'

'For sight of you.'

'Not touch?'

She felt ridiculously shy suddenly.

'Touch too,' she murmured, and then his arms were around her and his soft laughter was buzzing through her and the warm, familiar smell of him was enveloping her and she breathed easy for the first time in far too long.

Chapter Five

'We need to get back.' Hamlet leaped into the saddle and held out his hand to Ofelia. She took it and swung herself up behind him. 'Ah,' he cried, 'you're all wet!' She squirmed against him, rubbing the fjord water into his clothes, and he laughed. 'No matter – we'll soon dry out in this sun and wind.'

'There is no wind,' Ofelia pointed out. 'That's why it's taken us so damned long to get down the fjord.'

'There will be if I ride fast enough.'

'But then we'll be in company in moments and I have so much to say to you.'

He rubbed her knee where it rested alongside his own.

'And I you but there is time. Now you are here at last there is plenty of time. We have days to talk, nights too . . .'

The word, so full of promise, shuddered between them and Ofelia pressed herself tight against the prince as he kicked his horse into a canter, the others following discreetly behind. With an effort, she resisted the urge to rest her cheek against his back and sat up tall, responding to the rhythm of both horse and man as they headed down the path towards Roskilde.

'Besides,' Hamlet called back to her over the rush of air, 'there is little to say, save that I was wrong to press you, Ofelia. I knew what you felt and I ignored it. My father took me by surprise and then it seemed such an easy way forward and I would, you know, like you as my wife . . . '

'Hamlet!'

He held up his hand to stem her objection.

'But I know it is not what you want, so I accept that. We are bound by deeper ties than any posturing druid can create and that is enough for me.'

'Truly?'

He hesitated only a second.

'Truly, Ofelia . . . constable.'

'I am, then, reinstated?'

'You were never stood down; I was merely in a sulk.'

She laughed at his honesty.

'That is good as I have been taking charge these last months anyway – or trying to.'

'Such false modesty, Lia.'

'It is not.' Ofelia sighed, and looked sideways to the fjord. They were heading past Feng's boat and she glanced uneasily at his thick-set men and pushed herself up in the saddle to lean in close to Hamlet's ear. 'We do have to talk, and soon – not of us, but of Feng.'

'Feng?' Hamlet must have caught the urgency in her tone for he slowed the horse to a walk and twisted to look back at her. 'What of him? Is he prepared for the Norwegians?'

'He is prepared for something, Hamlet, for he and Wiglek are gathering themselves a personal war band. They keep to their own lodgings and train in their own ways and sit so tight around their hearth fires that no other can hear what they talk of. These are no king's troops, Hamlet, I swear it. Your uncles have some dark purpose in mind and your father must discover it for I fear, truly, that they plot to hurt someone. And I fear most . . . ' she tightened her arms around his waist ' . . . that they plot to hurt you.'

'Because I am Prince of Jutland?'

'Yes. Feng is a bitter man and a dangerous one.'

49

'Then thank Thor that I have my constable to protect me.'

His tone was light – too light.

'This is serious, Hamlet.'

He wiped the smile from his lips.

'Of course. I'm sorry, you are right, we must deal with it. I will talk to Father, I promise. But you needn't worry too much, Lia. Our spies suggest Norway has troubles of its own in its northern reaches and will no longer be looking abroad for battles. Feng's men can be disbanded and then he can go to Fyn and play at being a prince, far away from his scheming brother, and all will be well.'

It was as if a weight had been taken off her. Ofelia drew in a deep breath of spring air and stretched in the saddle.

'That is good to hear, Hamlet. Very good. When will you talk to the king?'

'Tomorrow. First thing. We will pay off Feng's men and send them on their way. But for tonight there is feasting to be had and Odin to be honoured in his great resurrection.'

Ofelia nodded against his back and held on as he kicked their mount into a canter again, heading for the royal estate. Tonight was a solemn feast indeed but even so Ofelia could not suppress her happiness at being back with Hamlet to celebrate it. As Lars had said, Feng and Wiglek were no longer her problem and she vowed to make the most of the evening ahead.

Despite her vow, Ofelia could not help a feeling of unease from creeping over her when she watched Feng coiling his way around the courtiers who were gathering for the great ceremony of Walpurgis. He had a snake smile for all the most important men and women but saved his especial slinking charm for the queen.

'How does she put up with him?' Ofelia asked Hamlet as she watched Feng whispering something into Gertrude's ear.

'How? To please my father, of course. And to keep Denmark safe. A flattered Feng is a happy Feng; and a happy Feng is, surely, a loyal one?'

Ofelia could see the logic to that but there was something unnervingly febrile about Hamlet's uncle tonight and she felt instinctively for the sword at her belt. Men were hungry from the nine-day fast and once the ale barrels were broached the drink would go to their heads fast. She prayed Gertrude had ordered the servants to bring the food swiftly after the great ceremony of resurrection but for now the tables were pushed back for the druids to take centre-stage. A number of the torches around the walls were being extinguished to plunge the court into a low light as all gathered together in a great circle to worship.

Ofelia tore her thoughts away from Feng. He was by Gertrude's side, head bowed as reverently as all the others, and even he, surely, would not risk the wrath of the gods by breaking the sanctity of Walpurgis. She drew in a deep breaths, stilling her ever-restless soul to contemplate Odin's great sacrifice. Servants were scattering herbs on the remaining torches and the air was filled with the heady scent of life and growth and summertime. Ofelia closed her eyes to focus on the Allfather and when she opened them again, she gasped at the sight before her. Otto had outdone himself.

Two druids were carrying in a great twist of ash to represent Yggdrasil, the World Tree, and tied to it, naked, was a third priest representing Odin. As the other druids chanted a low, pulsing thrum of ancient words, the representative of the great god was brought into the centre of them all and set before the hearth. Salts were thrown onto the flames, turning them blue and green and lighting up the druid's writhing body tattooed with mystical patterns.

A prolonged hush fell over the crowd, turning to awe-stricken gasps as, with a flourish, the Odin figure lifted the spear in his one free hand and rammed it into his own shoulder, drawing blood. The brave druid cried out in real pain but stayed fixed in his noble role as he stared down into the Well of Urd, represented by a highly polished copper mirror set upon the ground, to search for the runes – the secret of knowledge with which he would save the world for both men and gods.

Ofelia held her breath, drawn into the passion of his great suffering as Odin's blood ran down his chest. The druids chanted faster and faster, a pulsing drumbeat driving them on, and to Ofelia it seemed to beat out a dark warning as if the dead themselves were calling out to her. She looked again for Feng but he was no longer at Gertrude's side.

Out of the corner of her eye she saw the servants moving to extinguish the torches for the climax of the drama. Ofelia panicked. She looked for Hamlet and saw him, thankfully, near at hand with Lars at his shoulder, her brother's mop of fair hair bright in the firelight. But where was Feng? Or Wiglek? She scanned the circle of people and saw their men around the walls, hanging back as if ready for more than just witnessing the Allfather's great sacrifice. She felt for her sword and looked again to Hamlet and Lars. Both were lost in the ceremony and had been pulled a little way down the hall by the shifting crowd. Feng, however, seemed nowhere to be seen.

She saw him just as Odin flung back his head, flicking blood off the ends of his hair as he did so. Feng was no longer with Gertrude but stood at Otto's shoulder, his eyes fixed not on Odin like the rest of the hall but on his royal brother.

'No!' Ofelia gasped but her words were lost in Odin's sudden cry of exultation as he divined the runes and then the hall went black.

Ofelia's heart raced and she pushed her way blindly towards Otto but there were too many bodies in the way and it was too dark for her to be of any use. Every breath of every member of the court seemed louder than the greatest winds. Odin's cry died to nothing and all stood quiet. Ofelia put her hands pointlessly to her eyes and braced herself for tragedy.

But then the torches were flickering into life again and the druids were calling thanks to the gods for the birth of Trimilchi and people were stirring and pointing to the mirror where carved runes were now magically lying in the pretend pool. Odin was untied and cheered to the rafters. Ofelia looked desperately for Otto but there he was, cheering with the rest and coming forward to press coins upon the druids for their glorious theatrics.

'Was that not wonderful, Ofelia?' Lars asked, bouncing up at her side. 'Was it not awe-inspiring?'

'Yes. Yes, it was amazing.'

'I was so moved. Seriously. And now I'm *so* hungry!'

He looked keenly to the trestles being rapidly set up as servants, thankfully, came to the doors with great platters of meats, fish and bread. Odin was raised again and Otto lived still and the feast could begin but Ofelia could not seem to find it in her feet to move.

'Are you well, sister?' Lars asked, peering at her.

'Quite well, thank you, Titch. I was, er, moved too.'

'Come and eat. You'll soon feel better.'

Ofelia let herself be led to a bench, feeling numb. What had happened? Had Otto somehow saved himself? Or had she imagined the threat, caught up in the drama of the druids' play and her own weakness after fasting? Otto was chatting easily with both Feng and Wiglek and their men were scrambling to table with the rest. She felt foolish now and grateful she'd not had chance to speak her womanish fears to either her brother or Hamlet. She seized a goblet, grabbed a jug of the rich fruit wine that Zealanders made so well (there had to be something they were good for) and filled it to the brim.

Things got a little hazy after that. Ofelia tried to eat but her stomach, shrunken after nine days of privation, rebelled and she could only manage morsels. The wine, however, slipped readily down her throat and soothed her fears. It had been a long few months separated from Hamlet and perhaps that had clouded her judgement and made her more fearful of the world in some pathetic way. Well, no more. She drank eagerly to every toast and proposed a few of her own, and once the tables were pushed back she danced with Lars and Hamlet and even with Feng.

'You are merry tonight, lady,' he said, panting a little as he kept pace with her turns.

'Should I not be? Odin is risen, Trimilchi is come and Denmark prospers.'

'She does indeed. I am told the Norwegians have worries of their own so it should be a happy summer. It is good to see you so relaxed.'

'It is?' She stared up at him, stunned, but the dance moved on and she was whipped on to a new partner with little time to dwell on Feng's apparent kindness. Maybe he'd had a hard few months too; maybe he truly had been worried about the Norwegians invading Jutland? And who cared anyway, for here was Hamlet again, holding out his arms to her, and the days ahead could wait for this night was glorious.

He pulled her tight against him.

'I must have you, Ofelia.'

Her body surged at the urgency of his touch.

'And I you.'

'Come then – the night is warm and half the company are already in the bushes. No one will care if we leave.'

Ofelia glanced around, a little dazed, and saw that the hall was indeed emptying, some bound for their beds, set out in the many outbuildings for this great gathering, but many for the embraces of nature and each other. Summer was upon them, a time of bounty and fertility, and all wanted to make the most of it.

'Let's go!'

Ofelia made for the doors, Hamlet tight on her heels. As they dived out into the welcoming night she caught sight of Lars carrying a giggling girl into the woods beyond the compound and tugged Hamlet towards a different path. She might accept that her titch of a brother was a man now but that did not mean she needed to see the evidence of it.

They were barely into the trees when Hamlet fell upon her, kissing her neck and making her ache with desire.

'A little further,' she gasped.

'I can wait no longer.'

'You are a prince, remember?'

'I cannot remember. I can remember nothing but the look and the taste and the feel of you, beautiful Ofelia.'

For once she did not correct him but whirled around and stoppered his mouth with her own, and then they were falling to the mossy ground, clawing at each other's clothes and running desperate hands over each other's bodies. And as he entered her at last, Ofelia heard herself cry out in an exultation almost as great as Odin upon the tree.

'So good,' she murmured over and over when their passion was eventually spent and she lay in Hamlet's arms, hot and gasping.

'Not bad at all,' he agreed, running lazy fingers across her breasts. 'I might even do it again once I've got my breath back.'

'Promises, promises.' She looked up at the black skies through the still unfolding leaves of the beech trees. The moon was but a sliver and the stars mere pinpricks, winking on their joy and kindly offering little light to betray it to others. They were alone. 'I'm sorry we argued, Hamlet.'

'As am I.'

'Let's not do it again.'

He groaned.

'I would rather not, Lia, but you can be a hard woman to stay calm with, you know.'

'I know. I'm sorry.'

'Don't be. It's what makes you the woman I lo—'

'Hush! Don't say it, Hamlet.'

'It's just a word.'

'Words are power. Look at the runes – did not Odin suffer on the tree for nine days to gain their secrets? Words bind us.'

'And you will not be bound?'

She heard a flicker of sadness in his voice and leaped up, straddling him.

'I might. Have you any twine?'

She felt his instant arousal and, smiling, leaned over to kiss him but as her lips met his, a roar cut through the woodland – a high, dreadful shriek like a speared boar. They both leaped to their feet.

'Who hunts at this hour?' Hamlet demanded, looking frantically about him, but the darkness was absolute and the pinprick stars now seemed to be mocking them in their insubstantiality.

People were appearing between the trees, straightening clothes and huddling fearfully together. There was a terrible sound of some-one – or something – crashing through the trees and then they saw torches being rushed into the woods. Deep cries echoed unnervingly around the undergrowth until suddenly, sharp as the cry itself, came the sound of the king's war horn calling all warriors to duty.

'What in Hel is going on?'

Ofelia looked to Hamlet but already he was yanking on his clothes and she rushed to follow, grabbing her sword as she chased her lover from the woods, ecstasy forgotten in rising fear. They burst out into the compound to see a ring of torches and Ofelia's heart quailed for standing at the head of them, lit golden by the flames, was Feng.

'What's happened?' Hamlet gasped, breaking into the circle.

Ofelia followed at his shoulder and saw Feng's carefully selected war band fanning out from behind him to stand, swords drawn, around the courtiers. The cold fear was back in her belly.

'Where is my father?' Hamlet demanded when he got no reply. 'Where is the king?'

Feng folded his thick arms and looked straight at Hamlet.

'The king is dead.'

The courtiers gasped as Feng pointed and they saw Wiglek lead-ing four men from the woods bearing a body, a crumpled woman weeping in its wake. With horror Ofelia recognised the queen. All eyes shifted slowly back to the circle, looking to Hamlet, but Feng did not kneel to him nor speak the usual words: 'Long live the king.'

'How?' Hamlet challenged.

'I know not. Treachery it seems. My men heard his cry and went running but they were too late. He was lost already, struck through with a spear.'

'By whom?'

'I know not.' He looked hard at Hamlet. 'Sadly, I was still in the hall so cannot say and even for those without, the night stole away all sight.'

'Then where?'

'In the woods. The king, it seems, was celebrating summer like so many of you with his lovely woman.'

He gestured again to the queen – though queen no more – who had been taken into the arms of her ladies and was weeping piti-fully. Ofelia looked to Hamlet and saw his eyes narrow. He stepped closer to his uncle.

'You expect me to believe that my father, the High King of Denmark, was sporting in the woods?'

'Why not, prince? After all, his heir was doing so. And his heir's constable besides.'

Feng fixed them both in a sharp stare, malice in his eyes, and as Wiglek came up at his shoulder, broad arms folded, Ofelia knew with terrifying certainty that this murder was the dark plot she had feared. She'd been a fool indeed – not to suspect Feng, but to cease doing so. The serpent had struck and already his venom was seeping into Denmark. The wine was gone from her blood, the lust with it, and she must stand as a warrior now.

'This is a great tragedy,' she called, her voice clear and, thank Freya, steady. 'And we will work to find the culprit and bring him, or her, to justice. But for now it is our sombre duty to crown a new ruler, to crown King Hamlet.'

'King Hamlet,' came the response from the crowd but it was thin and uncertain. All eyes were on Feng.

'Where is the crown?' Ofelia demanded.

Feng looked straight at her.

'Where it belongs.'

With that he drew it from behind his back, held it high and

then placed it firmly upon his own head. At his side, Wiglek's eyes narrowed but he stepped forward a little to support his brother and Ofelia felt fury rise within her. All this time she had feared Feng was targeting Hamlet for being Prince of Jutland but the evil man had set his sights far, far higher – on the throne of Denmark itself. How dared he?

'Hamlet is Denmark's declared heir, Lord Feng. All saw him sworn in at Prince Geir's funeral. All acknowledged him. You cannot steal his rights.'

Feng's reply was steady.

'And I do not. I have no children of my own so he remains Denmark's heir. He can continue to learn his craft while he grows to full manhood as his father, my own brother, intended.' The court looked at each other. Ofelia heard a murmur of approval and her heart froze. Gods, but Feng was clever. 'Hamlet is my own dear nephew and Prince of Jutland. He will stand at my right hand in these troubled times and we will work together to keep Denmark safe and secure for all.'

'No,' Ofelia whispered but the crowd were all fixed on Feng.

Hamlet did not speak. What could he say to such a seemingly noble and practical solution? And, besides, Feng's men were drawing close, herding the crowd like sheep towards their new king, and in the darkness of this fearful Walpurgis Night there seemed no way to stop them.

'Long live the king!' someone cried. 'Long live King Feng!'

And with that, his war band lifted their swords high above their heads in approbation – or threat – and the sheep obediently bleated their response. Ofelia moved close to Hamlet, leaning gently against him and feeling him lean back in return, though neither looked at the other as they faced Feng.

'You swear your allegiance, Prince Hamlet?'

It was spoken as a question but there was no option to refuse. Hamlet looked left then right but he was hemmed in – trapped. Slowly he dropped to his knees.

'I swear.'

Feng smiled his serpent-smile and put a heavy hand on Hamlet's head in seeming blessing, though Ofelia saw his hairy knuckles whiten and knew how heavily he bore down on his "dear nephew". Already Wiglek was ordering their pet warriors to light a fire beneath Otto, calling all the druids forward to chant his obsequies with indecent haste to send the poor man into the realm of the dead, wherever that might be.

Ofelia clawed her fingers against her useless sword as the dear, much-loved king burned and Hamlet's future burned with him. She had been right to fear his uncles. She had known it and she had let it go, losing herself in the giddy pleasures of her lover. This was proof from the gods, if ever she'd needed it, that she should stand as guard, not girl, to her royal friend and he would need that now more than ever.

Chapter Six

Viborg, August 602

'Look, Hamlet – the stone is loose.' Ofelia wedged her fingers into the gap between the rock lintel and the giant stone door and pushed. The stone rocked. 'Come on – one big push and we'll be able to roll it away.'

She looked to him for help but he was backing off, hands held up to protect himself from the spirits inside.

'Don't, Lia. Come away. You'll wake the dead.'

Ofelia looked up at the great barrow curving up out of the rich earth.

'Exactly,' she said. 'That's exactly what I want to do. If this barrow holds the entrance to Valhalla then I want to find it and I want to stride inside and I want to drag my mother out by her burning dress and ask her a few damned questions.' He stared at her blankly. 'Do you not, Hamlet? Have you no questions for your father?'

He shifted awkwardly.

'Of course I do but none that require me to shake the very fabric of the earth.' He looked to Lars. 'Stop her, Lars, please. It's not right to break into a grave. The gods will be displeased and, Loki knows, we're in enough trouble without riling them further.'

Ofelia considered Hamlet curiously. He looked terrified but what he was saying made no sense. She went over to him.

'We are in trouble from men, not gods. We have nothing to fear from the underworld.'

'You don't know that.'

'Which is why I want to find out!'

She waved her arms furiously and Hamlet grabbed at them, pushing them down to her sides.

'You're obsessed with hunting down the dead but why, Ofelia? What can they tell us that we don't already know: that we are safe for now but danger is almost certainly on the horizon.'

He gestured across the vast moors of central Jutland to the very far line of sight where the sea was a thin strip of dark blue, like the damp hem of the sky. Feng had stayed in Zealand, lording it over his nervous new court all summer and letting his "heir" live quietly in Jutland, but they'd had word that he would visit for Lithasblot in a week's time and were on the lookout.

Peder had insisted that they move the Jutish court to inland Viborg not long after they'd fled Feng's sudden dominion. It was good, he'd said, for a prince to move about his land, which was true enough but they all knew that Viborg was also far easier to defend than Aarhus. Any "guests", welcome or otherwise, would have to come up one of the three rough roads from the east, west or south so would be seen far further in advance than if they pounced from the sea in a swift-moving boat.

Feng had sent Wiglek back to Jutland with Hamlet to help "protect" him but he had wanted none of such protection and when Peder had moved the court inland they'd left Wiglek in the Aarhus barracks to "guard the seas". He found reason to visit regularly, however, and Ofelia was certain that all he saw went straight back to King Feng. Not that there was anything more than the usual hard farming and training that made all Jutlanders the tough, stubborn folk they were. No one was disposed to rebellion, not even Hamlet.

'Feng will die,' he'd said to Ofelia on more than one occasion, 'and when he does I will be king. The gods will deliver in their own time.'

Ofelia wasn't so sure. The gods, in her experience, preferred men to weave their own wyrd.

'He would die quicker with a dagger in his back,' she'd retorted the first time but Hamlet had been furious.

'Never, Ofelia. That would make us as low as him.'

'That would be vengeance,' she'd flashed back. 'Feng killed your father, Hamlet; it is your duty to see the same delivered to him.'

'We do not know that.'

'Gods above! Of course we know that.'

'We have no proof.'

'We have all the proof we need in our hearts. Feng plotted every moment of that terrible night with skill and cunning and ruthless determination.'

'Perhaps, then, he will make a better king than I for I have none of those talents.'

He infuriated her at times like this, made her want to shake him until the pieces of his mind were loosened and fell back together in a more sensible shape.

'They are not talents, Hamlet, they are vices. A king should rule with justice and care as your father did. As you would.'

'As I *will*.' He'd taken her hands then. 'I know you think I am soft, Ofelia . . . '

'No, I . . . '

'You do and I can see why. But I am not soft, merely careful. I will ki—' He'd glanced nervously around; they'd been alone, it seemed, but there were always others listening and observing. 'I will challenge Feng if the need arises but in open battle, man to man, not in the dark spaces between honour.'

She'd felt shamed then. He had a nobler soul than she did but, then, his blood was royal. Mind you, so too was Feng's and Wiglek's so perhaps birth had nothing to do with it. Perhaps, in the end, it was simply about who was most prepared to act.

Shaking Hamlet off, she set her eye to the hole in the barrow entrance but it was too dark to grasp more than shadowy outlines. She beckoned to one of their small troop for a flint. They'd been out delivering harvest gifts to the poor shepherds and crofters on the moors and should be back in Viborg by now but this was far more important than dinner. Ofelia struck the flint and lit a taper, pushing it into the gap like a third eye.

'It looks like a corridor,' she called back to the others. 'A tiny corridor – a passageway perhaps.'

'Ofelia, come back now.'

Hamlet's voice sounded almost panicked and she looked over her shoulder.

'Is that an order, Prince?'

'It is. Leave the dead in peace, for who knows what trouble they may bring.'

'Less trouble than the living,' she growled, but the now familiar argument was interrupted by a cry from Lars.

'A ship!'

'What?'

Hamlet spun round to face her brother who had climbed up onto the barrow and was shielding his eyes as he stared out to the eastern seas.

'I see a ship sailing into the bay at Aarhus – the sail is red and gold.'

'Royal colours,' Ofelia said, scrambling up beside him.

'Feng,' Hamlet said dully. 'So he is come at last.'

'It looks like only one ship,' Lars told him, 'so he must be here without his war band.'

'Without *all* of his war band,' Hamlet corrected, 'and who knows what support his men have been drumming up locally.

We should never have left Wiglek in Aarhus; we should have kept him close.'

He paced around the base of the barrow, rubbing his hands, and Ofelia leaped down before him.

'Hamlet, be calm. The Jutlanders love you. Have you not visited many of them this summer? And have they not greeted you with joy? Feng is coming to taunt you with his power. If you wish, I can knife him in the – what was, it, the dark spaces between honour? If you do not wish, we will have to grit our teeth and be polite and hope he quickly grows bored of showing off and scuttles back to Zealand out of our way, preferably taking bloody Wiglek with him.'

Hamlet stopped his pacing.

'You are right, Ofelia. You are always bloody right.'

'Which is why I am your constable.'

'And not my wife.'

'Exactly.'

He looked at her curiously.

'Why are you not with child?'

'Hamlet!'

She flushed and looked with pointed fury at Lars and the others.

'It's hardly a secret. Why?'

His voice held an aggressive edge she'd rarely heard and he kept glancing across the golden moors to the strip of sea beyond. Feng's ship was clearly visible now. It would reach land soon so, crossly, she turned away from the barrow and made for her horse.

'We should get into Viborg.'

'And we will, but first answer my question.'

'Very well,' she snapped. 'Maybe my womb is as bitter as the rest of me?'

He considered this.

'Maybe but I know you, Ofelia – I doubt you'd leave such things to chance.'

'There are ... ways.'

'Spells?'

'Herbs.'

'You are binding your womb against me?'

'Not against you, Hamlet; just against your child.'

'You do not want my child?'

'No! I do not want *any* child, as I do not want any husband. But, Hamlet, why ask this now? Feng is coming and Wiglek will be more than ready for him. We must get back, prepare.'

'The best way to prepare against my uncle would be to add to my line.'

Still his eyes flickered restlessly to the ship. He was nervous, she knew, made anxious by his father's killer arriving, and who could blame him? But he didn't need to take it out on her. This was what men did, even honourable ones like Hamlet – they tried to shape you to their own ends and then blamed you if it didn't work.

'I agree,' she told him, planting her feet firmly in the heather. 'You should marry. Lady Agnete is as comely as ever. One word and she'd be yours and birthing royal babes within the year.'

'Ofelia . . .'

'Or pick a foreign princess. Get yourself a bride in your bed and a country at your back. Norway, perhaps, or Sweden? Lars will go as envoy, will you not, Lars?'

Lars looked nervously from one to the other.

'I will do whatever my prince commands,' he said eventually.

'If only your sister were as obedient,' was the curt reply. Hamlet stared at Ofelia for an agonisingly long time and then spun away. 'We had better go. We have a feast to order to welcome our glorious King Feng.'

He leaped into his saddle, kicked his horse straight into a gallop and was off down the slope into Viborg before anyone else could react.

'That went well,' Lars said drily.

Ofelia sighed and reached for Ansgar's bridle.

'Why won't he marry someone if he's so concerned about a bloody heir?'

'Why won't *you* just marry him, Lia?'

'Not you too, Titch?'

She made to leap into her own saddle but Lars held her back.

'It is a genuine question, sister. I do not understand.'

'That's because you're a man,' she growled then shook herself free, mounted and kicked Ansgar after Hamlet.

She must find him and make peace, for Feng would be upon them by the dinner hour and against him, at least, they had to stand united. She looked longingly back to the inviting gap in the barrow entrance but it seemed that the dead would have to wait yet again for there was trouble enough above ground without shaking beneath it for more.

'Mother!'

Hamlet stared, stunned, as the royal party rode into Viborg with not just Feng but Gertrude at its head. Ofelia was pleased to hear a note of hope enter his voice for, although he'd begrudgingly accepted her truce, he'd been snappish and foul-tempered all afternoon.

Feng's next words, however, killed any joy as dead as poor lost Otto: 'Mother and queen.'

'But . . .' Hamlet stammered.

'Gertrude has done me the honour of becoming my wife.' Everyone stared at Feng, slack-jawed, and he gave his slow snake-smile. 'We have been married since Midsummer. Did Wiglek not tell you the happy news?'

Hamlet glowered at Wiglek who stared implacably back. It was perfectly clear that he had deliberately kept the news secret and that Feng was relishing delivering it himself. His head was held ludicrously high, though Gertrude kept hers bowed and Ofelia could see why. At least her own mother had given herself to her dead husband, not to his killer.

She dared not touch Hamlet but moved as close to his shoulder as she could, hoping he would feel her support. They must be careful here. They must grit their teeth and be polite however much it galled them.

'Congratulations, my lord king,' she said, loud and clear. 'And my lady queen too. We wish you every happiness, do we not, Hamlet?'

She nudged at him and, like a puppet, he blurted out, 'We do.'

It had to be enough for now, surely, but Feng could not resist twisting the knife a little more.

'Oh, we are very happy. I thank the gods day and night for our good fortune. Especially night.'

Hamlet made a low noise in his throat, more animal than human, and Ofelia was hugely grateful when Peder fussed forward, bowing low and babbling about feasts and sleeping arrangements and plans for the royal stay. He guided the guests away to see them accommodated and Hamlet and Ofelia were saved from Feng, for a little time at least.

'Why?' Hamlet moaned. 'Why would she do that?'

Ofelia tugged him out of the courtyard towards their own rooms. As prince, Hamlet normally slept in a grand bed in the centre of the living half of the great hall but this afternoon that had been hastily made over to the king and, it seemed, his queen. Hamlet could simply have moved to Peder's second-best bed but he'd chosen, instead, to re-house himself with his men in the barracks. It seemed it had been a wise move and they rushed in there now, closing the doors behind them. A few of the other soldiers were around but they were loyal Jutlanders and could be relied upon not to report anything they overheard.

'Why?' Hamlet demanded again once they were further secluded behind his bed curtains.

Ofelia had now had time to think about this.

'I suspect it was her only option, Hamlet. Think about it – your mother has been royal all her life. She was raised a princess and made a queen through her own blood. As Rorik's daughter she is the true carrier of the royal line and to become a nothing would be hard for her to bear.'

'Not as hard as rutting with that boar every night.'

'That's just sex, Hamlet. If slave girls can stand it, a queen can too, especially if she gets a throne in return.'

'Is it worth so much?'

'Or so little.'

Hamlet yanked furiously at the blankets.

'How can you say that, you who will not marry for fear of being bound?'

She pulled the blankets straight.

'Gertrude, it seems, has no such fear. We must all find our own way in life, Hamlet.'

'So wise,' he spat, grabbing the blankets again and crushing them ferociously into a ball.

She left him then. He was hurting and there were no words, however wise, that could mend him. It would be a bitter feast tonight.

The court did its best. The musicians played loud and the skald outdid himself with an elaborate and thankfully long tale of Sigurd's conquest of the dragon Fafnir. Neither, however, could quite conceal the palpable unease of many of the courtiers. Wiglek's men ate with Hamlet's and the conversation simmered with an underlying violence that threatened to break out at any time. Only King Feng seemed truly to be enjoying himself, apparently drawing energy from the ill humour in the hall as a vulture would from battlefield carrion.

He had brought barrels of Zealand's fine fruit wine with him but Ofelia stuck to weak ale, mindful of the last terrible feast and determined not to let her guard down for even one moment this time. She saw Lars doing the same and was glad of it. They'd seated themselves at opposite sides of the hall to cover both the east and west doors and Ofelia had given her men strict instructions to stay on high alert and, especially, to watch the person of Prince Hamlet like hawks. She noted bulky Eric standing guard behind the king's table and was glad of it. She might not sport with him much these days but he was a good friend and a loyal soldier and she feared they may have sore need of those in the days ahead.

The meal done, however, and the skald finally talked hoarse, Feng pushed back his chair – knocking it carelessly against Wiglek's – and beckoned Hamlet close with all the appearance of geniality. Hamlet had been sitting beside his mother but both of them had been stiff-backed and silent and it was sad testament to the state of affairs between them that he went almost eagerly to his uncle's side instead.

The court was rising from the tables and Ofelia took the chance to move closer to the dais, hovering awkwardly with Lars until Feng called out easily to them, 'Lady Ofelia, Lord Lars – come, join us. Take a cup of wine. We should be friends. And I should thank you, for Jutland thrives under your care.'

''Tis Prince Hamlet who cares for her, my lord king,' Ofelia said carefully, 'and my uncle of course, Lord Peder.'

'Dear Lord Peder.'

Feng smiled over at the man Wiglek had pressured for the treasure to pay his foreign troops for mounting their coup. Lord Peder attempted a twisted grin in reply. Everyone waited. Feng watched the wine being poured and then turned to Hamlet.

'I am so pleased with you, prince . . . nephew, that I have chosen you for an important mission.'

'You have?' Hamlet asked, almost childlike in his surprise.

'I have. As you may know, I have long been in touch with King Aethelfrith of Bernicia and Deira in the land of the Angles. If you recall, King Rorik offered him shelter some years back and Aethelfrith has oft repeated his gratitude for that great service. He is also, as you know, married to the Lady Bebba, originally from this beautiful estate of Viborg in which we are now being so well entertained, and I am told she thrives with her lord husband and their children.'

He paused and looked around. Ofelia tried desperately to work out where his intentions lay but now the time had come Feng was bursting to reveal them.

'They have made it clear they would welcome an envoy from Denmark to formally cement an alliance between our two great kingdoms and I have chosen you, Prince Hamlet, to lead it.'

'An envoy?' Hamlet stuttered. 'To the land of the Angles?'

'To King Aethelfrith, yes. He is an important man and his power grows daily. He deserves an envoy of stature and you, my dear Hamlet, are second only to myself as king.' At his side Wiglek grunted crossly but Feng leaned heedlessly across him to stare at Hamlet, his eyes suddenly sharp. 'It is a great honour, Prince.'

Hamlet did not speak and Ofelia feared she would have to do so for him but then he gathered himself, pressed his hand to the diadem on his head, and bowed.

'And one I am delighted to accept. It will be intriguing, indeed, to meet this model of kingship.'

Feng caught the slight but had not the wit to respond.

'Good,' he eventually managed, and then Lars stepped forward to propose a toast to the great venture and the tension was drowned in ready goblets.

Ofelia raised her own with the rest but drank not. She knew better than to trust Feng these days. On the surface this mission could only benefit Hamlet; there must, therefore, be secrets hidden within its depths and she was determined to discover them before they undid him.

Chapter Seven

Hedeby, September 602

'You will like the Angles' land, Ofelia, truly. It is a fine place – so full of Danes you would swear you were at home, save for the great crags and hills. The gods must have been in a rare temper when they carved the land for it is wild terrain, though pretty, I suppose.'

Ofelia looked at Peder with surprise but his eyes were glued to the beach where Hamlet's ship was being prepared to sail on the morning tide.

'You've been there, Uncle?'

Peder nodded.

'When I was a young man.'

'You went in a trade ship?'

He flushed and tugged at his sharply trimmed beard.

'A raiding ship,' he mumbled.

'A . . . ?' Ofelia tugged on his arm, forcing him round to look at her. 'You went raiding, Uncle?'

His head went up.

'I did. Is it so strange?'

'Er, no.'

It was though. Peder had a sword but Ofelia had never seen him use it. He came down to the training yard from time to time but only to check the state of the armour and conditions of the barracks, not to fight a bout. He was a man of tally-sticks and runes and as far as she knew he always had been. She could not picture him in a raucous raiding band.

'Did you fare well?'

'We were moderately successful, yes. I could have made myself richer that way than by taking office.'

'So why did you?'

He grimaced.

'I am no sailor, Ofelia. I have no affinity with water. It is bad enough sailing Denmark's sheltered sounds; the wild Northern Seas terrified me.' He caught himself hastily. 'Though I am sure all will be well for you.'

'I am not afraid.'

'No. No, you never are. It is one of the things I admire in you, niece.'

'One of?'

Ofelia was more surprised than before for Peder rarely offered praise, or indeed criticism. Their uncle had been generous in his hospitality to her and Lars and determined in arranging their training and education but to date he had looked upon them with a sort of bemusement, as if uncertain why they were still here. Now, though, he patted her arm and coughed awkwardly.

'There are many things I admire about you, Ofelia – your courage, your tenacity, your individuality. You make your own way in the world, my dear, and that always impresses me.'

'Thank you,' she stuttered.

He coughed again.

'You might find it does you good, you know, to be in a new land. Away from ... ghosts.'

'Ghosts, Uncle?'

'I know you seek them. I've seen you, at nights, lying on the barrows as if you might sink through their ancient boundaries and into the underworld. It is not good for one so young to chase death.'

Ofelia swallowed. She had not known anyone had ever noticed her night-time whims.

'I do not chase death, Peder, but the dead.'

He shivered.

'That's little better. But perhaps in the Angles' land they will not call you so loudly. Oh, Ofelia, you will take care, won't you? You will keep yourself safe, and Lars too?'

Ofelia did not quite know where to put herself. She had not known he was so astute.

'Of course,' she assured him. 'Of course I will. And you too, Uncle, with Wiglek on your shoulder.'

'Ah, Wiglek needs me, for who else would count his beans so carefully? And, really, I am little threat to any man.'

'Uncle, you ... '

'Hush, niece, I know myself well. You need not worry about me. Keep your care for Lars – and for Hamlet.'

Ofelia looked across to the prince and felt the habitual tug in her guts he always seemed to cause in her these days. She'd had no chance to talk to him privately for he'd been determinedly caught up in preparations for the mission to the Angles any time she'd tried. She couldn't blame him, she supposed, but it hurt all the same and it was dangerous besides. They had to stand together against Feng or they would be lost.

She watched Hamlet now, talking with the handful of men Feng was allowing them to take along. An envoy, the king had insisted, should be accompanied by sufficient numbers to look imposing but not to threaten. He had deemed ten the correct number for this tricky balance, though to Ofelia it felt ridiculously few. Hamlet was a prince; he should have ten personal servants before anyone even considered his hearth troops. It worried her.

'I will do my best, Uncle. It seems a worthy mission but I fear Feng's intentions.'

'As you should. Sleep with your sword, Ofelia.' He patted her arm again then muttered gruffly, 'Your parents would be proud of you.'

Ofelia blinked, even more thrown. Peder never spoke of them.

'Thank you,' she managed, unsure what to say next.

Her eyes fixed on a strange-looking man coming along the beach. He was short and squat and walked with a limp and a wince, as if his left foot trod on nails every time he put it down. His eyes peered out from behind wild, dark hair and were fixed on the ship as lasciviously as if it were a naked woman.

'Captain Enok!' King Feng stepped away from the courtiers fawning around him and went to greet the man, shaking his hand as deferentially as if he were a fellow ruler. 'You are welcome. Lord Wiglek has told me much of your expertise and I am sure you are the man to trust with delivering my dear nephew safely to the land of the Angles.'

The captain bowed low, his left leg held at a strange, side-ways angle.

'I will battle Niort's waves on your behalf, my lord king. She is a fine craft.'

Again his eyes slid towards the ship.

'You would like to look her over?'

Enok nodded, almost drooled, and Ofelia felt briefly comforted by his clear love of the sea. Maybe Feng truly did have their safety at heart? But as the king drew the seaman away she saw Wiglek slide up to them with a small leather bag in his hand. Feng took it and pressed it tight against the captain's chest, so close to the man now that he seemed to be almost wrapped around him, and Ofelia could neither see the transaction nor hear the words spoken.

'What's in the bag?' she asked Peder.

'His payment?' he suggested, and that, she supposed, made sense but it looked very precious to Feng and she feared it held something of greater value to him than mere gold.

It suddenly felt very important to know what was inside that bag and, straightening her back, she went to join the party on the beach. The captain had been escorted on board the vessel and was running his hand along the gunwale, checking the rowlocks and leaning over to see the line of the great steering-board. He seemed very pleased with the craft and beamed readily at her when she approached.

'This is the Lady Ofelia.' Wiglek introduced her reluctantly. 'She will be travelling with you to the Angles' land.'

'You will?' Captain Enok asked.

'Indeed,' she agreed putting a discreet hand to her sword. 'I am Prince Hamlet's constable.'

'*You* are?'

He looked worriedly to Wiglek.

'You needn't worry about me, Captain,' Ofelia said, 'I can look after myself.'

The captain looked her up and down and gave a sudden, barking laugh.

'My sort of woman then!'

He winked lasciviously at her and the germ of a plan crept into Ofelia's mind. It wasn't one she liked much but these were hard times and she had to fight with every asset she had, including, it seemed, the ones she most liked to keep hidden.

'Oh, good,' she said, forcing herself to curl in closer to him, 'because you seem very much my sort of man.'

'He does?' Hamlet asked, but Ofelia forced herself to turn her back on him.

'Oh, yes.' She took the captain's arm. 'Is the ship a good one?' He nodded dumbly. 'Do show me.'

She could feel Hamlet glowering but he'd have to put up with it. He'd been avoiding her so he could hardly complain if she went for someone else. And, besides, it was for his benefit that she was doing this, as he would see soon enough.

Captain Enok was more than happy to take her round the ship

and not slow to make a move, sliding an arm around her waist as he guided her along the centre walkway and even squeezing her bottom as he helped her down to shore again. She jumped but kept her expression sweet.

'I hope to see you at dinner, Enok,' she said as they parted.

'Oh, I'll be there,' he agreed keenly. 'I get a hearty appetite the night before a journey.' He winked at her again and added, 'And not just for food.'

Ofelia managed an arch smile and headed off up the beach. She could hear footsteps crunching furiously in her wake and wasn't surprised when Hamlet grabbed her arm.

'What the hell are you up to, Lia?'

'Getting closer to the captain, of course. Wasn't it obvious?'

'Yes, it bloody well was. But why?'

She slowed and turned to face him.

'Because, Hamlet, he has secrets and we need to know the truth of them.'

'Secrets?'

'Yes. Wiglek gave Enok a bag. It's on his belt. There'll be gold in it but Feng seemed far too keen to ensure he kept it safe for it to be just that. I want a look inside.'

'And you plan, what . . . to seduce your way into taking a look?'

'I suppose so, yes, if I must.'

'That's ridiculous.'

Ofelia stared at him and noted his dark eyes bulging furiously.

'Are you jealous?'

'Of course I am.'

'Then it's you who is being ridiculous. I don't care for the captain. I don't even fancy him. It's just a means to an end, Hamlet.'

'Well, it's a poor means.'

'You can do it if you'd rather. I expect he'd have you every bit as eagerly.'

'No!'

'Fine. I will then. It's very simple. I distract him . . .'

'"Distract" him!'

'Yes. Distract him. You're right, seduction is the best ploy.'

'I'm right? I never ...'

'Because if I can get his clothing off, you can grab the bag.'

He squeezed her arm so tight she almost yelped.

'You expect me to watch you sport with the man?'

'No, Hamlet, I expect you to grab the bag.'

'I will not. It's a mad plan. I forbid you to do it.'

'Forbid me?' Ofelia narrowed her eyes and he flinched and let go of her arm. 'You forbid me to uncover something that might be vital to your safety?'

'Ofelia ...'

'That's my job, Hamlet. I'm your constable, charged with protecting you.'

'But ...'

He looked confused now and she stepped up close to him.

'I will do what I need to and if that means going all the way with the man then so what? It's not as if I haven't done it before, is it?'

'No,' he growled.

'So what's one more?' He looked even more confused and, with a quick look back to the ship to be sure they weren't seen, she darted forward and placed a swift kiss on his lips. He started but his eyes softened. 'It's just a ruse, Hamlet, to keep us all secure. Keep an eye on me, stay close, and when the time comes get the bag, yes?'

She pulled away but he grabbed at her.

'What if it doesn't work? What if he gets violent?'

Ofelia shook her head at his fears.

'As I told Enok, Hamlet, I can look after myself. Now, excuse me, I must dress for dinner. Trust me.'

'I can't. I think ...'

'Trust me.'

She kissed him again – fighting hard to resist the urge to linger against him forever – and then darted away. She did not relish the prospect of seducing Captain Enok but she was very much enjoying having something active to do. Feng had been in control for far too long and if it took some female wiles to stop him, so what? A soldier had to use every weapon in his – or her – armoury.

She drew the line at wearing a dress to dinner for fear of arousing Feng's suspicion but she left off her jerkin and chose her thinnest tunic, tied as tight as possible to show her modest curves. She borrowed some lavender water to make herself smell sweet and even put a little kohl on her lashes and bit her lips into swollen redness as she'd seen other women do when they were hunting a man. She'd never had to bother before. She found that asking if they fancied a little sport usually worked a treat but tonight there was more at stake than scratching an itch and she felt disconcertingly nervous as she headed to the hall.

'You look odd,' was her brother's greeting as he caught up with her at the door.

'You're too kind, Titch.'

He looked her up and down.

'Not odd,' he corrected himself, 'more ... pretty. What are you up to?'

'Can I not just look "pretty" – thank you by the way – for no reason?'

'You? No.'

'Fine, fine, I might have a bit of a plan but don't draw attention to it. Ah, Captain Enok!'

She went forward and was gratified to see the captain's eyes light up. He'd tidied himself, she noticed. He'd washed and changed into a fresh (or at least semi-fresh) tunic and had tied his wild hair back in a half-competent plait. He looked a little younger and a lot cleaner and she set herself straight to her task.

'You look very fine, Captain.'

'You're too kind. It's not every day I get to dine with royalty.'

He glanced towards Feng as they slid into places on the benches, clearly dazzled by the king who was showing him such favour.

'You have made journeys for King Feng before?' Ofelia asked.

'Once or twice, via Lord Wiglek, but just carrying goods or transporting soldiers. I have never crewed a prince before – nor his lovely constable.'

'And I have never sailed west, so it is new for us both.'

'Really?' His eyes lit up with genuine enthusiasm. 'Then it is a good job you are a part of this. The west is the future, Ofelia . . . I may call you Ofelia? Excellent. A wise king would build up this little port of Hedeby and my hometown of Ribe, further down in the south. It is a fine place, you know, or it could be with a little encouragement. A little gold.'

Ofelia spotted an opening.

'Are you looking to build there yourself, Enok?'

'Perhaps, in a year or two, when I grow too old to do battle with Niort and his sea creatures. I have a daughter there and she has a good husband and three growing children. I would like to see them more.'

'You are married then?'

'No. That is, no longer. My wife died a year back. I miss her.' He looked suddenly forlorn but then shook himself and added more lewdly, 'In all ways.'

'A man has needs,' Ofelia forced herself to say, keeping her voice low. 'A woman too.' His eyes widened and she smiled at him. 'But tell me of this hall you plan. It would take much gold, would it not?'

'I am saving.'

'So I see,' she said, running a light hand over his thigh and squeezing the bag that hung from his belt.

She felt coins and chunks of hacksilver, the curled shape of an arm-ring and something else – some sort of stick. Enok, however, was pulling away so she swiftly moved her hand across to his more personal possessions, rubbing gently. His eyes widened further.

'You seem to have treasure enough for me,' she whispered in his ear and felt him stir beneath her touch.

'Ofelia, we are in the royal hall.'

'For now . . .'

She let him go and turned back to her dinner but her mind was racing. What was the stick in the bag? It had felt like no ornament or piece of silver she'd ever seen and she could think of only one thing it could be – runes. Enok was carrying a rune-stick but for whom and to what purpose? And why, if it was a message for the Angle king, had it not been given to Hamlet as the king's envoy?

She was more certain than ever that she had to see inside the bag and redoubled her flirtation. She could see Hamlet glowering at her but shut her mind to that. This was far more important than his petty jealousy and she gave Enok her full attention for the remainder of the meal. As it drew to a close amidst a flurry of loud and hollow toasts to the success of Prince Hamlet's journey, she shuffled closer and placed her hand, again, on Enok's thigh.

'Have you ever done it on board ship?' she asked quietly.

He looked at her.

'Done what?'

She raised an eyebrow.

'Have you ever sported with a woman on board ship?'

'Once or twice,' he admitted, 'when I was a young man. But not for years.'

'Was it good?'

He looked at her and grinned.

'It was rather. Have you not?'

She shook her head and pouted her lips.

'Never.' She let her hand run higher. 'But I would like to.'

'We will be a considerable party on board though. We can hardly . . .'

'Surely the ship sits empty tonight?'

'Ah! She does, she surely does.'

'So we could . . .'

He was on his feet already, his royal host forgotten in a rush of lust.

'We could!'

Ofelia just had time to check that Hamlet had noted their hasty exit. His eyes, thank Frey, were tight upon her and the last thing she saw as Enok pulled her from the hall was the prince rising to his feet. She hoped he'd hurry. Now they were outside Enok was almost running, his limp far less pronounced as he made for the beach and the beautiful ship. Two men sat on deck guarding it but Enok dismissed them with little ceremony.

'I have charge now. Go, get yourself some ale.'

They needed little urging and were off to the hall almost as fast as their captain had arrived, leaving Ofelia alone with him. He lifted her aboard, scrambling keenly after, and she took a deep breath and set herself to her task.

'Gods, I want you,' he gasped.

'And I you,' she managed before he was grabbing at her tunic, shoving his callused hands beneath to grope for her breasts.

He was rough and unsubtle and she had to battle not to pull away. Hamlet's hands were callused too but he ran them so skilfully over her skin that the roughness teased her deliciously.

Don't think of that, she told herself, and bent to nibble at Enok's neck, taking the chance to check if Hamlet had marked where they had gone. She thought she saw a figure coming stealthily down the beach but Enok pulled her onto the boards of the deck before she could be sure. She would just have to trust that Hamlet would do as she'd said.

She rolled Enok over and straddled him, casting off her tunic so her slim body shone in the moonlight. He gave a rumble of appreciation and tugged at the ties of his trews.

'Let me,' Ofelia said, shuffling back and slowly, teasingly, undoing the laces. He moaned as she released him.

'Oh, God, that's good.'

She touched him lightly, letting her hand bump frustratingly against his belt.

'Ah, this is getting in the way. Here ...'

She put a hand to his belt to unclasp it but, even mad with desire, Enok stopped her.

'Leave it on.'

'But it will rub me when I ride you.'

He closed his eyes for a moment, clearly doing battle with himself, and then nodded. Ofelia watched, as keen to get her hands on the precious bag as he was to get his hands on her, but he pushed her aside and moved a few paces up the boat to stow it away in a casket. She had to move fast.

'Is that casket where you store all your treasures?' she asked as loudly as she dared. Where was Hamlet?

'Not all of them,' he said, closing the lid and turning back. 'Don't fret, I'll give you what you want soon enough.'

But he didn't move and, steeling herself, she dropped her breeches. He stared long and hard but then turned back to the casket and she saw a key on a cord around his neck. Damn! She moved closer, rubbing herself against him.

'Take me now,' she moaned into his ear and, thank Frey, it was too much for him to bear.

He pushed her across the gunwale, spreading her legs and pounding into her with desperate urgency. It was just the sort of rough, hard encounter she had always sought in the past but it seemed all those times with Hamlet and his slow, skilful caresses had changed her for now she felt exposed and used.

As you are using him, she reminded herself crossly, gripping the gunwales tight and forcing herself to make sounds of pleasure. It was too effective. He was going to be done in moments and Hamlet would not have time to get into the casket.

'Slower,' she gasped. 'It's so good, Enok. Do it slower.'

He obligingly calmed his pace, pausing to run his hands all over her in a way that made her flesh crawl but out of the corner of her eye she saw Hamlet peering over the gunwale behind. His face was pale and furious but he moved swiftly to lift the casket lid. Ofelia upped the noise, letting out a series of gasps and shrieks that sounded ridiculous to her own unhappy ears but were clearly music to Enok's for his pace increased again until, with a cry of his own, he was done. He collapsed along her back.

'Thor's hammer, Ofelia, that was good. You're amazing. I feel blessed, truly. This will be a succcessful voyage, I know it. What ship could not sail well with such an oblation to see her on her way?'

Ofelia squirmed beneath him.

'Indeed,' she squeaked. He was pulling her into his arms and kissing her. His breath was stale and foul, but he was clutching her so close and shaking so hard that she dared not pull away. 'Are you well?' she asked eventually.

'A little upset, that is all. I miss my wife, Ofelia. I miss her so much.'

The gods help her! This was all she needed. The sex she could just about manage but if he was going to pour his heart out she'd go insane.

'Let's lie down,' she suggested. 'You're worn out.'

'I am. I am worn out. I've not slept well since we lost her. It's like a bit of me is missing and I'm endlessly waking up looking for it.'

'Poor you. Here, rest your head. Let me cover you up.'

'Don't go.' He grabbed her hand. 'Don't leave me, Ofelia, not so soon.'

She had little choice but to lie down beside him and stroke his head as the shudders slowly subsided. She looked to the stars and prayed to kindly Balder for patience, but Balder either wasn't listening or was laughing at her, for she felt more and more irritated with every minute that passed.

Finally, to her great relief, the last shudder eased its way out of Enok and he slept. She lay there as long as she could bear and then slowly, carefully, slid away. He shifted but did not wake and she grabbed her tunic and let herself down off the side of the boat. Hamlet was crouched just below the figurehead, his brow drawn furiously tight but the precious bag, at least, in his grasp. She ran to him.

'Ofelia, you're naked!'

'So?' She tugged her tunic over her head. 'Better?'

'No.'

'Oh, Hamlet. Come on.' She pulled him a little further up the beach and reached for the bag. 'Have you looked inside?'

'No.'

'Why the hell not? Give it to me!'

She snatched it off him, half an eye on the boat in case Enok woke. She untied the drawstring, pulled the bag open and thrust her hand inside. Her fingers closed instantly around the stick she'd felt earlier and she drew it out. It was short but broad and cut cleanly in half to expose a flat, golden surface. The moon, thankfully, was large and bright in a near-cloudless sky and if she tilted the stick she could clearly see the runes scratched across the wood.

She heard Hamlet gasp and felt him draw closer as together they squinted at the carefully carved figures. For once Ofelia felt grateful to Peder for having insisted they all learned to read the mystical alphabet. She'd chafed at her lessons at the time, desperate to be outside, but she blessed his stern discipline now.

'"Please welcome Prince Hamlet into your family,"' she read, her voice quiet on the still air, '"and, when the time is right ..."' she peered more closely at the final strokes, unable to believe what she saw '"...kill him,"' she finished.

She looked at Hamlet.

'Kill him,' he echoed, putting out a finger to trace the few sharp strokes that demanded his murder. He stared at Ofelia. 'You were right.'

'It gives me no pleasure. I knew Feng was up to something but this ... He is not even man enough to do his own dirty work but must demand it of some Angle king?'

'It is not unusual to dispose of an unwelcome heir this way, Ofelia.'

'It is not right. And it will not happen.'

'You will take the stick?'

Ofelia shook her head. She peered again at the runes. They were very economical, each one conveying their meaning in a minimum of straight lines. It made them wonderfully simple to use – but wonderfully simple, also, to alter.

'If we take the stick Enok will be suspicious. He must know what he carries, even if not the meaning of it. He will check before we sail tomorrow and sound the alarm if it is not there. No, I have a neater plan.'

She reached for the belt that still sat at her side and took out the sharp knife she'd carried ever since Otto's foul murder. She had known it would be vital protection, if not quite in what way. Biting her lip in concentration, she put the lethal tip to the wood and cut.

'Ofelia . . .'

'Hush. I must not make a mistake.'

'But . . .'

'Hush, Hamlet. Two more strokes and . . . There!'

She blew away the flecks of sawdust and looked proudly at her handiwork. You could not tell her additions were later than the rest and a few days at sea would weather them further. 'Perfect.'

'What does it say?'

She handed it to him and slowly he read: '"Please welcome Prince Hamlet into your family and, when the time is right, see him wed." Wed? Ofelia, what have you done?'

'Saved your life.'

'But I don't want to marry an Angle princess.'

'You'd rather be stabbed in the back?'

'No! But there must be another . . .'

'There isn't. That is the only alternative rune that makes sense. And, besides, you should marry.'

'Why? So you can go back to rutting with strangers without me getting in the way?'

'No! Hamlet, I did that for you. I hated it.'

'Didn't sound that way.'

'I was dissembling. Making noise to cover any sound you made.'

'It was very convincing.'

'Good.' She glared at him; he glared back. 'Give the stick to me,' she said, holding out her hand. 'I need to return it to the bloody casket before we are found out and hauled before Feng. I am sure he would happily execute you here in Denmark if he had just reason.'

'I've done nothing.'

'You stole the treasure bag. That's theft. At the very least you would have your hand cut off – your sword hand. Now, give it to me.'

Sulkily he handed the stick over and she grabbed the bag and turned towards the boat but he stopped her.

'Please, Ofelia, there must be another way. I've told you, I don't want to marry. Or, at least, I do – but to you.'

'And I've told you, Hamlet, that I will never marry. When will you start to believe me?'

'So you'll rut with other men for me but you won't be my wife? That's twisted, Ofelia.'

'Not to me it isn't. I'm your constable, Hamlet. I do what I must to see you safe. It is my duty and my greatest desire for I could not bear it if you . . . you . . . Thor's fury, I have to go.'

She shoved the wretched rune-stick into the bag, yanked the drawstring tight and ran. Hamlet tried to stop her again but she squirmed out of his grasp to head down the beach and vault into the boat. Enok was asleep still but his head was moving from side to side as if he might wake at any moment and she dashed to the casket. She'd just slotted the bag inside when he stirred.

'Ofelia? Ofelia, where are you?'

'Here. I'm here. I'm just dressing.'

She held up her breeches as the casket lid shut behind her.

'Don't! You are so much nicer naked.'

The words reminded her painfully of Hamlet and it was all she could do to kneel down and kiss the portly captain instead.

'I wish I did not have to but, as you know, we sail early and I am not yet packed. I planned to organise myself before dinner but then I met you and thoughts of what I longed to do with you meant that I made a poor job of it.'

He smirked and pulled her onto him.

'Then let me do it to you one more time before you go.'

'But . . .'

'I will be quick.'

It was not the most romantic proposition but she could see little way out of it without putting him on alert so she had little choice but to submit and pray he was, at least, true to his word.

The next day they sailed. Captain Enok was in high spirits, humming as he supervised the loading of the soldiers and their goods and bowing jauntily to one and all as they came down to the beach to see off the Prince. Hamlet, by contrast, was dark-eyed and sombre. He bade his royal uncle the most perfunctory farewell and favoured his mother with nothing more than a curt bow.

'Take care of yourself, my boy,' she said, in a pleading tone.

Did she know of her new husband's plot? Ofelia wondered. Did she care? Was she so desperate to keep her own throne that she would sacrifice her son for it? Where, in all this, was the maternal instinct so many spoke of? Not in Gertrude, it seemed, nor in Ophelia's own mother either. In that, at least, she and Hamlet were united, though in little else.

He sat determinedly on the opposite side of the deck from her and did not even bid her a good morning or speak with her to check things were well with the men. Their little troop kept looking from one to the other of their leaders, confused, and Ofelia could only hope that three or four days at sea would force Hamlet to give up his sulk and talk to her again.

Captain Enok cast off with a flourish and beckoned her to sit with him at the steer-board. She crept up the deck, all eyes upon her, and set her face determinedly out to sea. Enok said the future was in the west and for now it seemed that hers was. Hamlet's too, not that he was thanking her for it. Who knew what would meet them when the boat touched land once more but it would, at least, not include Hamlet's murder and for that she would do what she'd done last night one hundred times over.

She looked out at the low waves beyond the curve of the port. Somewhere over these Northern Seas there was an Angle princess who would, if the plan worked, marry Hamlet and then, surely, he would stop pestering her for the silly ceremony. It was not as comforting a thought as she'd hoped and she was glad of the sharp air and spray of salt water to sting away her foolish thoughts as they left Denmark's shores far behind and headed to the land of the Angles.

PART TWO

Chapter Eight

Dinguardi, Bernicia, September 602

Weddings! Why did there have to be so much fuss? Flora didn't understand why they couldn't just be slotted into the usual routine of the day like any other piece of business instead of turning the whole estate upside down for what felt like forever.

She cut another stalk of rosemary, laying it alongside the rest to be sure it was the right length. Every bunch had three long stalks, three medium and three short. That way they formed a plump bundle in which all the tiny leaves had space to dry. Other people cut them all the same length and, whilst that appealed to Flora in theory, in practice it meant the herb was crushed so she had developed the three-three-three system – neat, orderly and effective.

Picking up a length of twine from the pile she'd cut earlier, she focused on tying the knot tight enough to hold the stalks, but not so tight that it bit into them. Perfect. She lifted the completed bunch, hung it on one of the hooks she'd cleaned before she started and reached for the next stalk. This, at least, was calm, controllable work and she was grateful to bury herself in it after the chaos of her father's wedding.

Her fingers itched at the thought of all the people who had been cluttering up Dinguardi for so many days and who looked set to do so for several yet. It was worse than a festival. At least Walpurgis, Yule and Lithasblot happened at the same time every year and with the same pattern of events. Flora still didn't like the way the beautiful estate on top of the crag above the sea suddenly filled with chattering, dancing, drinking people but at least they were kept busy in predictable ways.

With a wedding though there was no logic – no nine days of fasting, no twelve days of rituals to nurse the new sun into health, no patterns of prayers ordered by the druids to keep everyone in check. Instead, they all milled around, gossiping and speculating and creating trouble. And women were the worst. How could they spend so long debating what the bride's dress would look like? Why could they not just wait and see? And who cared anyway? It was a dress, the same as any other but with more gold thread sewn into it and much, much more fuss about whether it would fit.

Not that this bride had fussed. Flora had almost admired the girl for that though, in truth, it was more because she had not wanted to marry than because of a healthy disdain for dress patterns. Flora hadn't wanted her to marry either. Why did her father need another wife? He had an excellent one already and given how much he liked to moan about women there seemed little logic in saddling himself with a second.

'It's political, Flora,' Aethelfrith had said when she'd had a chance to ask him, back before the people had come and the world had gone wedding-mad. 'I have taken Deira by might, as you know, but now I must take her by negotiation too. King Aella is dead and his son fled so that leaves only his daughter.'

'Cathryn?'

'Cathryn, yes. If I marry her then the people of Deira will see that I do not intend to crush them or disupt their usual routines. I will be recognising the existing order of their society and they will therefore accept my rule more readily. Can you see that?'

Unfortunately, Flora had been able to see that all too clearly. Put this way, her father taking the Deiran princess as his wife made perfect sense but for some reason it still addled her stomach like fermented cabbage and she hated to see Lady Bebba, her tall, stately mother, having to sit in the same hall as the fiercely pretty little Cathryn.

She glanced across the herb-room to where Bebba stood working on the marjoram, tying bundles with a quiet concentration that soothed Flora nearly as much as her own work. She had been surprised to find her mother in here when she'd arrived as she was usually the only one up at dawn, but was happy to work alongside her. Bebba understood about working in silence. She did not chatter like the other women and Flora loved her for it. She wasn't sure how a woman was meant to act when her husband of fifteen years wed another but it seemed to her that Bebba, with her elegant, smiling acceptance, had at least minimised the fuss and for that she was hugely grateful.

Bebba looked up, as if sensing Flora's eyes upon her, and smiled. 'Are you hungry, Flora?'

Flora shook her head. She wasn't sure she'd ever be hungry again, she'd eaten so much food. With new guests arriving every day of last week there'd been constant feasts and that had been before the wedding eve feast and of course the wedding itself. So much fuss; so much waste. Flora had kept herself busy working with the kitchen servants to arrange distribution of the leftovers to the locals as far out from Dinguardi as she'd been able to persuade the soldiers to ride. The people, at least, would appreciate this wedding for it had been a cold winter in Bernicia and they were all far too thin.

'Me neither,' Bebba said. 'We'll just stay here, shall we?'

'Yes, please.'

The herb-room was Flora's favourite place at any time but especially today. It was a shrine to the goddess Eyra, physician to the gods, and Flora strove to learn a little more of her healing magic whenever she could. The neat building led into the garden, which was encircled all around with a low fence to keep the fierce sea winds from damaging the delicate leaves of the various herbs and, coincidentally, kept it separate from the rest of the compound.

All around she could hear people hefting themselves up from their makeshift beds, groaning and scratching and starting up with the chatter already. Now the wedding was over they would dissect what had happened in much the same way as, beforehand, they had speculated about what was to come. It was all so very pointless and Flora was far happier in here with her quiet, sweet-smelling, totally un-opinionated herbs.

'There you are!'

She flinched as her sister burst in with a whirl of skirts that sent the carefully laid out lengths of twine flying to the floor.

'Udela! Look what you've done.'

'Who cares, Flora? It's just string. There are far more important things to worry about. What did you think of the wedding? Was the dress not divine? Though her face less so. She's a pretty thing but not when she scowls; it quite ruins the effect.'

'Perhaps, Udela, she didn't really care, what with being made to marry her father's killer.'

'Flora! You can't talk about Father like that.'

'Why not? It's true.'

Udela tossed her hair, as corn-blonde as Flora's own but far more assiduously tended.

'So? When will you understand that truth is not always the best guide?'

Flora did not bother to reply. She would never understand that because it was stupid. If everyone just spoke the truth life would be far, far simpler.

'Mother!' Spotting Bebba, Udela rushed across and enveloped her in a fierce hug. 'Oh, Mother, how *are* you?'

Her voice, Flora noticed, had that strange tone to it that seemed

94

to say that her sister cared if Bebba was well but also hoped she was not. That must be this malleable truth nonsense again. Bebba let herself be hugged then politely detached herself.

'I am well, thank you, Udela.'

'Did you sleep? I'll wager you didn't sleep a wink, did you? How could you with Father ... well, you know ... '

Flora frowned. That was another thing people like Udela did – deliberately not say things.

'*I* don't know,' she said.

'Flora! Don't be so crass. Poor Mother.'

'You brought it up.'

'I know but at least I was subtle.'

Flora opened her mouth to protest but Bebba caught her eye and gave her a quick wink and she closed it again. She thought carefully. Last night Father had been in bed with his new wife. She knew that because the whole court had put him in there, with the men all cheering and Aethelfrith hurrying them away and Cathryn glowering even more than at the ceremony.

Flora knew what he'd had to do to her for she'd seen it enough times at feasts. You could never go to the latrines without stumbling over some couple locked together. It looked a messy business but everyone seemed to like it so, as with the pattern on a wedding dress, Flora had decided she would just wait and see what it was like when her time came.

'Father was doing his duty,' Bebba said quietly to Udela.

'But it's not that simple, surely?' her sister protested.

'It is if you let it be.'

'But *you're* his wife.'

'One of them.' Udela gave a furious squeak and Bebba took both her hands in her own and held her daughter until she stilled. 'Listen, my sweet one. It is not easy, you're right, and I hope that when you marry you have your husband to yourself, but I am not, you know, put aside. Your father needed to cement relations with Deira and this is the best way to do so.'

'But why could Cathryn not just marry Earnfrith?'

'Your brother is only twelve, Udela. It is a little young and we needed to move fast for the people of Deira are restless and we do not want a rebellion. If that happened, we would have to send our men to fight. Many lives would be lost on both sides and many women would be left widows. It is better, surely, for one woman to suffer a little blow to her pride than for so many to lose their protectors?'

Udela huffed.

'It just seems so unfair on you, Mother.'

Bebba smiled.

'Perhaps but I can take it, my sweet. Thank you, though, for your concern.'

Udela hugged her again and this time Bebba squeezed her elder daughter tight. Flora watched them. She felt an uneasy suspicion that she should join in – girls seemed always to be in huddles with each other – but they looked very well as they were and she felt she was more likely to get in the way.

'Would you like a drink?' she offered instead. 'I have fresh apple juice.'

She pointed to the press in the corner into which she'd squeezed some of the apples from the barrels this morning.

'Please, Flora,' Bebba said. 'That would be lovely.'

Udela accepted a goblet too. Her eyes kept darting to the doors as the shadows of people heading to the great hall to break their fast continually crossed the gap beneath, but she sat down with Bebba and Flora between the trestles and sipped thoughtfully.

'What if Cathryn has a child?' she asked eventually.

'I'm sure Cathryn *will* have a child,' Bebba said, 'probably several, and that will be all to the good for my womb, it seems, can hold babies no longer. Cathryn is young and healthy and your father needs more children. More boys especially. One is not enough to guarantee the succession.'

Flora felt a surge of alarm.

'Is Earnfrith going to die?'

'No, Flora! Of course not. He is quite well, but in the future . . . who knows? Men must go to war sometimes and not all of them come back. You know that.'

Flora nodded; she did know that. She had counted her father's hearth troops out and back in again too many times not to know for certain that some were lost each time – on average about one in every five. And that number rose steeply if the common people had to go too, for they had little in the way of armour and their weapons were often poor swords passed through so many generations that their edge had been worn right away, or farm tools adapted ineffectually for battle. Barely one in two of them came back, even from a victory. The mathematics of war were not good.

'But princes rarely die,' said Udela complacently, 'because everyone else fights to keep them safe.'

'King Aella died,' Flora pointed out. 'That's how Father got Deira and why he's married Princess Cathryn.'

'Flora!'

'It's true.'

'That doesn't mean it needs to be spoken of aloud.'

'So we all just sit here thinking it but we cannot say the words?'

'Yes. Saying the words makes it more real.'

Flora ground her teeth in frustration.

'That cannot be, Udela. It either is real or it is not. Words cannot make it more so.'

'You're strange, Flora.'

'*I* am strange? You are the one trying to bend reality.'

'Girls, girls, hush now,' Bebba interrupted. 'You are not children anymore to be squabbling this way but young women. We must not fall out but take care of each other.'

'You're right, Mother,' Udela gushed instantly. 'So right. Now, shall we all go to the hall? We should be seen, you know, or people will talk.'

'People will talk anyway,' Flora said wearily.

'Of course. It's called being sociable.'

'It's called being nosy.'

'Girls!' Bebba warned again but a low cough outside the door stopped her and she scrambled to her feet, Udela and Flora just behind, as Aethelfrith sidled in.

'Good morning, wife.'

He took Bebba's hand and kissed it formally.

'Good morning, husband. I hope you . . .' Bebba faltered, gathered herself. 'I hope you are well.'

'I am, thank you. And you?'

'Very well. Flora and I have been tying herbs.'

'Good. Good.'

Flora looked curiously at her father. Bernicia's king was tall and wide-shouldered and usually dominated any room he was in, especially one as small as the herbery, but this morning before their mother he seemed unusually stooped and uncertain.

'I have a gift for you, Bebba,' he said now.

'For me?'

Bebba looked confused and no wonder. Everyone knew a new wife received a bride price the morning after her wedding but Bebba was not a new wife.

'For you, yes. I would like to gift you this prosperous estate of Dinguardi to be held as your own. I know it is your favourite residence and I would like you to have it as assurance of my . . . my continued regard for you and your security within this, my kingdom.'

Flora looked at Bebba and saw tears well in her mother's eyes.

'Thank you, Aethelfrith,' she stuttered.

'It is my pleasure and I hope we can still spend much time here. Together. I mean, I know it will not be as simple as before but . . .'

'It will be as simple as we make it,' Bebba said, composed again, and Flora thought she had never been prouder of her mother.

Aethelfrith, too, seemed reassured by her calm.

'I am blessed indeed,' he said and kissed his wife's hand again. 'May I escort you to the hall to break your fast?'

98

'Me? But what of . . . of Cathryn?'

Bebba choked a little on the name but got it out.

'She is resting,' Aethelfrith said. 'I thought maybe my daughters could go and see her.'

'Go and see Cathryn?' Udela spluttered.

Aethelfrith's eyes narrowed dangerously.

'Yes, Udela.'

'Why would I go to see *her*?'

'Because I asked you to.'

He glared at her and Udela swallowed.

'Of course. I mean, yes, Father, whatever you suggest.'

'Good.'

'Now?'

'Now.'

Udela gave a curtsey and headed to the door. Flora made haste to follow.

'Thank you,' Aethelfrith said, but when Flora glanced back she saw him already turning to Bebba, taking her elegant face between both his hands.

Flora watched for a moment before Udela dragged her away but afterwards the picture stayed in her mind. Her father loved her mother but had taken another wife; her mother loved her father but had let him. Now they had to negotiate the days ahead between them. Whatever her mother said, it all felt very complicated. And now they must visit the new wife too.

'I cannot believe Father thinks this is a good idea,' Udela fumed as she stomped across the bustling compound towards the bower Aethelfrith had assigned to his reluctant bride. 'What on earth are we going to say to her?'

'I don't know, Udela – you're the one who always wants to talk.'

'But not to *her*.'

'It's not her fault, surely?'

'Well, no, but she's taken our mother's place, Flora – we can hardly be seen to condone that.'

'Mother's place is assured. Did you not just hear Father gift her all of Dinguardi? And he is taking her into the hall on his arm. It is perhaps Cathryn who actually needs us most.'

Udela tossed her hair and stopped just short of the bower door to glare at Flora.

'You do know what she was doing with Father last night?'

Flora coloured.

'Of course I do.'

'They were together. Naked.'

'I know, Udela. Hush.'

'He put his ...'

'Hush! It is you who are being crass now.'

Udela gave her a sly grin.

'Just making sure you know, Flora. We will be wed soon and I wouldn't want you going to your wedding bed unprepared.'

'You're too kind.' Flora considered her sister. 'Do you want to do that, Udela?'

Now it was she who flushed.

'I don't know. I suppose so. Everyone else does and I do want to get married.'

'There's no rush.'

'I'm eighteen, Flora. I don't know what Father is waiting for. I'll soon be too old for anyone to want me.'

'Hardly! Mother has seen thirty-three summers and Father clearly still wants her.'

'And yet he beds another.'

'That's politics and you know it.'

'Yes, well, I wish he'd get on and "politic" me. Now, are we going to visit this damned girl or what?'

'I don't know,' snapped a voice from the other side of the door, 'but either get on with it and come in or sod off!'

Udela gasped. Flora smothered a giggle and stepped up to the door.

'We'll come in then,' she said and did so.

The bower was not especially large and was almost entirely taken up by the huge bed. Cathryn looked childishly tiny against the big pillows and Flora edged forward.

'Good morning, Queen Cathryn.'

'Co-queen,' Cathryn retorted.

'Queen nonetheless. You are honoured.'

'I am forced.'

Flora liked her honesty.

'You are,' she agreed, sitting tentatively on the end of the bed, 'but at least this way you still get to rule your own people.'

'My father's people.'

'No,' Udela said from the doorway where she hovered still, '*my* father's people. He won them in battle.'

'And me besides.'

Cathryn's voice was fierce but she pulled the covers up tighter around her and Flora wondered what she had endured last night.

'Are you . . . well?' she asked.

'What do you think?'

'I don't know, that's why I asked.'

Cathryn squinted at her and then looked to Udela.

'She's always saying odd things like that,' Udela told Cathryn gruffly.

Flora couldn't see what she'd said that was so odd but at least Udela came a little closer.

'I am alive,' Cathryn said eventually to Flora, 'which is more than my father is. And I am safely housed, which is more than my exiled brother is.'

'Well, then, that is good.'

Again Cathryn looked to Udela who gave a low laugh.

'My sister's a bit simple,' she said.

'I am not,' Flora protested. 'I'm far better at mathematics than you are and I can speak three languages and I know every herb under Odin's skies. It's just that everyone else likes to make things unnecessarily complicated.' She looked from cowering Cathryn to glowering Udela. 'Look – it is clear that no one likes this situation, correct?' She received two grunts of assent. 'But it is how things are so surely we are best finding a way to get on with each other?'

'Just like that?'

'Why not?'

Udela bridled but Cathryn sat up a little straighter.

'You mean, be friends?'

'If you'd like that.'

Cathryn shook her head.

'Not friends.'

'Compatriots perhaps?'

Neither Cathryn nor Udela answered but Udela sat on the bed and Cathryn pointed to the floor where her shift lay in a heap. Flora bent, picked it up and handed it to her.

'Thank you.'

Udela fidgeted with the covers as the other girl made herself decent and then blurted out, 'What's it like?'

'What?'

'You know ... marriage.'

Cathryn snorted.

'Rough.'

'Oh.' Udela fiddled with her hair then added, 'Lady Annis says it is fabulous.'

'Yeah, well, maybe Lady Annis has a better husband than I.'

'Or maybe Lady Annis is a better wife.'

They stared each other down and Flora rose and moved to the window opening, pushing back the leather curtains to avoid the strained atmosphere within. The window faced east and she could see the sea sparkling in patches where the sun peeked between the clouds. There was a ship moving at some speed far out across the bay and she wondered who was sailing at this time of the morning and then noticed with a start that the sail was not the blue and white of her father's craft but red and gold.

'A ship!' she cried, letting the curtain drop and running for the door.

'Flora?' Udela called after her but she wasn't listening.

She sprinted across to the hall and burst inside.

'A ship, Father! There's a foreign ship in the bay.'

There were many people in the hall, gathering around the hearth to eat bread and cheese and chunks of ham, and everyone froze and looked her way. She quailed beneath their stares but this was important.

'Father . . .' she started again but already Aethelfrith was up and heading towards her, his men falling in at his back.

He swept Flora up with him without breaking stride and headed straight out and across the compound to the palisade fencing at the seaward side of the great fortress. The lookouts had clearly seen the ship too and were heading their way.

'Too late,' the king rapped at them. 'My daughter's pretty blue eyes work far better than yours.'

He brushed them aside and stepped up to the fence. He was tall enough to look over the top but Flora had to stand on her tiptoes and was glad when Aethelfrith lifted her as if she were a little girl again and not sixteen summers old.

'There!' She pointed. The ship was closer now and the sail clear to see, for her at least. Her father was squinting and she pointed her finger impatiently. 'There!'

'What colour is the sail?' Aethelfrith demanded.

'Red and gold.'

'Danish then. Interesting. Is it just one ship, Flora?'

She scanned the sea all around.

'Just one,' she confirmed, 'and it is heading this way.'

'Excellent. Odin smiles on us for it must be from King Feng.' He turned to the court, setting Flora back on her feet, and looked for Bebba. 'You remember Feng, my dear?'

'Otto's younger brother? Of course.'

'Otto's younger brother and now High King of Denmark. I have been exchanging envoys with him. I owe Denmark a duty of gratitude for sheltering me in my exile and they could prove a useful ally as we seek to enlarge out borders. With Danish assistance we could, perhaps, push all the way to the west coast.'

The court roared approval. The west was held by two Celtic kings – Aedan of Dal Riata in the north and Rydderch of Strathclyde below – and it had long been an Angle dream to take one, if not both, of their kingdoms and seize the land from coast to coast. That would create a North Angle kingdom to rival those of the East Angles and the South Angles, and Aethelfrith was sure he was the man to realise the dream. His eyes shone now and they were not the only ones. When Flora looked around she saw a smile on even Cathryn's face as she stood at the back of the assembled Bernicians and Deirans, united in their thirst for land far more than they would ever be by a mere wedding. And all because of one little ship.

'Shall we go down to greet them, Father?' Flora asked.

'We shall,' he agreed, 'we shall all go at once.'

Ever impetuous, Aethelfrith made straight for the big gates of the elevated compound as guards skittered ahead to grind them open for him and the court scrambled to follow, many with their breakfast still in their hands. The king took the looping path down to the beach with long strides so that Flora had to almost run to keep up.

'Who do you think it is?' Udela asked, panting by her side.

'It's Danes,' Flora said as patiently as she could.

'I know that but what sort of Danes?'

'I don't know – we'll soon see. Hopefully peaceable ones.'

'They'll have to be; there look to be very few of them.'

'Eleven,' Flora agreed, counting.

'You can see that from here?'

'Can you not?'

Udela shook her head.

'Are they men?'

'I think so. Warriors. But their swords are sheathed. That one at the masthead looks to be their leader.'

'Where?' They'd reached the beach now and the ship drew

close. 'Oh, there, yes, I see him. A man, yes? A young man.' She leaned so far forward that she almost tipped herself over. 'A very handsome young man!' She clutched at Flora and leaped up and down excitedly. 'Oh, Flora, I think I'm in love.'

Flora groaned. Her sister truly had no grasp on reality. This young man – a prince if the diadem on his brow was anything to go by – was indeed nice-looking but he had not yet even landed on Bernician soil. It was impossible for Udela to be in love with him.

'You should wait until you meet him to decide that, Udela,' she cautioned.

'Oh, I cannot wait!'

'It will not be long.'

The ship was coming towards the shore at speed, hoping to crest up onto the beach without the need for ropes, and the waiting court edged back to clear the way as, with a crunch and a spray of sand on either side, it landed.

'See,' Flora said to Udela but her sister was already gone.

Chapter Nine

Udela was at Aethelfrith's shoulder when the Danish prince leapt ashore, doing her best to look demure and, Flora presumed, bride-like. It didn't help her much, however, as Aethelfrith introduced himself, then Earnfrith who was busy admiring the ship, before adding a sweeping 'and my two daughters' in their general direction. Bebba, fortunately for Udela, was a little more astute.

'You may remember the girls from our time in Denmark?' she suggested.

'I do,' Prince Hamlet agreed. He spoke in a Norse very similar to their own with only a few odd words and a sharper, more clipped accent to mark out the Danish strain of the language. He looked at Udela. 'I believe you are about my own age, princess?'

'I am eighteen, Prince.'

'As am I.' Udela beamed as if this fact alone determined their compatibility and even more so when Hamlet went on, 'I remember us playing together as children.'

'So do I,' Udela agreed eagerly, though she had not mentioned it earlier. 'I am delighted to rekindle our acquaintance.'

'And I, though I hope you will not push me into a lake this time.'

Udela coloured furiously.

'I did that? Goodness, I am so sorry. I'm sure it must have been an accident.'

'Oh, no, it was quite deliberate. You were cross with me for beating you in a race.'

Udela looked horribly flustered now; it was very amusing.

'How horrible of me,' she managed weakly but the prince smiled.

'Not at all, Udela. I expect I deserved it. I was probably being insufferable about my victory.'

'Almost certainly,' agreed one of his warriors, stepping up at his side, and Flora was astonished to see it was a woman.

She was almost as tall as the prince and wore much the same warrior's clothing. Her dark-blond hair was held back in many braids, each one fastened with a bead at the bottom, and she carried herself like a man, albeit a graceful one. Her face, however, was delicately featured and distinctively female and her voice had a disarmingly soft lilt. Flora stared at her, fascinated.

'You remember the Lady Ofelia?' Hamlet asked Udela who was gawping as openly as Flora. 'She looked a little different back then,' Hamlet allowed. 'Still in dresses and still, perhaps, in some small way biddable.'

He threw a sideways glance at Ofelia who ignored him.

'More fool me then,' she said, bowing to Aethelfrith. 'Greetings, my lord king. I am Prince Hamlet's constable. Delighted to meet you.'

She stuck out her hand and Flora watched, amused, as Aethelfrith took it uncertainly.

'You are a warrior, my lady?'

'I am.'

'You fight well?'

'I do. I accept challenges too if you wish me to prove it?'

Aethelfrith looked at her in disbelief.

'You are challenging me?'

'No, my lord. I am simply saying that if you wished to test my mettle, I would accept.'

'I see. Well, maybe later. For now you must all be hungry.' Some fierce nods from his unexpected guests restored his equilibrium. 'Excellent, excellent. Come up into my hall and we can break fast together.'

The prince looked around him as everyone began to move up the beach towards the path.

'You keep a large court, Aethelfrith,' he commented.

'It is not usually so. You come at a busy time for we have been celebrating.'

'Father married yesterday,' Udela said, looking hopefully up at the prince.

What response did she expect, Flora wondered – for him to say: 'Ooh, what a good idea. I wish I could do that'? Her puppy dog eyes seemed to suggest so but Hamlet looked straight past her to Bebba, standing a little way back but looking every inch the queen.

'A second wife,' Aethelfrith said crisply. 'Queen Cathryn is from Deira whose lands I have recently joined to my own so it seemed prudent to join our families too.'

'Congratulations,' Hamlet said, all manners, though his eyes lingered on Bebba.

The king hastily turned him towards the hall, leaving those behind to panic themselves into place as no order of precedence had yet been established for Aethelfrith's wives. Udela solved it by seizing Flora and marching close behind the king and his handsome guest. Earnfrith was still looking at the ship and did not even notice his father go, giving Bebba the chance to pull him into line, herself at his side. The Lady Ofelia slotted in behind with a young man with floppy hair even blonder than Flora's own, who looked so like the she-warrior that he must surely be her brother, and Cathryn was left to follow alone.

Once in the hall, Udela made a sly move round Aethelfrith to seat herself on Prince Hamlet's other side and Flora grabbed the opportunity to do the same with his fascinating constable.

'Have you always been a warrior?' she asked as servers brought food forward and the Danish girl took a large helping.

'Since I turned ten, yes. It was easy for me then since I was taller than all the boys but most of them have now outstripped me, sadly. Even my little brother does so these days.'

'This is your brother?' Flora asked, looking to the man with the shock of hair sitting on Ofelia's other side.

'This is Lars, yes.'

Lars gave Flora a wide smile and started to speak but more breadcrumbs came out of his mouth than words.

He slapped a hand across his mouth and tried frantically to swallow. Ofelia laughed loudly.

'Very smooth, Titch. Now Princess Flora will think we Danes are all savages.'

'I will not,' Flora protested. 'I should not have spoken to Lars when he was not ready to answer.'

He finished his frantic chewing and took away his hand.

'You are too kind, my lady.'

'Is it possible to be *too* kind?'

Lars blinked. Ofelia laughed again.

'That is a very good question. Is it possible, Titch?'

'Don't call me that,' Lars said, flushing. Flora saw Ofelia jump but Lars was speaking again now. 'I suppose if you were kind to your enemy by releasing him and then he turned and stabbed you, you might have been too kind.'

'Or your enemy not kind enough?'

Now Lars laughed.

'True. That is very true, princess. I like the way you think.'

'Then you are probably alone in that,' Flora told him. 'Udela, my sister, says I am odd.'

'Perhaps it is she who is odd?'

'That's what I tell her,' Flora agreed happily, then looked at her sister, who was desperately trying to break into an earnest conversation between Aethelfrith and Hamlet, and felt guilty.

'But she is not odd, you know. She is very sweet and gentle and pretty.'

'And is making the most of that,' Ofelia said drily. 'I hope Hamlet will notice her soon.'

'Why?'

'It would be good for him. He needs a sweet, gentle, pretty woman.'

'Ofelia,' Lars said, his voice dark with some sort of warning, not that she seemed to care.

'It would be good, Flora, would it not, if there were to be an alliance between our countries?'

'Oh, yes,' Flora agreed, pleased to be able to show her understanding of diplomacy, 'for with Danish help, Father could take the lands all the way to the west coast and create a kingdom of North Angles to rival those in the East and the South.'

'Could he indeed? And what would *we* get in exchange?'

Flora considered.

'What do you want?'

Ofelia looked surprised and Lars gave another laugh. He had a nice laugh, low and resonant as if it came from somewhere deep within him.

'This girl asks good questions,' he said and Flora felt herself glow with pride.

'We want . . . ' Ofelia started, but at that Lars seemed swiftly to turn sober. He put a hand on his sister's arm and leaned across her.

'We want to see as much of your father's kingdom as possible, Flora, for we have heard it is very beautiful and first impressions certainly bear that out. I have never seen such hills as this one we are upon now.'

'This! Dinguardi is quite high, I suppose, but if you want hills we should ride to my father's new estate at Aet Gefrin. It is set in the shadows of the highest hill I have ever seen and there is an ancient fortress upon its top that must surely have been there when the gods roamed the earth.'

'Amazing. Will you take us?'

'I will ask my father. He will be delighted, I am sure, as he is very proud of his new buildings and will love the chance to show them off.'

She was rewarded with another of Lars' delicious laughs but, in stark contrast, Ofelia had gone rigid, a piece of ham hock halfway to her mouth.

'My lady, are you well?' Ofelia was gazing at the king and as Flora looked across she saw a funny-looking man, short and stout with a sideways walk, approaching Aethelfrith. 'Who is that?'

'Captain Enok,' Lars supplied. 'He piloted our ship here.'

'What does he want with my father?'

'I don't know,' Lars said. 'It looks as if he has something to give him but surely Hamlet is the envoy?'

'You'd have thought so,' Ofelia agreed tightly, her eyes fixed on the funny-looking man as he bowed low before the king.

Flora, Lars and Ofelia were not many paces away but with so many in the hall the background noise was too loud for them to hear what Captain Enok was saying. They could, however, clearly see the stick he withdrew from the leather bag at his belt and held out to Aethelfrith as reverently as if it were made of pure gold.

'What's that?' Lars asked.

Ofelia did not answer but Flora saw Aethelfrith turn the stick and saw it had a flat side and, upon that, the magical promise of carvings.

''Tis runes,' she said, adding, 'Father cannot read them.'

'What?' Ofelia's head whipped round so fast that one of the beads at the end of her braids caught Flora's chin and she flinched. 'Oh, no, I'm sorry. Did I hurt you?'

Flora stopped herself from putting her hand to her stinging skin. 'No, no.'

'Good. Did you say the king cannot read runes?'

'Yes.' Sure enough Aethelfrith was looking in puzzlement at the stick. 'But Mother can.'

Ofelia's head swung back almost as fast, though this time Flora knew to duck away and avoid the clattering beads. She watched as Aethelfrith handed the stick to Bebba who turned it carefully to the light and read. It seemed to take her ages. The stick was not long so the message could hardly be extensive and Flora could only assume her mother was checking it carefully.

Next to her, Ofelia seemed to be actually holding her breath but at length Bebba looked up and across to Udela and she seemed to release it in one go – more a sigh than a breath.

'Do you know what it says?' Flora asked her.

'Me? No!'

The denial was vehement but Ofelia sounded like Udela when she told their mother she'd completed her sewing and had actually done little more than finger the needles and daydream. Flora still couldn't see why people had to lie but this looked more important than needlework and she forced herself not to ask anything more. Prince Hamlet, she noticed, was as fixed upon Bebba as Ofelia was, but when Bebba looked towards Udela he flushed and his head snapped round to look straight at Ofelia instead. For a long moment the pair stared at each other in much the way Flora had seen two hounds do when squaring up for a scrap, then Ofelia broke off and turned back to Flora.

'So, princess, tell me more about Bernicia.'

Her voice was super-bright, like a torch when oil was added. It seemed Flora wasn't the only odd one here this morning.

The day was spent riding out with the new arrivals to show them the beautiful Bernician countryside. Aethelfrith assured Flora they would move inland to Aet Gefrin once the majority of the wedding guests had left but in the meantime there was plenty to show Prince Hamlet and his little band of warriors around Dinguardi. They all seemed perpetually amazed by even the lowest hills or cliffs and took great delight in driving the horses up them to look out from the top.

'Do you not have hills at home?' Flora asked Lars as they made for yet another.

'I thought we did before but now it seems we have merely slopes.'

'And barrow graves,' Ofelia put in from her other side. 'We have many of those. The dead live close to the surface in Denmark.'

Flora thought about this.

'We have a few,' she said, 'but they are dwarfed by the real hills.'

'Good,' Lars said crisply. 'If you ask me the dead live too close to the surface in Denmark, at least for some.'

Flora caught the sideways glance he threw his sister but Ofelia refused to do so.

'My uncle told me the gods were having a tantrum when they created the Angles' land,' she said, 'and now I see what he meant.'

'Not a tantrum,' Flora protested. 'A party.'

Ofelia looked out over the crags at the edge of the Cheviot Hills and laughed.

'A party? Yes, that is better. What think you, Hamlet, were the gods partying when they made this land?'

Hamlet looked back from his position higher up the hill track. He gave Ofelia a sharp look and then wheeled his horse round to join them, sending Udela, who had been at his side, into a tantrum of her own. She glared at her sister but for once Flora didn't care for she was too busy watching the prince and his constable exchanging combative looks even to notice anything else. It seemed curious that Hamlet should have appointed Ofelia to such a significant office if he didn't even like her but maybe she was a very skilful warrior.

'A wedding party, perhaps,' he suggested, so lightly that his words seemed almost snatched away on the breeze.

'Oh, not a wedding party,' Flora said. 'They are no fun.'

Ofelia gave a strange yelp.

'See, Hamlet! Flora agrees with me.'

'You do not like weddings either?' Flora asked her.

'Not one bit. They are so sickly-sweet.'

'And so messy,' Flora agreed. 'And noisy and chaotic.'

'So you do not wish to marry?' Ofelia demanded excitedly, surprising Flora.

'Oh, I would be happy to marry if my husband were a good man. It is just the wedding ceremony I would not like. I would prefer to step out quietly, two people and a priest, and pledge our troth before the gods without all the ceremony and fuss.'

'How wise,' Hamlet said. 'Is that not wise, Ofelia – not to object to an idea but to mould it to suit oneself? Does that not sound a fine plan?'

'No,' Ofelia snapped and Flora crumpled a little.

'I only meant for myself,' she said hastily. 'Others I am sure like the ceremony. My sister, for example, would make a beautiful bride.'

She tried to direct Hamlet's attention towards Udela but it was fixed on Ofelia.

'Ofelia is the opposite to you, princess. She would be happy with the wedding but does not want the marriage.'

'Oh.' Flora looked to Ofelia who was bristling like a cornered cat. 'Well, Ofelia is a warrior, so she is married to her sword.'

'Exactly!' Ofelia leaned over in her saddle, grabbed Flora, and placed a smacking kiss on her forehead. 'That is exactly it, Flora. I am married to my sword and it makes a fine husband for it is ever ready to defend me, is always polished to a high sheen and asks no more of me than that I wield it well.'

Flora was delighted to have pleased this mercurial Dane but uncertain exactly how she had done so. Hamlet, by contrast, looked far from pleased.

'A sword is a sharp bedfellow,' he said.

'Even better,' came Ofelia's retort and with a snort Hamlet kicked up his heels and rode forward to rejoin a delighted Udela.

'Must you rile him so, Ofelia?' Lars asked wearily but his sister had kicked her own horse into a gallop and was already gone.

Lars looked apologetically at Flora.

'She's a bit wild sometimes.'

'I don't mind. Do you want to gallop too?'

'No. No, I am happy here if you are?'

Flora thought about it.

'I am,' she agreed.

Ofelia intrigued her but her constant changes of pace were exhausting and for now Flora was more than happy to let her ride on ahead.

There was another damned feast on their return, of course, but the long ride must have shaken down the mass of food in Flora's stomach for she found herself ravenous and ate with a will. Many wedding guests had lingered in Dinguardi, attracted by the new arrivals – and the fine food they merited – and so it was a merry gathering.

Only little Cathryn looked unhappy. Aethelfrith had chosen to sit Bebba on one side of him and Cathryn on the other and Flora's older, more experienced mother appeared to be coping with the situation far better than the new bride. Flora considered what Hamlet had said about Ofelia not wanting marriage and longed to ask her more but they had been formally seated tonight and Flora, to her surprise, was between Prince Hamlet and her brother Earnfrith on one side of the top table with Ofelia between Cathryn and Udela on the other. The three women did not seem to be getting on at all well but Flora had little time to worry for she was painfully aware of the fraught conversation with Prince Hamlet on horseback earlier and was determined to be more charming tonight.

'Tell me of Denmark,' she suggested politely as the first course was served.

'You do not remember it?'

'Barely. I was only five when we returned to Bernicia. I think I remember the boat trip home, for porpoises followed us half the way, but nothing of Denmark.'

'That's a shame. It is a wonderful country.'

'And you will be High King there one day.'

'Perhaps.'

'Perhaps? Are you not the heir?'

'I am in word, yes, but words can be twisted.'

'That's true,' Flora agreed. 'So often people seem to say one thing and mean another. I do not understand it.'

'Do you never lie, Flora?'

'I try not to. Sometimes I think maybe I should for it seems people don't always want to hear the truth.'

Hamlet's laughter was sudden and unaffected. His eyes lit up with mirth and Flora noticed, a little uncomfortably, that Udela was right – he was a handsome man. His face was strong-boned, with cheekbones as high as Bernician crags and eyes the colour of new-turned earth. Flora loved new-turned earth. She felt suddenly confused and turned hastily to her food.

'So you may not be king then?' she asked once she'd composed herself.

Hamlet's smile faded.

'I would like to be. My father was a good king. Very good.'

'He died?'

'He was murdered.'

'Oh!' Flora dropped her eating knife with a clatter. 'Oh, Hamlet, I didn't know. I'm so sorry. Who did it?'

'They never found the killer but I know who it was. Or, at least, I know who ordered his death, which was a worse crime.'

'So can you not bring him to justice?'

Hamlet looked at her, through eyes that had turned as cold and dark as clay.

'I can and I will but it will take time and patience and cunning.'

'That sounds hard.'

'I suppose it does. I apologise but cannot really talk more of it.'

Flora nodded.

'Very well. What then shall we talk of? Ships, perhaps, for Earnfrith loved your ship, did you not, Earnfrith?'

Her brother leaned forward eagerly.

'I did. I do.'

Hamlet smiled at him.

'Very well then. I would be delighted to talk ships. Thank you, Flora.'

'For what?'

'For not prying. I appreciate it.'

'My pleasure,' she managed though it seemed a curious thing for which to be praised. He had said he could not talk of it so there was nothing more to say. And people thought her odd!

She joined in happily with their talk of ships and Earnfrith's eager questioning of the prince made the dinner pass far more swiftly than she'd expected. She was weary though. It had been a long and busy day, packed with new people, and she was hugely grateful when Aethelfrith finally announced he would retire and everyone began to scramble for the best beds as servants obligingly folded them out around the edges of the hall and in the outbuildings.

Aethelfrith bowed low over Bebba's hand and then rose, held out an imperious arm to little Cathryn and strode from the hall. Flora wanted to go to her mother but Bebba had slid out of the side door and into the night before she could pass through the crowd and join her.

'Marriage,' a voice said by her side and she turned to see Ofelia also watching Bebba leave. 'I dislike it, Flora, because it makes women second best and I *despise* it when it makes them third best.'

Flora stiffened.

'Mother is secure in her own worth. Just this morning Father gave this burgh and all its lands over to her personal keeping.'

'But she still has to do what he tells her.'

'So? Don't we all have to do what someone tells us, save for the king – and even he is subject to the gods. The important thing, I think, is to keep something of yourself for yourself and then, surely, the rest is just playing games.'

Ofelia made a strange sound, half huff, half laugh.

'You are very wise for your age, Flora.'

Flora frowned; that was the second time today someone had called her so. But before she could puzzle over what they meant her father's reeve approached, bowing low.

'I have ordered a bed for the Lady Ofelia to be put into your bower, princess. Does that suit?'

'Of course,' Flora agreed. 'Udela and I will be happy to share with our guest.'

She turned to smile at Ofelia but saw that the she-warrior looked panicked.

'Oh, no. No, that is not necessary. I will sleep with my men in the barracks as I always do.'

'But, Ofelia, they are very rough. It is far nicer in our bower – we have feather beds.'

'I would sink into one of those.'

'And soft covers.'

'My cloak is soft enough, thank you.'

'And a brazier.'

'Heat makes my skin prickle.'

'Oh.' The other girl's vehement refusal stung but Flora tried to be politic and not show it. 'Well, whatever suits you best.'

Ofelia looked pained.

'I did not mean to offend you, Flora. It's just that I am their constable; I should keep them in my charge.'

'Can your brother not do that?'

'Lars? He's only sixteen.'

'It's old enough.' Flora looked at her curiously. 'Do you not like women, Ofelia?'

'No! That is, I'm not sure. I like you, Flora.'

She felt herself flush.

'Well, that's good. Sleep where you wish, truly.'

The reeve wrung his hands.

'Only, the king did order the bed in your chamber especially, princess.'

'He did?'

'For the Lady Ofelia's particular comfort.'

Ofelia looked decidedly *un*comfortable at that. Her eyes darted around the hall and then came suddenly to rest upon the slantways figure of Captain Enok who was standing a few paces away, his head cocked strangely on his thick neck and his eyes fixed upon her as a mouse might fix upon a tasty piece of cheese.

'Ah, well,' Ofelia said loudly, linking arms suddenly with Flora, 'if the king insists I sleep with the ladies then I suppose I must. Udela, we are to share a bower tonight.'

'We are?'

'The king insists upon it.'

'Oh.' Udela looked put out but then gave a sly smile. 'Good – you can tell me all about Prince Hamlet.'

'I can, for I know him all too well. What would you like to know?'

She led them both past Captain Enok, who seemed to droop as they went by, and out into the night.

'I want to know everything,' Udela said breathily and Flora sent up a silent prayer for fortitude.

However weary she might feel, she feared sleep could be a long time coming tonight and, sure enough, they were barely inside the bower before Udela was firing off questions like arrows. Was Hamlet a good fighter? What did he like to talk of? Did he swim? Did he like hawks? Did he like butterflies? No matter seemed too small for her. Ofelia did her best to answer and Flora did her best to ignore the babble and sleep but then Udela asked, 'Has he had many women?' and Ofelia gave a strange strangled cough that jolted the other girl awake again. Flora sat up and looked at her.

'You?' she asked.

Udela squealed.

'You've bedded Hamlet?'

Ofelia shrugged.

'A few times. Nothing serious. Just as, you know, training partners.'

Udela gaped at her.

'Do all soldiers do that?'

'No! It just ... happened.'

'Will you marry him then?' Udela asked, horror writhing through her words like snakes.

'Oh, no. I won't marry anyone.'

Udela looked relieved, if confused.

'Ofelia doesn't like marriage because it makes a woman second best,' Flora told her sister.

Udela giggled.

'Well, I'd gladly be second best to Prince Hamlet. Is he, you know ... good?'

Ofelia chuckled.

'He scratched an itch well enough.'

'What?'

'Nothing. In my experience, Udela, he is good, yes, but you will have to try him for yourself.'

'Ofelia! A princess cannot "try" men.'

'Then I am glad I'm not a princess.'

'Have you tried many?' Flora asked, intrigued anew by this unusual she-warrior.

'Enough.'

'And it's fun?'

'Oh, yes, if you throw yourself into it.'

'Throw yourself into it,' Udela repeated earnestly as if learning this advice by rote.

'But you will find out soon enough, I'm sure.' Ofelia leaned towards her and spoke in a low voice. 'We are here, you know, to broker an alliance between our two countries – and how best is such an alliance joined?'

'With a marriage,' Udela breathed.

'Exactly.'

'You think Prince Hamlet looks for a bride?'

'It is possible, is it not? And your father seeks Danish help, I believe, to take the west?'

'He does,' Udela squeaked. 'He really does.'

'Then I do not see why not. Indeed, I very much hope it is something your father may suggest.'

Her voice had taken on a strange edge, Flora noted, but Udela was dancing around the chamber so maybe her sister had imagined it.

'Oh, I hope so!' Udela gasped. 'I so, so hope so. Oh, how will I ever sleep a wink tonight?'

'You should,' Flora said hastily, 'or you will have sacks under your eyes.'

'I will! Oh, gods, I will! I must sleep. I must!'

She flung herself back onto her bed and Flora laid her own head gratefully on her pillow but within moments Udela was off again and it was late before any of them had a chance to surrender to sleep. Flora was, therefore, still abed when a servant came knocking at the bower door the next morning. She leaped up and let the sunshine in with the young man, amazed at herself for it was a long time since she had missed a sunrise.

'Message from the king, my lady. He wants to see you in the hall on urgent business.'

'Me?' Udela asked, leaping up faster than Flora had ever seen her sluggish sister tumble from her bed.

The servant bowed low.

'He asked for the Princess Flora.'

'Flora?' Udela spat. 'Why her?'

'I know not, my lady. I am but the messenger.'

'You're sure you heard right? Flora not Udela?'

'Flora, princess. He said it very clearly and I always listen very carefully since the time I thought he'd asked for cheese and actually . . .'

'Enough,' Udela snapped. 'Tell the king that both his daughters will be with him shortly.'

'Very well.'

The messenger backed gratefully away and Udela rounded on Flora.

'Why you?'

Flora spread her hands wide.

'I don't know, sister. Why don't we go and ask?'

'Yes,' Udela agreed as their maids scrambled in. 'Why don't we?'

But still she mumbled protests and complaints and the moment they were dressed Flora was grateful to head for the hall and escape her. She went inside to find her father seated on his chair of office, her mother at his left side and Prince Hamlet at his right. Aethelfrith stood up as she approached and opened his arms to her.

'Ah, Flora, welcome! Come closer, my dear, come closer. I have news ... great news. You are to be wed, daughter – wed to Prince Hamlet.'

Flora stared at him, stunned. She sought for words but found none and the only sound that greeted this royal pronouncement was a strangled squeak and a loud thud as, behind her, Udela fainted away.

Chapter Ten

Aet Gefrin, September 602

'Why you?'

Flora closed her eyes and prayed to Balder for patience. Those two words seemed to be the only ones Udela had spoken to her since her father's shock announcement four days ago and they were getting, if that was possible, even whinier and more furious every time. Flora had had enough.

'I don't know, Udela,' she snapped, 'why not ask Father since it was his decision?'

Udela pouted.

'You did something to influence him, I know you did.'

'Like what?' Flora reined in her horse and stared at her sister. 'What on earth do you think I could have said to Father to talk him into marrying me to the prince? I don't even *want* to marry the prince!'

Her voice had risen alarmingly and she put a hand over her mouth in case her father heard her but he was far too busy talking to Hamlet up ahead. The court was processing to Aet Gefrin, to celebrate the wedding in Aethelfrith's new palace, and Flora was meant to be riding beside her groom to show them off to the people as a betrothed couple. Her father, however, was far more interested in talking to Hamlet than in riding behind him between his own two wives and had swiftly disrupted the order of the entourage, leaving Flora to ride with Udela and suffer her bitter resentment.

'Of course you want to,' she spat now. 'How could you not want to? Look at him!'

Hamlet was handsome, that much Flora knew, but since the betrothal his face had looked more like a mask than a man's. When she tried to look into his eyes she could only get so far, as if he had leather curtains keeping anyone from looking too deeply. And he was ever on alert. Flora had kept an eye on him and she could swear his hand twitched for his sword at least one hundred times in the course of a meal. That, to her, spoke of someone with secrets to keep and she did not like secrets.

'I doubt his intentions,' she whispered to Udela now, looking nervously around to see if they could be overheard, but they were riding up the narrowest part of the Glen valley and there was room for only two mounts abreast so they were safe enough.

'You do?' Udela asked.

'I do. And Father's besides. Think, Udela – why would he not marry Prince Hamlet to his eldest daughter?'

'I told you why – because his youngest has bewitched Hamlet in order to get him for herself.'

'Udela! Don't say that. I'm no witch.'

'You might be. You're forever at the herbs and you know more about them than is natural!'

'Only because I work hard to learn. I look to the goddess Eyra for inspiration and assistance but I do no magic, Udela, I swear it.'

She looked around even more fearfully. Here, in the ancient Glen valley with its streams and falls and caves, magic always felt close and she had no wish to claim – or be claimed by – it. When she'd been small she'd heard a skald tell the tale of how the ancient peoples who'd lived in Aet Gefrin had been enslaved by an army of dwarves sent by the gods to recruit people to work their jewel mines. By day they had lived normal lives but by night they had been dragged from their beds by the dwarves and marched, in a half sleep, deep under the huge bell-shaped hill to dig for jewels to make amulets for the goddesses.

Few could last more than a week of such a harsh regime before they left their minds beneath the hill and threw themselves, babbling, into the River Glen. The dwarves had cared not, they'd just taken the next handful of people – men, women, children, it mattered little – and those left behind had not known what ailed the poor creatures or who might sicken next. Then, finally, one young boy, born under a black moon, had been able to resist the dread magic and only played at falling under its spell before returning home and warning the others of what was dragging their loved ones into insanity.

The villagers had ringed their houses round with ash and vervain to keep the dwarves away and so their tyranny had ended. The story had made Flora shiver with fear but it had also impressed upon her the importance of knowledge. Herbal lore had saved these people's lives and she had vowed to learn all she could in case one day she was called upon to use it. So far in her sixteen years, she had helped people with agues and sniffles, with spots and growths, with rashes and cuts and boils, but never yet against the forces of darkness. She had studied all she could so that if the time ever came she would be ready, but she was no witch for her sole aim was to resist magic not to invoke it.

It was one of the reasons why Prince Hamlet worried her. He had come here with a rune-stick newly carved and golden and with, it seemed, her wyrd carved upon it. She had not seen the figures herself but Bebba had told her that they had asked for marriage. The runes had reached out from a Danish stick and bound themselves around her life as surely as the dwarves of Aet Gefrin had bound themselves around the locals to enslave them to their will, and Flora did not like it.

'Father chose to give his younger, less significant daughter to this prince because he doubts him. It is very clear. He does not wish to waste you upon him, Udela, so he has passed him on to me.'

'You think so?'

It was the first time Flora had seen even a glimmer of a smile on Udela's face in the last four days.

'I know so.'

'You think Hamlet is evil?'

Flora considered.

'He does not seem so but evil comes in many guises and too often they are sweet. Did not Odin disguise himself as a nursemaid to have his way with the maiden Wrinda? And was he not exiled from the land of the gods for ten years for his transgression?

'He did. He was.' Udela leaned closer. 'But what will Hamlet do with you?'

Flora shuddered.

'I don't know but Father says that the wedding will be in two days' time so I will soon find out.'

Udela's eyes glinted wickedly.

'Perhaps he is in some way misshapen.'

'I don't think so, Udela.'

'Or perhaps his seed is poison and will curdle your womb. Or perhaps he is part-troll and you will give birth to . . . '

'Udela!'

Flora's protest was so loud that even Aethelfrith looked back.

'Flora!' he called crossly. 'What are you doing lingering there, shouting like a hoyden? Come up and ride with your betrothed as you were bid.'

Flora longed to protest that it was he who had forced her away but dared not. Instead, she went meekly forward and took up her place at Hamlet's side. If she were honest with herself, as she tried always to be, she was rather enjoying taking precedence over her sister, who had always been so insufferably superior, but she was afraid of the price she was going to have to pay for this petty joy and so could not make the most of it.

They must be close to Aet Gefrin now for she saw three children high up on the curve of the hill, pointing and waving. She lifted a hand to wave back but they were already gone, heading down to tell the estate-workers that the royal party was on its way. And now the path swung round the curve of the hill and opened out onto a plateau and before them was another, smaller hill atop which sat Aethelfrith's new estate of Aet Gefrin.

'It's magnificent,' Hamlet said to Aethelfrith, looking up at the fenced compound. 'Truly. I have never seen anything like this place. It feels as if it is the heart of the world.'

Flora stared at her betrothed. Whatever her reservations about the Danish prince, he spoke true now. Aet Gefrin rested below the bell-shaped hill like a heart beneath a goddess' great breasts, cushioned and safe and vibrant with life in the late-afternoon sun. Aethelfrith beamed.

'It *is* the heart of the world, *my* world, and it will beat out its power from the east coast to the west before my time upon its throne is done.'

'I hope to see it, my lord king,' Hamlet told him.

'I hope you will help me make it happen, prince – son.'

Hamlet smiled and bowed his head in acknowledgment of the compliment but his eyes shifted past Flora to his men and Flora knew without looking that they would have found Ofelia. Hamlet's eyes always found Ofelia and Flora feared he and his constable were plotting together and that somehow she was being drawn into their plans.

'The wedding will be in two days,' Aethelfrith said clearly for all to hear.

'Would it were tomorrow,' Hamlet replied.

He sounded sincere and looked at Flora with kindness but his words seemed as slick as a skald's, sliding around on the truth like a skater on ice. She did not, *would* not, believe Udela's fool tales of poison and trolls but she was unsure why this prince wanted her for his wife. Then again, why did any prince want a wife – for alliance, for power, for profit?

She watched Hamlet as he rode into Aet Gefrin with her father, waving and bowing humbly to all, and wondered what he was thinking. He had not asked for gold as her dowry but instead for warriors to join his little band. He claimed he wished to train his own troop to best support Aethelfrith and Aethelfrith, delighted not to have to part with any of his precious treasure, had readily agreed. Flora, after some hard and unflattering bargaining, had turned out to be worth twenty men complete with swords, armour and a horse apiece.

The horses, Flora knew, were worth a good deal but she wasn't sure if men were of a higher or lower value as no one had counted out their dowry in warriors before. They had certainly not fitted in a chest for the betrothal ceremony and Flora had stood with them all ranged around her (the horses had, thankfully, been left in the stables), feeling very small as the match had been blessed by three druids. She hoped they would not be there at the wedding ceremony, not to mention the wedding night.

Two days to go. Two nights. Flora's stomach contracted as if she had swallowed nettle-juice. She had not looked for this marriage and had expected to see Udela into a wedding bed long before she turned back the covers on her own. She'd been relying on her sister's inevitably lurid descriptions to prepare her for a wife's role but now she must forge the path herself and she feared its tangles and spikes.

That night, she lay in the bower with Udela and listened to the wind howling up the glen as if issuing a warning. Udela had talked herself into snores, as grumblingly cross in sleep as she was awake, and Flora was alone. Once the funny captain of their ship had returned to Denmark, Ofelia had insisted on sleeping in the barracks and Flora had been glad of it. Like Hamlet, Ofelia seemed to talk loudly of her joy in the forthcoming marriage but fill her words with dark meaning, like a rogue thread in the weft, breaking the smooth pattern of her meaning. Flora was still intrigued by the she-warrior but now she had been pulled closer to her flame she felt the heat of it as well as the light.

The whole world seemed to have gone off kilter these last few days and Flora was struggling to keep her balance. First her father had taken a new wife, then a handsome Danish prince had sailed in with a she-warrior at his right hand, and then, almost before the sun had taken a full turn of the dial, Flora had found herself betrothed.

If she had disliked the chaos of Cathryn's wedding, she was dreading her own. Tomorrow would be a tumble of gowns and shoes and jewels as she was prepared for her big day and as Flora stared out of the window towards the great bell mountain she longed to climb out of bed and run up and up to the ancient fortress at the top, to hide there until it was all over. Fear of the dwarves held her beneath her covers but still sleep would not come.

In the end, she got up anyway and, wrapping her cloak around herself, went out into the darkness. Walking might tire her enough to sleep and she set out on a circle of the compound. A bored guard looked up from his post at the gates but she gave him a little wave and he sank back onto this stool, leaving her alone with the night. Or nearly.

There was a light burning in the chamber that had been assigned to Flora's mother. Bebba, she knew, would have preferred to stay in her own burgh of Dinguardi but could hardly have left Flora to be wed without her so had dutifully joined Aethelfrith and Cathryn's court. It seemed that sleep eluded her too and Flora headed gratefully in her direction but as she passed the barracks, the sound of whispered voices sent her scuttling against the wall of the pigsties opposite. Heart pounding, she crouched down, listening intently. Two people were having a hissed but heated conversation against the barracks wall and she was pretty sure she knew who they were.

'It's how we planned,' one was saying and Flora caught the excitable lilt of Ofelia's voice.

'How *you* planned,' the other countered. Hamlet, it had to be. Flora held her breath in her chest and leaned as far towards them as she dared. 'I didn't choose this marriage, Ofelia. I don't want it.'

'Because you don't know what's good for you. Would you have preferred the alternative? No?'

What was the alternative? Flora wondered. Udela? What was so bad about her? She was prettier than Flora and fuller-figured and far, far more eager to take a husband. Or Ofelia herself? Why would Hamlet not choose her? He could never stop looking at the woman and so what if she wasn't a princess, did it really matter so much? Ofelia's next words, however, stopped her foolish worries over feminine charms.

'It's the only way, Hamlet,' she hissed, 'the only way to see him dead.'

Flora froze, her whole body pressed tight against the pigsty. The beasts within, sensing her presence, were starting to wake and snuffle. Any minute now one of them would squeal for attention and the Danes would discover her – and then what? It was clear they had no qualms about murder and she had already put the guard off alert so they could dispatch her in moments. She had to go.

She looked longingly towards the little light in her mother's window but to reach Bebba she would have to pass the plotters. There was no alternative but to creep back around the sties and return to her own bed. But then she heard a gasp and a slap and a fierce cry of protest, and Ofelia shot past her at pace, sending the pigs squealing anyway. Hamlet took a few steps after her but then stopped, barely an arm's length from Flora. The moonlight fell on his face and she saw on it a look of such anguish that she sighed in pity. Instantly he turned to look at her.

'Who's there?' His hand shot out and grabbed her, yanking her roughly into the silvery light. But then, seeing who it was, he loosened his hold. 'Flora? What on earth are you doing out here?'

'I couldn't sleep. I was . . . restless.'

'Nervous?'

'A little, yes. I didn't expect to be wed so soon.'

'Nor I.' He gave a sigh. 'Come, Flora – we're disturbing the pigs and they'll have half the compound awake if we don't leave them to settle. Will you take a cup of wine with me?'

'Now?'

'It might help you sleep. Your father has kindly left a jug in my bower.'

'You are inviting me into your bower?'

'We are, you know, to be wed.'

'Not for two days.'

Hamlet glanced up the valley to where a thin sliver of light was topping the hills.

'One day, I'd say. Wine?'

The pigs were jumping up against the wall now and Flora could hear people stirring in the nearby bowers. Her father would be furious if she was caught out here and it was too far back to her own bower for her to make it unseen.

'Wine,' she agreed and followed Hamlet through his door.

She took care to leave it ajar. The prince did not look to have dark deeds on his mind but she already knew he was a man who found it easy to dissemble so she wasn't taking chances. Even so, it was good to talk.

'So you do not want to marry me?' she said as he lit a torch.

He froze at her words and the taper burned down, scorching him so that he yelped. Despite her fears, Flora had to bite her lip to hold in a giggle as he leaped up and down like a child, waving his singed fingers. He gave her a rueful smile.

'What makes you think that?'

'I heard you say so.'

'Ah.'

He flapped his hand ineffectually at the air.

'Mustard-seed,' she told him.

'Sorry?'

'You need mustard-seed on that finger to stop it swelling. I could fetch you some but not until it is light.'

'Thank you but I've known worse.' He sucked on the skin and looked at her. 'I'm sorry you heard that, Flora. It is not because of any lack in you. You are sweet and pretty and astute and funny and will make an excellent wife.'

'But not for you?'

He shuffled awkwardly.

'I suppose I'm not ready to wed so soon.'

She grimaced.

'So if you are not ready and I am not ready, why are we marrying?'

He gave a little laugh.

'Perhaps because others are ready? And, really, there are worse fates, are there not?'

He came a little closer but Flora put up her hands to keep him at bay.

'Like death?'

'Sorry?'

'I heard you, Hamlet – I heard you and Ofelia say that you want him dead. Who is "him", Hamlet? Who do you plot to kill? Is it my father?'

'No!'

'Because I will tell him. If you come any closer, I will scream louder than any pig and everyone will come running and I will tell them all.'

'As you should.'

That confused her.

'So you *are* plotting to kill the king?'

'Yes,' Hamlet agreed almost wearily. Flora opened her mouth to scream but he was upon her in a flash, his hand pressing over her lips and his body forcing hers against the wall. Fear coursed through her veins but his eyes, when he stared pleadingly into her own, were kind. 'But not King Aethelfrith. Not anyone here in Bernicia, nor the land of the Angles at all.'

She struggled and he stepped back a little but kept his hand over her mouth.

'Listen, Flora, it is best you know anyway if we are to wed. And best you know now so that if you hate me for it, you can still withdraw from the match.' She frowned up at him and he gave her a reassuring smile. 'I will let you, you know. If you will listen carefully to what I have to say then I will leave it to you to decide whether or not the marriage still stands. If you wish for no more of me, then tomorrow I will go to King Aethelfrith and withdraw from our betrothal, to my own dishonour. Is that agreed?'

She looked into his eyes but saw nothing more than an honest plea. She nodded and slowly he took his hand away. She stood, dumb, and saw him relax a little.

'Thank you,' he said. 'Wine?' She nodded again and he fumbled to pour her a gobletful, pressing it into her unresisting hand before backing off again. 'A seat?'

She shook her head. She wanted to be ready to flee if need be.

'I want one thing only from you, Hamlet: the truth. No lies, no half-truths, no omissions, just straightforward facts.'

Now it was he who was nodding.

'A fair request. So listen – I told you back in Dinguardi that my father King Otto had been murdered, did I not?'

'You did. You said you did not wish to talk of it further.'

'And I did not, but it seems maybe I should. I told you, also, that I knew who killed him but had not been able to bring them to justice. That, Flora, is because the man who had my father murdered was my uncle, King Feng. He had it all carefully planned. He and his brother Wiglek had soldiers in place – foreign soldiers, in their own pay – and they had my father slaughtered in the bushes like an animal, then Feng seized the throne – *my* throne – before the sun was even up upon the poor corpse. There was nothing I could do save bend the knee. But I will not bow to a usurper like him for long. It is King Feng I want dead, Flora. Can you understand that?'

She nodded.

'I would feel the same.'

'You would?'

His eyes sparked with a hope that made him look suddenly very young – and very handsome.

'Of course I would. Indeed, I do. Such a man deserves to die.'

'There is more.'

'More?'

'Feng sent me here to your father on a supposed mission of friendship but we discovered . . . '

'We?'

'Ofelia and I.'

'Of course.'

He looked askance at that comment but continued speaking.

'Ofelia and I discovered that he had charged the ship's captain with a rune-stick for Aethelfrith – a message demanding my death.'

Flora pictured the stick, dark on one side and golden-fresh on the other, covered with the runes of Hamlet's wyrd.

'What did you do?'

'We changed it. We changed the sentence held within the runes from requesting my death to my marriage.'

'Death was your alternative?'

Hamlet frowned.

'You heard that too?'

'I did. Well, I suppose marrying me should, at least, be better than that.'

'Far, far better.'

Hamlet suddenly stepped forward and clasped his hands around her own where they were clutching the stem of the goblet. His face was close to hers and the dark wine reflected onto it by the torch-light made it glow a dark, almost bloody red. She shivered.

'I don't want you to die, Hamlet.'

'Then the choice is yours – either wed me as planned or give me leave now to gather my men and flee before you tell your father of our crime.'

'Is it a crime to save your own life? It seems to me that it is the only sensible course of action.'

'Then you will let me flee?'

'Do you want to flee?'

'No.'

'Do you, then, want to marry me?'

'Yes.'

There was no hesitation in his reply and to Flora's shame that made her heart leap like a spring bug. With the lies stripped away, she liked this man. He had dared to twist the runes of his wyrd towards her own and she was ready to embrace that.

'You would not rather marry Udela?'

'No! She seems a little ... excitable. I would not be comfortable with a woman like that so I asked your father if I might take you instead.'

'You did?' Flora let this little droplet of information sink into her like the finest wine, warming her through. 'You want me?' He nodded. 'Not Udela?'

'No.'

'And not Ofelia?'

Again she looked for hesitation; again none came.

'Not Ofelia. She is more man than woman for she has no heart.'

'So you are saying men have no hearts?' Flora teased.

Hamlet smiled at it and she felt absurdly glad.

'Some men do.' He removed his hands from hers, prising the goblet away and setting it aside before retaking her fingers and pressing them to his chest. 'Do I?'

Flora stood very still, feeling for the pulse of his lifeblood as she might with an ailing creature, save that they never stood so close, nor made her own heart quicken as it seemed to be doing now.

'You have a heart,' she confirmed as calmly as she was able.

135

'You are wrong,' he corrected her, his voice low. 'Not now – now *you* have that heart.' She looked at him in disbelief but his eyes were earnest. 'Truly, Flora, for I know no other more deserving.'

She shook her head.

'I am young, Hamlet, and a little simple perhaps but I am not stupid. Hearts are rarely given to those who deserve them most.'

He laughed and placed his other hand around her waist, drawing her gently in against him.

'Will you at least let me try to give you mine?'

It was a fair request and she wanted to tell him so but her own heart was racing so fast it was stealing all her breath and she could only nod. And then his lips were upon hers and her whole body felt alive to his touch and she happily gave herself to his kisses. She had not expected to wed so soon but now it seemed she was ready. Very ready.

'Hamlet,' she whispered.

'Flora?'

'Will you take me now – as wife, I mean?'

'Now? Before our wedding?'

'*As* our wedding – just you and me, without all the fuss and craziness of the court.'

He ran a finger down her cheek.

'There will still have to be fuss and craziness.'

'I know but that will be for them. This will be for us.'

'It is what you want?'

'Oh, yes.'

'Then, wife, I am yours to command.'

And, lifting her in his arms, he carried her to the bed and kissed her again and there, in the dark and the peace of the night, Flora was wed and finally, in Hamlet's arms, she slept. Secrets, it seemed, she liked well enough so long as she was on the right side of them.

Chapter Eleven

Aet Gefrin, November 602

Ofelia pressed the tiny silver coin deep into the earth and begged Thor to send war to Bernicia. Her sword grew rusty with all this damned peace and her soul with it. Training had slackened with the first frosts and all Ofelia could see before her was night after night spent around the hearth fire listening to skalds telling of others' adventures instead of carving out her own.

She'd told Hamlet they should head back to Denmark before the winter Wild Hunt came and they were stranded in the Angles' land to see it out, but he'd insisted that they weren't ready. He had spies crossing the seas and they'd reported that his death had been widely cried abroad and Wiglek had declared himself Prince of Jutland in Hamlet's stead. Feng presumably also had spies crossing paths with theirs on the whale road so must know it not to be true but it suited them to wipe Hamlet from the people's memory. With no hope of his return, Danes would be more likely to bow to Feng and Wiglek's yoke ... and that meant they needed a great force in order to fight back.

Ofelia disagreed. They'd do better to strike before Hamlet's uncles got a tighter grip on his country and, besides, they had men enough now. They been part of a skirmishing party sent to harry the enemy at Aethelfrith's western borders and had been so successful that the delighted king had added another ten men to their personal troops. With their original ten and the twenty from Flora's dowry they were now a band of forty – enough, she was certain, to mount a surprise attack on Feng. Hamlet, however, wanted at least twenty more but no further attacks had arisen and how was he to win warriors sitting round the hearth fire joking with Aethelfrith and cuddling his cute little wife? It drove Ofelia mad to see him wrapping her pretty blonde hair around his fingers and looking into her pretty blue eyes like some ordinary sap.

Ofelia brushed earth over her coin to keep it safe for Thor and backed away from the tangle of tree roots the locals used as a shrine, praying the great war god was watching for she needed his help badly. There was still time to wage war before winter blanketed the ground and they all needed combat. The men grew too fat sitting around the royal estate and too soft without an enemy to sharpen their swords upon. And as for Ofelia – she itched for action. Any action.

She'd found an obliging couple of lads among Hamlet's new troops to sport with. Aart was a little small and Seaton a little simple but they were both lively and robust. Somehow, though, it never seemed enough. War, yes, that was definitely what she needed. What they *all* needed.

'Lia? What are you doing out here?'

Ofelia rose to her feet and turned to face the new arrival.

'I could ask the same of you, Hamlet.'

'Isn't it obvious? I'm looking for you.'

'Oh.' She brushed dirt off her tunic. 'Why?'

'Does there need to be a reason?'

She thought about this. There hadn't used to be such a need but these days it no longer seemed natural for them to spend so much time together. It was her own stupid fault for rutting with him back at Walpurgis of course. She'd known it was a bad idea but hadn't realised quite how bad. Somehow with Hamlet it didn't work the way it did with other men. With them she was always able to enjoy a romp and then go easily back to being barrack-mates, as she would if they'd just played knucklebones. With Hamlet, though, the intimacy seemed somehow to leak into normal life.

They'd done it too often, she'd decided. They'd let it become a habit and now it was a habit she was having to break. She'd seen men grow so used to drinking wine that a few days on campaign without would see them pining and struggling to function and she'd always thought it pathetic. No man – or woman – should have to rely on a drink to be able to live their life, nor on another person either. She'd known that from the moment her mother had flung herself into the flames after her husband, as if her own life was no longer of any value without his to parcel it up in. Truly pathetic. No, it was a good job she and Hamlet had stopped sporting together and if things were a little awkward then so what? They would recover.

'What were you doing?' Hamlet asked when she didn't reply.

'Praying.'

'Oh. For what?'

'War.'

'Right. Why?'

'Why? Because war is what we do, Hamlet – what we're trained for. You wouldn't ask a skald why he wants to tell his stories, would you?'

'A skald does not risk his life when he stands up to tell a tale.'

'But he does risk his reputation. And, besides, if he does not entertain for too long he may fall out of the way of it. He may forget how to deliver his plots and his characters and his elegant phrases.'

'As you forget sword swings and axe hacks?'

'Not that. We train still but there is a difference between fighting on the yard with blunted swords and opponents who are actually friends, and combat to the death in battle. There is not the same . . . *bite* to our practice sessions.'

Hamlet smiled.

'You are bored, Lia?'

'Restless,' she allowed. 'And a little trapped. You cannot even see the sea here, Hamlet.'

'You miss the sea?'

'I miss *Denmark*. Do you not? Do you even still send spies?'

'Of course I do but there is little new to hear, save that Feng is still on his stolen throne and Wiglek still parades his stolen title. We are better here for now.'

'*Better*, Hamlet? Has Bernicia so easily become home to you?'

'No! It is comfortable, yes, convivial even . . . '

'With your little wife?'

He stiffened.

'Flora is not "little", Ofelia, not in any way. She is strong and funny and brave, not with a sword perhaps but with what she believes in.'

'Believes in? Such as?'

'Her herbs, healing people, doing good.'

'Doing good?' Ofelia spat.

'What's wrong with that?'

'Nothing. It's very worthy. But how much good can herbs actually do, Hamlet? Can they win land? Can they see off enemies?'

'Perhaps not but they can heal warriors who work to do so and that is valuable. Not everyone can fight with a sword, Ofelia.'

'And you prefer your women not to?'

'No! Don't be ridiculous. This isn't like you, Lia. When did you worry about being a woman? You are yourself, as Flora is herself. Isn't that enough?'

'For you, it seems.'

Hamlet's eyes narrowed knowingly.

'You're jealous?'

'I am not! If you want to play herbwives with Flora that's up to you.'

'Well, actually it was *you* who chose this wyrd for me. You who wrote it in the runes and bound me to it.'

'To stop you from being killed!' Her voice rose, flinging itself against the trees and echoing up the valley. She caught herself, turned back to her offering. 'You are disturbing my prayers, Hamlet.'

'Prayers for war?'

'As I already said, yes.'

'Then I am less disturbing them than answering them.'

'What?' She spun back and saw that his eyes were shining. 'Are we sailing for Denmark?'

The shine faded a little.

'No, not that.' She went to protest and he put a hand to her mouth to stop her. His touch seared across her lips, as fiery as a kiss, scorching the words in her mouth before they could form. 'I'm sorry but we are not ready yet to attack Feng. We will, Lia, I promise it, but he and Wiglek are firmly entrenched and we need more men. There may, however, be a chance on the horizon for us to win some.'

'How?'

His fingers were still on her lips, grazing them as she spoke. Slowly he removed them and she had to fight her own desire to snatch them back.

'It seems this King Aedan of whom Aethelfrith has told us is rising up.'

'The one in the north-west?'

'That's it. Ruler of a kingdom called Dal Riata – a proud little place by all accounts, making a name for itself with a clutch of monasteries.'

'Monasteries?' Ofelia asked, stumbling over the unfamiliar word.

'Places where Christians gather to live in communities and dedicate their lives to prayer.'

'Their *whole* lives?'

'So I'm told.'

'Why?'

'I'm not sure. It's part of what the White Christ wants.'

'He sounds a funny sort of god.'

'Oh, he is. He wouldn't suit you at all, Lia – he wants everyone to live in peace.'

'Then he must be very foolish. Does he not understand men?'

'They say he lived among them.'

'When?'

'I don't know. A long time ago. They say he lived with men and then he died for them.'

'In battle?'

'No. On the cross, as a criminal.'

Ofelia laughed.

'A *very* funny sort of god. I'll stick with Freya, thank you very much. And Thor.' She glanced over to where she'd buried the coin. 'You said war, Hamlet. Does that mean this Christian king, who believes in peace, is attacking us?'

Hamlet gave her a rueful smile.

'It seems his beliefs are more flexible than he would like his borders to be. He fears Aethelfrith's intentions in the west.'

'Rightly so.'

'Yes.' Hamlet looked at her, his face suddenly intent. 'Oh, Ofelia, it *is* good to talk to you. You understand things. Your mind works in the same way as mine. I wish ... ' He stopped talking, drew in a deep breath. 'No matter. Would you like to see the sea again?'

The sudden change of subject threw her.

'The sea, Hamlet?'

'Yes, the sea. You said you missed it, did you not?'

'I said I missed Denmark.'

'Well, it's a clear day – perhaps we will see her too.'

'How? You're talking nonsense, Hamlet. Are you going to call up Odin to give us a ride on Sleipnir into the skies?'

'Not quite, but we *can* get closer to the gods.'

His eyes drifted up the great slope above their heads and suddenly Ofelia understood.

'You wish to climb the bell?'

'I do. I want to see the ancient fortress at the top and I bet you can look out for miles from there. We might even spot Feng living it up on his stolen throne, waiting for news of my death.'

'News that he will never hear. Oh, Hamlet, yes! Come on, we can show him our alive-and-kicking arses from the top!'

She turned to head out of the trees, making for a rough herder's path up the side of the great hill. It was a good idea to climb it. Why sit moping in something's shadow when you can conquer it instead? She struck out, her legs newly energised by the challenge, her spirits lifting with every upward step. She could hear Hamlet behind her, his breath coming thick and fast, and the sound of it pushed her on faster.

'Come on, Hamlet – you're as slow as a worm.'

'A worm?!'

His breathing grew louder and suddenly he caught her by the ankle and brought her down. 'Ha! Who's the worm now? What are you doing wriggling around in the grass, worm?'

She sat up slowly.

'Admiring the view,' she said, pointing to where already they could see out across vast stretches of meadow and woodland towards a sliver of dark blue on the horizon. 'Is that the sea?'

He turned to look and she seized her chance to grab him round the knees and bring him crashing to the ground, sitting astride his hips then to keep him prisoner.

'Worm!'

He grimaced and grabbed at her, trying to pull her off, but she had the advantage of height and pushed his arms above his head to pinion him to the sloping ground. She felt the flush of victory and, hot on its heels, a new, more intense heat as she became aware of her body against his, their faces so close she could feel his panting breath upon her lips. One tiny move forward and they would . . .

She stood up, releasing him and stepping swiftly away, her breath coming faster than it had done while climbing the slope.

'Stop lying around there, lazy bones, or we'll never get to the top.'

'What if I'm happy here?'

'Then you're weak. Come on – you said you wanted to see the ancient fortress, so let's go and see it.'

She set off again, turning her face determinedly towards the slope, and was relieved to hear Hamlet heave himself to his feet and follow. It was good to be out here away from the tangles of a foreign court. She felt alive again, free. It must be the air, fresh against her skin, and the pleasure of climbing higher than you could ever go in Denmark that was making her head so light.

'You're going too fast, Ofelia,' Hamlet called.

She turned and looked at him labouring up the great rise.

'No, you're going too slow. Come on – there's the top. We're almost done.'

But they weren't. As they crested the rise they saw to their horror that there was another yet to climb.

'The gods are playing with us,' Ofelia said, looking up. 'They've moved the mountain.'

'Maybe we'll never get to the top,' Hamlet said. 'Maybe they'll move it every time?'

Ofelia looked to the next summit. She could see the stone walls of the fortress ringing it and, beyond, the crumbling roofs of some ancient dwellings. Were the gods there? Was this a test?

'Let's try the next rise. If it moves again, we'll surrender and leave them be.'

Hamlet groaned.

'It's a long way, Lia.'

'No further than we've come already. See, that's Aet Gefrin all the way down there with the people as small as bugs beneath our feet.'

Hamlet nodded.

'I see the appeal of mountains – I feel on top of the world up here.'

'We're not on top yet. Come on!'

'You'll kill me, Ofelia.'

'I thought you were fit? *Come on*!'

She grabbed his hand to tug him onwards and, with a squeeze of her fingers, he moved in her wake. It was steep and they both found words hard to form so walked in silence, linked together as they climbed relentlessly upwards. This time, thank the gods, the top did not move. The stone walls stayed solid in their eyeline and grew as, breath swelling in their chests and thighs aching more than after even the hardest training bout, they approached the top.

The sun, which had been overhead as they'd started out, had curved its path and was now descending behind them. When they finally reached the thick stone wall and peered over a crumbling section, they saw long shadows cast from the abandoned buildings within the fort.

'No gods?' Hamlet asked.

Ofelia shook her head.

'I can see none and cannot believe they would live in such run-down shacks.'

'Trolls?'

'No. Trolls like it below the ground not up here in the skies. Let's climb over.'

Ofelia scrambled over the wall and ran into the centre of the compound, exhilarated by the space. She couldn't remember ever being alone in such a vast area before, save perhaps on the Jutish moors. Up here there was an amazing sense of a whole estate devoid of all lives bar their own. Many of the timber buildings were rotting away, walls caved in and roofs at sickening angles, but she could still make out the shapes of a great hall, of byres and bowers, of sties and stables. Here in the Angles' land it seemed the dead did not hide away in barrows but danced around the hilltops and she cast around for their shapes between the ancient timbers.

'Isn't it fantastic?' she asked, turning back to Hamlet who was treading more carefully between the buildings.

'Is there anyone here?'

She looked again for ghosts but if they were here they had danced shyly off on the soft Bernician breezes.

'Just us.'

She went to meet him. Her body felt alive from the climb and her head giddy from the great height they'd reached. She felt alive, excited, reckless.

'Just us?!'

He raised an eyebrow and the simple movement set her body flaming with desire. Habit, she reminded herself. Hamlet was like the most potent wine, calling to her, promising her thrill, joy, release – enslavement.

She ran to the far side of the compound and pushed herself up onto the stone wall to see over the other side.

'There's the sea! Definitely the sea. And somewhere out there is Denmark. We need to send our signal to Feng.'

She looked for footholes in the stone and started to climb in earnest.

'You're really going to bare your arse to him?'

She looked down.

'Aren't you?'

'Isn't it a bit . . . childish?'

A little of her euphoria dropped out of her.

'Childish?' She stepped back down. 'Maybe. But what else can we do, Hamlet? You won't attack.'

'I *can't* attack.'

'Why? Because you're chicken?'

'No.' His voice was exaggeratedly patient. 'Because we don't have enough men to secure victory. I would just be leading us into death.'

'You think it better, then, to stay cosy around here?'

'It's hardly cosy, Ofelia. We are going to war.'

'So you say but I see no evidence of it.'

'You would if you paid attention to Aethelfrith instead of going off sporting with Aart and Seaton.'

She jumped. She didn't think he'd noticed and was perversely pleased he had but she wasn't going to allow herself to be censured.

'Aethelfrith is boring.'

'And Aart and Seaton are clearly not.'

'No. They're very . . . energetic.'

'And that's all that counts with you, is it?'

'It's a start. And it's not as if you haven't got a wife tucked up obligingly in your bed every night.'

'No, it isn't, and if you'd agreed to it, that wife would have been you! And let me tell you, Ofelia, I'd have shown you energy then – night after bloody night.' He grabbed her by the arms. 'But you wouldn't have that, would you? You'd rather be rutted by strangers who fill your body and leave your heart untouched. Well, Ofelia, you needn't worry because your heart is so cold *nothing* will ever touch it.'

She gasped and went to hit him but he was holding her too tight. She could feel herself trembling in his grip though whether from anger or fear or something else altogether she could not tell.

'I will do what I want with my life and my body and my ice-cold heart, and none of them are anything to do with you, Prince Hamlet.'

'Oh, but they are, Constable Ofelia. You fight at my side; your actions could endanger me.'

'I always fight well. *Always.*'

'But do I?'

'What?'

'Your heart may be ice, Ofelia, but mine is not. I love you.'

'Hamlet, don't . . . '

'It's true. I've tried to fight it these last, strange weeks, but I cannot. I love you, Ofelia. I love . . . '

'Hush!'

'Make me! I love you, I love you.' She tried to put her hands over her ears but he held her still. His body was lean and strong against hers and his breath hot against her lips as he said the dread words over and over.

'Quiet,' she pleaded, but still his lips formed the words until there was nothing to do but cover them with her own.

His response was instant, his kisses so passionate she lost herself gladly in them and when he let go of her hands, she flung them round his neck and together they sank to the ground beneath the great walls of the ancient fortress with only the skies and the gods and the wisps of ancient ghosts to see and smile upon them.

By the time they headed back down the bell, Sol had pulled the sun right behind it and they only just beat her to the ground. Ofelia knew she had a stupid smile on her face and battled to hide it but when they finally headed through the gates of Aet Gefrin all was in far too much chaos for anyone to notice something as trivial as a smile. Ofelia grabbed Eric's arm as he passed.

'What's happened?'

'Haven't you heard? Where have you been?'

"With the gods" she wanted to say but instead she grunted, 'Training run.'

'Mighty long one. Hope you're not too tired. Aethelfrith says we ride out tomorrow.'

'Ride out? Where?'

'North. King Aedan's troops are on the march and we must cut them off. We go to fight, Ofelia – we go to war!'

She looked to the skies. So Thor had heard her prayers, made just this morning though now it felt a long, long time ago. Well, good. She'd longed for action and here it was. She glanced at Hamlet.

'It seems, Prince, that I will fight at your side again.'

He smiled and led her into the mass of preparations.

'I would have no one else do so.'

Chapter Twelve

The Borderlands, November 602

'Left side!'

Hamlet's cry whistled into Ofelia's consciousness, his familiar voice blade-sharp against the roar of battle, and she spun just in time to duck the hack of an axe. Her shoulder muscles twitched as if feeling the ghost blow but threw themselves behind her own sword swing as she pounced on her assailant. Off balance from his attack, he was exposed and she was quick to drive her blade between his ribs. Blood spurted in a crimson arc before her, gloriously fresh and pure, as he fell, face in the mud and soul already halfway to Valhalla.

Ofelia did not envy him one bit. Valhalla would be a wonderful rest but she was in no mood for resting at the moment. She was alive with the battle. It buzzed through her veins so that her body seemed attuned to every minute detail of it. She bobbed lightly from one foot to the other, seeking her next opponent. Here he came – a big man, loping towards her with a fool grin on his fat face as if he thought she'd be easy meat for the ravens. She smiled.

I'll have you, she thought. *I'll have you straight away.*

The big ones were usually the easiest. They could sometimes move fast but rarely change direction. And they always, always made the same mistake this one was by noting her slim frame and thinking they had to do little more than a desultory swing of the blade to dispatch her. It made them lazy – perfect.

Sure enough, here he came, blundering forward on his great big feet, making a direct charge, sword held high. It was a matter of moments to side-step, twist and impale him under his sweaty armpit. He went down, eyes wide in horror, not so much at his own death as the manner of it.

'Easy mistake to make,' Ofelia told him as she wrenched her sword out of his sucking flesh. 'Better luck next time.'

She looked quickly about her. The battle was on a wide field so the shield wall had swiftly degraded into one-on-one scraps. She saw Hamlet being drawn away from her by a wiry opponent and edged back towards him. She was sworn to protect him and, besides, after these last days – and nights – on the campaign trail her body felt utterly attuned to his. They had been careful. Aethelfrith was a man of the world but he might not take kindly to his son-by-marriage being quite so close to his constable so they had kept carefully apart at bedding-down time, waiting for all to sleep before sneaking away to lose themselves in each other. Ofelia was desperately short of sleep but existing on a heady sexual energy that seemed – for now at least – to be not just a substitute but an improvement.

Now she noted a second Dal Riatan heading towards Hamlet and ducked around to head him off, swinging her sword into his arm. He was quick though – too quick. He twisted so that the blade simply tore away the fabric and squared up to her. So that's how it was to be. Good.

Ofelia eyeballed him and he met her gaze with a dark, focused look of his own. He wore a thin diadem around his helmet – a prince then, a worthy kill. She saw him size her up with a practised glance

150

and set his feet a little wider. Her heart beat with the peculiar joy of the battlefield: a keen piercing sense of utter dedication; a fierce certainty both in her own ability and in the release of knowing that if she failed, she would not be here long to suffer the consequences.

There was nothing to lose in combat so long as you gave it your all. The outcome was either the affirmation of victory or the ecstasy of a warrior's death. Either way there was a party at the end of it. People only struggled if they had things – or, more often, people – they did not want to leave behind. Too many times she'd seen men going to their graves weeping for what their wives or children would do without them, instead of embracing the glory of their own passing. It made for a messy death with more snot than blood and Ofelia hated to see it. Dependence on others made you weak and then – then you lost.

She took a step towards her opponent, eyes fixed on his, made a feint, saw the way he moved, the way his balance tipped naturally to the right. She could use that. Now he feinted and she met his thrust square on, lifting her blade to take his, feeling the clash buzz down her arm. Good. She was ready for a decent fight.

He thrust for real and she dodged, spinning back with a low strike to his legs. Tear his thigh and a man was all but yours, but he saw the move and parried, trying to cut up and under her ribs but she was too fast. She felt her breath come in short, fierce spurts and focused utterly on her opponent, matching his every move. She caught him frown and felt a flash of triumph. He hadn't taken her lightly but he'd still underestimated her. He was shocked – shocked and therefore vulnerable. Time to move in earnest.

Ofelia called up her favourite sequence, the one she'd practised with Hamlet time and again. A short jab at the chest, followed by a backswing to the left arm and then, as he tipped away to the right, a twist of the wrist to slash across the throat. It worked perfectly and again the crimson arc of the kill curved across her sight as the man fell, crumpling at her feet as if begging her, too late, for mercy. Such was war: kill or be killed. Clean, simple, straightforward.

Ofelia glanced around. This was the most dangerous time for, flushed with your own victory, it was easy to lose sight of the battle as a whole. Too many were cut down whilst gloating over their success – Odin's punishment for pride. She glanced left and right but the battle seemed to have sucked away from them like a turning tide and for a moment she and Hamlet stood alone in their small patch of the field.

'You bagged a prince, Ofelia,' Hamlet said, pointing to the helmet. 'Nice work.'

With another glance around she reached down and removed it. The limp head fell back on the unnatural hinge of the severed throat and she turned away. She might delight in the delivery of the blow but not in seeing its effect. The diadem was wedged tight onto the helmet and slick with blood so she struggled to remove it. She looked to Hamlet for help but his eyes were fixed on the field.

'They're retreating.'

'Already?' Ofelia glanced to the skies. Time could slide past in a battle, each moment locked into your own mortality lacking connection to the rest, but it did not usually disappear altogether. Sure enough, the sun was not yet at its height; the day was still young. 'I thought these Dal Riatans were meant to be formidable foes?'

'Perhaps something has happened?'

Ofelia looked to the diademed helmet in her hands.

'This surely isn't their king?'

The dead man was young, twenty-five summers at most, and hadn't Aethelfrith said King Aedan had been long on his throne?

'Maybe someone else killed the king.'

Ofelia felt a flash of jealousy but smothered it. What did it matter who killed him? If victory had been secured this easily Aethelfrith would be in a generous mood and handing out warriors in abundance to the son-by-marriage who'd helped. If they were quick they might yet make Denmark before Yule and then she could kill the king who really counted.

'Let's go and see.'

Together they headed towards Aethelfrith's standard. Men were coming from all corners, most looking as dazed as Ofelia felt, their sword arms twitching restlessly. On the far side of the field the enemy milled and Ofelia kept a tight eye on them. Was this some Celtic trick? She knew little about these native peoples, save that their hair was unnaturally dark, like ravens' feathers, and some of them at least worshipped the strange new god who preached peace but let his people ride to war. Perhaps this Christ had had enough and told them to stop. Ofelia almost laughed out loud at the idea but a trick seemed more likely so she wasn't ready for the ease of mirth yet.

They found Aethelfrith amongst his hearth troops, watching the field with as much suspicion as they, but now a white flag was being raised and it seemed, in truth, as if victory belonged to the Bernicians. Ofelia felt strangely cheated. She clutched the prince's helmet to her chest and watched as a messenger came picking his way across the bloody grass towards them, arms outstretched and head bared.

He wore a long, near-white robe, somehow unblemished by the gore of the battlefield, and she saw that his feet, as he lifted his robes high, were clad in sandals as if he were at home on his farm and not at war. Most curious of all, the front part of his head was shaved completely, down to the softly pink skin.

'Why's he made his head look like his arse?' Ofelia demanded.

Several people laughed but Aethelfrith held up a hand to silence them.

'He's a Christian,' he told Ofelia. 'A monk.'

Ofelia looked quizzically to Hamlet.

'From the monasteries I told you about.'

'Where they devote all their lives to prayer? What's he doing here then?'

'I think we're about to find out.'

Sure enough, the man drew close and dropped to his knees before Aethelfrith.

'Greetings, my lord king.'

He spoke their language but with a curious upward lilt, as if he were singing. Aethelfrith squinted at him but no offence seemed intended.

'You surrender?' he demanded.

'We call a truce.'

'Well, we don't. Surrender or die.'

'King Aedan would parley with you.'

'Parley? This is battle. The time for parley is done. Tell your king to draw his weapon and stand like a man or turn and run.'

'He believes he could be of use to you.'

'He could,' Aethelfrith agreed. 'My sword needs blunting.'

His men roared their approval and looked to the monk but the man just bowed his shiny head before their guffaws and waited until they died down. Ofelia saw his lips moving in private supplication and wondered if he was talking to the White Christ.

When all was finally quiet the man looked up again and said, 'Will you parley, King Aethelfrith?'

The king looked around at the sparse scattering of corpses.

'Have I won?'

'If you wish to see it that way.'

'What other way is there?'

'We could simply say that peace is the victor?'

Aethelfrith growled low in his throat.

'This Dal Riatan king sends me a fool as a messenger. Out of my way, idiot. I came here to fight, not to juggle words.'

He lifted his sword to the monk who, again, bowed his neck before it. Aethelfrith let out a roar of fury and this, at least, sent the man to his feet. He backed off, hands spread.

'You are the victor, King Aethelfrith, and King Aedan begs leave to speak with you.'

'Thank Odin! Very well, he may approach, but tell him that if he doesn't speak more sense than you this parley will end swiftly – and bloodily.'

'Yes, my lord king.'

The monk bowed and backed away but caught the straps of his sandals in his long gown and fell flat on his back. Aethelfrith roared again, this time with laughter. He turned to Hamlet as the hapless envoy rescued himself and fled, his back now thick with mud.

'This should be easier than I thought. The west will be ours by sunset if they are all such dolts. What sort of god is the White Christ if these are his priests?'

'I'm not sure, but he'll be chewed up by Odin and spat out if the Allfather decides he's worth bothering about. Tell them they can all go and live in their monasteries on the western isles and we'll have the mainland and defend it for them.'

'Quite right,' Ofelia agreed, though she had no idea where the western isles were. 'We'll do the sword work and they can use their knives for shaving arses onto their heads.'

The men laughed again but then fell silent. Ofelia turned and saw, crossing the grass towards them, a tall, lean man with a shock of hair as silver as a treasure-hoard and a well-trimmed beard to match. He was old, surely too old to do anything more than tell tales to children in corners, but he walked with mesmerising assurance, despite holding one arm inexpertly bandaged across his chest. The crown on his head was rich with jewels, each as large as a thumbnail and as bright as Bifrost, the rainbow bridge to the land of the gods. They proclaimed him a king and Ofelia looked awkwardly at the royal diadem on the helmet still clasped in her hands.

The Dal Riatan king bowed low to Aethelfrith and then turned to her.

'May I?' He held out his hands and she felt compelled to place the bloody helmet into them. The king looked down at it, head bowed, and then, with sudden, piercingly accurate violence, wrenched the diadem from the helmet and held it aloft. 'You killed my son,' he said straight to Ofelia, though his voice, lilted like the monk's, held no malice.

'I did, my lord king,' she agreed, 'else he would have killed me.'

He bowed his head in acknowledgement of this truth.

'You must have fought well.'

'He was a worthy opponent and will rest merrily in Valhalla.'

The monk, hovering behind his king, made a strange gesture across his chest, as if quartering himself, but Aedan gave a faint smile.

'Maybe he will.'

'King Aedan!' The words hissed out of the monk as if he'd been stabbed.

'Is he well?' Ofelia asked.

Aedan glanced back.

'He does not believe in Valhalla. For Christians, men go to join the angels in heaven according to their behaviour in life, not the manner of their death.'

'It is not dissimilar. If a man – or a woman – lives with valour and courage they will rest merry with the gods.'

Aedan gave a soft laugh.

'I had forgotten the old ways.'

Ofelia frowned.

'Old?'

'Pre-Christian.'

'We are not pre-anything. We . . .'

Hamlet coughed loudly.

'Did you come here to discuss religion, King Aedan?'

Aedan turned to him.

'I did not. You are?'

'Prince Hamlet of Jutland.'

'A true Dane?'

'Is there another sort?'

'Oh, yes – the sort that leaves Denmark and steal other people's lands instead.' Aethelfrith's Angles drew a sharp breath and reached for their swords but Aedan put up his hands. 'And do so with great might. I understand that. I am Dal Riatan. My people once came from Ireland in the east and took our kingdom for their own. I can hardly blame yours for doing the same from the west.

It is the way of things. It is simply where our people meet, King Aethelfrith, that concerns me.'

'And me,' Aethelfrith agreed, stepping up to his counterpart.

They were height for height, Ofelia noted. Aethelfrith was broader, younger and uninjured but the Dal Riatan did not seem fazed by any of this.

'Then it is good we talk. Shall we sit?'

Aethelfrith looked around. They were in the middle of a groaning battlefield with nothing to sit upon unless you wished to pull up a corpse. King Aedan, however, simply sank to the ground, his legs crossed beneath him and his back straight. Six young men of varying ages sat down in a semi-circle behind him. All looked expectantly at Aethelfrith who gave a shrug, gestured Hamlet and Earnfrith to his side, and sank, rather less elegantly, onto the ground opposite them.

Ofelia felt a start of guilt as Earnfrith took his place next to his father. This was the young prince's first battle. He was here simply to carry water and bandages so should not have been in immediate danger but last night Aethelfrith had charged her with looking out for him. She'd resented the charge, certain he had picked her out to be nursemaid solely because she was a woman, but had accepted it all the same. And then, in the heat of the battle, she'd forgotten all about him. Thank Odin he'd had the sense to keep himself alive. Unlike Aedan's son.

Ofelia looked at the diadem, still held in the Dal Riatan king's hands. It was hers. She'd won it fair and square but even she was sensitive enough to know that now was not the time to demand her rights. She shifted round to stand behind Hamlet and watch the progress of this curious parley. King Aedan opened it.

'I am, as you see, in no state to continue fighting.' He held up his bandaged arm. 'But while withdrawn from the fighting, I had the chance to watch both my men and yours, King Aethelfrith, and they are well matched. It struck me, quite simply, that they would do better on the same side.'

Ofelia saw Aethelfrith sit up straighter.

'Against whom?'

'Against Strathclyde of course. King Rhydderch's lands border both yours and mine. Join together and we trap him. Divide Strathclyde and we are both victors – I gain lands to the south of my kingdom and you, King Aethelfrith of Bernicia and Deira, you extend your kingdom all the way to the west coast. It is what you want, is it not?'

Aethelfrith leaned forward.

'How do you know that?'

'How does anyone know anything?'

'You have spies on me?'

'Of course. As you do on me. Need we pretend otherwise?'

Aethelfrith looked to Hamlet who shrugged. Who could deny the truth of what the Dal Riatan said? Ofelia decided she liked King Aedan. He had picked himself a strange god but she appreciated his frankness. Aethelfrith, however, was not convinced.

'You wish to ally with me against Strathclyde?'

'I do.'

'And you go about this by attacking me? Why not simply request a parley?'

Damn, Ofelia thought, that was a good point. She looked to Aedan who gave a rueful smile.

'This is, I admit, my second plan. My first was to kill you, seize Bernicia and Deira and then, with all that might at my disposal, take Strathclyde as well.'

Aethelfrith looked to Hamlet again and Ofelia caught the look of astonishment on his face. What Aedan said was clearly the truth but it was rare for it to be spoken aloud in this way.

'What changed?'

'I now understand that you are too strong for me to overcome. If I cannot defeat you, I would like to join with you.'

'Not only can you not defeat me, King Aedan, but you have been defeated by me.'

'Called a halt to battle.'

'Ceded the victory. It is for me to dictate terms, if there are to be any.'

The man did not even blink, simply asked, 'So what are your terms?'

Aethelfrith thought.

'If we succeed, I get the larger part of Strathclyde. And Dal Riata submits to me as overking.'

Aedan shook his head.

'Never. Dal Riata stands alone.'

'Then let us fight again.' Aethelfrith got to his feet. 'Come, King Aedan – you and I. Let us settle this now.'

Aedan looked up at him and slowly lifted his bandaged arm.

'You know I cannot.'

One of the men at his back stood forward.

'But I can, Father. I will fight him. I will settle this with the Angle.'

He took two steps towards Aethelfrith who drew his sword but, with impressive agility, the older king was up and between them.

'No so fast, Tuathal. I have lost one son already today.'

'And will not lose another but will instead gain a kingdom.'

Aethelfrith was on his toes, testing his battle legs and flexing his shoulders. He had to be twice the age of the prince squaring up to him but he was strong and experienced and Ofelia would put her hack-silver on him winning this bout. Hamlet was scrambling up too and Ofelia reached round to yank Earnfrith away, mindful, albeit rather late, of her promise to take care of him.

'Will Father fight that man?' he asked her in a hushed whisper.

'If he can.'

All five of Aedan's other sons were up, bristling with purpose, and suddenly this royal gathering had all the marks of a hearth-side brawl. The funny little monk was scuttling up and down like a mouse and Ofelia didn't blame him. If things kicked off he'd be the first to be dispatched. Peace is the victor indeed! She reached for her own sword, weighing it in her hand, ready to pounce the moment the first blow was struck, but Aedan and Aethelfrith were still facing each other and those around were frozen, waiting for the signal.

'I will fight you, King Aedan,' Aethelfrith said, 'or we will all fight and you can trust to your sons to keep you safe.'

It was a sharp move. Not honourable, perhaps, with the Dal Riatan clearly injured, but sharp. Unless, that is, the old king took the gamble that of the nine royal warriors here, one of his seven was most likely to survive and take the day – and all the land.

'Not if I have anything to do with it,' Ofelia vowed under her breath, flexing her sword-arm again. She was ready. But Aedan, it seemed, was no gambler.

'I agree,' he said clearly.

'Agree to what?' Aethelfrith demanded.

'I agree that you can be High King if we take Strathclyde, so long as Dal Riata has full autonomy as a client kingdom.'

'Father!' Prince Tuathal protested but Aedan put up an imperious hand to silence him.

'It makes sense, Tuathal. If we succeed, King Aethelfrith can establish a kingdom of Northern Angles that will keep us all secure. Then we can look north for future conquests. I am sure that our High King would support us against the Picts, would he not?'

Aedan looked to Aethelfrith who gave a gracious bow of his head.

'Of course he would. This could be a worthy alliance, Aedan, for us both.'

He seemed satisfied and waved his sons to put down their swords. Aethelfrith did the same and, with great reluctance, Ofelia returned her blade to its scabbard. It all seemed suspiciously easy.

'Shall we meet again to agree full terms?' Aedan suggested. 'Maybe at Disting?'

The mouse-monk squeaked again at the mention of the spring festival of planting but Aedan ignored him.

'At Disting,' Aethelfrith agreed. 'But for now – a drink?'

'Why not?'

Aethelfrith waved a hand and several men hurried off towards his battle tents to summon servers. Ofelia felt as if she were not in real life but in a druids' show, save that no one would make a show with so pathetically little action. Was this the damned White Christ in action? She glanced to the skies, begging the gods for release from this awkwardly civilised gathering. Was she truly about to clink cups with their foe in the middle of a half-fought battle?

It seemed so, for here were servers rushing forward with goblets and jugs of ale, presumably from the barrels Aethelfrith had brought to toast their victory. That, she supposed, was exactly what they were doing but it was the strangest victory celebration that she'd ever attended and she accepted her own drink with little enthusiasm.

'To alliance!' Aethelfrith proposed, his spirits visibly rising as his curious victory became more and more solid.

'To alliance!' Aedan echoed and a mumbled chorus backed them up.

'We should mark this with a marriage,' Aethelfrith said, drinking deep. 'My son will soon seek a wife.'

He clapped Earnfrith on the back so heartily that the lad staggered. Aedan looked down at him.

'Is he not a little young?'

'He will turn thirteen in the autumn and he is growing fast.'

'Hmm,' Aedan said, letting his eyes wander to his own sons, all grown men. 'I have three daughters, Aethelfrith, but two are married already and the other . . . she would not be suitable.'

Prince Tuathal snorted and looked to his brothers, muttering something in their own language. Ofelia could not make out the words but it was clear from the rough response that it was not complimentary about their sister.

'Mairi is thirty-seven summers old,' Aedan said, glaring them into silence.

'And has given herself as bride to Christ,' the monk put in, folding his hands with punctilious delicacy against each other, fingertip to fingertip.

'Given herself?' Ofelia asked. 'Your god ruts with your women?'

Maybe this Christ wasn't such a sap after all, she thought, but the monk gave a gasp of horror, almost a sob, and Tuathal laughed.

'No, my lady warrior. She has given herself to chastity, to honour Christ.'

Ofelia stared at him.

'How does that honour him? Surely if he has given her a body he wishes her to use it to its full ability?'

Tuathal nodded keenly while the monk mouthed manic prayers against this blasphemy but Aedan just smiled again.

'Mairi feels that if she married she would have to serve her husband and not her spiritual lord.'

'Ah.' That Ofelia understood. 'Fair enough, but chastity – really? Doesn't she get bored?'

Tuathal turned to his brothers, speaking again in their own language, clearly translating. They all laughed then Tuathal said something to his father who raised an eyebrow at him and turned back to Ofelia.

'We have not been properly introduced, my lady.'

'I am Lady Ofelia and am, like Prince Hamlet, from Jutland. My parents . . . died when I was young and now I serve the prince as his constable.'

'Is that usual in Denmark?'

'To have a talented warrior as constable? Yes, it is.'

Again King Aedan smiled.

'To have a *woman* as constable? But, then, if you are a talented warrior – as you must be – that answers my question. Are you married, my lady constable?'

'No! Nor will ever be. Like your daughter, my lord king, I have no wish to stand second to a husband.'

'Shame,' he countered. 'My youngest needs a wife.'

He gestured to a red-faced young man who was being jostled

forward by his brothers. He flashed Ofelia a defiant stare from the brightest green eyes she had ever seen then lost his nerve and looked down. Tuathal, however, was still all swagger.

'He undertakes, my lady, to be sure you are not bored.'

Ofelia stepped up to Tuathal, hand to her sword hilt, trying desperately to keep a lid on her rapidly boiling temper. She was not here as casual entertainment for these boorish Celts. She planted her feet and looked up at him through her lashes then, quick as Thor's fire, shot out a hand and grabbed his manhood, twisting just enough to make him squeal.

'I can keep myself more than amused without some bum-fluff Celtic husband, thank you, Prince.' His eyes bulged and she let go and stepped back. 'Apologies, King Aedan, but I am here as one of King Aethelfrith's warriors, not as a plaything for your sons.'

Aedan bowed low.

'It is we who apologise, my lady. Is it not, Tuathal?'

Tuathal mumbled pained agreement and Aethelfrith stepped hastily forward.

'But I do have a daughter in need of a husband. Udela is eighteen years old and ripe for the marriage bed. She is a biddable girl . . .' he paused to glare at Ofelia who cared not; the last thing she wanted to be was a biddable girl ' . . . and would make a suitable wife for Prince . . . ?'

'Gartnait,' Aedan supplied. 'Prince Gartnait.'

'Excellent, excellent. If you agree, we can celebrate the betrothal at Disting. I shall bring Udela with me. You will not, Prince Gartnait, be disappointed in her.'

Ofelia ground her teeth. Udela, she knew, would be delighted at the news but, even so, Ofelia hated to see her talked of as a piece of flesh, offered for the boy's gratification.

'You will not,' she agreed loudly, 'for she is strong and clever and a true royal.'

'And very pretty,' Aethelfrith added.

Ofelia gave up. She was sick of this. She withdrew towards the tents, leaving the men to their posturing, but to her surprise King Aedan followed her.

'I apologise again, my lady, for my sons' behaviour. They are not used to she-warriors.'

'Clearly.'

'This should be yours, I believe.'

She looked down to see him holding out his lost son's diadem and took it awkwardly.

'I am sorry for your loss.'

'As am I, but such is battle. That is why I was keen to stop it.'

'Because your god prefers peace?'

'Because *I* prefer peace. It keeps more people alive.'

'It keeps more people in *this* life,' Ofelia corrected him. He nodded thoughtfully. 'The old ways?' she suggested.

'I am not condemning them. Indeed, sometimes I miss them. I was a dutiful servant of Odin once.'

'And you have turned from him? Why? Why would you do that for a White Christ who dislikes fighting and drinking and rutting?'

Aedan laughed. He laughed a lot, she'd noticed, even at this difficult time.

'He does not dislike rutting, my lady Ofelia. It is simply that some people choose to devote their lives to his service.'

'But why? Is he so vain that he must have this constant devotion? Why would he give a life just to demand it for himself? He seems a very greedy god to me.'

Aedan drank his wine.

'It isn't quite like that,' he said eventually. 'There is much to be said, you know, for forgiveness and living in harmony. Imagine a world without war.'

Ofelia shuddered.

'I would be rendered utterly useless.'

'I'm sure that's not true.'

'I am a warrior, my lord. I fight.'

'And well, it seems.'

Ofelia turned the diadem awkwardly in her hands and looked to the rest of the group. They were draining their cups so, praise Odin, this strange meeting would soon be done. And yet now she found herself curiously sorry to part from this interesting king.

'Tell me then, King Aedan, what is so good about this Christianity of yours?'

He, too, glanced towards the group then turned back to her.

'There is much that is good in it, much that is worthy. It teaches us to be kind to one another, which cannot, surely, be a bad thing? But, in truth, for a king it has one big advantage – power.'

'Power?'

'The church grows daily and across many kingdoms. It has rules, common rituals, a hierarchy. A priest in Dal Riata can talk with a priest in Ireland or Francia or Roma and they can understand each other. They create a web and, if a ruler complies, that web can hold him up very high indeed. The priests have sway over the people, Ofelia, so if I have sway over the priests, I have the people too. It is a new way – collaboration, cooperation, coordination.'

'All things you are clearly good at,' Ofelia allowed.

'I have learned to be.'

'Are you, then, chaste?'

At that Aedan laughed loudest of all.

'Have you seen all my sons? No, Lady Ofelia, I am not chaste. I am with you in the belief that chastity is – how did you put it? – a waste of the body God granted us. And I shall tell my daughter, Mairi, that when next I see her.' He held out his hand. 'It has been a pleasure meeting you.'

Ofelia took his hand firmly in her own.

'And you, my lord king.'

'It is a shame you cannot marry my boy but you would, perhaps, be a little overwhelming for him. Wear the diadem, Ofelia, and I shall instead consider you one of my sons.'

With that he was gone to gather up his men and, with much bowing, retreat from the field.

Ofelia stood and stared. The gods had surely played tricks on them today, the White Christ along with the rest, and she was unsure yet how it would turn out. Udela, at least, would be happy, though this strange Princess Mairi, this bride of Christ, perhaps less so.

Chapter Thirteen

Dunadd, December 602

Mairi unclasped her hands, feeling them tight and sore from the fervency of her prayers, and raised her head to look up at the statue of the Virgin, her chosen namesake. As ever, she drew strength from the expression of boundless love upon the blessed saint's beautiful face. She had bought the statue from a priest visiting Iona from Rome itself. It had been costly (she still blenched at the memory of her father's shouting when he'd found out just *how* costly) but was worth twice as much. Whoever had carved it must have been blessed by the hand of God Himself for His goodness shone clearly from the Blessed Virgin and brought light to even the darkest of days.

'Hail Mary, Mother of God,' she murmured. 'Bless my family this day and bring my father and brothers safely home from the wars.'

She fixed her gaze on Mary's face, longing for a sign, but the saint did not move. She looked sad, though, and Mairi felt a terrible pang of foreboding strike her so hard it was all she could do to stay upright on her knees before the altar. What if her father had lost? What if the Angles had defeated him and were even now marching on Dunadd? She had heard terrible stories of the pagan peoples. They were harsh and ruthless and intolerant. They took what they wanted: property, land, goods, women. Her royal status might not be enough to protect her, nor her faith.

The Angles, a priest had told her the other day, were God's scourge on wicked Christians who broke his laws or showed insufficient devotion, and Mairi greatly feared that applied to her. Had she not sworn, years ago, to give herself as a bride to Christ? And yet here she was, still living as a princess in the luxury of Dunadd. What kind of devotion was that?

She had given in too easily to her father's refusal to allow her to travel to the blessed St Brigid's nunnery at Kildare; had chosen to believe her stepmother's kind insistence that Christ could be as well served here on the royal estate as within a religious order. She had let herself be seduced by the comfort and ease of Dunadd and had compromised her private vows. Now the Angles were coming to scourge her and she deserved every violent act they could commit upon her poor, feeble frame.

'Mairi?' She heard Dorothea's voice through the fog of her own misery and guilt. 'Mairi, are you well?'

She felt a hand on her arm and, looking down, realised she was shaking all over. But so she should be. She pushed her stepmother gently away and fixed again on the statue of the Virgin. Her knees ached from the cold stone beneath them, her bones shivered with the frost of the morning and her fingers, as she pressed them urgently together again, were drained of blood, but she cared not.

'Hail Mary, Mother of God. Hail Mary, Mother of God . . .'

She would do better, she vowed. If God sent her father home safely she would renew her petition to enter the nunnery, and if he refused her again she would run away. She gave a little nod of determination but then remembered that 'Honour thy father and thy mother' was one of God's own commandments, sent to Moses in the desert, so which was the greater sin – disobedience to her father or to her own vows? The walls of the chapel seemed to press in on Mairi and she murmured her prayers faster and faster, snatching at the words to hold her up.

She half sensed Dorothea rising and moving to the door but cared not. Mairi stared up at the Virgin, drawing strength from her kind eyes, and then suddenly, through the thin window on the east side of the chapel, a shaft of light, pure and fierce, broke in and shone directly on the statue, bathing the Virgin in a golden glow that reflected down onto Mairi at her feet.

'She hears me!'

Mairi cast up her arms to the saint. Her prayers were answered. Their men would surely be safe and the Angles turned away. No barbarians would come to violate her poor, weak flesh. She felt a flash of something like disappointment at being robbed of the drama and ground her knees into the stone to punish herself. Oh, she was weak, so very weak. She had endured long, empty weeks after the men had marched off to war but that was no excuse. She was, indeed, seduced by court life, not just its luxury but the company it offered her. Her feet were so firmly of clay that even in this ecstatic moment of heavenly communion the sinful ways of the flesh called to her.

Mairi flung herself flat on the floor before the glowing saint, begging forgiveness. Dorothea had returned to her side and was saying her own prayers now, praising God and beseeching Him for her husband's safe deliverance. So her prayers had been for Aedan too, Mairi noted – though she would doubtless be thanking God not with devotion but by leaping into her returning husband's arms. The night the army arrived home would be a noisy one. Mairi hated it, lying in her bed in the hall, trying to meditate on God's goodness, as all around panting and squeals of lust filled the air, muddling her prayers. Everyone here was so carnal. Could they not see that the path to true happiness was to forswear all bodily pleasures?

'Nunnery,' she said, leaning forward and forming the word so clearly that her lips brushed the icy stone beneath her.

She welcomed this kiss from the church itself. It was time to devote herself to it entirely. Slowly she raised herself, stretched out her sore limbs and brushed the frosted dirt from her gown.

'Shall we break our fast?' Dorothea suggested from behind her.

Mairi turned to look at her. So carnal!

'I am hungry for no more than God's holy blessing, thank you.'

Dorothea smiled.

'Lucky you. I, by contrast, am eager for cheese. The dairymen produced a fine new recipe yesterday and I am keen to try it. We should get to the hall before it is all gone.'

Mairi did not deign to answer but, to her annoyance, her stomach gave a low, hollow rumble. Dorothea smiled again and took her arm.

'Come, sweet one. 'Tis no shame to keep the body nourished. Let's go to the hall.'

Mairi nodded; Dorothea spoke true. Had not Christ fed the people with loaves and fishes? She let her stepmother take her arm, grateful for the support for she felt a little shaky after the miracle, and moved out into the icy sunshine. She blinked furiously against the onslaught of light and looked about her.

They must have been praying some time for they had entered the chapel before the sun was halfway over the horizon and now it was heading for its modest winter zenith. The royal estate of Dunadd was alive with the business of the day. To her right the swineherds were braving the jostling of their charges to pour swill into the troughs and one was chasing an escaping piglet across the compound. The creature was remarkably agile despite its stubby legs and tubby belly and kept ducking away just as he pounced. Mairi laughed and Dorothea looked at her.

'It is good to hear you happy, Mairi.'

The man finally made a successful grab for the piglet and hefted it awkwardly into his arms, kicking and squealing furiously at its capture.

'I think my father will come home today,' Mairi said.

'The Holy Mother told you that?'

Mairi inclined her head.

'I believe so.'

'Then let us make haste. If you are right, the men will be hungry and I must check provisions with the kitchens.'

Mairi frowned.

'Is food all you think of, Dorothea?'

Her stepmother looked cross.

'You know it is not, Mairi. Don't be foolish. I am steward of Dunadd in your father's absence and must see it run well. It is my duty as wife and as queen.'

Her voice was sharp and rightly so.

'I'm sorry,' Mairi said hastily. 'I know that and you do it very well. I am still a little lost in my prayers.'

Dorothea smiled.

'It is a gift, Mairi, to pray so fervently, but do not overindulge yourself in it. Come.'

She hastened towards the hall and, with their arms still linked, Mairi had little choice but to hasten as well. Her mind raced too. Was it possible to overindulge in prayer? Surely not? It was all very confusing. One thing she did know though – Dorothea had been unendingly kind to her from the day she had been brought to Dunadd as wife for Aedan thirty-five years ago and had readily taken charge of a grieving two-year-old stepdaughter. She had been not much more than a child herself then and, looking back, Mairi could see that she must have been overwhelmed by her new life as Dal Riata's queen. But if so, she had never let on.

'Dorothea,' she asked now, 'were you scared when you married my father?'

Dorothea slowed her steps a little.

'Scared? Oh, yes, sweet one, I was terrified. But excited too. I was keen to leave my father's estate and rule one of my own – and who could want better than Dunadd?' She beamed around at the great compound. 'I have been very happy here.'

'And, God willing, will be for many years yet,' Mairi said quickly.

'I pray so, though I grow old, Mairi.'

'You do not,' she protested instantly, though she knew it to be true.

Dorothea had been fifty-four summers on God's earth. Her once black hair was now white as the snow that already covered the hilltops to the north and her body was frail from bearing Aedan eleven children and grieving the deaths of two of them. Sometimes these days she struggled to rise from prayers and had to turn to Mairi for assistance. If she left for a nunnery who would her stepmother have to lean on? Was it fair to leave the woman who had cared for her as a child just when she needed care in return? Was *that* over-indulgence in prayer? Mairi quailed at the difficult choices before her. She must pray for guidance.

She looked longingly back to the chapel even as Dorothea pulled her towards the great hall. Then something caught her eye way down the river valley below. A flash of light and then another and another as if angels were dancing at the riverside – but this was no visitation by angels.

'Father!' she called, stopping dead in her tracks.

She felt Dorothea's arm pull against hers.

'Where?'

'There in the valley. See, the sun is catching their armour.'

'God be praised! God be praised, the men return!'

Dorothea lifted her voice and it stopped the whole estate in its tracks. The swineherds froze amidst the heedless beasts; the women paused at their weaving frames, shuttle halfway across the warp; even the men cutting wood stopped, axes raised over their heads. All looked to Dorothea and then dropped whatever they were doing and came running. She grabbed Mairi's hands.

'You said they would come. Did you not just say it?'

'The Virgin told me,' Mairi agreed. 'She shone her light upon me.'

This announcement spread speedily through the crowd jostling to the palisade to see the men approaching and people called God's name to the skies. It set Mairi's heart alight with joy. The estate at Dunadd was declared as Christian and blessed as such by the great Columba himself, God rest his soul, but Mairi knew that many of her father's people still practised the old ways.

Most men still wore Thor's hammer around their necks and many women preserved the old domestic superstitions. Often when she made her way to the chapel at dawn Mairi would see bowls of oats left out for the sprites and there were always women placing round pebbles into the gods' circles on the stone at Achnabrek, to pray for conception of babes or safe delivery of babes or even men with whom to make babes. Children were still all many of them thought about. Mairi had tried to direct them to intercede with the Mother of Christ, but they would simply mutter cursory prayers and scuttle back to their silly circles.

'Why would I ask help of a *virgin?*' one lady had scornfully demanded of Mairi when she'd challenged her about it. 'God's hardly going to impregnate me, is He? And certainly not if my Brecc has anything to do with it.'

Then she'd waddled off, big hips rolling, to go and rut like an ignorant animal as if it was all she was on God's earth to do. And maybe it was. Maybe God only communed with a few and if Mairi was blessed to be one of them she must work doubly hard to hear Him and save the souls of those too subsumed in the flesh to understand. She was pleased, however, that they could all now see that she was chosen by God. Perhaps then they would listen when she tried to spread His word. In truth, though, all anyone seemed interested in was the fast-approaching war host and Mairi was left with little to do but join the rush to open the gates and welcome them in.

It took some time. The army was, praise God, still large, and the gates, even held fully open, were narrow. Her father and half-brothers came first, riding high on their horses, with the rest following on foot. Mairi noted that Aedan had one arm in a sling but he swung down easily enough from his horse so could not be too sore wounded. Women and children jostled to reach their own men and the air was filled with the noisy joy of reconciliation.

Mairi spotted a few darting desperately around, seeking in vain or being diverted to the covered wagon at the back where those who had returned in body only were laid out; she felt for their loss. She would ask the priest to hold a memorial service later, outdoors so that all could attend. It would offer comfort to the grieving and draw the community together and some might take Christ more fully into their lives. Wounded hearts, Mairi had noted, were often open hearts and it was as well to make the most of that – for their own good.

She had stayed tight against the fencing to avoid the first crush of arrival but now that people were peeling away in tight family knots the compound was clearer and she approached her father. He had dismounted and was embracing Dorothea, though as she drew closer Mairi saw that it seemed to be more a case of his wife holding him than the other way round. Aedan's silver head was tight against his wife's shoulder and she was stroking his back as she might a child's. Mairi remembered Dorothea stroking her own back when she'd cried for her dead mother in the night in those early years, and to her sudden shame found she could not remember the grief so much as the comforting feel of soft hands. But why did her father need that comfort?

She scanned the boys surrounding the royal pair, counting off her stepbrothers. There was Tuathal, the eldest and fiercely aware of it. Then the twins, Baithene and Conaing. There was young Eochaid Buid, still so short that the others teasingly called him "the dwarf", and green-eyed Gartnait, his fierce protector, but where was Bran? She ran forward and grabbed Gartnait's arm.

'Where's Bran?'

He turned sorrowful eyes upon her and she saw tears sparkling in their jade depths and felt them leak straight into her heart.

Suddenly she remembered Holy Mary's face this morning, before the glow of her revelation. She had looked so sad. Had Mairi not been filled with foreboding then at how sad the saint had looked? Now she knew why.

'Dead?' she whispered. He nodded. 'God have mercy upon us.'

'It's a little late for that,' Tuathal said, joining them. 'In this instance, sister, God had mercy on the Angle warrior who slew him.'

'Curse him!'

The words flew out of her before she could stop them. The old ways were pervasive even for one who guarded herself so carefully against them.

'Curse *her*,' Tuathal corrected.

'What?'

'Bran was killed by a she-warrior.'

'A . . . ?' Mairi was lost for words.

'A she-warrior,' her eldest brother repeated harshly. 'A fearsome one yet a lovely woman. Gartnait wanted to marry her.'

'I did not,' the lad protested.

'But she turned him down.'

'She did not!' Gartnait protested again, louder. 'She said she would marry no man.'

'She is given to God?' Mairi asked. 'That is, whichever god she worships.'

'No. She is given to her sword. Perhaps Gartnait has had a lucky escape. He gets a Bernician princess instead.'

Mairi looked at her half-brother.

'You are to marry?'

'Apparently.'

'To a pagan?'

'A pretty one, or so her father says.'

'Fathers always say that,' Tuathal scoffed. 'Did not our own tell King Aethelfrith that Mairi could marry?'

'What?' Horrified, she looked from Tuathal to Gartnait. 'Did he truly say that? Does he plan it?'

Gartnait took pity on her.

'No, sister. He said you weren't suitable for marriage.'

'Oh.' Mairi should be pleased, she knew. 'In what way am I not suitable?'

'Because you have given yourself to Christ.'

'Right. Good. I have.'

'And because you are old and dry,' Tuathal added nastily, 'and your womb has probably shrivelled so you'd be no use as a wife anyway.'

Mairi gasped. She itched to slap her smug half-brother but reminded herself fiercely that Christ had counselled turning the other cheek and dug her hands into the fabric of her dress. And now, thank the Lord, her father had pulled away from Dorothea and she could leave Tuathal and his taunts and go to Aedan. She curtsied to him.

'God be praised, Father, for your safe return.'

'I deserve that praise, daughter, for stopping the battle, else you might have lost more than one brother.'

'I will pray for Bran's soul.'

'Will you miss him?'

The king's voice was tight. She looked up at him.

'Of course I will miss him, Father.'

'Or are you just glad for his soul?'

'I ... Both, Father. I will miss him for myself but pray he rests safe in God's glory.'

'Not in Valhalla?'

'No! Father?'

Aedan's eyes were glinting dangerously. His fingers went to something around his neck and she saw to her horror that he wore a charm depicting Thor's hammer, threaded onto a cord. Had the Angles worked some pagan charm on him and turned him back to the old ways? She thought fast.

'You are grieving, Father, as are we all, and you are hurt besides. You must be hungry. Come into the hall and eat.'

She sounded like Dorothea, she knew, but she could think of nothing else to do. Aedan, however, did not move.

'What have you done in our absence, daughter?'

Mairi swallowed and looked over for her stepmother's support but Dorothea kept her eyes fixed on the ground.

'I have prayed, Father. I have prayed every day for your safe return.'

'What else?'

'Father?'

'What else have you done, Mairi? What have you done of use?'

She felt tears rise and battled them.

'Prayer *is* of use. Are you not here safe?'

'Bran is not.'

'For which I am truly sorry but such is war. If you sued for peace, as Christ taught us, then ...'

'Then the Angles would be upon us in time to celebrate Yule here in Dunadd, daughter, and how would your prayers serve you then? They like virgins, the Angles – revere them even – for about as long as it takes to sacrifice them to Odin.'

'Father!'

She fell to her knees before Aedan. He glared down at her and then suddenly shook himself. He reached out and pulled her back up, hugging her roughly against him.

'I'm sorry, Mairi. 'Tis grief for Bran speaking. You are right. Peace keeps people alive. I know that. It is why I called a halt to the battle; why I agreed to an alliance with bloody King Aethelfrith and his cocksure Angles. It is even why I agreed to submit to him as High King if we defeat Strathclyde.'

'Submit, Father? To pagans?'

'To *strong* pagans, Mairi. What other choice do I have? Do you want your damned peace or don't you?'

He banged his injured arm furiously against his chest and she rushed to soothe him.

'Of course, Father. Of course I do. We all do. I am sure you did what was wise.'

'Wise?' He sighed. 'I thought so at the time but the long roads home have made me less certain. Is it better, Mairi, to live in peace beneath the yoke of a foe or to die attempting to throw it off?'

She gaped at him.

'I don't know. I ... I will have to think on it, pray for wisdom.'

'Pray? Of course – pray. You are good at that, Mairi.'

It did not sound like a compliment.

'Truly, Father, the Virgin Herself spoke to me this morning. She told me you would return and here you are. And she foretold Bran's death.'

'How?'

'She looked sad.'

'She looked sad? The sad-looking statue looked sad? That is some miracle! Worth all those hours of prayer, would you not say, to see a statue look sad?'

He was mocking her, Mairi knew. She'd endured such scorn too many times and from too many people to doubt it. Such was the thorny path of the missionary and she must bear it as best she could though truly she feared for her father's soul. She thought he'd embraced Christianity. Had the great Columba not been his advisor for years? Had they not, together, sponsored the building of many wonderful churches and monasteries so that almost every western isle had at least a hermitage upon it to God's great glory? He was a good, Christian man, she knew he was. He was just battle weary.

'Food, Father?' she tried again, taking a step towards the hall, but he reached out and grabbed her arm.

'Did you prepare it?'

'Me? No, I ...'

'Did you, then, choose the menu?'

'No, Father.'

'Have you, perhaps, been weaving?'

He gestured to the frames, abandoned by the women for the embraces of their returned husbands.

'Not today, Father. I was ...'

'Praying. I know. And yet still Bran is dead. It is time, Mairi, that you considered more useful pursuits that could advance your family's fortunes. Like marriage.'

'No!'

'No?'

'I mean, please, no, Father. I am given to Christ. I wish to enter a nunnery. I ...'

'A nunnery? Not this again. You are a princess, Mairi. That is your calling. Your mother, bless her soul, birthed you as a princess and it so weakened her body that her second child stole her from us. You are her sole legacy in this world and you wish to hide away in a nunnery?'

'It is not hiding, Father, truly. It is to God's honour and ...'

'And what of *my* honour? I am sick of it, Mairi, sick. I fight wars, I claim or cede victories, I lose sons to keep Dunadd and Dal Riata safe – and for what? For you, my eldest child, to closet herself in a chapel and wear her virgin knees red-raw in prayer to a God who cannot, despite all His teachings, bring us actual, real peace.'

Aedan's face was scarlet with fury, his whole body bristling with it. Mairi tried to back away but he still had hold of her.

'Who has been speaking to you, Father?' she asked. 'Who has turned you against God?'

'The Angles,' came the curt reply. 'The Angles have made me see sense. They have cut down my son and cut away my foolishness with him. I was a fool. Christ has made me a fool and I am punished for it.' He turned to his remaining sons, yanking his injured arm out of the sling and punching it at the skies. 'Forget alliance, forget cooperation and forget bowing to bloody Aethelfrith as High King. We start mustering men now. As soon after Christ's Mass as the snows allow, we attack again.'

'No, Father,' Mairi begged. 'It is not the way.'

Aedan shook her so hard that her teeth rattled.

'It is *my* way and you, daughter, make the most of your praying because when this is done, I will give you to an Angle and then, at last, you will be useful to me.'

Chapter Fourteen

Aet Gefrin, February 603

'This way, my lady. Be careful. Do not stumble, not in your condition.'

Flora felt gloved hands on her back, guiding her up the narrow pathway, and had to suppress a giggle at the sight they must make: a procession of heavily clothed women feeling their way through the pre-dawn light with flowers frosting in their hair and more clutched in their hands. The air was laced with ice, the frozen ground crunched underfoot and low clouds massed threateningly in the night sky, blocking out all but the boldest stars. She wasn't sure how she'd been persuaded into this but everyone else had seemed so sure it was a good idea that she hadn't had the heart to protest.

'The light's coming,' someone called from further down the line. 'Hurry.'

Flora felt twenty pairs of feet pick up pace, willing her forward, and did her best to speed up her frozen limbs, though if the light was coming it was doing so by very small degrees. There was perhaps a pinkish tinge to the white ground ahead of her but nothing more to reveal her way through the trees. She reluctantly unwrapped her hands from her fur-trimmed cloak and put them out in front of her as she forged on, aware of the weight of others' expectations.

It had taken only a few moments from Hamlet's grand announcement last night for the first woman to sidle up to her.

'Congratulations,' Lady Annis had said, squeezing Flora's shoulders and dropping hearty kisses on both her cheeks. 'Such lovely news.'

'Thank you,' Flora had said, placing a hand on her still-flat belly. 'We're very pleased.'

That had been something of an understatement. It was closer to the mark to say that when the midwives had been sure enough for her to give Hamlet the happy news, he'd been ecstatic.

'A baby, Flora? Truly? Our baby?'

'A baby,' she'd confirmed, touched by his naïve wonder. 'It should arrive around harvest time.'

He'd picked her up and spun her round and round, then suddenly stopped and set her down, smoothing her hair back with sudden nervousness.

'It's fine, Hamlet,' she'd assured him. 'I'm not ill. In fact, I feel very well.'

She did. So far she'd had none of the sickness of which others complained. Perhaps it was the catnip and angelica she took infused in her breakfast ale or perhaps the gods were just feeling benevolent towards her but either way she intended to make the most of it while it lasted.

'That's excellent,' he'd said, kissing her, then hugging her, then kissing her again. 'It's all excellent. I shall ask your father to call a grand feast to tell the world.'

So he had, that very night, and the world seemed every bit as pleased as Hamlet. Especially the women.

'So,' Lady Annis had said, leaning in close, 'you'll be going to the rings tomorrow then?' Flora had looked at her uncomprehendingly and Annis had laughed. 'The rings, child. You must know about the rings?'

Flora had shaken her head and looked round for Bebba who'd hurried up to them, smiling. Other women had been drawing close and Flora had suddenly found herself at the centre of a crowd.

'There's a rock up on the plain,' Bebba had explained, 'that's marked with the rings of the Ancients. They represent life – the sun, the pond, the womb.'

Flora had frowned at her.

'You mean they're fertility symbols?'

'They are.'

'But I'm already with child.'

'*You* are, yes.' Flora had looked around the eager little crowd and begun to understand. 'When a woman is newly with child,' Bebba had gone on, 'she can lead others to the stone to ask the gods to bless their wombs with the same joy. It is an ancient custom and perhaps a little foolish but there is no harm in it.'

'No,' Flora had agreed, looking again at the women.

Lady Annis had lost a daughter last year and the gods had not yet granted her a replacement. A young woman at her side was newly wed, another almost at the end of her childbearing years and yet another had endured several babes dying in her womb. All looked as if they knew, as clearly as Bebba, that the ritual was foolish but still hoped, every bit as clearly, that it was not. Who was she to deny them their dreams?

'When do we go?' she'd asked and small ripple of pleasure had gone around the gathering.

'Tomorrow. Before dawn.'

'Before dawn?' Flora had echoed, horrified.

She might not be feeling sick but she was tired all the time and had not been springing out of bed as early as she once used to. Besides, it had been threatening snow these last days and everywhere was finger-deep in frost.

'Before dawn,' everyone had affirmed, unwavering, and she'd had little choice but to agree.

It had been very hard forcing herself out of the warmth of Hamlet's arms into the cold and dark but she was waking up at last and now the light truly was coming. She stepped out of the gloom of the trees and up onto the plains just as a thin sun appeared over the far horizon, sending rays dancing through the icy mists hanging above the grass. She gasped.

'Is it not beautiful?' Bebba said, stepping out at her side.

'Propitious,' someone else corrected her and suddenly the other women were pushing past and tumbling towards a group of low stones glowing pale pink in the new day. 'Come, Flora, you sit in the centre.'

Flora squinted at her mother but Bebba shrugged and took her arm to lead her forward. Thankfully someone produced a rich fur for her to sit upon and, with much giggling, she was handed up into the centre of the low rocks and sat solemnly down. She drew her cloak around her and watched as the other women plucked the best of the poor early flowers and placed them in the frozen wells in the middle of myriad ring marks carved deep into the stones. Flora stared at them, trying to imagine the long-ago hand that must have etched these circles into the land. How had they lived? What had been their beliefs? Their dreams? Babies, she supposed, just like the women around her now.

She heard more giggling and saw that several of the young ladies of the court had brought not just flowers but long, smooth stones. These they were inserting into the little wells within the rings in a symbolism no one could mistake. One of the older women tutted but the girls rounded on her.

'Oh, come, my lady, we all know what truly has to happen to plant babies in our wombs so why hide from it?'

Flora noticed Udela flushing and peering intently at the stones sitting wonkily in the smooth holes as if they might somehow tutor her in the ways of the flesh. She wasn't sure why her sister had come but supposed that if she was betrothed it was as well to put in a good word with the gods and, besides, Udela hated to be left out of anything.

'My Marc said this ritual is silly,' someone confided as the women drew back and began to form a ring around the rocks.

'That's as may be,' another replied, 'but I bet he'll be waiting for you when you get back, all set to do his part in it!'

She wiggled her stone in its hole and they all shrieked with laugher. Flora smiled. It would be a merry breakfast for sure if all the husbands were waiting to scoop their wives back into bed on their return as she hoped Hamlet would be waiting for her. She might not need him for the ritual but she was getting colder by the minute and could think of few nicer ways to warm up.

Marriage, she had found, suited her well. Being with Hamlet made her happy. He was lively and kind and fun. He made her laugh and he did surprisingly nice things to her. The marriage bed, it turned out, was a perfectly pleasant place to be. It had seemed a little confusing at first, knowing how everything was meant to fit together, but she had insisted Hamlet give her detailed instruction and together they had worked their way to some sensations she had not known were possible.

The thought of this warmed her a little as she sat awkwardly on her rock throne surrounded by flowers bobbing in icy little wells as the women linked hands to turn three times, sunwise, around her. She saw Udela, flushed with thoughts of her Dal Riatan betrothed, and Lady Annis beside her looking more sombre. To her surprise, Bebba was similarly focused and Flora realised with a pang that her mother still hoped for more children from her shared husband.

Across the ring, Cathryn was visible in the middle of the young women doing her best to look above it all, but secretly every bit as determined as the rest. Babies were a woman's most valuable commodity – her greatest gift and her surest source of power – and everyone here, beneath the quiet hilarity, knew the truth of that. It thrummed through the dancing and the giggling, and if they were all noisy with their own giddiness, they were sharp with intent beneath. Flora felt her own part in this ancient ceremony charged with new responsibility and sat up a little straighter in case her earnest participation in some way helped those who needed it most.

They returned to the compound as the pink early light was easing into a grey day, to find the men supping mulled ale around a brazier. One by one they pounced on their wives and peeled off in pairs until Flora was left with Udela, Bebba and, to their shared discomfort, Cathryn. Aethelfrith had chosen to spare himself the public spectacle of choosing between his royal wives and as Bebba and Cathryn strode off in opposite directions, Flora could not help wondering if he would visit them both and in what order.

It was not a welcome thought and she was grateful when a low voice called to her, 'You look cold, wife,' and she turned to see Hamlet in the doorway to their little bower.

'I'm frozen,' she agreed, and ran to him.

She was inside before she realised, a little guiltily, that she'd left Udela on her own but it was not long now until Disting when her sister would ride out to her betrothal, beautiful in the new gown she'd been fussing over all winter long and more than ready for her lucky groom. Besides, Hamlet was here and Udela was swiftly chased from her thoughts by the touch of his hands upon her.

'How was the ritual?'

'Cold.'

He smiled.

'The problem,' he said, reaching round for the cords that held her gown in place, 'is that you have too many clothes on.'

'Too many?' She giggled. 'You think we should have gone to the rings naked?'

'I think, if you had, the men would not have waited in the compound but followed you up the hill.'

She giggled again. Her gown fell to the floor and Hamlet clasped her against him, his hands running all over her chilled skin and warming it instantly.

'That would have ruined the magic,' she protested weakly.

'Not for the men! Now, little one, you should be resting in your condition.'

He scooped her up and laid her on the bed, then stood back a moment to look at her before tugging off his clothes and leaping in at her side.

'Your job is done,' she reminded him, touching her belly.

'Best, though, do you not think, to be sure of it?' he responded. As his hand covered hers and then moved lower she could only murmur in agreement.

She must have slept afterwards because the next thing she knew her maid, Darelle, was bustling into the room, shaking her awake with unusual roughness.

'My lady, my lady, wake up, please! You need to come to the hall immediately.'

'Why?' Flora mumbled, fighting her for the covers. 'What's the hurry?'

'I'm not sure,' Darelle said, 'but there are men in the yard and not a little fuss. Listen.'

Flora sat up and, sure enough, she could hear the sounds of men milling around outside.

'Messengers?'

'Riders,' the girl said. 'Your father's own, my lady, and he's pacing the hall like a cornered boar. I thought you should come.'

'You thought right.' Flora forced herself out of bed and looked around. 'Where's Hamlet?'

'Your husband went to the barracks a little time ago. He said he had to train but I was not to wake you. I didn't mean to disobey, truly I didn't, but then ...'

'It doesn't matter, Darelle. Here, help me dress.'

The girl stepped forward and, with only the slightest of raised eyebrows, picked up Flora's undershift and gown from the floor where Hamlet had cast them earlier. She held them out and Flora went eagerly forward to put them on. The air felt, if possible, colder than it had before dawn and, once clad, she lifted the leather curtain to look out. The clouds had finally loosened their hold on their burden of snow and it was falling softly to the ground, coating the tangle of messengers in incongruously soft flakes. How on earth were the men training in this?

The messengers outside had now surrendered their horses and were heading to the hall. Flora waited impatiently to be laced into her gown and pushed her feet into their warmest boots. Others were rushing into the compound and as she stepped outside she saw that all the women and older men of the estate were making for the hall too. There were few younger men to be seen and she assumed they were all at swordplay in the barracks and prayed they would not soon need it for real.

In the hall all was chaos. Everyone seemed to be talking at once and all Flora could hear clearly was the unmistakable wail of her sister in distress. She couldn't see her for the press of bodies, so she grabbed the arm of the nearest lady.

'What's happened?'

The lady turned and Flora saw it was Cathryn and cursed her impatience but it was done now.

'It seems,' Cathryn said a little breathlessly – she had clearly been roused in as much haste as Flora – 'that the Dal Riatan has turned traitor.'

'What?'

'The riders say King Aedan is, even now, marching an army of three hundred upon us, hoping to catch us in our winter slumber.'

Flora put a self-conscious hand to her bed-mussed, blonde hair.

'An army? But don't we have peace negotiations with him at the new moon?'

'Not anymore,' Cathryn said darkly and gestured to where the crowd had fallen back from the wrath of their king.

'How dare he?' Aethelfrith was roaring. 'How dare he call a halt to my valiant troops only to scuttle away to his damned Celtic lands and drum up more of his own? It is cowardly and it is dishonourable and it is a bloody pain in the arse! Well, to Hel with him. I didn't want this alliance anyway and now I can take his life instead.'

Those around cheered in nervous encouragement, all bar one.

'But my betrothal,' Udela wailed. 'My poor, dear Gartnait.'

'Your "poor, dear Gartnait" is a traitor and a bastard, daughter, and you must forget him.'

'But we are to be wed!'

'No longer,' Aethelfrith growled. 'I would not welcome him into my family but grind his miserable bones into the mud! And the rest of his brothers with him. Scum!'

'Father, no!'

'Silence, Udela. If you can't shut up and let a man speak then you can piss off back up the hill to play babies with the gods.'

'But if I don't . . .'

'Silence!' Aethelfrith's roar cut off even Udela and everyone cowered again. 'Why am I surrounded by women and greybeards? Where are my men? I need my men.'

'They're in the barracks,' someone dared to volunteer.

'Training? Good. They're going to need their skills, every last one of them.'

They all stared and it was Bebba who dared to step forward and ask, 'What will you do now, my lord king?'

Aethelfrith looked at her, his eyes as icy as the weather beyond the hall.

'I will summon every last man in my lands – my *extensive* lands – to do his duty. And fast. But first I will find someone to lead out a noble band to delay the invaders long enough for me to complete my muster.'

'Someone?' Flora whispered, but Aethelfrith's hearing was sharp and he spun round and fixed his eyes on her.

'Someone bold and brave and skilled,' he declared. 'Someone to stand as my true son and be a hero for us all.'

The ragged crowd managed a cheer at that and Aethelfrith turned back to them, his humour already improving with the prospect of action. Flora, however, stared at him in horror. He couldn't send Hamlet into the jaws of a Celtic army; he just couldn't. She had to get to her husband first. Edging around the hall, she made for the doors at the far end, slipped through them, and ran for the barracks as fast as her shaking legs would allow.

Chapter Fifteen

'Five!'

Ofelia watched as Hamlet held his hand completely steady to show off the five knucklebones balancing precariously upon its back. The other men in the circle groaned good-naturedly.

'You've got Loki's luck this morning, Prince,' Eric complained, reaching out to tap Hamlet's hand from underneath and send the bones rattling to the cold earth.

'Must be the news that you are to become a father,' Lars said. 'The gods are smiling on you.'

'Only in pity,' Ofelia snapped.

She was fed up. Back in Aet Gefrin she barely got to see Hamlet at all. He was forever in Flora's bed and now news of this damned baby had been announced it was all anyone seemed to be talking about. The others stared at her and she glared back.

'What? I only mean that soon he'll be pacing up and down here with a wailing babe, not practising his gaming skills, so the gods are favouring him while he has the chance.'

'He'll not be pacing,' Eric said. 'That's what nursemaids are for.'

'And mothers,' young Aart put in.

'Flora will be a very good mother,' Lars added.

Ofelia frowned at her brother.

'How do you know? It's not as if you've got a mother of your own to measure her by.'

A couple of the other men sucked in their breath but Lars did no more than pick up the knucklebones and roll them round and round in his big hands.

'Perhaps, sister, that makes me more objective in my assessment.'

'Perhaps,' Ofelia grunted, aware that she'd gone too far even by her own standards. 'I'm sure Flora will produce a fine babe.'

'And care for it too,' Lars agreed, running one hand through his blond curls. 'She told me last night that she wishes to nurse the little prince or princess herself.'

'She told you that?' Ofelia frowned at her brother again. This was worse than she'd thought – the boy was growing soft hidden away here in Aet Gefrin. 'Why on earth would Flora be discussing nursing babes with you?'

Lars shrugged easily.

'I don't know. Given the announcement, it seemed an appropriate topic of conversation.'

'I see.' Ofelia shifted on her fur rug, feeling itchy suddenly. Damned animals were full of fleas even when they were dead. 'Are you going to take your turn, Titch, or just sit there thinking about babies?'

'Grumpy, Lia! I'll play, don't you worry.'

Lars rolled the bones around then tossed them in the air and flipped his hand over to catch them. Two clattered straight to the floor but two others landed on his hand and shivered there until the fifth hit Eric on the cheek, making him jump and knock into Lars, sending the bones flying.

'Eric!' Lars protested.

'What? Is it my fault if your throwing is crap?'

Lars, ever slow to rise to a taunt, laughed.

'Nope. Your go.'

Eric scooped up the bones and shook them in his hands. Ofelia flinched. Normally she liked to hear the rattle of the playing pieces but today they sounded hollow and irritable. Or maybe that was just her. She stared at the bones as Eric threw them high, wondering at the man or woman who had once used them unthinkingly to grip a knife, or a lover or, indeed, the bones of those who'd gone before them. Were we all just doomed to become our descendants' playing pieces? Had someone, somewhere in Denmark, turned up the bones of her parents and was even now trying to catch them on the back of his hand as Eric was doing?

She pushed into the circle, slamming her hand down over the rough playing surface.

'We should be training.'

She glared round at the men but no one met her eye, not even Hamlet. They'd all been slow to the barracks this morning after whatever nonsense the women had been up to at dawn and even once they'd arrived they'd seemed reluctant to train. She understood. The snow made feet slip, the cold crippled your grip on the sword, and if you fell, the damp soaked into your tunic. But so what? There were solutions to all these petty problems. Fitting spiked plates to your boots gave you a better grip if you took the time to tie them on. Hands stayed warm if you fought hard enough; and if you didn't fall, you didn't get wet. Simple.

'Hamlet, we should be training.'

'I know,' he agreed, 'but breakfast was big for once and we should let it settle in our stomachs first.'

This was seized upon eagerly by the others who, Ofelia noticed, huddled a little closer to each other as if bracing themselves against her. And Hamlet spoke true. After a lean few weeks, his baby-feast last night had been welcomed by those over-wintering at Aet Gefrin and there had been plenty left for a rich breakfast this morning too. They were right to enjoy the sensation of a full belly but even so . . .

'Food will keep you warm while you fight.'

'What's the point, Ofelia?' Eric moaned. 'In a week's time we ride into the borderlands to talk terms with King Aedan. We will be out in the snow and cold every hour of every day and night so why not store up our warmth while we have it?'

'Because if you sit around here you will get fat and stiff and the ride will be twice as hard. You know that, Eric.'

He groaned.

'I do but would one day really hurt?'

'No, it would not. But tomorrow you will say, "But one day didn't hurt us yesterday so why not one more?" And one more and . . . '

'Enough, Ofelia.' Hamlet pushed himself up. 'We understand. We will train, will we not, men?'

The men rolled their eyes but began grudgingly getting up from their furs and looking around for their swords. Ofelia felt momentarily mean but she was right, she knew she was. No good came of indolence. The only way to get back to Denmark was to work every day, even the cold ones.

'Thank you,' she said. 'I promise you'll be thanking me too when you're celebrating Walpurgis at home on Jutland.'

This summoned a lame cheer from Eric and some of the others. Hamlet, however, hesitated.

'Walpurgis, Ofelia? That's only three moons away.'

'So? Surely once this treaty with Aedan is agreed we can attack in the west and win ourselves enough men to sail? After the last victory we have fifty and a good campaign should win us twenty more, all trained and armed. How many do you need?'

'That would be enough,' Hamlet agreed but his voice was tight.

'So what's the problem?'

He kicked at the knucklebones abandoned on the floor as the men went to don their practice swords.

'Flora is due at the end of summer, Ofelia. Around Lithasblot the midwives think. I'm not sure she should sail until the baby is born.'

'Lithasblot? You want all of us to wait until the harvest is in so your little wife can have her baby in Bernicia? Why, Hamlet? He will be the heir to Denmark and should be born there and shown to the people as their future High King.'

'True . . . That is true.'

'And Flora will still have ages to go at Walpurgis. It will be quite safe. She's not ill, Hamlet, just having a baby.'

'*My* baby.'

'Don't we know it?'

'As we should. It is a matter of great pride to me.'

'It is a matter of simple biology. If you pump enough seed into a girl it's bound to happen.'

'True, because Flora, unlike you, does not take poison herbs to stop it from doing so.'

'Because Flora, unlike me, is not a warrior. How would I fight with a swollen belly?'

'I don't know. I suppose you would have to stop for a time, as if you were injured only more fun.'

'More fun? You think pushing a baby out of bits made as tight as you like them is fun?'

'Ofelia! Sssh. This is inappropriate.'

'Sorry. I forgot I was your shameful secret.'

'By your own choice. You could have been my much-respected wife and proud carrier of Denmark's heir if you'd chosen, but you did not. Flora is content to be so, so be pleased for her – as I am. Now, are we training or what?'

'We're training,' Ofelia agreed furiously, stamping over to her bed to fetch her sword.

She'd kick Hamlet's arse and his bloody pride with it. And if he thought she was jealous he was wrong. This wasn't about winning his stupid heart; she'd done that once before and it wasn't a prize she valued. This was about staying focused on the important things – on slaying Feng and avenging Otto and imposing a just and lawful rule in Denmark under Hamlet as High King. Surely all that was so, so much more important than some mewling baby?

She grabbed her sword-belt, buckling it on furiously, and reached for her practice sword from its hook on the wall, but as she did so the door flew open behind her and she jumped and dropped the weapon. It fell to the ground with a clatter, point towards her, and she jumped back in horror. No warrior should face his – or her – own sword point; it was a bad omen.

Ofelia turned angrily to see who had brought the evil gods into the barracks and saw Flora standing there, the morning light shining prettily behind her, making her honeyed hair glow. Oh, the gods were feeling tricksy this morning for sure.

'You're letting the cold in,' she snapped, stepping in front of her fallen sword before anyone else noticed it.

'I am,' Flora agreed, not even looking her way. 'I'm afraid I am. Hamlet!' She ran lightly up to him and grabbed at his arms. 'Hamlet, don't do what he asks.'

'Who?' Hamlet pulled her close. 'Don't do what who asks, little one?'

Little one? Ofelia thought. *Gods!* But Flora ignored the endearment.

'My father, Hamlet. He is on his way to ask a boon of you but you mustn't agree. He will ask you to accept a command. It means certain death.'

Certain death! Interesting. Ofelia pushed the fallen weapon under her bed (it was only a practice one after all, it meant nothing) and grasped her true sword firmly in both hands as she went to join Hamlet and Flora.

'What command?' she demanded.

Flora looked to her.

'It's King Aedan of Dal Riata,' she said. 'He's on the attack.'

'Are you sure? We have a truce with him.'

'*Had* a truce with him. He has broken it. Dispatch riders are in the hall now, talking to Father. He's furious. He's ranting fit to bring the roof down about cowardice and treachery and vengeance.'

'And he wants Hamlet to deliver retribution?' Ofelia rubbed her hands. 'Excellent. There will be reward here for sure, Prince.'

'No!' Flora let go of Hamlet's hands to grab Ofelia's instead. 'Think about it, Ofelia – we have no warriors here.'

'We have these men. And very fine they are too.'

Ofelia gestured around the barracks to Aethelfrith's twenty hearth troops and Hamlet's own band of fifty but Flora shook her head almost pityingly.

'The messengers say Aedan is bringing at least three hundred men. You would be annihilated.'

It was strange hearing little Flora talk of war but she had a valid point. Not that she needed to be told so.

'Not if we use cunning as well. There are traps that can be set, especially if you know the land well.'

'Which you do not.'

'No, but some of these men will.' Ofelia turned to Aethelfrith's troops to demand, 'Which of you are Aet Gefrin born?' But all of them shrank back, looking more like toddlers than warriors. 'None of you? No one is prepared to step up to this challenge?' The men looked awkwardly at each other but still did not volunteer. Ofelia put her hands on her hips. 'So what do you propose then? How about we all sit here playing knucklebones in the warmth and wait for them to get right up to our doorstep? Then what? Maybe the serving lads and the maidservants and the pregnant princesses can help us fight them off. Would that be better?'

'I'll go,' Seaton called.

'Thank you, Seaton,' Ofelia said. 'At least someone sees sense.'

A few laughed at the irony, for simple Seaton was the one least likely to see sense around here, but they did turn to debating the problem amongst themselves and Flora seized Ofelia's arm, pulling her and Lars closer to Hamlet.

'You are right, Ofelia,' she said. 'Someone must go but not you. Please, not you. This is not your fight. It is a Bernician battle and you are under no obligation to take it on.'

'That is true, Ofelia,' Hamlet said. 'Do we want to lose our carefully recruited army in a fool's attack? It might mean we cannot return to Denmark for another year.'

'Which is what you propose anyway if we must wait for your babe to be born.'

Ofelia shook herself free from Flora's grasp as the other woman looked to Hamlet in surprise.

'You do not wish your son to be born in Denmark?'

'See!' Ofelia cried. 'Even Flora is braver than you, Hamlet.'

'*Even* Flora?' she protested. 'You don't need a sword to be brave, Ofelia.'

'So I've heard,' Ofelia agreed wearily. 'You can be brave healing people with herbs or some such but I doubt they'd be much use against King Aedan unless you can put a charm circle around Aet Gefrin?'

'Ofelia, I'm no witch!'

'Shame.'

'Leave it, Ofelia,' Lars snapped. She looked at him in surprise. 'You're being spiteful and it doesn't suit you.'

Ofelia was even more stunned.

'I am being truthful, Lars, which no one else seems to want to be. King Aedan is apparently on his way with three hundred troops. We are here at Aet Gefrin with seventy. We are warm, well fed and highly trained, which in these circumstances makes us worth at least twice our actual number, but they are tough odds all the same. The rest of our possible troops are scattered across Bernicia and Deira, half buried in their farmhouses by snow and unlikely to reach us within the turn of the moon. Correct?'

'Correct,' agreed a deep voice and all of them sprang apart as Aethelfrith strode into the barracks. He went straight to Ofelia. 'I am glad someone is thinking clearly, constable, for all is madness in the hall.'

'Udela is upset,' Flora supplied.

'My spoiled daughter is wailing the bloody place down, stupid girl,' Aethelfrith said. 'So what if she is robbed of her handsome groom? Grooms can be found in any royal marketplace and are nothing compared to what I stand to lose – my kingdom, my throne, my life. And all your lives besides. Aedan has played us for fools. He called a halt to our battle, not to parley but to buy himself time. Devious bastard!'

His voice teetered between hatred and admiration then hardened.

'But he will not win this time. This time I will muster all the might at my disposal and I will fight him and I will not stop fighting him until I have crushed him and every one of his numerous bloody sons into the dirt of their stupid Christian graves.' He glared round at Hamlet's men. 'But first I need a troop who are strong and brave and wily enough to hold back the advance and buy us the time we need to muster. And in you at least, constable, it seems I have a suitable leader. Will you take the command, Lady Ofelia?'

She stood to attention.

'I will, my lord king, if there be just reward.'

'There will be *mighty* reward. Gold and jewels and . . .'

'Men?'

'And men, yes. You wish to retake Denmark, do you not?' Ofelia hesitated but Aethelfrith clasped her arm. 'I am not stupid, constable. Feng thinks he is my ally but it was Rorik who sheltered me in Denmark and Rorik was Hamlet's grandfather. Hamlet is my son-by-marriage, my daughter carries his child, so why would I not want him on the throne? It seems Feng wrote his runes foolishly, does it not?'

His eyes bored into Ofelia but she stood firm before him. If he had any suspicions about their mission in his lands they mattered little to him. Especially now he needed them.

'Fifty warriors,' she said.

'That is what you will take against Aedan?'

'That is what I want when I succeed in holding him back.'

'Done.'

Damn! She should have asked for more.

'One moment,' said a quiet voice – Hamlet's. 'This is my command to decide upon, constable.'

Ofelia faced him.

'I think not. King Aethelfrith offered it to me and I have accepted.'

'You would ride without me?'

'I would rather not but I will if I must. If you prefer to stay here and play husband, Hamlet, I shall ride alone.'

His eyes flickered to Flora who put a hand nervously to her belly.

'And if you win?'

'The fifty men are yours. It will be my gift to you and, more importantly, to Denmark.'

'Ofelia . . .'

He was looking at her with such intensity, his eyes full of all the things she knew he wanted to say if they were only alone. But they were not.

'It is your choice, Hamlet. Maybe Flora is right. If it is such a fool's pursuit then it is best you do not die with us.'

'Ofelia, no!'

He closed his eyes for a moment, clearly battling with himself, and when he opened them again they fixed on Flora. For a dread moment Ofelia thought she had lost him but he simply took his wife's hands and said: 'I must go, Flora. I came here with my men and must stick with my men.'

'Ofelia is not a man,' Flora said.

'She is in this respect,' was his response, then he covered Flora's mouth with his own, drawing her tight against him so that Ofelia had to look away for fear of, after all, falling prey to jealousy. Hamlet spoke true: she rode out as a man, a warrior and a constable. And if, by chance, she also had Hamlet to herself for the turn of a moon, then so be it.

Chapter Sixteen

The Borderlands, March 603

Ofelia looked up to the stars and wondered if the gods were hanging from them watching and, if so, if they blessed these endeavours. She would find out soon enough. If the gods smiled on them, they would come back down this hill as heroes; if they did not, they might be thrown down it as corpses. She sent up a prayer not, for once, to her own goddess Freya or to warlike Thor or the Allfather Odin, but to Loki – most mischievous of the gods. Loki succeeded by cunning and guile and audacity; they would need all of that and more tonight if her plan were to succeed.

Ofelia slowed her pace. Over these last moon-turns in the land of the Angles she had grown used to seeing the land rising around her in bulbous hills and stark cliffs but climbing the damned things never seemed to get any easier, especially with the weather warming up, and she couldn't afford to breathe too heavily. There would be sentries and if this, the darkest part of the night, shielded them from view, she would not gift their ears with the sounds of an advance.

Lars, behind her, missed her change of pace and tumbled into her back. She tripped and caught her foot in the long grass but his hand in hers kept her upright and they shuffled on in silence. Ofelia gave his fingers a grateful squeeze and tried not to wish they were Hamlet's gripping so securely around her own. He was behind Lars with Eric after him and the rest of the thirty-strong troop in careful file behind, all holding hands so as not to lose each other in the night. If the gods were watching they were probably laughing at this little parade, like children behind a nursery maid – save that children had no swords, nor lethal secrets in the packs on their backs.

Ofelia adjusted the weight of her own pack and pushed on up the hill. Again her thoughts drifted to Hamlet, again she tried to force them away, but with nothing to fix on but the stars above and the grass beneath it was hard. He'd been at her side at the bottom of the hill, focusing as intently as the rest as she'd gone over the plan one more time, but when they'd moved into their human chain he'd slid quietly but very deliberately behind Lars so that his hand was not in hers and her very skin ached with awareness of that absence.

He'd been this way from the moment they'd ridden out of Aet Gefrin, Flora waving them off in a dress the colour of the spring sky. He'd been polite to Ofelia, had walked with her and listened to her and shared command in a most respectful and open way. Anyone new to the war band would have thought them excellent comrades but Ofelia knew that Hamlet was holding back his true self. There was none of their usual ease, little teasing or joking and no touching whatsoever. Not a handshake, or a clap on the back or a friendly jostle. He did not sit with her or bathe with her or lie anywhere near her when they all rolled up in their cloaks at night.

If the others noticed they did not mention it. Why would they? They were men on the march, not gossiping girls at the weaving frames. And the march they were on was into dangerous territory in which an enemy with ten times their own number could strike at any moment. There wasn't much joking from anyone. Only Lars had paid any attention and she'd found him sleeping close up to her as he'd used to do when they'd first lost their mother to the flames and had been grateful for it.

Tonight, though, no one was sleeping. After too many long, anxious days scouring the borderlands for Aedan and his host they had spotted them making their slow, loud way down a long valley half a day's walk away. If the Dal Riatan army had kept clanking along and their own lighter, mounted troop had taken the path towards them they would have met well before sundown. That, however, would have been suicide.

Aedan had placed multiple outriders and small bands up on the hills to either side. He was taking no chances. Ambush would have been a very tempting prospect with so many men crammed into such a narrow cutting but he was as alert to the possibility as they and the hills were too bare for the defenders to stand a chance of surprising them. Not that it mattered – ambush, at least of the classic charge-down-the-hill type, was not Ofelia's plan. All they'd needed had been for Aedan to select the perfect camp.

And he had. Too clever a campaigner to back his troops up against a river or trap them in a valley, he'd had them march, complaining loudly, up a hillside to light fires on its leeward slope so as to prevent an unexpected advance up the valley. Ofelia, Hamlet and their men had spied on them from a far-off hill with some satisfaction.

'Will it work?' Eric had asked as they'd watched their quarry lighting cooking fires.

Ofelia had shrugged.

'Conditions are perfect – no rain in the skies, a nice spring breeze and a thin moon. If it doesn't work tonight it never will.'

'Small comfort,' Eric had grunted, but she wasn't here to give comfort but to lead the action and that's exactly what she was doing now.

Once they'd been sure the enemy camp was settled in, they'd turned the horses and ridden in four smaller groups around the back of the hill, reassembling as Sol pulled the sun below it. There they'd tethered the horses in a thick copse and set about readying the weapons they'd need. It had been a relief actually to get on with things. The animal fat Ofelia had insisted they all carry had, despite its tight wrapping, started to moulder in the otherwise welcome sun and to stink horribly. Ofelia had been beginning to fear that, however stealthy they were, the enemy would sniff them out but hopefully by the time they smelled them now, it would be too late.

She focused on placing her feet carefully in the dark, ignoring the lingering stink from the pack on her back and the equally lingering stink of Hamlet's cold attitude.

'You wanted to act as a man, so you should expect to be treated as a man,' he'd told her when she'd confronted him a few nights into their march. And it was true, she supposed, though she'd thought they were capable of greater subtlety than that. Ah, well – she'd rutted with Eric a few times instead and it had been fine. A little perfunctory perhaps but out on campaign all you needed was the crush of someone else's flesh against your own to remind you of the joy of staying alive. And soon she would need that more than ever for they were reaching the top of the damned hill and would soon tip over it and see the fires of the Dal Riatan camp – the perfect target.

Ofelia looked back to Lars and whispered one word: 'Sentries.' She felt him nod and heard him turn to repeat it down the line. Aedan would surely have put a lookout on the hilltop but if they were lucky it would be a disgruntled little band and easily dispatched. Lars tugged at her hand.

'There!'

Their feet had stepped up out of grass and onto a rocky escarpment at the top of the hill and just along it, set into a hollow in the stone, was a small fire. There looked to be three men around it, though only one was upright enough to be awake. Perfect. Ofelia touched Lars and then Hamlet to lead them forward from the group. She felt Hamlet stiffen but he could hardly complain – it was the only silent way to give the command.

It was still pitch black, the stars offering just a milky wisp of light, almost enough to pick out the blades of their three knives as they drew them and crept, bent low, towards the fire.

'Poor buggers,' Ofelia muttered to herself but this was no time to show mercy.

They got as close as she dared and then she gave the order, whispered still so as to alert no one down in the camp below. They all moved fast. The two sleeping men did not even have time to wake before Hamlet and Lars dispatched them to eternal rest and Ofelia's victim had time only to open his eyes wide to his own wyrd before it seized him. He gave a small gurgle but Ofelia silenced it with a kiss as she sent him to the gods. For a moment she wondered where his poor soul had taken her last blessing but this was no time for seeking the dead, rather for sending others to do so.

With all three sentries gone, Lars went back to collect the chain of men and they gathered around the flames, stoking it up with the wood the dead men had kindly left to hand. They made sure that all but the leaders kept to the shadows so that if anyone down below chanced to look up they would see just three figures above them, supposedly keeping them safe. How wrong they would be.

'Packs,' Ofelia ordered in a whisper.

Everyone drew them off their backs and laid out their precious haul. It had taken some time to fashion so many but it would be worth it. They had one chance at this and had to be well prepared.

'Ready?'

'Ready,' came back the answer like the hiss of grass snakes.

'Then let's do this, as fast and as accurately as we practised it.'

She'd made them drill it over and over. They'd complained then but no one was complaining now with three hundred enemy soldiers some fifty paces below.

'Will they reach?' someone asked nervously.

'If you draw the string properly,' Ofelia shot back. 'It's time.'

They rose and paired off, one of each pair with a bow, the other with a quiverful of arrows, the feathers of each one carefully primed with the ripe animal fat. As one, the fifteen arrowmen bent to the fire to light the fat on their first arrows. One caught, then the next and then the rest. For a moment they were all mesmerised by the blossoming of light in the darkness but they had to move fast. They strung out swiftly along the hillside, lighting a second arrow each as they did so. The bowmen took their first missiles, lifted them high, and with a thwock of well-drawn strings, sent them arching into the sky like shooting stars.

Loki will surely like this, Ofelia thought as she fired her own arrow and turned to Eric for her next.

She was already firing her third when the first found its target, plunging into a shelter strung between two bushes and firing the waxed linen instantly. Shouts of alarm rang out as the fire arrows rained down. A few fell uselessly to the ground but others hit more shelters or caught at cloaks or packs. The Dal Riatan men were crammed in close together and the hot, fatty flames spread mercilessly. Ofelia could almost see Loki dancing for glee amidst the panicked enemy as they scattered and rolled and made desperately off down the slope to the river below. And then the wagons, parked wonderfully tightly to one side, caught as the flames found the cheeses and hams they must be carrying. They flared up eagerly, sending great sparks into the air and illuminating the devastated camp.

'Last ones,' Ofelia urged, 'and then we must go.'

Already men were lumbering up the hill towards them, intent on vengeance. Eric handed Ofelia the last arrow and she sent it up in one last, glorious trajectory of devastation before they were all turning and heading back down the far slope, under the blessed cover of darkness once more.

'It worked,' someone gasped at her side and Ofelia thought it was Hamlet, though she could not see him and the tone of his voice was lost in his struggle for breath. 'Thor be praised, it damn well worked. You're a marvel, Ofelia.'

And then whoever it was had gone and it was all she could do to focus on her footing in the grass. The danger was not over until they'd reached the horses and even then not for some hours afterwards when they knew they'd made their escape but she cared not. She felt as if she could run forever, as if she were a very fire arrow herself. *You're a marvel, Ofelia – a marvel.*

The sun was high in the sky before, exhausted and panting with thirst, Ofelia finally allowed their jubilant troop to stop by a quiet stream to rest. They plunged straight into the water, horses and men together, and gulped it up.

'Do you think this stream leads back to the river at their camp?' Seaton asked. 'I hope it does. I'll send them this with my blessing.' He planted his feet in the shallows and pissed into the stream with a high-pitched laugh. 'Use that to douse the flames on your charred provisions, Dal Riatan scum!'

The others cheered him eagerly, if still mutedly. No one was more aware of the possibility of an ambush than those who had just performed one. Aedan would have men out everywhere hunting them down and they had to stay vigilant. They were hugely vulnerable and Ofelia knew her tight command would be more important now than ever but she felt horribly weary. She longed to throw herself down on the soft ground in her cloak and sleep and sleep, to forget enemies and battles and troublesome princes, but that was not a luxury she could afford if she wanted them all to stay alive.

'Rest,' she instructed, 'and get some food. Lars, Eric, you take lookout to the west for now. Hamlet, you and I are to the east.'

He opened his mouth to protest then seemed to think better of it and followed her meekly to a suitable spot on a small rise above the clearing with a good view of the thankfully deserted plains beyond.

'Do you think we did enough?' she asked, scanning the terrain for riders.

Who knew where Aethelfrith was now and how they would ever

meet him. Had this all been for naught? They were a wandering band in a strange country, buzzing like wasps around the huge beast they had just stung. Where was the marvel in that?

'I think we did all we could have done and more. We will, perhaps, have struck few death blows but an army cannot march for long without its food.'

'So now they will raid the villages. Perhaps all we have done, Hamlet, is to deflect their onslaught for a little while onto those less able to take it.'

'Ofelia,' he asked gently, 'why this doubt? We did well last night – *you* did well. Aethelfrith will be delighted with you.'

'And you? Are you delighted with me?'

'Of course. It worked beautifully. The arrows burned as they should and met their targets perfectly. It should hold Aedan up for ages and that is exactly what we were tasked with doing. Aethelfrith will reward you well.'

'Fifty warriors?'

'That's what he promised.'

'And then we can head to Denmark?'

She still had not looked at him but she heard him sigh.

'Exactly so.'

She spun around to face him.

'You do not want to?'

'I do.'

'Why the sigh then? Why the evasion? Do you not wish to be High King of Denmark, Hamlet? Are you afraid of it? Would you rather loll around Aethelfrith's heels like a lapdog than take your own rightful throne?'

'No!' He grabbed her arms, pinning them to her sides, and shook her. 'No, Ofelia, I would not rather that, but I will not rush our plan just to reach Denmark's shores a few months sooner, for if I do so, we will surely get no further than her beaches before we are cut down and it will all have been for nothing. We will be dead and Flora with us.'

'So? Why should you care? You only married her to keep a grip on your own life.'

'True. But when I took her as my wife she became a part of that life and now she will perpetuate it for me in my child.'

'Your precious bloody child!'

'Yes, Ofelia, my precious child. It is the way of mankind to care for his own offspring – or for most of mankind. Some, it seems, are born without such feelings.'

'You think I do not care?'

'I know you do not. You have shown me so too many times for me to doubt it and now I am done. Caring for Flora does not come from as deep a well inside me as caring for you once did, but she returns my care and so the waters flow rather than stagnating.' He dropped Ofelia's arms and stepped back. 'I am done,' he said again.

'Done caring for me?'

'Yes. It is best.'

'For whom?'

'For us both. I will cease annoying you with my apparently pathetic need for love, Ofelia, and you will cease disappointing me by withholding it.'

'I do not . . .'

Ofelia's voice faltered. What he'd said made sense. She did not love him; had sworn not to love him. But must the line between loving and not loving be so absolute? She had cut his marriage into the runes of his life, yes, but had not meant to cut her own dismissal from it.

'Can we still, you know . . .'

She moved closer but he leaped away as if she were a fire arrow.

'No, Ofelia. No, we cannot. We are comrades now . . . friends, I hope . . . but no more than that.'

'Never?'

'Never. You will have to scratch your itches elsewhere for I can no longer satisfy them.'

'Because you are done caring for me?'

'Yes! Yes, Ofelia, I am done. All done. For always. Now leave me be. I will keep watch. You feast with the men. You deserve the glory. It was a clever plan and well executed. Eat. Drink. Rut if you must. There are plenty who will oblige you, I am sure, but not me. I am done. I am . . . '

'Done,' she finished for him. 'I understand. Watch well.'

She pushed past him and headed back into the clearing to celebrate with the other men who knew to take a victory as they took a life: as the start of something, not the end. She didn't need Hamlet anyway. Marriage had dulled him and the last thing she needed was dullness. She would eat and drink and . . . and seek out Aethelfrith to claim her reward. Last night's ambush had been but a skirmish. The decisive battle still lay ahead and, as a warrior, she must focus on that.

Chapter Seventeen

Dinguardi, April 603

Flora had never seen the point of fighting before. It had seemed to her the height of foolishness to charge at each other with sharpened blades as if they might be in some way more eloquent than words. If the gods had put so much work into crafting the human body, why deliberately fling it into the path of blades and arrows and clubs? Why let it be mangled for the sake of an extra field or a made-up title? Finally, though, she did see the point – for if you were out fighting then you were at least doing something and even if you came back mangled you didn't drive yourself mad living in a void.

Hamlet and his troop had ridden out a long time ago – twenty-six days to be precise. Flora was notching them off on a rune-stick and was beginning to fear she had not selected a long enough one. In that time Aethelfrith had called his muster and men had filed into Aet Gefrin in reluctant droves until, three days ago, their king had decided he had an army big enough to face Aedan's and led them out, trumpets blaring, to follow Hamlet's brave advance guard.

Flora, Udela and Cathryn he had sent with Bebba to her hilltop burgh of Dinguardi for their own safety and Flora was glad to be back on the coastal estate. With spring finally on its way, the air felt fresher here than at Aet Gefrin and the gods did not seem to loom constantly over them as they did in the hills. The waiting, however, was every bit as long. No word had come of Hamlet before the main troop had left and Flora could only hope that he had not engaged with the enemy. He might, however, have been a hero and she did not know. Did that matter? Was he any less heroic for her ignorance of it? Her father believed messengers to women were a waste of valuable military resources so one would only come if it were to tell them to flee and there would be little comfort there.

War had never bothered her much before. Her father had ridden out many times, seeking conflict in every corner of his borderlands, and she had just got on with her day-to-day life without thinking too much about it. The herbs had still grown, the warp had still awaited the weft, Udela had still whined and all had been as it usually was. To her shame she had sometimes even felt cross when the men had ridden back in, bringing noise and more chores to be done and demanding constant attention and praise.

Now, though, she longed to see Hamlet come riding in at the gates and tortured herself with images of how it would feel if the horses finally arrived and his was not one of them. It was most uncomfortable. Was this love? she'd asked herself over and over when sleep would not come and memories of hideous wounds she'd seen from battles past would insist on imposing themselves over her recollections of Hamlet's fine limbs in her bed at night.

If this was love, it was a curious and inconvenient emotion; a slippery, amorphous, changeable thing that no classification system, however rigorous, could ever label to any satisfactory degree. Herbs you could name according to their properties and every time you found a plant with the same smell and texture and shape of leaf, you recognised its derivation. It conformed. Rosemary was rosemary wherever you found it and whoever picked it and whether you ate it with lamb or fish or crushed it beneath your feet in a dance. Not so love.

Hamlet made her feel newly aware of herself and of the world around her, as if she were gaining far more from both. Her problem, therefore, lay in her fear of having that all taken away by the slash of a sword or, perhaps, the constant, clever manoeuvring of his constable. Because perhaps the worst torture of all lay in Flora's mind, which insistently imagined Ofelia out there with Hamlet, going through who knows what together and comforting each other who knows how.

'Flora?' She looked up to see her mother gazing kindly at her. ''Tis a dry day – shall we go herb gathering?'

Flora nodded and heaved herself to her feet. She felt little inclination to seek out lemon balm or borage but she should go. If nothing else, it would pass the time.

'You are weary?' Bebba asked.

'Weary of hearing nothing.'

'Ah, yes. It is hard, especially with a babe on the way.'

Flora put a hand to her belly. It was swollen into a small mound, thankfully unlike the bulge of too much feasting. She felt it constantly, testing it against her usual shape; seeking proof of what all the midwives assured her was true. Logically, it did not seem to be in any doubt. Her courses had always been very regular. She charted them against the moon and they always came when it was almost returned to fullness. Four moons had swollen and faded now with no bleeding from her so she must be with child but she wanted more proof. Other women were forever jumping and rolling their eyes and insisting baby was kicking at them. Not so for her.

'I can't feel it,' she complained.

Bebba rushed over to her.

'It will come, sweet one. You will feel him soon enough, though it might only be as the tiniest flutter at first as if a bird were trapped within you.'

Flora recoiled. She did not want to feel a bird trapped within her.

She'd seen them in cages in the kitchen, throwing their poor little bodies against the bars again and again until they broke their own wings and, with them, their spirit. She never ate them when they were served, for it would have been like swallowing down distress, so she did not want them inside her by any other means.

'Won't the baby feel trapped?' she asked Bebba anxiously.

'No! No, the baby will feel warm and safe and cocooned – like moths before they come out and spread their wings to the skies. Babies love it in the womb; why else do you think they cry so when they come out?'

Flora grimaced.

'I'm not sure this one will ever come out. I'm not convinced it's even there. What if Hamlet comes home from the wars keen to recount his tales of heroism to his baby and there is none?'

Bebba took her in her arms and held her close.

'There *is* a baby, Flora, and it is well and will be born safe once the men are returned.'

'To here or to Denmark?'

'That, sweet one, I cannot tell you. It is between you and your husband.'

'And Ofelia.'

Bebba pushed her daughter gently away and tipped her chin up so that Flora must look at her.

'Imagine Ofelia as a man, Flora. Would her closeness to Hamlet worry you then?'

Flora shook her head.

'But Ofelia is not a man, Mother.'

'She is in her own mind, and it is the mind, you know, that counts the most.'

'I know,' Flora agreed. 'But what if, in his mind, Hamlet feels . . . '

'The gods save us, not Hamlet again!'

Udela wafted in like a raincloud and flung herself onto a bench. Bebba frowned at her.

'Is your sister not allowed to speak of her husband?'

214

'Of course she's allowed but it's not very sensitive of her, is it? It's not at all kind, not when my marriage has been stolen from me by the treachery of my poor bridegroom's greedy father.'

Flora did her best not to laugh. Was her sister truly imagining the young man forced to march behind his royal father, spitting and cursing at a lost Bernician bride he had never even met? But then she reminded herself that Udela had thrown herself into loving this unseen groom from the moment her father had told her of his existence. Was her love any less painful for being entirely imaginary? The mind, after all, was what counted the most. She went over to Udela.

'It is very hard on you, I know.'

Udela looked surprised but delighted.

'It is, Flora. It is very hard. You have seen my betrothal dress. It is magnificent ... and now it is left mouldering in a chest because the wretched Dal Riatan king has broken the truce as if I were nothing. It is so unjust.'

'At least you do not have to go and fight.'

Udela shuddered.

'Can you imagine? I don't know how Ofelia does it – she is unnatural.'

'Udela!'

'Well, she is. She's a man stuck in a woman's form.'

'See!' Bebba said to Flora, who smiled gratefully.

Udela, however, was on to this immediately.

'She worries you, Flora?'

'No.'

'She should. It's not right, her going off with your husband and leaving you here. That may be the way they do things in Denmark but over here in civilisation ladies wield needles, not swords. Only one sort of woman follows the troops on the road. Mind you, it sounds as if Ofelia is more than capable of whoring if she chooses.'

Despite herself, Flora bristled on the Danish woman's behalf.

'Surely it cannot be whoring if you choose the path unpaid, Udela?'

'What?'

'If it is for your own pleasure, freely undertaken, it is not whoring.'

'Hark at you! Such a lady of the world these days. So you don't mind, then, if Ofelia ruts with Hamlet?'

'Udela!' Bebba was over to her elder daughter in a trice and to her astonishment Flora saw her mother's hand raised. Bebba controlled herself but ordered, 'Apologise at once.'

'Why?' Udela asked sulkily. 'I was just asking an honest question.'

'There was nothing honest about it. You were trying to upset your sister.'

'But it's the truth. Ofelia told us so herself the first night she was on our shores, did she not, Flora?'

Flora flinched at the memory.

'She told us she *had* rutted with Hamlet, not that she still did so.'

'So she doesn't now?'

'I don't know,' Flora admitted. 'I haven't asked.'

'Quite right,' Bebba said, her voice calm but iron-hard. 'It is not for you to know or care. Men do not see bedding as we do. For them it is all of the body, not the mind, and the mind, remember, counts for more.'

'So you think he is then, Mother?' Udela asked slyly.

'I did not say that. I have no idea either way but what I do know is that it is not Flora's concern. She is Hamlet's wife and she carries his child – that is a sacred bond.'

Flora reached for her mother's hand.

'Thank you,' she murmured.

'It is the simple truth, Flora, and you will be sure of it again once Hamlet is back at your side. The waiting is hard but news must surely come soon.'

'Surely!' Udela agreed, adding a mumbled, 'Sorry, Flora,' before perking up to ask, 'If Father defeats Aedan, will he enforce the alliance?'

'It will be less an alliance than a subjugation,' Bebba said.

'Oh. Will a subjugation include a marriage agreement?'

Bebba reached out and took Udela's hand in her free one.

'It might well do, Udela. Fret not, you will be wed soon enough and with child just as your sister is.'

'As your sister *might be*,' Flora corrected grumpily.

"Might" was the most she seemed able to be in this empty life – she *might be* a wife if Hamlet were still alive; she *might be* a princess if her father thrived; she *might be* a mother if the supposed babe were truly there.

A sound beyond the hall doors made her look up. She listened hard. Was that a horse? She let go of Bebba's hand and ran to see, her mother and sister hot on her heels, but when they got there they could only watch forlornly as a wizened old trader rode up on a ragged mule.

'Not exactly a victorious army,' Udela sneered, and Flora sighed.

'Maybe they will never come.'

'That's no way to think, Flora,' Bebba chided and she bowed to the admonishment.

She felt as hollow as the endless days and she hated it. Udela and Bebba retreated back inside but Flora leaned on the doorframe and watched as the trader began unrolling knives and tools from his pack with a pleasing precision belied by his decrepit appearance. The baker's son, a young lad left behind to mind the ovens whilst his father rode to battle and who was clearly relishing the responsibility, came swaggering over and the pair began to barter over a serrated knife.

Flora watched curiously. Life went on. Bread must still be sliced whoever had baked it and hay must still be scythed whoever's land it grew upon. She was being self-indulgent moping about when there were herbs to gather and balms to mix and cloth to weave. She pushed herself upright to fetch Bebba and head out to look for borage and that's when she felt it – a flutter. Tiny, perhaps, and less like a trapped bird than a tickling feather, but a flutter all the same.

She put a hand to her belly. There was nothing to be detected against her skin but she felt it deep within, stronger now. A flutter as if her baby were reaching out, finally, to greet its mother.

'Hello,' she whispered. 'Hello, baby.'

And though she knew she was imagining this every bit as much as she had imagined Hamlet riding home victorious or lying mangled on a bloody field, she felt sure that their baby smiled a reply within her.

Chapter Eighteen

Degastan, April 603

Ofelia had decided to abstain from sex until a full victory was secured. Many men swore by abstinence to keep them sharp and hungry and it had seemed as good a time as any to test the theory. So far she wasn't convinced. It had been ten long days since the night of the arrows and all that abstinence had done was to make her feel listless and more easily distracted. Now that they were at last on the cusp of battle, however, it might pay off. She hoped so.

This, she swore, was the biggest battle she'd ever heard of, let alone stood up in. The fire arrows had, praise Loki, kept Aedan in sufficient disarray to allow Aethelfrith time to gather a mighty force. Ophelia's little band had found them after three anxious days of searching and been welcomed like heroes into their protective folds. But Aedan, too, had come back stronger than ever and Ofelia could swear there were at least a thousand souls facing each other across the vast fields at Degastan.

The noise was intense as both sides screamed insults and clattered swords against shields until Ofelia's mind seemed to rattle with them. Aethelfrith was making a stirring speech about unity and honour and she tried to focus on him but all she could hear was the din of weapons and the beating of her own blood around her body. She waited for the usual pulse of battle joy but all she felt was a sort of dark determination to make it to the end of this alive.

She picked at her new armour, gifted to her by Aethelfrith in honour of her band's achievements on the 'night of the arrows' as the skalds were hailing it. The arrows had fired their imagination as brightly as they had fired the Dal Riatan cheeses and Ofelia's name had hovered above many a hearth fire in the long nights building up to this great confrontation between the two rival armies.

She had found it uncomfortable to be so lauded and prayed that the gods would grant them a victory glorious enough to seize the skalds' attention away from her own petty triumph. Now was the time to find out if they would. The Dal Riatans were starting to advance, strange blue marks painted on their faces as if that would somehow scare the Angles. No chance! Though there was something a little unearthly about the way their eyes blazed out above the colour as they advanced and as Ofelia adjusted her grip on her sword she felt her palm slick with sweat and had to wipe it hastily on her tunic.

She took a step forward and her fellows went with her, locked together in a tight shield wall. Not Hamlet though. He was with their own, original band and Ofelia was in command of the fifty warriors she had won from Aethelfrith. They were good men, fierce and strong, but she did not know their ways and was having to rely on standard training, not knowledge of each individual. It should work better this way – predictable, more reliable – but surely not one of these new men would die for her and her back felt exposed even with all fifty of them covering it.

'You are a marvel, Ofelia,' she murmured to herself, plucking the words out of her memory and drawing strength from them. She *was* a marvel. She was quick and agile and highly skilled. She belonged here, at the head of these men, and she would prove it today. Now.

The clash of the first blade against her own hit her like a dose of cold water: icy-sharp and very, very welcome. Her body flowed into the motions of war and she felt herself come alive at last. Her palms were totally dry now, her resolve fierce. She cut down her first foe in moments and shifted with the rest of the wall to stab at the next enemy to charge them. Training, rules, precision – this was how battle should be. It was better to have no one you cared for close. Better still to care for no one. Save perhaps Lars and . . .

The spear came out of nowhere and stabbed straight at her hip. Aethelfrith's armour deflected the point but the impact dug into her bone and made her cry out. The man to her left stepped in and swung with deadly accuracy, slicing the top off the spearman's head. Brains glooped over his face, smearing his blue paint as he fell to his knees, thankfully giving Ofelia the time to recover herself and get back into the rhythm of battle.

Cut and drive. Cut and drive. The wall held and she held with it. Her hip ached but it was little enough compared to the pain in her arms. She was not built for wall-to-wall fighting. She was better in open combat where her agility gave her the edge, rather than stuck beneath the weight of her shield trying to force her way over fallen bodies to fell more. She could not stop, though, could not leave a gap that would expose her fellows. Cut and drive. Cut and drive.

At least the enemy seemed to be falling back, collapsing even. At some point she heard trumpets, saw white flags waving, but at the centre of their own line Aethelfrith was roaring them on. He would not agree to a surrender again, real or staged. There would be no end to this battle until the last Dal Riatan had either fled or been cut down and the field truly belonged to the Angles.

Before them the front line was falling apart and men were either turning to run or standing alone. Good. Ofelia wrenched her shield free of the wall at last and flexed her shoulders as she faced a large Dal Riatan. He licked his stupid blue lips and came charging forward. Easy. A dart to her side, a backward slice and his thigh tore open sending him lurching to the ground, neck helpfully exposed to her eager blade.

She drove down so hard that it pierced through to his collar bone and stuck fast and she struggled to wrench it out. Another Dal Riatan was coming at her and she needed her weapon. She pulled harder and felt it budge but it wasn't free yet. In desperation she kicked sideways and caught a lucky blow to the man's knee. He staggered and, praise Thor, she pulled her blade free at last and swiped blindly at the new foe, sending him toppling over.

Almost she closed her eyes in thanks but just in time recollected herself. The Dal Riatans had worked out that Aethelfrith was in no mood to cease fighting and were battling for their lives. It was hard to flee from a front line and they stood their ground, seeking instead the door to Valhalla. Fine. She'd open it for as many of them as wanted to try her. If only her legs weren't so weary or her arms so very sore.

She could draw back, slide behind the mid lines and take her ease, at least for a time, but that was surely cowardice. She might be cold and uncaring but she was no coward. She faced the next man – shorter than her and so slim you could fit two of him behind his shield. He wore no paint but his eyes were jade green and seemed to pierce into hers, seeing her tiredness.

'Dance with me, maid,' he hissed in her own tongue.

She blinked, surprised, and he thrust, catching her arm. She blocked but felt the flesh burn and saw blood ooze onto her sleeve. Bastard. She drove furiously at him and, caught out, he took a step back and tripped over a corpse, falling flat on his back. Ofelia stood over him and looked straight into his pretty green eyes as she thrust her sword through his throat. He burbled a last prayer, in his own language this time, and Ofelia had chance to note the diadem on his helmet. Another prince. Well done her. Suddenly she remembered those jade eyes, now staring unseeing past her, and realised guiltily that this was Gartnait, Udela's intended.

'Whoops – sorry, Udela,' she muttered.

The moment seemed weirdly amusing and she felt a laugh burble ridiculously in her throat, rasping up and out of her dry mouth.

She looked around. Only a few were still fighting. The battle was almost done. Gods, she was tired. And thirsty, so thirsty.

She glanced back and saw someone coming running up with a pail. Water – gods be praised! She checked around her but no one approached and as the boy ran up she snatched the goblet floating in the blissful liquid and drank deep.

'We've won,' he gasped at her. 'Father has won!'

'Earnfrith?'

The young prince was filthy and had a streak of blood, hopefully not his own, down the side of his face.

'It is a great victory, Ofelia, they will sing of it for years to come. Father will rule from the east coast to the west and I after him, and I will . . . '

The man moved so fast it was as if he came out of nowhere. Maybe he did. He was near-naked and caked with blood as if he had died once and was risen again to exact vengeance and he cut poor Earnfrith's words off his shoulders before the prince even knew anything of it. His young head bounced to the ground and the pitcher fell from his instantly limp hands, dousing his innocent face clean of the old blood so that it lay pale and bright on the ground before her. Ofelia stared down, horrified.

'Ofelia! Right side!'

She heard the voice in time but her body would not respond. The cut Gartnait had dug into her arm bit like fire as she tried to lift her sword and all she saw as she turned towards the blade she knew was coming, was a flash of fury as Hamlet threw himself before her. Then all was black.

Chapter Nineteen

Bebba's burgh, April 603

Aethelfrith, Flora discovered, was happy to send messengers to his women when they came crowing victory. Several men also took it on themselves to bring the news in the hope of reward so the women in Bebba's burgh were treated to several jubilant announcements within one day.

The first to return were warriors, men who had fought and who spoke of the ferocity of the attack, of the gore of wounds and corpses and the ache of muscles. Behind them came the skalds who had clearly watched from the hillsides, harps kept carefully out of the way of chance sword swings, and who told of Aethelfrith's great speech and the clash of the two lines, of the fall of princes and the coming of the Valkyries to take the souls of the dead to Valhalla. The first men, Flora noted, could remember only the fine detail and the second the shifting patterns of the encounter but their message was the same – victory for the Angles against the treacherous Dal Riatans, and glory and land for King Aethelfrith and his people.

Flora, giddy with relief at the news, drank far too much of her mother's finest fruit wine at the impromptu feast that night and fell asleep at the table. Hamlet, it seemed, was alive and well and feted both for his bravery at Degastan and his part in the 'night of the arrows' before it. The skalds loved that tale and it was clear they had had longer to work on it for the words were richer and the rhyme fuller and the truth of the event already sinking into insignificance against its symbolic import.

Ofelia, they said, had led the ambush like a very Valkyrie, hot for the souls of warriors, and Loki had ridden the first arrow himself, urging it plumb into the middle of a Dal Riatan cheese big enough to sustain twenty soldiers for a week and melting it into a stinking pool. It seemed unlikely but who cared when it was told with such finesse? Flora was only sorry she couldn't keep awake to hear more.

Bebba took her to bed in the bower she would soon share with Hamlet again and Flora burrowed gratefully under the covers, letting her now pronounced belly sink into the feather mattress.

'I'm so tired,' she muttered into the folds of the blanket.

'It's the relief,' Bebba said. 'It's understandable. Rest, sweet one.'

'Where's Udela?'

'Gone to bed in a huff.'

'Poor girl.'

The skalds had told of Dal Riatan princes littering the battlefield, jewelled diadems mired in mud and blood. It had seemed from the way they told it that none had survived so they were unlikely to be available for truce-sealing marriages to Bernician princesses, even ones with betrothal gowns ready to hand.

'Skalds always exaggerate,' Flora had assured her sister. 'They won't all be dead.'

'I bet my Gartnait is,' had been the dark answer and there had been little Flora could do to rouse her sister from her determined misery.

Only one thing niggled at Flora as she gave way to sleep. The dead princes had not all been on the enemy side. Hamlet was safe, that much all had assured her, but one soldier had hoarsely confessed that he'd heard Earnfrith had been cut down.

'That cannot be,' Bebba had said. 'He was not to be part of the fighting. He was in the camp, that is all. Aethelfrith promised me.'

'I may be mistaken, my lady,' the poor man had stuttered, and everyone had agreed that he probably was, but rumours rarely came out of nothing and, watching Bebba carefully, Flora had been sure her mother was thinking the same and prayed her brother had suffered an injury and no more.

Earnfrith was so young his voice had not yet taken on the low tones of a man. Many was the day he'd sat with Flora in the herbery, playing with the soldiers he tried to carve out of sticks. She could picture him now, his tousled hair flopping forward as he bent over his knife; she could catch the sound of his inconsequential chatter and couldn't believe she might never hear it again. And it would break Bebba's heart if her only son was lost after only thirteen summers. Not only that, it would cut away much of her power in Bernicia. Earnfrith was Aethelfrith's heir and while that remained the case, his mother's position was secure. But things could swiftly change and if he was dead it would be both tragedy and jeopardy for poor Bebba.

Cathryn was keeping to herself but making it quietly apparent that she had a swelling belly to rival Flora's. If Earnfrith was truly dead and the new child was a boy then, despite Bebba's seniority in both years on the gods' earth and as Aethelfrith's wife, Cathryn would take precedence. And Flora – Flora would be in Denmark with Hamlet and unable to do anything to support her mother. Bebba was a strong woman, she knew, but was she strong enough to bear that? Was anyone? Flora reached a hand out of the blankets and fumbled for her mother's, which closed around it, warm and dry.

'You do know, Mother, how much I admire you?'

'You do? Thank you, Flora.'

'And . . . and love you.'

Her mother's grip tightened.

'And I you, Flora, very much. You have grown into a fine young woman – though one, I think, who does not sleep enough. Shall I stay with you?'

'If you are happy to.'

'I am. I have had enough of battlefield tales for one day and there will be a hundred more stories once the army returns in full. I will take some peace here with you while I can find it.'

She released Flora's hand and lay down at her side then began singing softly as she had always done when Flora was a child. It was a sweet, soothing sound and she let herself drift gladly upon it.

It was still dark when she half woke to hear someone banging furiously on the bower door. She pulled herself up reluctantly and rubbed at her eyes, trying desperately to see.

The banging came again and then a voice called, 'My lady! My lady Flora. Forgive me, but you must come. Your husband calls for you.'

'My husband?'

Flora battled to full consciousness. Hamlet was here? She must go to him, now, but her limbs felt so dull and her head so heavy and it was so dark this must surely be some strange dream. She felt movement beside her and caught the fresh smell of her mother as Bebba stumbled across the bower and lifted the latch. If this was a dream, then Bebba was in it too.

Flora threw back the covers, hoping the cold would rouse her rebellious body from sleep, and swung herself round to sit on the edge of the bed. The world spun a little and then settled as the door opened and she saw one of the stable lads framed in the entrance, revealed by the light of the torch he held high in one hand.

'What do you want?' Bebba demanded.

The lad shook visibly.

'Beg pardon, my lady, but Prince Hamlet is here and calls urgently for his wife's help. It is his companion. She is sore

227

wounded, I fear.'

'She?' Flora asked and then answered her own question. 'Ofelia. Of course.'

'You will come?'

Flora nodded. Bebba draped a cloak around her shoulders and offered her arm and together they went out into the compound. All was in darkness, save for lights blazing in the stables over by the gates. The lad picked up his young legs and Flora did her best to match his urgent pace though her belly felt like a stone at her waist and her head was still thick with tendrils of sleep. The moment she stepped into the stables, however, all this was seared from her by the burn of pure shock.

Ofelia was lying just inside the door, covered tightly in a blanket like a babe in swaddling. Flora could see nothing of her bar her face but that was enough. On one side it was as pale as the brightest moon but the other was darkest red where the flesh had been ripped away. Flora saw the white line of the she-warrior's jawbone in the gaping wound and a dark, matted sheen where blood had seeped up into her hair and knitted itself into her plaits like a dye. The wound seemed to be moving and as Flora forced herself to step closer she saw maggots feasting upon the rotting flesh at its edges.

'Eyra help her!' she cried and Hamlet, crouched at his constable's head, looked up and leaped to his feet.

'Flora! Oh, Flora, thank the gods you are here. Ofelia is hurt.'

There was no answer to such an understatement. Hamlet tugged her towards the shrouded body and, transfixed, she crouched at Ofelia's side. She could see a shallow rise and fall beneath the blanket but otherwise there was little sign of life about the woman.

'They are eating her!' Hamlet cried, his voice shrill as he snatched at one of the maggots and crushed it to nothing beneath his fingers.

Flora put out her hand to touch his. So long she had dreamed of touching him but not like this. Never like this.

'Leave them, Hamlet.'

He stared at her wild-eyed.

'She is not dead, Flora. They cannot have her.'

'They can. It is good. They only eat the rotten parts so they will cleanse the wound.'

'They will?'

'Truly. And then it can knit together healthily.'

'It can?'

'All else being well, yes.'

Flora stared helplessly into the hole that had once been Ofelia's face, but now Hamlet was grabbing at her.

'I brought her to you, Flora, because you can heal people. You know so much about herbs and you're so caring and so clever with your hands. You can save her, can't you?'

Flora looked from Hamlet to Ofelia and then back to Hamlet again. Not a word of hello, she noted. Not a word of concern for her. Not even a kiss of greeting, just 'save her'. A bitter, Udela-like bit of her did not see why she should. Hamlet looked near out of his mind with distress and she hated that his damned constable with her breeches and her sword and her spiky self-centredness could so affect him.

If she died, a tiny, evil voice whispered in her ear, *she would have no further hold over him.* But then she looked to the wound and her heart turned over at what Ofelia must be suffering and all hesitation vanished. Perhaps someone, somewhere, was caring for her brother as she could now care for Ofelia and she owed it to the gods to do all she could.

'I can try,' she said and looked to the stable boy and guards who had gathered to see what was going on. 'We must take her to the herbery. It is clean there and I will have all I need. Have a pallet set out – fast. Clean coverings, please, and cloths, plenty of them. And water, warm if you can. We will need to move quickly.' She looked to Hamlet. 'Is it just her face?'

He shook his head.

'Her side too. It was a vicious attack.'

'How did she escape?' He did not answer but she noticed for the first time that he was holding his sword arm across his chest. 'You are hurt too?'

'I had to help her.'

'Of course you did. Come, we can tend you too. Mother, will you come with us?'

Bebba stepped up firmly to her side.

'I will be proud to, Flora. Whatever it takes.'

It was a long night and a hard one but Flora had learned herbal lore for years and soon forgot it was Ofelia on the bed and Hamlet pacing at its foot, and focused on all she knew. The maggots had done their fierce work and the flesh of the face, if gaping, was fresh and could be gently cleaned with water infused with burdock. Ofelia half woke and cried out, so Flora gave her as much poppy juice as she dared and, gritting her own teeth, ordered Hamlet to hold the sufferer's hands tight as she worked on.

The jawbone was broken. Flora forced herself to reach in and ease it back where it had hinged apart. There was little she could do to splint it in such a position but the two jagged edges seemed to fit together as if relieved to be reunited and she hastily padded around it with linen soaked in honey and comfrey, to try and keep it in place as it knitted together.

Ofelia's eye worried her the most for the wound went right up to its very edge and the brow was smashed open. It looked as if it had, at least, done its job in defending the orb beneath for Ofelia seemed able to open and close the lid but she was delirious and there was no way of determining clearly what she could see. Flora rinsed it with salt water and bound it over with strip after strip of linen to keep the light at bay in case it was more damaged than it looked.

She had to cut away the matted hair well past Ofelia's miraculously unscathed ear and in the end it seemed sensible to cut it all off. She handed the plaits one by one to Bebba who freed the pretty beads off the ends and dropped them carefully into a clay pot. They rattled inconsequentially but it was a relief to them both to be able to save something.

When Ofelia's face was clean and bandaged as best as they could, Flora pulled back the blankets and looked down at the blood that had clotted in all the beautifully crafted rings of the she-warrior's chain mail.

'We have to get this off,' she said to Hamlet.

'I'll get the smith. We can cut it.'

'Is it not a very expensive object?'

'Not compared to her life.' Flora recoiled at the ferocity of this reply and Hamlet caught himself and, for perhaps the first time in this reunion, looked properly at her. 'Sorry. I'm sorry, Flora. You're amazing, truly. I am . . . am not myself.'

'I know. I understand.'

'You are a good woman.'

She gave a little sigh.

'Too good perhaps.'

'No!' He leaned down and dropped a soft kiss on her lips. 'No, Flora, never think that.'

She smiled at him.

'The smith then?'

He nodded and was gone, returning a little later with a sharp cutter, like the jaws of an animal cast in metal. He bent to the mail and, tongue between his teeth in concentration, cut slowly and carefully through one ring at a time until, at last, they could peel it away from Ofelia. Next came the tunic. Flora considered suggesting Hamlet look away and then reminded herself that Ofelia's body was nothing he had not seen before.

It was perhaps Flora therefore who was more shocked by Ofelia's form. It was not so much the wound, which thankfully looked superficial, especially in comparison to her poor face, as the hard ridges of muscle across her stomach and shoulders. It should be no surprise, this was a warrior after all, but Flora had never before seen a woman's body so clearly delineated and could not stop herself from staring.

'Is it bad?' Hamlet asked anxiously.

'What? Oh, no. No, it will heal. If she survives. She is very hot, Hamlet. Fever has a hold on her and we can do little but keep her cool and pray that she is strong enough to fight it off. I will give her borage and bee pollen and the poppy juice will keep her comfortable but she is in the hands of the gods now.'

'I will make a sacrifice,' he said. 'It is near dawn and the gods will be at their most attentive.'

He took a step towards the door but Flora stopped him.

'I think you would be better staying here and talking to her. She needs to know she is safe, that there is something – someone – to fight her way back to.'

He looked at her for a long time then nodded and shuffled back to Ofelia's side.

'If anyone can fight, it's Ofelia.'

'I'm sure.'

'She's fought all her life.'

Flora busied herself with tidying her herbs. She saw Bebba slip quietly from the room and did not know whether to bless or curse her mother's tact.

'Really?' she managed to reply.

Hamlet nodded.

'She lost both her parents when she was just nine. She has largely looked after herself since then. And Lars too.'

'From the age of nine?' Flora asked, drawing closer to the bed despite herself. 'Why? What happened?'

'Her father was killed in a hunting accident and her mother ...' He clutched at Ofelia's hand as if seeking her permission to speak on but she did not move and he decided for himself. 'Her mother threw herself onto the funeral pyre right in front of her. It was hailed as a glorious act, the ultimate sacrifice, but for Ofelia ...'

'It was abandonment,' Flora whispered. Hamlet nodded. 'You were there?'

'Right there. I held her back, Flora, else she might have gone in after Lady Sigrid. I held her for ages and I felt her body twitch and I swear I heard her poor mind screaming as she tried to work out what had just happened, but she never cried, not once. She did for her father but not for her mother. It was as if the heat of Lady Sigrid's burning body seared her daughter's tear ducts shut.'

'Hamlet, don't!'

'I'm sorry.' He held out his hand to her and she took it and let him draw her down onto his knee so that she was caught between him and Ofelia. 'I wanted you to understand a little more about her – about why she is as she is.'

'And why you are as you are with her?'

'I'm sorry for that too. I did not, you know, lie with her when we were away. I told her that if she wanted to be a man among men, I would treat her as such. She didn't like it.'

'You have, then, lain with her since ... since ...'

'Since we married? May I be honest with you, Flora?'

'I would very much rather you were. I cannot bear lies. They send things in all sorts of confusing directions and I do not like being confused.'

He nodded.

'You are a wise woman.'

'On the contrary, I am a very simple one; it is others who are not. I would like your honesty, Hamlet, please.'

'Very well. Yes, I have lain with her. Not often but perhaps too often. I am as tangled up in her as if we shared limbs, Flora, and it seems I can do little to escape that. But it is not love, not really. I thought it was once but she made it very clear she could not love me back.'

'But ...'

'Ofelia will not love, Flora, not since her mother.'

'You believe that?'

'I believe that she believes it.'

'But Lars ...'

'Lars is different. Ofelia loved him before that dread night and nothing will change that. And, besides, loving Lars takes nothing away from her.'

'Loving someone surely only enhances a person?'

'It enhances you, Flora. At least, I feel it does. Loving you has certainly made me a better person.'

'You love me?'

'Yes. Truly. Not with tangles, perhaps, but with honesty.'

'That is all I want.'

'Are you sure?'

Flora thought about it. She wasn't. She'd seen the anguish in Hamlet's expresison as he'd begged her to save Ofelia and what she truly wanted was for him to feel as strongly about her.

'No, Hamlet, I want more, I think, but if we are being honest then I do not – yet – feel tangled in you, so why should you feel tangled in me?'

Hamlet gave a low laugh.

'You really did mean honesty, didn't you?'

'It's best.'

'It is.' His arm tightened around her waist and his fingers found the bump and spread wonderingly across it. 'Our child?'

'If the gods see it safe into the world.'

'Oh, they will. We are owed a new life, little one, for too many have been taken.'

He looked to Ofelia but his words had reminded Flora of some-one else, someone she hardly dared ask about. But she had to know.

'Hamlet, is my little brother alive?'

She had been going to say 'dead', but it seemed, somehow, to be inviting the answer. It made little difference, however. How could it? Hamlet's hands tightened further around her and she felt his head shake against her shoulder.

'Earnfrith was killed, Flora. I'm so sorry.'

'But how? I thought he wasn't to be part of the fighting?'

'He wasn't. It was a rogue attack, right at the end as he was bringing water to . . . to . . . '

His words petered out but she saw him staring past her to the bed and knew. Earnfrith for Ofelia; it seemed a poor exchange.

'I killed the bastard,' Hamlet said. 'I cut him right through the middle. I avenged your brother's death, Flora.'

Hamlet offered her this like a gift but she did not want it.

'It won't bring him back.'

'No.'

She felt the pain of Earnfrith's passing like the worst kind of nettle sting all across her skin, and fought to resist it in case it consumed her.

'Father must be very sad.'

'He must. He is masking it in fury. I pity the Dal Riatans at the negotiations.'

'They are happening now?'

'The two sides are gathering, yes. I must head back soon but I wanted to get to you.'

'You wanted to get Ofelia to me.'

'That too.'

It was honest at least. She had said that's what she wanted and she must stick to it. And if she could not save Earnfrith then Ofelia would be the beneficiary of her lost love.

'I will nurse her for you.'

'I know it. I will do everything in my power to speed the talks and, indeed, there cannot be much left to say. I am to fetch Udela but I know not why. I tell you, Flora, there are precious few men left fit for her to wed after this dread battle and it will be a bitter truce indeed.'

Chapter Twenty

Borderlands, April 603

'Hail Mary, Mother of God. Hail Mary . . . '

For once reciting her favourite prayer offered Mairi no comfort. She was cold and tired and ached from hours in the saddle. It was the glorious festival of Easter tomorrow and she should be on her knees in vigil for the resurrection of the Lord but an order had come from a shivering messenger that she must make haste and ride south for her father needed her.

It was good, she supposed, to be needed, especially after Aedan's continued mutterings about how useless she was before he had ridden off to war, but she longed to know why. The messenger, a gruff fellow who'd given his name as Allan, had had no further information and she could only remember her father's threat to 'give you to an Angle' and pray that he had forgotten that and wanted her for the spiritual consolation she could offer.

The battle, it seemed, had not gone well. Allan had been singularly uninformative on that front too, though he must surely have been there so could at least have reported what his eyes had seen. His refusal to do so felt ominous.

'Halt!' she called out to him now. 'Please, halt. I must rest.'

'It is not far now, my lady. We should be in camp before sundown.'

Mairi eyed the sun. It was not even near the treetops yet.

'That is too long. I must rest and I must . . . relieve myself.'

'Oh. Of course.'

He was embarrassed now. Well, good. So was she but if this was what it took to make him stop for a while then she could live with it. Allan called their little party to a halt and a guard came to hand her out of the saddle. She waved her maid to her side and the girl scuttled over, twittering. Mairi's usual maid, a sensible, god-fearing woman near her own age, would have been far preferable but she was pregnant for at least the fifth time (Mairi had lost count) and could not ride so far. Mairi was, therefore, stuck with this chit, a gangly girl called Lynet who seemed to be terrified by everything and had barely even pulled herself together enough to choose her mistress's gowns or de-tangle her thick, dark hair. Not that such frivolities mattered to Mairi but she was royal and should look royal even on the road. It was the least she could do for her father in his time of need.

'Let us retire into the woods a little,' she said to Lynet, indicating the thick trees to the side of the road.

'Into the woods?' the girl said, as if Mairi had suggested they step into hell itself.

'Yes, the woods, Lynet, unless you expect me to relieve myself at the roadside?'

'But what if there are wolves?'

'There probably *are* wolves but not this close to a well-frequented highway. And, besides, God will protect us.'

'From the wolves?'

'Yes.'

'How?'

Mairi squinted at her.

'What do you mean, how? With His grace and all-seeing care, of course.'

'Oh. Right. All-seeing?'

'Yes, Lynet. You are a Christian?'

Lynet shuffled her feet.

'I think so.' She looked at Mairi and swallowed. 'I mean, yes, of course, my lady.'

'So you know then that Christ has shone His light on the world, including these woods. And that there are no such things as trolls or wood sprites or whatever else it is you fear.'

'But there *are* wolves.'

Mairi sighed.

'Fine. I'll go alone.'

'No! Oh, no, my lady, it is my duty to care for you.'

'Come along then.'

Mairi strode into the trees, Lynet twittering in her wake though she shut up the moment they broke through into a small clearing and saw God's light slanting down through the trees and falling in soft rays upon a blanket of deepest blue flowers.

'Oh!' the girl gasped, dropping to her knees.

Mairi made haste to join her. It was a miracle. A sign. An Easter blessing. She clasped her hands together and looked up along the lines of heavenly light, lost in the glory of it.

'Praise be to you, Lord Jesus, for shining this your glorious light upon your poor unworthy subjects.'

'Why unworthy?' she heard Lynet mumble but cared not to reply.

Mairi felt the warmth caress her face like a lover and revelled in the bliss of it. This was love. This was a holy communion with all it took to be human and it was far, far more rewarding than messy, noisy, frenzied bedplay with some sweaty man.

'Is this your God at work?' Lynet asked, staring around her in awe.

'*Our* God,' Mairi corrected her. 'He will love you if you turn to Him.'

'That's nice. Now, it looks like rain over there so shall we get on and relieve ourselves?'

Mairi groaned but the irreverent girl had a point. Through the trees to the west she could see dark clouds forming and could do without adding wet clothing to her current discomforts.

'My lady,' Allan called through the grove, 'are you done? We need to push onward. We do not want to be out on these roads after dark or it will be more than wolves we have to worry about.'

Mairi looked apologetically at the sunbeams, hoping God would forgive her for her companions' base concerns, but the clouds engulfed them at that moment and the heavenly light was snuffed abruptly out. Mairi felt she might cry but Lynet was tugging at her skirts and there was no time for tears, holy or otherwise.

If she were in a nunnery, she thought as she crouched awkwardly over the foliage, trying not to empty herself onto the beautiful flowers, she would not have to put up with this. Everyone would be busy with preparations for the glories of Easter and life would proceed peacefully according to the pattern of the canonical hours.

'Oops, I think you've got a bit on your skirts.'

Mairi ground her teeth and prayed for patience until this wretched journey was done.

When they finally rode into camp at nightfall, however, she instantly wished herself back in the bluebell glade with nothing worse than an irritating maid to bother her. There were men everywhere and all of them, it seemed, lying groaning on the ground or sitting clutching at stumps of mangled limbs as if they were misshapen babies. Where were all the healthy ones?

'Gone,' Allan said shortly when she asked him. 'Fled for home and good luck to them. No one would want to stay in this hell.'

'And yet you brought me here?'

'King's orders, my lady, and I'm sure someone will have found you a tent to protect you from the worst of your people's suffering.'

Mairi looked at him askance but was too overpowered by the

stink of the camp to challenge what she strongly suspected was insolence.

'I did not ask to come here,' she said stiffly. 'I did not ask anyone to come here. I do not seek war. Indeed, I begged for peace, according to Christ's word.'

'Was Christ's country ever attacked by the Angles?' came the dark reply.

Mairi decided that now was perhaps less the time to save souls than to get to her royal father without giving way to nausea at the stench all around. Someone had to retain a sense of dignity.

'In here, my lady.'

Allan stopped outside a rough tent and indicated to go inside. Mairi stared. There were charred holes in the tent's roof that surely rendered it useless against the rain that was now starting to fall with bleak persistence and only half the walls seemed to be in place so that she could see inside to a press of angry-sounding men. She felt her insides curl like autumn leaves dying round the edges and looked up for God's assistance, but found only dark, cold drops of water.

'Send her in,' a voice snapped – her father's. 'And tell her to look pretty.'

Pretty? Mairi's hand went to her wet headdress, her chapped lips and wind-stung cheeks. She was worn out, hungry and, frankly, terrified, and her father expected her to look "pretty"? How was she to achieve that? And more to the point, why?

'Best get down, my lady.'

Lynet had clearly heard the order too and as Mairi dismounted she rushed up to tug at her clothing in a way that only sent it more askew. Mairi brushed her off.

'I look as God made me, Lynet – that should suffice.'

The girl looked sceptical but there was no time for more as they were being ushered inside the tent and the eyes of what felt like a hundred men were upon her.

'Mairi! Here, daughter.'

She saw Aedan dead centre and made her way towards him but it was packed beneath the ineffectual roof and she had to push past every dirty, sweaty warrior so that she became quite flushed. Her lips, at least, would no longer be blue.

'This is Princess Mairi.' Aedan introduced her to a clutch of people. They were as big and hairy as the rest but did at least look to have found some cleanish clothes and drawn a comb through their extravagant locks. 'This is King Aethelfrith . . .'

'*High King* Aethelfrith,' the big man corrected him with a wolfish smile. He stared her father down.

'High King Aethelfrith,' Aedan forced out.

Mairi looked to her father in alarm. He had lost then. He had lost to this barbarian, God help them all.

'And this,' Aethelfrith said, gesturing to his right, 'is Prince Hamlet of Jutland who stands here at my side as my most trusted commander and my son-by-marriage in place of my own trueborn son, who was cut down in battle.'

'As were four of my sons,' snarled Aedan.

'Four?' Mairi gasped, looking to him with horror, but Aethelfrith spoke over her.

'Yours, at least, were men, standing in the lines, both armed and armoured. My boy was carrying water – offering comfort to all after the battle was done.'

'The battle was *not* done,' Aedan shot back, 'because you refused our surrender. Your son's death is on your conscience not ours.'

The men behind Aethelfrith jostled forward furiously but the prince – Hamlet, was it? – put up a hand to silence them.

'Death in battle is no one side's fault,' he said. 'We have all suffered losses and must work now to ensure there are no more.'

He spoke with icy calm in the same Norse tongue as the rest, though his voice was heavily inflected. Had the Angle said he was from Jutland? Was that in Denmark? Mairi studied him curiously. He was a young man, fully formed with the broad shoulders of an experienced warrior but no lines on his face as yet to drag his features downwards. He held his sword arm a little awkwardly but stood tall and looked about the company with a curiously distant air, almost as if he were somewhere else in his thoughts. She didn't blame him; who wouldn't want to be somewhere else?

'Quite right, Hamlet,' Aethelfrith growled. 'Now – borders.'

The men around the two kings began bickering loudly and Mairi slid sideways to avoid their coarse voices and flying spittle. Rain was falling heavily on the flimsy roof and pouring through the holes on whichever unfortunates were jostled beneath them. It soaked into hair and clothes so that a claggy steam began to form in the space between linen and heads. This, Mairi imagined, was what the antechamber to hell looked like. She felt herself shrivelling in despair as she edged as far to one side of the assembly as she could. To her surprise she collided with another woman, huddling every bit as miserably against a soggy bush that was attempting, poorly, to form the fourth wall of the dreadful shelter.

'Oh, er, hello,' Mairi stuttered.

The woman looked up at her; she was only half Mairi's age at a guess. Like her, she was bedraggled but somehow the water glowed on her young face, making her dark blue eyes glisten and her smooth skin sparkle. Her damp dress clung to her ripe curves and her lips, pouting against the discomforts of this wretched gathering, looked irritatingly full. Her blonde hair had been darkened by the damp but her plaits were smooth and carefully threaded with little jewels, making her look far more the princess than Mairi. Immediately she regretted speaking to her but it was too late now.

'Hello,' she replied in the language of the Angles, a rough-edged, harsh-sounding jumble of consonants with little musicality.

Mairi knew it well for her father had hired her a tutor, saying that it paid to know your enemy, and the idea had intrigued her. She and Tuathal had been the only ones who had truly listened and she looked around for him now with a sense of rising fear. If Tuathal were here she would know it, everyone would know it. Tuathal was loud and opinionated and always at their father's

242

shoulder, asserting his rights as heir. Was he, then, one of the four sons lost to this dread battle? She turned away.

'Hail Mary, Mother of God, have mercy on his soul. Hail Mary . . .'

'What are you saying?' the pouty girl demanded.

'I am praying,' Mairi said stiffly in the Angle tongue.

'Praying? Oh. To which god?'

'To *the* God, the only God. And to the mother of his son, Jesus Christ.'

'Is he not a god?'

'Who? Jesus? He is God's holy son.'

'But not a god?'

'No. Well, he is one with God. And the Holy Spirit.'

'A third god? You said there was only one?'

'There is. It's a trinity, a union.'

'A union of gods?'

'No!'

Mairi glared at the girl who looked boldly back at her.

'Are you a Christian then?' she asked, looking Mairi up and down with open curiosity.

'I am. It is the only true faith.'

'So you believe. We have our own gods, thank you. And they are, it seems, more powerful than yours.'

'They are not!'

'Why, then, do we stand the victors?'

Mairi swallowed.

'It's not that simple.' The girl raised an eyebrow at her. Mairi changed the subject. 'So who are you?' she demanded. 'And why are you here?'

'I am Princess Udela, Aethelfrith's eldest daughter, and I am here to marry into your house. Or at least, that was the plan. It seems, however, that your father has lost all his marriageable sons to the sword.'

Mairi stared at the girl.

'Those are my brothers you talk about so lightly.'

'So? I lost my brother too.'

'One brother.'

'One is enough – or do Christians prefer multiple deaths?'

'Of course not,' Mairi snapped but she felt unpleasantly ashamed of herself. She drew in a deep breath of sour air and placed her hands carefully together. 'I am sorry for your loss.'

'Oh. Thank you. I am sorry for yours too. And for losing my betrothed – your brother. We should have been sisters, Princess Mairi, and now . . . '

Her eyes filled with tears and Mairi looked awkwardly around, uncertain what to do. She fumbled in the pocket at her belt and drew out a linen square. It was a little soggy but less so than anything else in this dank tent and she proffered it to the Angle princess. Udela snatched at it and dabbed delicately at her glistening eyes.

'Thank you. You're very kind.'

Mairi felt a little glow of pleasure then reminded herself that this girl was on the enemy side and looked guiltily over at her father who was, thankfully, too deep in argument to notice. She tried to edge away but Udela grabbed at her arm.

'Are you married, Mairi?'

'No.'

'Widowed then?'

'No.'

The girl looked at her with undisguised astonishment.

'But you're old.'

Mairi tugged self-consciously at her headdress.

'I have chosen not to marry, thank you.'

'Oh!' Something seemed to spark in Udela's dark eyes. 'You're the one who's given herself to Christ?'

'That's right. It's a noble . . . '

'How strange!'

'What?'

244

'Is it just you, or are there a few of you? Does he . . . you know . . . you all at once?'

She nodded suggestively downwards and Mairi recoiled in horror.

'No! It's not like that. I am chaste. I have known no man.'

'Gods alive! Poor you.'

'There is nothing poor about it. On the contrary, I am freed from the base concerns of the flesh and enriched instead by spiritual ecstasy.'

Udela snorted ungraciously.

'Ecstasy? Are you sure your priest doesn't . . . No? Ah, well. Mind you,' she went on huffily, 'I've never done it either. And now, with Gartnait dead, I'm not likely to for ages yet. I hate war.'

'Gartnait is dead?'

'Yes. Awful, isn't it?'

'It is. He . . . '

'That's the second husband I've been robbed of. I should have married him over there, Prince Hamlet, but my little sister stole him away from me. So unfair. I mean, look at him, Mairi. Isn't he handsome?'

She pointed a finger and Mairi looked. Hamlet was still stand-ing with the rival kings but he was staring into the steam above their heads so that he seemed momentarily haloed by it. He was, Mairi supposed, a good-looking young man if your thoughts were earthbound. His jaw was firm, his cheekbones high and his eyes rich brown and filled with an affecting sadness.

'He's a prince too,' Udela went on, 'and heir to the High Kingship of Denmark. If he takes his throne, Flora will be queen and I won't even have Gartnait.'

She began to cry again and Mairi looked around for escape but found none. The arguments were gaining in volume and sword hilts were being rattled. She feared for all their lives. Then suddenly, amidst the chaos, she saw why God had sent her here and felt a blissful calm descend on her soul. She must speak up for peace at

Easter, the most holy of times, mediate in Christ's blessed name before these men tore themselves apart. Filled with the Holy Spirit, she pushed her way back to her father's side and stepped boldly between him and Aethelfrith.

'Peace!' A stunned silence fell. 'Can we not settle this like civilised people?' she demanded, trying to remember the Angle words. 'Our differences are but earthly concerns.' The Angle king spluttered but said nothing. Emboldened, Mairi raised her hands to her rough audience and let God's Holy Spirit lift her. 'Christ said, "Blessed are the peacemakers",' she pronounced. 'So let us follow His example and . . .'

'Christ?' Aethelfrith roared. 'What the hell has this Christ to do with it?'

'Christ is God's own son,' Mairi told him, willing him to listen.

If she converted the Angles to Christ she could snatch a victory from the jaws of defeat. Would that not be glorious? Would her father not sing her praises all over Dal Riata? And would he not reward her with entry into the blessed nunnery at Kildare? She took a step towards Aethelfrith and reached for his hand. It was huge, callused and unpleasantly damp but she grasped it keenly.

'If you accept Christ into your life, King Aethelfrith, you will know redemption.'

'I will know I'm gone mad,' he snapped, yanking his hand away, 'as you, girl, are gone mad.'

Mairi swallowed but had not Christ explained that the path ahead would be hard? She could not surrender at the first insult.

'It can be hard, for the uninitiated, to understand but God will shine His . . .'

'Mairi!' Aedan's voice was a roar and his hand was fierce as a claw as he grabbed at her neck and yanked her backwards. 'You shame me.'

'No, Father. Do not deny Christ or . . .'

'Silence!' He pushed her to her knees before Aethelfrith. 'You wanted a bride to seal our "alliance", Aethelfrith – well, here's one for you. She is foolish, yes, but royal and her blood will bind us well enough.'

'No, Father,' Mairi begged.

'I said, silence!'

His hand tightened on her neck, squeezing tears from her eyes as Aethelfrith stepped up and looked down at her.

'She's not much of a prize.'

'Oh, come, she's healthy and she has all the right holes.' Mairi's eyes widened in horror but she dare not speak again. 'And she's a virgin. That, surely, is worth something?'

She remembered him telling her that pagans sacrificed virgins to Odin and felt her whole body begin to shake in fear, but now Aethelfrith was grabbing her chin, yanking it so that she was caught between the rough hands of the two kings and it was all she could do not to break down in sobs.

'She's in good shape,' the Angle allowed as if she were a horse. She cowered back but Aedan's hand was rigid on her neck. 'But who will I marry her to?'

'You said Prince Hamlet stood here as your son.'

'My son-by-marriage, King Aedan. He has my own Flora for wife and she is even now carrying his child.'

'Then he is blessed with a fecund woman and can afford to take a second.'

'Father!' Mairi wept but there was a dark light in Aedan's eyes and she knew this bitter battle had blinded him to her.

Aethelfrith nodded.

'I have two wives myself – one older to run my affairs and one younger to warm my bed.' He spun around. 'What say you, Hamlet?'

The prince stared vacantly at his lord.

'Of what?'

Aethelfrith's eyes narrowed.

'Of marriage.'

'It is a fine estate.'

'Good. That is settled then.'

'What is?' asked the Dane, blinking as if returning to them.

'Raise her, Hamlet,' Aethelfrith urged.

The Dane looked at Mairi, shivering on her knees. She saw something like pity in his brown eyes as he held out a hand to her.

'What are you doing down there, princess? Women should not be so abased. Come, rise.'

He held his hand closer to her and she had little choice but to take it. He lifted her to her feet and the men in the tent cheered as one. Hamlet looked around, confused.

'Is all well?'

'Very well,' Aethelfrith agreed. 'Terms are set and this marriage will seal them for us all.'

'Marriage?'

'We shall celebrate it tomorrow.'

'But . . .'

'Then we can all go home and see to our wounded, can we not, Hamlet?'

Aethelfrith's words sounded fraught with a meaning Mairi could not divine but Hamlet appeared to understand him completely.

'Very well,' he said, 'I will marry her.'

His clear reluctance matched her own but even so it pierced her heart. The wail of furious protest, when it came, was from Udela's pouty mouth but it resonated through Mairi like a sword cut. She had come here dreaming of nunneries and was to leave a wife – and a second wife at that. What had she done that was so wrong for God to forsake her in this way? And how, in the paws of a man, would she ever redeem herself?

Chapter Twenty-one

Mairi had intended to spend all night on her knees, begging the dear, risen Lord for forgiveness from whatever sins she had committed to be condemned to this barbaric match, but her weak flesh must have succumbed to sleep instead for she woke with a start to the clatter of the camp breaking their fast. She stared up through the holes in her shelter in horror. How could that be daylight, albeit it a murky, grey version? She'd only lain down on the filthy fur that passed for her bed to ease out her aching back after the long ride and somehow she had dropped off and not stirred all night long.

She covered her eyes with her hands as shame washed over her. No wonder God had forsaken her. She could not even resist her fleshly failings long enough to say one prayer. And at Easter too. She was weak and unworthy and the dread day ahead would be a just punishment.

'Ah, there you are, sleepy head!' Lynet bustled up, all smiles, clutching a gown before her as if they were in the most luxurious bower in the land and not a stinking half-tent beneath dripping trees. 'We need to get going if we're going to make you lovely for your happy day.'

Mairi blinked up at her, searching for the words to convey just how wrong everything Lynet had said was, but it seemed she'd been struck dumb. Not that Lynet cared.

'Still, good job you're rested. It does wonders for the skin and, after all, you'll have little chance of sleep tonight.' She leaned closer. 'You're a lucky woman, my lady – he's a fitting man to take to your bed.'

'He must be half my age, Lynet.'

'As I said, you're a lucky woman. I could hear the Lady Udela weeping over in her own camp which, in truth, is an excellent thing for you as it will make her pretty eyes all swollen and red. You'll outshine her for sure.'

Mairi frowned at her.

'I do not need to "outshine" anyone, Lynet. Such desires are mere earthly vanity.'

'I suppose so but we are, after all, on the earth, my lady, so why not?'

Mairi sighed and looked away; the girl would never understand.

'We are *very much* on the earth,' she said, forcing herself to stand up on the soggy ground. It wasn't raining anymore but water still hung menacingly in the air and the clouds were low over the camp. Good. She couldn't have borne sunshine. She looked at the dress Lynet was holding out. 'Is that, then, my wedding gown?'

Lynet grimaced.

'It's not as fine as I'd like for a princess such as yourself but it's the best I can do. The pack got sodden yesterday and I've no way of washing it but I've brushed off all the mud – see.'

She thrust the dress at Mairi who saw that Lynet had, indeed, removed the surface dirt but it had permeated the fabric with far too great a determination for a thin girl with an improvised birch brush to tackle; the once proud red fabric was now a dull, mottled brown.

'Lovely,' she said dully.

'Luckily,' Lynet pressed on, undaunted, 'your headdresses are mainly dry and I put in some neck-chains. Not your best ones, sadly, in case we were robbed on the road, but pretty all the same. Of course, it would be usual for the groom to present you with some jewels . . . ' She looked out behind the flapping piece of fabric that passed for a door, to the men grunting and groaning around the campfire. 'I'm sure Prince Hamlet would be keen to honour you but where's he going to find jewels out here?'

'I need no jewels,' Mairi said stiffly. 'God's nature is jewel enough for me.'

'I'm sure, but you know jewels *are* the workings of nature, are they not, for they come from under the hills, so really . . .' Lynet caught her tongue and ground to a halt. 'Anyway, the neckchains are very pretty. Shall we have a go at washing you?'

She indicated a pail that had been set outside the door to catch the rainwater. Mairi shivered.

'We shall not,' she said, 'for I must pray.'

'But, my lady, King Aethelfrith wants us ready by midday and there is much to do first. Your hair, for a start, is very tangled and will take . . .'

'I must pray! It is Easter morning. On this great day Our Lord Jesus Christ rose from the dead and ascended to sit at God's right hand in Heaven.'

'He did?' Lynet looked nervously towards the grey skies as if she might see him passing by.

'Of course he did. I thought you said you were a Christian?'

'I am! I just didn't know it was today.'

'Well, you should have. It is the most important day in the Christian calendar and I do not care if I go to my husband naked if it means I still have time for prayer.'

Lynet giggled.

'I imagine he'd like that.'

'Lynet!'

The maid pouted.

'Well, he would. My sister's been married twice now and she says men would have women naked all the time if they could. Imagine!'

'I'd rather not. Now, lovely as it is talking to you, Lynet, I must to prayer.'

'Where?'

Mairi stepped over to the doorway.

'My father must have an altar of some sort?'

'You think?'

'Of course.'

Mairi looked around the camp, her confidence faltering as she took in the bleak state of it in the cold daylight. They were in a clearing of rough scrubland set between low hills. Their own camp was in the trees to the north side, with Aethelfrith's notably larger one to the south on raised, less marshy ground. The two sides were separated by a strip of land about ten paces wide and two lines of sour-faced guards. Otherwise there were few visible distinguishing features and nothing that might stand out as a holy shrine.

'But how did he pray for success in battle?' she asked. Was her father mad?

'This was not his original camp,' Lynet told her. 'This is merely where he has been forced to come for the peace negotiations.'

'Ah. Of course.' Mairi looked back at her maid. 'How do you know that?'

'I was, er, chatting to some of the men around the fire last night after you'd gone to sleep. They were keen for news from home and it seemed kind to offer them that small comfort.'

She was blushing furiously.

'Is that all the comfort you offered them, Lynet?'

'Almost all. That is, I did nothing wrong, my lady. It was just a kiss. Well, a few kisses. But he's a lovely man and his father has a farm out at Ardnackaig and he needs a wife to help him run it. And oh, my lady, I'd so love a farm of my own! I wasn't naughty though. Well, not very. Just enough to, you know, make him want more.' Mairi stared at her and Lynet stuck out her bottom lip mutinously. 'A girl has to take care of herself as best she can in this world.'

Mairi sighed. That much was true.

'God bless you,' she said. 'I hope he is true to you.'

Lynet beamed.

'I hope so too. Oh, my lady, I'm so pleased I came here with you. Thank you for picking me.'

'I didn't . . . ' Mairi started to say and then stopped herself. She was rarely thanked and it was a pleasant experience. 'I am glad something good has come of this,' she said instead.

'More than one thing – there is your own marriage, my lady.'

'Hmmm.'

Mairi scanned the camp again and spotted her father commanding a group of men wrestling some large logs into the central area. They set two stumpy ones three paces apart and, with loud grunts, hefted a long trunk on top.

'An altar!' Mairi cried in delight.

Someone produced a cloak, which they draped over the top, and then Aedan sent them all off across the grass. Mairi watched, intrigued, as the mucky, mutilated young men began to pick bluebells and primroses and bring them back to scatter around the makeshift altar. She felt absurdly touched and then remembered that, sweet as this might be, it was all to celebrate a marriage for which she had no desire. Her father could dress up this absurd mock-chapel as nicely as he liked but it would not mask the fact that he was forcing her to marry a man against her will. Against God's will.

Or was it? Did God, after all, want her to marry this Danish prince – this pagan, already wed, Danish prince? Did He, perhaps, want her to carry His word into the Baltic lands? That would be a calling indeed . . . but how would she know? She looked longingly towards the altar but couldn't bring herself to head out there in front of all those men, even to pray.

'Perhaps I'll just conduct private prayer in here,' she said, backing up against her rough fur bed. 'God hears us wherever we are.'

Lynet nodded earnestly.

'And perhaps, my lady, I could tend your hair while you do it?'

Mairi looked to the bone comb the girl was brandishing and, with a sigh, nodded her consent. Out here in this strange wasteland full of soldiers she was no longer sure what was the right way to go about things and it seemed simplest to submit to those who did. She dropped to her knees, clasped her hands together and closed her eyes to pray – but her dark hair was very knotted and Lynet was very thorough and the constant tugging made it almost impossible for Mairi to concentrate.

She screwed her eyes even tighter shut, to focus on God and to stem the tears of pain, mortification and fear leaking from her. God had spoken – she would go as missionary to the land of the Danes and if that meant enduring a hairy, sweaty man in her bed then there could be worse ones than Prince Hamlet. Something deep inside her shifted pleasurably at the thought and she was glad of the next sharp tug of the comb to stop it.

'Hail Mary, Mother of God. Hail Mary ... '

Her prayers, such as they were, were halted by a kerfuffle outside and her eyes opened as her father strode in, a wide smile plastered across his face.

'Good morning, daughter dear. A fine day for a wedding.' Mairi looked pointedly up through the holes in the roof to the drab skies above but said nothing. 'You are praying?'

'Yes, Father.'

'Good, good. Asking for God's blessing on this sacred match, I'm sure.'

She inclined her head. His anger last night had frightened her but this forced good humour was, if anything, more unsettling.

'It is Easter, Father,' she dared to say.

'Is it? God be praised, is it really? You lose track of time terribly out here. It is hard to know one day from another.'

'I can see that.'

'But this is wonderful news. A blessing indeed. If God sent you to us on the day of Christ's resurrection then he must like this match well, must he not?'

'I did wonder if that was so myself,' she admitted.

'Well, wonder no more. It is a joyous sign, daughter, and we should offer thanks for it.'

Mairi gazed up at him. His certainty was so beguiling. But had not the devil tempted Christ with easy solutions?

'We should offer thanks for it,' Aedan repeated, and an edge of steel crept into his voice leaving Mairi in little doubt about her options. Whatever God thought felt horribly hard to ascertain but what her father felt was as clear as mountain ice.

'We should.'

'I will fetch the priest.'

'Priest?' Mairi's heart surged. 'You have a priest, Father?'

'Oh, yes. A monk from Iona.'

'Iona?' What joy was this?

'He's gone a little loose in the head, poor lad – hadn't seen battle before and this was a hell of a one to start with – but he's holy enough. Fetch Father John,' he said to one of the men at his back who scurried off. 'Dress yourself, Mairi, and we will meet at the altar.'

'Yes, Father.'

'Pull the gown tight, girl. And leave your hair loose. And do you have some of that stuff your stepmother puts on her eyes to make them look darker?'

'We do,' Lynet said eagerly.

'Excellent. If you must go to the Angles, Mairi, you should go shining.'

'Shining?' she repeated incredulously. But the maid was already rustling assiduously in a casket and there was little Mairi could do but submit to her ministrations.

Mairi stepped nervously out into the camp a little time later, not exactly shining but definitely feeling bright against the clutch of

255

soldiers gathering around, keen for a little joy after their harsh days in this purgatory of a camp. Her dress might be muddy but it was of best quality, close-woven wool. Her hair felt strange left loose and not caught up in a headdress and she was horribly aware that the streaks of grey that she'd recently found in it were all too apparent without her habitual plaits to hide them in. Despite that, however, she liked the way the breeze lifted it from her neck and the feel of her silver diadem against her exposed forehead. She had no mirror so could not see how Lynet had painted her but the men who eyed her as she passed looked appreciative enough. Mind you, they hadn't seen a woman for weeks so would probably appreciate the ugliest old hag if only for relief from the monotony of their own kind.

'You look beautiful,' Lynet told her.

It was a lie, of course. Mairi had never been beautiful even as a young girl, but she appreciated it all the same for she had never before felt more exposed.

'Very presentable,' was Aedan's comment as he offered her his arm before she stepped out into the no-man's-land between the camps, and that, at least, she believed.

She moved forward with him, trying to pretend the muddy grass was a rich tapestry and the makeshift altar was a glorious chapel and the mutilated men lining her way were Dal Riata's most prominent courtiers. This was not a wedding any girl would dream of but, then, she'd never dreamed of a wedding so what did it matter?

She kept her head high and looked determinedly forward. King Aethelfrith was standing before the altar with Prince Hamlet by his side and, Lord help her, but her groom looked even more handsome in the daylight. Udela was on his other side, looking, if possible, even more reluctant to be here than Mairi herself and now Aethelfrith nudged the Bernician princess forward to join Lynet as Mairi's attendants. Every part of the Angle girl's body fizzed with anger and Mairi found time to wonder at the madness of this situation. Udela would give her teeth to marry Hamlet and Mairi the same not to, and yet here they were, in each other's place, at the mercy of men's plans.

'You look nice,' Udela said, more as an expression of astonishment than a compliment.

'Thank you,' Mairi said anyway, and by now they were before her groom and it mattered little what Udela thought.

Hamlet nodded kindly enough to her and Mairi did her best to smile at him.

'Good people!' a voice called in melodious Celtic. Mairi turned eagerly to it and saw a scrawny young man in a torn monk's robe standing behind the tree-trunk altar with his hands held high and a wild look in his eyes. 'We are gathered here on this glorious day of Christ's passion . . .'

'What's he saying?' Aethelfrith demanded loudly, cutting the monk off.

Aedan translated.

'Passion?'

'It is Easter today, my lord king.'

'High King.'

'It is Easter today, my lord high king.'

'Eostre? Of course! How marvellous. And how apt.'

'Apt?' Mairi asked, confused.

'Of course.' He came up to her. 'What better way of celebrating this union than with the great festival of fertility?'

He winked lewdly then, to her great astonishment, grabbed her face in both his hands and planted a loud kiss upon her brow.

'Fertility?' she choked out, confused.

'Of course fertility. Fertility and renewal.' He looked at her as if she were stupid. 'Eostre – Goddess of Spring, bringer of crops and fruits and babies. I bet you'd like a baby, wouldn't you? It's not too late, you know, and Hamlet here has good seed – just ask my daughter.'

Mairi looked desperately to her father who cleared his throat.

'So, shall we recommence?'

'The lady looks confused,' Hamlet said.

Mairi *was* confused. Who was Eostre and what on earth did she have to do with this sacred day?

'Easter is when Christ was resurrected from the dead and ascended to God's right hand in Heaven,' she explained.

'Did he?' Aethelfrith asked. 'Good on him. Just like Odin.'

'What?'

'Odin, child – died on the Tree of Knowledge and was born again.'

'No, that's Christ. He was crucified for our sins and . . .'

Aethelfrith waved this away.

'Whatever you say. It's all much the same in either version, is it not? We can celebrate the two together – we with our gods and you with yours.'

Mairi gaped at him.

'But it's not like that. Our God is the only God.'

'Enough!' Aethelfrith's voice broke over her like a thunderstorm. 'There is no need to be greedy. We will tolerate your White Christ but you must also tolerate Odin and Thor, Freya and Frey.'

'Now who's being greedy?' Mairi mumbled but did not dare speak it aloud.

'We *do* tolerate them,' Aedan said loudly over her. 'Of course we do. There is room at the altar for all.'

Mairi stared at the flower-strewn ground, unable to believe what she was hearing. Her father was a very Judas. Poor blessed Columba would turn in his sacred grave if he could hear his old friend denying the core principle of their faith like this. One God, now and forever.

'Let's get on with it then,' Aethelfrith said. 'I've two barrels of mead want emptying and I don't care who the toasts go to, gods or men, dwarves or trolls. It'll all taste the same anyway. Hamlet . . .'

He ushered the prince forward and Mairi found herself deposited at his side. She looked up into the eyes of the young man with whom she would now, apparently, share her life and could not quite believe this was happening. Yesterday her main concern had been not to destroy God's beautiful bluebells with her bodily waste and today she found herself with a marriage bed to contend with – and a marriage bed, besides, in a blood-stained army camp in enemy borderlands.

All she wanted right now was to escape into the safety of her dear chapel at Dunadd, kneel beside Dorothea and pray the prayers that the church had sent for man's consolation. She realised with a fresh jolt of pain that she might never see that chapel again, never see Dorothea, never even see Dunadd. From here she would ride south-east with her new husband and his Angle tribe to the sea and in Denmark there was not one Christian soul to sustain her in her faith. Her knees seemed almost to give way beneath her and it was all she could do to stand upright as the wild-eyed priest recited an approximation of the marriage service.

'Will you, Mairi, take this woman, erm, man to be your husband?' He fixed her with his strange, wild stare. 'Will you?'

'I . . .'

Aedan stepped forward.

'She will. Of course she will.'

The priest looked at her and for a moment the haze in his poor eyes seemed to clear and he sent a piercing question straight into her heart – will you? – but Aethelfrith drew his sword halfway from its scabbard and the monk flinched and was lost again.

'Do you, Prince Hamlet, take this woman to be your wife?'

'I do.'

Hamlet sounded weary.

'Then,' said the priest in a babble, 'I pronounce you woman and man and wife and husband and . . . and together in God's holy ordinance. Amen.'

'Amen,' Aedan said loudly.

'Amen,' came the rough chorus from behind him, echoed with guttural vowels and what sounded suspiciously like laughter from the other side.

'Excellent,' Aethelfrith said. 'Give her a kiss then, man.'

The ill-assorted crowd seemed to lean in and Mairi quaked before them. Then she felt strong arms holding hers and looked up to see Hamlet.

'It'll soon be over,' he said, 'thank Freya.'

'Freya?'

'Goddess of love,' he said on a half laugh, and then he pulled her against him and pressed a kiss onto her lips.

It was mercifully quick and not as sweaty or as stinky as she'd expected. Indeed, Hamlet's skin was clean and his lips felt smooth against her own. He smelled of pine and leather and hearth fires in wintertime, and his hold on her was steady and reassuring as the men all around cheered and cracked lewd jokes.

'You do not want this marriage either?' she asked him in an undertone.

'Honestly?'

'Of course.'

'Then, no, I do not.'

'Right. Good.'

Mairi wasn't so sure now that honesty had been what she'd wanted at all. There should be some comfort in their shared antipathy to the match but if so it was hard for her to find. She put her hand to her lips and felt his mouth there still. He was her husband now, whatever he felt about it, and tonight it would take more than a kiss to make it truly so. It would not soon be over at all.

It was a rough, raucous wedding feast. There had been no time to send out a hunt so they had to make do with skinny birds plucked from the trees, cooked in garlic leaves and served straight from the fire. There was no wine, just a strong ale that seemed to coat the inside of Mairi's mouth whenever she drank it. But she drank it all the same for it dulled the jagged edges of the fear grinding inside her poor virgin body.

The other two women at the feast seemed merry enough. As

the day wore interminably into night Lynet planted herself firmly on the knee of, Mairi could only assume, the young man she had kissed last night. Mairi watched her. Lynet seemed so at ease there, ruffling the man's filthy hair and giggling at every word he said while rewarding his increasingly wandering hands with kisses. Kisses! Hers, she suspected, would not be the only virginity lost tonight and she envied Lynet her eagerness.

Even Udela seemed to have cheered up a little. Someone had woven a garland of flowers for her blonde hair and she had seated herself on the now dismantled altar and proclaimed herself to be Eostre. Mairi had no idea what the wretched goddess was meant to be like but from the way men were flocking to kiss her feet and, indeed, as high up her shapely legs as they thought they could get away with, it was nothing decorous. Was that any way for a princess to behave?

Mairi drank more ale and tried desperately to meditate on Christ's glorious resurrection but a skald had taken the grassy floor now and was telling a most lewd story about the deplorable goddess Freya sleeping with four dwarves in exchange for a gold necklace. Mairi desperately wished she could not understand but the priest, his robe torn open to the waist to reveal his thin-boned chest, took it upon himself to translate anyway with, as far as she could tell, some embellishments of his own that he surely could not have learned on Iona and lewd hand movements that needed no translation. Angle and Celt were united at last in roaring their approval, brought together it seemed by nothing more than base bawdiness.

Mairi pictured the nunnery at Kildare – a remote community, separated from this corrupt world by fences and seas and rules of order and propriety. She thought of a simple chapel with white-robed women lined up before an altar to sing a psalm, voices raised as one to the glory of God. It was a lost dream and she looked out across the men and wept into the darkness for the pity of it. But then Aethelfrith rose and she was yanked back into reality.

'Bed!' The Angle king spoke the word with something like

surprise, as if he'd only just remembered the purpose of the day but he rapidly warmed to the idea. 'Bed! The groom must take his bride to bed.'

The motley wedding guests – those who were still sensate – roared their approval. Mairi felt the last tiny piece of herself shrivel up like the final leaf on the tree and rose stiffly. She had drunk more ale than ever before in her life but it had not been enough. Maybe nothing would have been enough.

She saw Lynet leering at her from her man's lap like a pretty demon. She saw Udela climb down from her Eostre throne, glaring at her as if she had stolen her favourite gown. She saw Aedan nodding her on with guilty kindness on his face, and she saw Aethelfrith drawing closer and closer and saying 'bed' over and over like a creature from a nightmare. A bird bone had caught in his beard and seemed to signal a desperate plea for help every time he spoke. Mairi could not turn her eyes away from it.

'Shall we?' Hamlet's voice was gentle but no less ominous.

Mairi felt her heart hurl itself against her ribcage and wondered if she could die from fear and, if so, if it could be before she was made to strip naked before this fertile Dane. He had her by the arm now and was tugging her out of the tent and towards her own shelter and the same besmirched rug on which she had woken up this morning a virgin. Ten years old she'd been when she'd first sworn herself to Christ. She had lasted twenty-seven years since then and all for this – a forced marriage in a bloody field to a pagan prince.

'Might as well get it done,' Hamlet muttered and Mairi saw him reach into his breeches and shift whatever he kept in there.

She knew what it was, of course. Men seemed to have little shame about even this most private part of their bodies. Never, though, had she been this close to one – or wanted to be. They'd reached the tent and he tugged her inside. Someone, maybe Lynet, had found a cleanish blanket and strewn it with the same flowers as had been on the altar earlier but nothing could make it look inviting to Mairi.

'Shall we lie down?' Hamlet suggested. Mairi stared at him.

It was dark but someone, sadly, had left a smouldering brazier in their rough shelter and she could see him all too clearly. 'It would be best.'

'I don't want to.'

'You want to do it standing up?'

'Is that possible?'

'Well, yes. But for your first time . . . It *is* your first time?'

'Yes!'

'Right. I thought so. Let's get you undressed then.' He reached for her gown, pulling the ribbons expertly apart and easing it off her shoulders so she stood in just her shift. 'Shall I take that one off or shall you?'

'Must we?'

'Yes.' He darted impatiently forward and pulled it up and over her head, leaving her naked before him. She crossed her hands over herself and he tutted. 'Better just to get on with it, Mairi.'

'I don't want to.'

'So you said. Am I so hideous?'

'No! It is not you, Hamlet . . . husband. It is only that I made a vow when I was young – I promised myself to Christ. That is, I swore an oath of chastity so as to honour God for all my life.'

He shrugged.

'So? Things change. I swore myself to someone when I was young too but she did not want me. I have had to change my path and it seems you must too. Now come, let us get this over with and then we can sleep. And in the morning, we can ride for home.'

'*Your* home.'

'Yours too now.'

'But I don't want . . . '

'Enough, Mairi.' Hamlet picked her up and placed her none too gently on the bed. 'Do you think I wanted to leave Denmark? No. Do you know why I did? Because my uncle slaughtered my father and I had to flee for my own life. I made a new home and so must you.'

He was fumbling with his breeches now. Panic engulfed her and she retched, spewing ale and tiny bird bones all down his front. He sprang back, cursing.

'Sorry! I'm sorry.'

'You should be.'

'I ... I don't want to.'

It came out on a sob. She closed her eyes and waited for him to force himself upon her, to take what was, after all, his. Nothing happened. She heard Hamlet take off his soiled shirt and fling it outside then, slowly, he lay down next to her.

'We won't then.'

'What?'

'I'm no rapist, Mairi.'

'But ... '

'But what? You do not want to and in truth I do not much want to either, so we won't. Good night.'

'That's it?'

'Yes.'

'But my father and King Aethelfrith and ... '

'Are they here now?'

'No.'

'So ... It is our marriage, Mairi, to do with as we will. I have a wife already and you, it seems, have this Christ – for all he wants you.'

'He *does* want me.'

'Good. Then sleep.'

'But ... '

'Odin's teeth, Mairi, are you never satisfied? You have your way. You can keep your virginity if it matters so much to you. Good night.'

And with that he turned on his side and pulled the blanket up over himself, sending the flowers tumbling onto Mairi. She lay in the dark, staring at the unmoving bulk of her new husband against the glow of the brazier. God, it seemed, had blessed her with a reprieve. She was saved. She picked up a primrose and tore the petals off one by one, scattering them over her untouched breasts, and tried to thank Christ for His mercy upon her. But yet again on this strangest of days she could not find the words to reach Him.

Chapter Twenty-two

Bebba's burgh, June 603

Ofelia lay, eyes closed, listening to the soft murmur of chatter between Flora and her mother, enjoying the gentle rise and fall of their voices more than any music she'd heard. She loved the back and forth of their words, the undertones of quiet laughter and the soft easy teasing. Her mind was fuzzy still from the remnants of the fever that had held her for, so Flora had told her, two whole days and nights and the Bernician Norse sounded sufficiently alien to her to let the sense drift and just enjoy the cadence of their voices. She could live here forever, floating on the conversation – if only she didn't need the latrine. And if only doing so wasn't pathetically weak.

She prised open her right eye. The left one was still swathed in bandages. Flora had suggested removing them yesterday to check her vision but Ofelia had stopped her. She'd burbled about needing more time to heal but in truth she was afraid – afraid she'd be blind on one side and therefore useless as a warrior. No one would want to fight with someone who couldn't protect their flank. It was cowardly, she knew, but she wanted one more day when her full recovery was still an undisputed possibility, when she could rest in this cocoon of illness and not have to face what it might mean to be out in the real world again.

She did her best not to move so Flora wouldn't notice and rush to her side. This last day, as she'd felt less and less like a trapped insect was banging against the inside of her own skull, Ofelia had derived curious pleasure from watching Flora at her work. Ofelia hadn't been in the herbery before, scorning it as a blatantly female domain, but she had to admit it was a lovely place to be.

Large window openings made it lighter than most buildings and it smelled wonderful, as if the gods (or rather Flora) had gathered all that was good in nature and concentrated it in this one neat space. It was as immaculately organised as any barracks and Flora moved about it with quiet purpose, snipping and grinding and mixing with an intense concentration that brought remarkable authority to the face Ofelia had previously thought of as almost vacuously pretty.

Right now, for example, Flora was adding ingredients to a carved wooden bowl and grinding them beneath some sort of bulbous stick so that they released a scent like the headiest dusk.

'Marjoram?' Bebba suggested, moving into Ofelia's narrow line of sight.

'I thought camomile,' Flora replied, looking to her mother for agreement.

Ofelia watched as their two heads drew together over the shared project and felt an ache sharper than any in the severed flesh on her side or face. Something suspiciously like a tear leaked out of her unbandaged eye and she put up her hand to bat it away. Flora turned instantly.

'Ofelia! You're awake. How do you feel?'

Sad, she thought, envious, bitter, angry. Yes – angry. That was her strongest emotion. She called up a picture of her mother's lily-white hem being yanked out of her own childish fingers as Sigrid leaped gladly away to death and snatched at the anger that burned with it, holding it close to strengthen herself.

'Better,' she managed to say aloud.

'Good. That's very good.'

'But I need a piss.'

She saw Flora flinch at this use of coarse barracks language and was momentarily glad but, really, what sort of victory was it to shock the kindly woman who had nursed her so devotedly.

'Sorry,' Ofelia mumbled.

'It's fine,' Flora said, smiling at her in a way she didn't deserve, 'I'll fetch the pot.'

'Can't I go to the latrines?'

Flora shook her head.

'It's too far.'

'It's about twenty paces.'

'Which is too far if you've been lying down for days. You'd fall in the mud and then you'd get your bandages all mucky.'

'And look like an arse.'

Flora smiled.

'That too. Do you need help to get up?'

'No!'

'Fine.'

Flora held the pot out and retreated to the door with Bebba to give Ofelia some privacy. She sat up and swung her feet to the floorboards. Her head spun a little and her legs, when she tried to take her weight upon them, shook. Damn.

'Er, Flora . . . '

'Yes?'

'I might need a hand after all.'

Flora gave a little chuckle but came over and supported her with surprisingly strong arms as she crouched like an infant. Ofelia looked at the swell of Flora's belly and remembered Lars speaking of her before the battle when all had been knucklebone fun and daring plans.

'You'll be a good mother, Flora,' she said.

'I will? Thank you, Ofelia. I hope so.'

She helped her patient back into bed and quietly removed the pot. She took it to the door and Ofelia heard the contents slosh onto the ground outside.

'Won't it damage the herbs?' she asked when Flora came back in.

'No, actually. Certain herbs – borage and sage, for example – flourish with a little human watering.'

'They do? How on earth do you know that?'

'Mother told me.'

Flora looked towards Bebba who smiled back at her.

'And my mother told me. I suppose someone must have spotted them growing near latrines and worked it out.'

Ofelia nodded and lay gratefully back on her pillows once more. Mother to daughter. It had never occurred to her before to wonder about the knowledge she had lost to that pyre. She had hazy memories of Lady Sigrid with a needle, darting it in and out of the fabric as quick as a dragonfly, pulling thread into beautiful patterns behind it. If she'd lived, would she have passed that skill on to Ofelia? Loki help her, she might even now be sitting on a stool meekly sewing birds onto her husband's finest tunic as a present for when he returned from the wars. Perhaps it was a good job her mother had died!

'You do not have to stay with me all the time, you know,' she said to the two women. 'It must be very dull for you.'

'Not at all,' Flora said. 'It is good to have something useful to do.'

'I am your project?'

'I suppose so, if you want to see it that way. And it is going very well, though it may suffer some setbacks now that you are fully awake and trying to move around.'

She grinned at Ofelia who grimaced back.

'You don't approve of my moving around?'

'Not yet. It was a terrible injury, Ofelia, and you cannot rush healing.'

'It doesn't feel so bad.' She put her hand to her side and flexed the skin beneath the bandages. It tugged a little but nothing she couldn't bear.

'The wound to your side is superficial.'

'Then . . . ?'

Flora put her fingers to her face and Ofelia found herself mirroring the action. She felt the wad of bandages and pressed down. Pain seared instantly across her skin; if, indeed, there was skin left there.

'Is it very bad, Flora?'

'I've seen worse.'

'But . . . ?'

'But it's bad, yes. Your jawbone was broken. I tried to reset it but I don't know if I've succeeded. It may set squint.'

'Squint? Ah, well, it's not as if I want to attract a husband, is it?'

'I'm sure you will still be beautiful.'

'Me? Gods, Flora, I think you must be the blind one. I've never been beautiful.'

'*I* think you are. And so does Hamlet.'

Ofelia felt herself blush and the heat fired uncomfortably across the covered part of her face.

'Hamlet thinks I am many things – stubborn, irritating, foul-tempered . . . '

'And beautiful.'

'Don't be ridiculous, Flora. It's not like that between us.'

'Only because you won't let it be.'

'No, I . . . '

Flora put up her hand.

'Don't fret, Ofelia. Hamlet has talked openly to me of this. I know how it is between you two and I can live with it, as Mother has to live with Cathryn.'

'Where is Cathryn?'

Flora smiled.

'She went back to Aet Gefrin the minute she heard of the victory. She says she prefers it there, that it's more civilised.'

Ofelia considered this.

'The hall is finer, I suppose, and the buildings newer and perhaps more cleverly designed, but it has not the grandeur of Dinguardi.'

'I agree,' Bebba said. 'And by the time I am done, the hall here will be twice as fine – and all the other buildings too.'

'You are going to rebuild?'

'I am. They are calling it Bebba's burgh now, you know, and if it is to bear my name it shall do so in style. I have lost my son to war and will soon lose my daughters to their husbands' estates but I can leave a lasting legacy here, carved into the land for all to see.'

'And to admire,' Flora said, tucking her arm under her mother's and kissing her cheek. 'I hope I can return from Denmark to see it.'

'And I that I can travel to Denmark to see you – and my royal grandchildren.'

They looked fondly at each other and Ofelia turned her face away from the glare of their simple love. This damned herbery was indeed fiercely female and suddenly she itched for the rough ease of knucklebones and swords. At least the men asked nothing more of you than skill and bravery, both of which could be acquired with training and willpower.

She put a hand to her face once more. Flora was being kind, she knew. The wound must be hideous and would scar her for life. Little children would duck away from her and then, as they grew older and bolder, would dare each other to go close to her. She'd done it herself. There had been an old Jutlander with no nose and his top lip all gnarled in on itself and she had often taken a dare to dash up and touch him. She'd thought only of her own foolish bravery and the admiration of her peers and nothing for how he must have felt as a warrior turned freak.

Once he had shouted something at her. She'd dashed back to the others swearing he'd cursed her, but when she'd thought about it in the dark and quiet of that night she'd known that what he'd actually said was: 'Why don't you just sit down and talk to me?' She wished now that she had. His story would have been of far more value than her comrades' empty cheers. And now that would be her story too. No one would be able to look at her, not even Hamlet, and he would wish in his heart of hearts that he had shown mercy and finished her life instead of making his fool's dash to save it. And so would she.

'Ofelia? Ofelia, you're crying!'

'I'm not. It's just my eye aching from doing the work of two.'

Flora said nothing but dabbed the moisture away with a cloth and fetched a compress to lay upon her forehead. It was cool and soothing but it blocked Ofelia's sight, leaving only imagined images of her own deformity, and she pushed it off impatiently.

'When will they be back, do you think?' she asked.

Flora picked up the compress from the floor with her usual composure and took it over to the bench. The girl was so like Hamlet sometimes; no wonder she made him such a good wife.

'It shouldn't be long now,' she said, more to the herbs than to Ofelia. 'Hamlet was bidden to attend the peace negotiations and is determined to help conclude them swiftly. I have sent word that your fever has broken so he does not rush back needlessly. It must still be dangerous out there, with soldiers from both sides having flown from the battle, and he needs to stay alert.'

Flora began grinding her herbs again and Ofelia watched, lulled by the repetitive movements. Bebba spoke a few quiet words to her daughter and then slipped out of the door, doubtless to go and see to her estate. Ofelia thought of her quiet determination to create a beautiful palace here on a rugged seaside rock and admired her for it. It seemed there were more ways than marriage for a woman to make her mark on the world. If Ofelia could not fight again she should think on that, though it seemed an awful lot harder work than the heady rush of battle.

She must have slept again for she woke to see Bebba had returned and was speaking urgently with Flora.

'How far away?' the young woman asked and Ofelia felt a rush of joy, swiftly chased by fear.

She put a hand to her face but the bandages were still in place. Good. Flora sensed the movement and turned to her.

'The men are on their way back. Scouts have seen my father's banners so we can expect them soon.' She looked to Bebba. 'Do you think Udela will be with them?'

'Not if she is married – she will be gone to Dal Riata.'

'I suppose that will please her,' Flora said, a little forlornly, and it struck Ofelia anew how odd this woman's world was. She might not have returned from battle but only if she had been dispatched to the gods, never to go and live out her earthly life in a spouse's land. A memory surfaced sharply in her mind – a pair of jade green eyes staring blankly up at her from the mud. She swallowed.

'I think you may see her back, Flora,' she said. 'I believe Prince Gartnait was killed.'

'Really? How do you …' Ofelia looked to the ceiling beams where myriad bundles of herbs hung from orderly hooks. 'You mean, you killed him?'

'I had to. It's battle, Flora.'

'It's pointless.'

'It is not. How else can we defend ourselves?'

'Or attack others?'

'One side always has to attack.'

'Why? Why do they? If no one attacked, no one would have to defend and then everyone could just live their own lives in their own lands and be content.'

Ofelia opened her mouth to protest against Flora's naivety but there was a certain logic to what she'd said and Ofelia's brain was still too befuddled to counter it.

'Maybe with the peace negotiations concluded they can now,' she said eventually.

'Let's hope so,' was the curt reply and Ofelia felt sorry for having upset her kindly nurse.

Flora had been nothing but good to her. If she'd spoken true earlier then she knew that Hamlet had been with Ofelia since his marriage and it would have been so easy for her to take quiet revenge. The wrong herb here, the wrong potion there, and Ofelia would have departed this world with no one apparently to blame but the warrior who'd inflicted the original wounds. And yet here she still was.

Mind you, if pretty Flora had seen the mess her face was now perhaps she thought herself secure in Hamlet's affections, especially while ripe with his child and with her own pretty features glowing as if lit from within.

'I'd like to get up,' said Ofelia.

Flora looked at her.

'You couldn't even get to the pot.'

'Not fully up, but onto a stool. Please, Flora. I don't want to greet them home while confined to bed like an invalid.' Flora sighed but came over and drew back the covers to help her. 'And can I get dressed?'

'I have a robe that . . . '

'Properly dressed. In a tunic and trews.'

'A gown would be easier with that wound.'

Ofelia grimaced.

'Then Hamlet would think I had been replaced by someone else.'

Flora laughed.

'I doubt that but it might shock him. Have you never worn a dress?'

'Not since I was nine.'

'Of course. Hamlet told me about your mother.'

'He did?'

'Yes, and I'm very sorry. It was an unforgivable thing for her to do.'

'You . . . you think so?'

Ofelia was stunned to hear this opinion expressed. She felt the little herbery blur around her, the plants seeming to dance and whirl, and clutched for Flora's hand to steady herself.

'Yes, I do. She was grieving, of course, so perhaps she was not in her right mind, poor woman, but she should not have left you and Lars. That was not right.'

Ofelia held on tighter. She looked up at Flora and slowly the plants seemed to fall still.

'Everyone said it was a glorious act – the ultimate sacrifice. A woman who follows her husband into death will feast with him for all eternity.'

'In which case, it seems to me that it was you who made the sacrifice.'

Ofelia felt tears fill her poor overworked eye again. For so long the ducts had been sealed by the fire but her damned injury seemed to have broken them open and they were becoming far too active.

'You really think that, Flora?'

'Don't you?'

'I don't know. I don't believe I thought about it at all, just felt, felt . . .'

'Betrayed?'

'Angry.'

Flora nodded slowly.

'You were right to be. What your mother did was selfish and irresponsible and cruel.'

'Flora,' Ofelia heard Bebba warn her daughter in a low voice, but no warning was needed. They were the most glorious words Ofelia had ever heard.

'It's all right,' she said, using Flora's strong arms to pull herself to standing. 'It's all right, Bebba. Flora speaks true and I bless her for it.' She looked at her nurse. 'You are a remarkable woman, Flora, and I am so, so glad that Hamlet has you to care for him for you will do it ten times better than I ever could. Thank you.' Flora looked bewildered. 'Truly, thank you.'

Ofelia put an arm around the girl and hugged her. Flora responded, pulling her into a ready embrace, and Ofelia drew in the soft feel of her and wondered if she'd ever been held in this easy way before. For a moment she caught the threads of a memory of her mother before she had run into death's fiery embrace but it dispersed instantly and she pulled back and straightened her shoulders.

'Tunic and trews?' she asked.

'If you must,' Flora agreed and went to fetch them.

It took some considerable effort to get Ofelia dressed but by the time Aethelfrith's triumphant party rode into Bebba's burgh she was seated on a high-backed chair fetched from the great hall especially and padded with rich furs as if she were a queen and not a mere, deformed soldier.

Flora and Bebba went out to greet the men and Ofelia was left alone for a seeming eternity before at last a shadow fell across the doorway. She looked up, expecting Hamlet, but saw Flora standing there instead, looking as dazed as a dormouse facing the spring sun.

'What is it?' Ofelia asked.

'It's Hamlet.'

'Is he well?'

'Quite well, yes. He's ... '

'He's what?' Ofelia demanded.

'He's got someone with him.'

Ofelia frowned. What on earth had got into her nurse?

'Who? Who's he got with him?'

'His wife.'

Now it was Ofelia who gaped. She stared at Flora who stared back.

'But *you're* his wife,' she stuttered eventually.

'It seems I am now *one of* his wives.'

'But ... ' Ofelia felt as shocked as Flora. 'He has married again?'

'He has,' said an all-too-familiar voice and suddenly there he was, next to Flora and drawing her into the herbery while casting guilty backward glances over his shoulder. 'I was forced to,' he went on, his voice so low Ofelia had to strain to hear it. 'Your father, Flora, was determined to seal the alliance with a marriage, and with all his sons dead King Aedan had only a daughter to offer.'

'But why you?'

'With Eamfrith sadly lost, I was the only kin to the king available.'

'Kin by marriage.'

'As I pointed out, but that didn't seem to matter to Aethelfrith. Oh, I don't know – it was a peculiar situation and I was distracted and it all happened so fast. I'm sorry.'

Ofelia looked from Hamlet to Flora and was struck by the absurdity of the situation.

'Well,' she said firmly, 'she cannot be as good a wife as the one you have already.'

Hamlet put his arm around Flora.

'That is very true, Ofelia. She does not in any way match up to Flora and I care not a jot for her.'

'Hamlet!' Flora protested. 'That's not very kind.'

Ofelia squinted at Flora. Goodness, the girl was too gentle for her own good.

'It's not meant to be kind, Flora,' Ofelia told her sternly. 'And you should be glad of that.'

Flora sighed.

'True. But ... '

'Besides, she's ancient,' Hamlet confided, 'and very grumpy and Christian too. She goes on about her damned god all the time. She even ...' He stopped himself. Ofelia was curious but he was too quick for her. 'But how are you two? I was so relieved when the message came that your fever had broken, Ofelia, and you look well. So much better than ...'

He shuddered.

'Than when my face was a gaping hole?' she suggested.

'A gaping, maggot-infested hole,' Hamlet agreed.

Ofelia felt sick.

'Maggots?'

'Fantastic creatures,' Flora said briskly. 'Part of the healing process.'

Ofelia put a shaky hand to her bandages.

'Are they still in there?'

'No! All gone. Your flesh should be knitting up nicely.'

'I will be hideous.'

'I don't think so. The wound did not touch your eye or your nose or your lips so there will be no evident deformity.'

'You said I might be squint.'

'A little,' Flora agreed awkwardly.

'But, then, you have always been a little squint,' Hamlet teased, and Ofelia smiled gratefully up at him. Gods above, it was good to have him back.

'Thank you, Hamlet,' she said.

'For what?'

'For keeping me alive.'

He smiled.

'It would have been a shame not to for you are so good at living, Ofelia.'

She felt another damned blush flare across her poor damaged face and pushed herself more upright in her chair.

'When do we get to meet this little Christian of yours then?' she asked.

Hamlet rolled his eyes.

'I know not. She has gone to pray. She likes praying. Loki knows why she has to do it so often. With only one god to pray to, he must be bored stiff of her damned voice.'

Ofelia grinned.

'I will look forward to asking her,' she said, and for perhaps the first time since she'd woken in Flora's beautiful herbery she felt a desire to be back out in the world again.

'*I* won't,' Flora said in a small voice, and Ofelia looked away as Hamlet gathered her in his arms and murmured reassurances.

The exchange of voices, low male butted up against higher female, was not as soothing as the lilt of mother and daughter earlier but it felt solid, real. Ofelia remembered Hamlet telling her he was done with her after the night of the arrows and tried to be glad of it. He belonged to Flora now and that was as it should be.

As for herself, he had saved her life and she should repay him with the sword she had sworn to him on Frey's boar way back in Denmark. She must get well and she must learn to fight again, to protect both Hamlet and the wife she had written into the runes of his dear life.

Chapter Twenty-three

Bebba's burgh, September 603

'It softens the skin?' Flora asked, eyeing up the small pot the trader was holding out.

'Truly, my lady, it does. It lets the belly spring back into place as if there'd never been a babe inside at all. My wife's birthed five now, the gods have mercy on us, and she looks as lithe as if . . . Well, I won't lie to you, my lady, she's not as lithe as when I first married her – but then, neither am I.' He patted his rolling gut and laughed. 'But you'd swear she'd only had one. And it's all down to this oil.'

Flora took the little pot.

'May I smell it?'

'Of course, of course. I'm no thief, my lady, just an honest trader selling honest products.'

Flora carefully drew the neat stopper and sniffed.

'Lavender?' she asked.

'Very soothing.'

'And is that dog rose?' She smelled again. 'And agrimony?'

'It is! You know your herbs. But there are a couple of other ingredients besides.'

'Which you aren't going to reveal to me?'

'I'd be a fool to, would I not?'

Flora smiled.

'You would. What price then?'

They set to haggling. Flora didn't really have the energy for it but she knew the worth of such a lotion and wasn't going to pay over the odds. She settled with the trader and moved away, looking for somewhere to sit for her back was aching and she needed the latrine again though she'd been just before they all came down to the beach market. She put a hand to her back and looked hopefully for a tree stump or mound. She had grown so large that she feared if she had to sit on the sand she might never get up again.

'A stool, Lady Flora?'

She looked around to see Lars coming towards her carrying a three-legged stood carved with a beautiful design of inter-twined leaves.

'You're a miracle!'

'Hardly. I spotted that you looked a little weary and had this to hand.'

He set the stool down, checking for an even spot, and then offered her his hand while she sank onto it. She let out a sigh of relief.

'Perfect. Thank you so much, Lars. Where did you buy this? It's beautiful.'

'It's yours.'

'Oh, no. I couldn't possibly ...'

'Please. I'd like you to have it. And it's from just over there so I can easily buy another.' He crouched down next to her. 'I find I am getting a little too stiff of limb to sit on the floor for knucklebones these days.'

'These days?' She looked at his bright face and golden curls and laughed. 'You are hardly old, Lars.'

'Maybe not but battle takes its toll on a man.'

Flora sobered.

'Too great a toll, I fear. I wish there were no wars.'

'Me too.'

'Truly?'

'Of course.'

'I don't think your sister would agree with you.'

'Perhaps not but Ofelia has ever sought danger. I would prefer to live my life as a simple farmer if I could.'

'So why do you not?'

'I will one day but for now I am sworn to Hamlet and must see him to his throne. Then perhaps he will let me retire to tend cattle and bore my children with tales of former glories that they will never believe of their dull old papa.'

Flora laughed.

'It sounds wonderful, but you will, you know, need a wife.'

Lars dug his fingers into the sand and sent it trickling through them.

'Plenty of time for that,' he said gruffly.

'No one has caught your eye?'

He shook his head and leaped up, shaking the sand from his hands.

'I'd best go and secure another stool before they pack up.'

Flora reached out for him.

'You don't have to, Lars. It is kind of you to lend me this one but you are welcome to have it back.'

'No. No, it is yours. Good day, my lady.'

And with a funny little bow he was gone, weaving off between the boats and the trestles full of goods until she could see him no longer. She looked down, confused, to his footprints in the sand but now Ofelia was coming over to her, brandishing a shiny knife.

'Look what I got, Flora. Is it not magnificent? The trader says it could cut a throat with only the slightest pressure.'

'Delightful.'

'*Useful.* What have you got?'

'Scented oil.'

'Delightful!'

'*Useful.* It softens skin. The trader sold it to me for my ever-growing belly but I thought of you too, of your ... '

'Shhh!' Ofelia threw herself down on the sand. 'No one else knows how ill my skin looks.'

Flora sighed. Ofelia still wore her bandages in public though they had, praise Eyra, been able to uncover her eye, which was unharmed save for a jaunty scar across the line of her eyebrow. Her jawline, too, looked to be mending only a little askew but the skin on her cheek was red-raw and criss-crossed with scar lines.

'You are a warrior, Ofelia, and you live amongst warriors who have seen all the horrors of the field. You think they haven't guessed what lies beneath the linen?'

'That's different from seeing it.'

'You will have to take the bandages off if you insist on going back to war.'

Ofelia shrugged.

'That will be different. No one will be looking at me when there's a deadly enemy to focus on. And when I come face to face with Feng he will think the forces of evil themselves have come for him.'

Flora sighed at Ofelia's bloodthirsty delight. Hamlet was preparing to sail on Denmark and although for a time Ofelia's injury had given Flora ammunition in her bid to delay the departure, the she-warrior had now declared herself fit. Plus, Aethelfrith, hot from his triumph against the Dal Riatans, was eager for further conquest and with his own lands secure had turned his rampant energy to Hamlet's concerns.

'You should strike now,' he'd told his son-by-marriage not long after Ofelia was first up and back dining in the hall. 'Hit Feng as he settles in for the Wild Hunt. All men are looking inwards to their stores and repairs at this time of the year and you can catch them by surprise. You could be on your own throne by Yule with Flora at your side.'

'And Mairi?' Hamlet had asked mildly.

'And Mairi, yes. In fact, it is useful you have her for maybe Flora should not sail, so near to her time.'

'You would have me leave your daughter here and make the Dal Riatan princess Queen of Denmark?'

Aethelfrith had at least had the grace to look discomfited by this. Mairi had been at prayer – as always – but Flora had been with them and he'd glanced sideways at her.

'Flora should be queen of course,' he'd said, 'but she can follow on with the child in springtime once you are secure and she can be welcomed in safety.'

'You're too kind, Father,' Flora had said.

He'd missed her sarcasm and, patting her leg, told her, 'Naturally I care for you, Flora, and would have you well looked after but if Hamlet waits until spring, Feng will be more firmly entrenched and his army stronger. It has been nearly a year since you landed on my shores, Hamlet, and you have done great work for me but now I must release you to fight your own battles.'

Hamlet had been tempted, she'd seen, but perhaps more from fear of Aethelfrith's loudly spoken opinions than from any true desire to hasten the attack.

'Do you want to be king?' she'd asked him in bed later on.

'I do! Of course I do. It is my wyrd and I will fight for it but I am a cautious man, Flora. Trying to seize a country, albeit your own, is no easy matter even with great men at your back. I must be sure conditions are right. Defeating Feng is one thing; winning over the people is another. Peder writes that Wiglek is throwing his weight around as Prince of Jutland and he is doubtless sowing all sorts of evil thoughts in people's minds to poison them against me. If I sail with an heir already born I am more likely to be accepted.'

'What if it is a girl?'

'It matters little. It proves my fertility.' She'd raised an eyebrow at him in the moonlight and he'd tugged her close. 'That's how it will look to them. I cannot wait to welcome our child, be it boy or girl, and would rather see it safely into the world than sail without you. I am, perhaps, too soft-hearted to be a great king.'

'Rubbish,' she'd told him. 'Kings *should* care, then they can tend their country rather than simply rule it.'

He'd kissed her then, over and over.

'As I've said before, Flora, wife, you are a wise woman. I will prepare to attack but will wait for you to birth the babe before I sail. Although,' he'd added, burrowing beneath the covers to tap on her belly, 'if you could hurry up, little one, it would help for Aethelfrith is right about catching Feng by surprise.'

Flora had laughed then but now, with the ships all but ready, the men eager for war and the babe still firmly inside her, it did not seem so funny. All eyes seemed to be fixed impatiently upon her and she was grateful that for today at least the market would distract them all.

'Perhaps we can try the oil later?' she suggested to Ofelia.

'Why not? It can't hurt. Thank you, Flora.'

Flora said nothing in reply but thought, as she had many times over these last weeks, how much softer Ofelia had become – not exactly caring but certainly kinder. At least she had with Flora. With others she could still be merciless and with one person in particular. Even now Flora saw Ofelia's eyes narrow as she spotted her favourite prey and wished she had the energy to get up and move away.

Princess Mairi was such easy meat for Ofelia. Hamlet's curious second wife was old – nearly as old as Bebba – and very thin with thick, straggly hair the colour of charcoal and ash. She was about as much of a threat to anyone as a scared mouse but it gave Ofelia great pleasure to toy with her.

'Mairi!' she called now, all fake cheer. 'Mairi, what have you bought?'

Flora fully expected the Dal Riatan woman to walk away as she usually did whenever Ofelia was near but to her great surprise Mairi hurried over.

'I've found a great treasure,' she said. 'A very great treasure.'

'You have? Where?'

'Over there, with the dark-skinned man near the shore. Have you seen Hamlet? I need silver urgently before someone else gets it.'

'What is it?'

Mairi looked dramatically from left to right and leaned in to hiss at them, ''Tis a piece of Christ's True Cross.'

'His cross?' Ofelia asked.

'The one he was crucified upon for our sins.'

'Really. Where was he crucified, Mairi?'

'In Jerusalem.'

'Where's that?'

Mairi frowned uncertainly and then recovered herself.

'The Holy Land, of course.'

'And where's *that?*'

'In the east somewhere. Far away. The man has sailed for weeks to bring it to these shores. He was heading for Dal Riata as he knows there are many people of the true faith there but he heard I was here and came to offer it to me first. Me! Imagine.'

'Imagine,' Ofelia said drily.

Flora longed to intervene but the two women loosed words at each other so fast that there was little chance.

'So I must secure it before anyone else does,' Mairi was insisting.

Ofelia looked out across the beach.

'I don't think there'll be much competition. Most people here can find bits of wood for themselves.'

Mairi glared at her.

'This isn't just a bit of wood, Lady Ofelia – this is a piece of the True Cross.'

'How do you know?'

'He has travelled many weeks and . . .'

'What does it look like then?'

'Like . . . like . . .'

'Like a piece of wood perhaps? Like this one, for example.'

Ofelia picked up a splinter of driftwood from the sand.

'No,' Mairi said, though she flushed darkly. 'Not like that. It is in a casket.'

'Ah! A casket! So if I, say, put this piece of wood in a casket, how would you tell the difference?'

'Because that is just an ordinary bit of wood.'

'No, it isn't. It's from Christ's True Cross.'

'It is not. You just picked it up from the beach!'

'As your precious trader probably picked his up when he landed this morning.' Ofelia turned to Flora. 'I think I might start trading, you know. Which way to Dal Riata? There are clearly riches to be made there.'

'Ofelia!' Flora said. 'Don't be cruel. This might well be a piece of this cross Mairi speaks of.'

'Thank you, Flora,' she said but Ofelia was far from done yet.

'Or it might not. It might, for example, be a piece of Yggdrasil – the great Tree of Knowledge.'

'Ofelia!' Flora snapped.

Poor Mairi looked close to tears and Flora felt sorry for her. She'd moped around Bebba's burgh looking miserable ever since she'd arrived. Hamlet had persuaded Aethelfrith to assign her her own little bower and she spent most of her time within it. Even her maid had left, romping off with a young soldier in need of a lively wife, and Mairi had made no effort to befriend anyone else. This morning was the first time Flora had seen her look animated and Ofelia was spoiling it for her. She reached for her purse.

'How much is he asking for it, Mairi?'

The woman fixed on her, dark eyes suddenly glittering with hope.

'Half a pound of silver.'

'How much?! Mairi, I could buy herbs to cure an entire army with that. Have you haggled with him?'

Mairi looked even closer to tears.

'You cannot haggle over a piece of the True Cross.'

'*I* can,' Flora said. 'Come on, let's go and find this trader and see if we can strike a deal.'

She pushed herself up off the stool with an involuntary groan and Mairi put up both hands.

'No, please don't. I'll find Hamlet.'

Ofelia, still lounging on the sand below them, laughed.

'There's no way he will give you half a pound of silver for a piece of wood.'

'It's *not* just a piece of wood!'

Mairi's voice was shrill now, desperate, and Flora tried to steer her away from the other woman.

'Ignore Ofelia. She's just a warrior. She doesn't understand these things. Come, where is this trader – let's talk to him.'

Mairi looked reluctant but the lure of the precious item was too much for her and she led Flora over to a tiny man with skin the colour of hazels and a long, thin moustache that he had oiled up on either side of his sly-looking mouth. Flora sat down her stool and looked him up and down.

'I hear you have a piece of Christ's cross for sale?'

'I do, my lady. Very special it is. Very precious.'

'May I see it?'

'Of course, of course. But do not touch it, please. It is old, very old.'

'How old?'

'Six hundred years, my lady.'

'Six hundred?' Flora considered the wood in the box, a mellow dark brown but far from the silver colour you usually saw in ageing wood. 'And it is from . . .?' She glanced to Mairi.

'Jerusalem,' Mairi supplied eagerly.

'Exactly,' the man agreed, nodding his head up and down so the curly ends of his moustache bobbed like squirrels' tails.

'What trees grow in Jerusalem?'

'Sorry?'

'Trees. What trees grow there?' He looked at her blankly. 'I am just wondering what tree this sacred wood came from.'

'Oh. Oh, I see. Yes. What tree ... Pine, I believe. Yes, pine.'

'Pine? But pine is a softwood.'

'Sorry?' he asked again.

'A softwood. It would never last six hundred years without treatment.'

'Jerusalem pine would.'

Flora had to admit he was a fast thinker. But not a clever one.

'A shame then that this is oak.'

'What? How do you know?'

'Does it matter? 'She turned to her companion. 'It's a fake, Mairi, a trick.' Mairi stared at her and then, to Flora's great surprise, frowned. 'Are you not glad we found out? You could have wasted so much money.'

'But I would have had a piece of the True Cross.'

'No, you would not. It is oak, you see, and ... '

'I see! I see, thank you very much. You are very clever and I am very lucky to be spared. Yes, I see!'

Her lilting voice reached a near-scream and Flora cowered back.

'What's wrong?' she asked.

Mairi shook her head and drew in a deep breath.

'I just thought ... oh, never mind.'

'But I *do* mind.'

'Very well then – I thought I'd found something precious in this godforsaken country. I thought it was a gift, a sign to me that I was doing the right thing here. And it was not. It was just a rogue taking me for a fool. And maybe I am; maybe I am a fool. I thought I could convert people, thought I could spread God's word, but no one is interested. No one!'

'I am interested.'

'You are?'

'I am. It sounds a very orderly religion.'

'Orderly?'

'Yes. Shall we walk?' People were staring at them and Mairi still looked red-faced and wild-eyed. Flora picked up her stool and took a few determined steps towards the edge of the makeshift market. 'It is very pretty along the beach,' she went on, 'and the midwives tell me I need to keep moving or the babe will never come.'

'Babe? Oh, of course. Does it hurt?'

'Not yet.'

'It will. It is God's punishment on Eve.'

'Who's Eve?'

'She was the first woman on earth,' Mairi said, allowing Flora to edge her past the outer line of trading boats.

'What did she do wrong?' Flora asked.

Mairi gave a sigh.

'Are you really interested?'

'Yes! We have so many gods and they all seem to work against each other and you can never be sure from one day to the next what will please them.'

'Christ is pleased if you come to him openly and humbly and repent your sins.'

'Sins?'

'Wrongdoings. Like stealing or coveting your neighbour's goods or adultery.'

'Adultery?' Ofelia asked, bobbing back up between them.

'Go away, Ofelia,' Flora said.

Ofelia ignored her.

'What's adultery?' she asked Mairi.

'Sleeping with another woman's husband.'

'Ah, I see! Like you have?'

'No.'

'Yes. Hamlet was Flora's husband and you slept with him.'

'I did not. I . . . I . . .'

Mairi ground to a halt. Ofelia's eyes glittered dangerously.

'He's not bedded you?' She looked triumphantly at Flora who couldn't quite believe it, though Mairi's red cheeks seemed to testify to the matter and Ofelia was in no doubt. 'Loki laughs,' she cackled, 'he's not made you his wife!'

'The priest made me his wife,' Mairi said coldly.

'Perhaps but you are not a *true* wife until the match is consummated. Did you repulse him too much for him to get it up?'

'Ofelia!' Flora protested.

'You are pretty old after all and if you're still a virgin you must be rather shrivelled and . . . '

'Ofelia!'

'It was my choice actually,' Mairi said icily. 'I told him I am given to Christ and he respected that.'

'He can't have been very tempted.'

'Ofelia, stop it,' Flora begged. 'You are being horrible.'

'So? Did you not hear her, Flora? Her marriage to Hamlet is as much a sham as that rogue's piece of cross. You should be delighted.'

In truth, Flora *was* delighted but it was hardly the time to say so.

'It is none of my business. Now go away and bother someone else, for I am talking to Mairi. Come, Mairi.'

She led the older woman determinedly out onto the stretch of beach away from Ofelia and everyone else.

'Wait til Aethelfrith hears of this,' Ofelia called, still bent on mischief.

'No!' Mairi spun back, looking genuinely terrified. 'No, you can't tell him . . . '

'Oh, I can.'

'But you won't,' Flora told her firmly, 'because if you do, who do you think will get into trouble?'

'Mairi, of course.'

'Think, Ofelia. Can Mairi insist on consummation? No. Can Hamlet? Aethelfrith will see it as his fault and he might fall out of favour – which would be good for none of us.'

'Perhaps she's put a spell on him.'

Mairi made a strange motion across her chest and gave a little whimper.

'Don't be silly, Ofelia,' Flora said and turned her back on her once more.

Really, the she-warrior could be so tiresome. It was convalescence that was the problem. Even now that Ofelia was getting back into training she was bored and restless and took it out on whoever she could, but picking on Mairi like this was hardly fair.

'She won't say a word,' Flora said to Mairi, fighting the urge to ask her how she could have resisted Hamlet and thanking Freya that she had. She felt remarkably bouncy suddenly and walked out along the beach, turning her face to the sea breeze and welcoming the soft give of the sand beneath her feet. 'So this Eve woman ...'

'She lived with Adam in the Garden of Eden,' Mairi said, reluctantly falling into step beside her. 'That was a paradise on earth with all they could want freely available save for one tree they were not allowed to eat from.'

'Why?'

'It was the Tree of Knowledge.'

'So why weren't they allowed?'

'Because it is better that some things are kept for God alone.'

'What things?'

'Bad things. Sins.'

'But surely if man has knowledge of sins he will learn to avoid them? Without knowledge he is helpless.'

'No, because God will protect him.'

'But why would he stop doing so just because we knew things? And did we not know some things, like which plants to eat and where to find water and ...'

'Yes, of course. We could eat all the plants there save for the Tree of Knowledge.'

'So there was no arsenic?'

'Sorry?'

'If you eat arsenic it kills you. Was there, then, no arsenic in the Garden of Eden?'

'I suppose not. Look, Flora, thank you for your interest but I think you're concentrating on the wrong things and not grasping the point of this story.'

'Which is?'

'Which is that the serpent tempted Eve to want knowledge and she ate of the tree and persuaded Adam to eat of the tree too and God sent an angel . . .'

'A what?'

'An angel. A pure being in white with a halo of gold around his head to mark him out for his goodness.'

'Right. That must have surprised them.'

'I imagine so for the angel cast them out of paradise to do battle with the forces of evil.'

'Oh. That was a bit harsh.'

'Maybe, but it turned out well in the end because God sent his son Jesus to live as a man and to die upon the Cross to save us.'

'Save us from Adam eating the fruit?'

'Yes.'

'Even though *we* didn't eat the fruit?'

Mairi frowned.

'We did in the sense that all humans are weak. We are all tempted and all eat of our own particular fruit.'

Flora considered this. It seemed a strange, mixed up religion to her.

'So God sent his son to be a man and to die as a man to stop the punishment that he'd come up with in the first place?'

'Sort of. He sent His son to save us.'

'That's nice.'

Mairi beamed.

'Isn't it! So you see . . .'

'But then the son became a god again?'

'Yes. He was dead for three days and three nights and on the third day He rose again. It was a miracle.'

'Not really.'

'What?'

'Well, it wasn't really a miracle because he was a god in the first place. It would have been more peculiar if he hadn't gone back to that, wouldn't it?'

Mairi gave a deep sigh.

'I don't think you're understanding this properly, Flora.'

'Well, I don't think you're explaining it properly, Mairi.'

It wasn't like Flora to snap but really Mairi was infuriating. Flora *was* interested in Christianity. Lots of people seemed keen on it so it must have something to offer but the way Mairi explained it, it made no sense.

'Why is there still sin then, if Christ died to save us?'

'Because men are weak and women more so.'

'Mairi! That's not true. If that's what Christianity teaches then I want nothing to do with it.'

Flora glanced back down the beach. With all the conversation she hadn't noticed how far they'd come. The boats looked very small as they began to push out into the light waves, market over. There were only a few people left below Bebba's burgh and even they were turning for the cliff path.

'I'm tired,' she told Mairi. 'I'm going to rest a while.'

Blessing Lars for the stool she still held, she set it down and sank gratefully onto it. Her legs felt limp and her back sore and as she sat she felt her baby kick out. She rubbed at her belly.

'All is well, baby. Mama's here. Rest awhile.'

The baby, though, seemed to be turning somersaults. Mairi stood over Flora and looked down at her.

'It's moving.'

'Yes.'

'That's disgusting.'

'It's perfectly natural, Mairi.'

'It's still disgusting. How do you bear it?'

'Bear having a life growing inside me? I love it. I feel very blessed. The gods have granted me a part in the act of creation and I am honoured by them. They will see me safe.'

'Your gods will?'

'They stand more chance than your woman-hating White Christ.'

Mairi huffed.

'You have misunderstood me, Flora. It is not that . . . '

But Flora put up a hand to silence her. Her head felt light and her belly was churning with more than the babe. She felt two parts hungry and three parts nauseous and looked up the beach towards Bebba's burgh. Even the great rock looked small from this distance and she wondered a little desperately how she was ever going to get back there. Perhaps she just needed more rest.

She closed her eyes and concentrated on murmuring soothing words to the babe who slowly settled and grew still once more. Her belly itself, however, seemed to pulse occasionally. It was not a cramp, nor she was sure a birthing pain, but maybe a sort of practice.

'Not here,' she muttered to her belly. 'Please, not here.'

She looked again towards Bebba's burgh. Surely someone would notice she was gone and come looking for her? But the men, Ofelia included, would be training and her mother would have much to do sorting the supplies bought at market. No one would really miss her until the evening meal and that was some time away yet.

But she wasn't alone out here, she reminded herself. She looked round for Mairi but the other woman was up in the dunes. She seemed to have found herself some driftwood and twine and had fashioned them into a rough cross and stuck it up on the rise of the dune. She was on her knees before it, hands clasped together and face turned to the skies, lost in her own world, and Flora was reluctant to disturb her. A little more rest would do her good anyway.

The next twinge, however, was stronger than the last. Flora was no expert but she'd heard enough birthing tales to be pretty certain what was happening. She pushed herself to standing.

'Mairi!' The woman on the dunes did not seem to hear her. 'Mairi!' she called louder. 'Mairi, please help me.'

'I am at prayer.'

Mairi didn't turn around and her voice floated, almost ghostly, down the sand.

'I think my baby is coming.'

Mairi paused at that and looked over.

'Your act of creation?'

'Yes, I suppose so. Mairi, I need to get back.'

'That's fine. Go ahead.'

'But . . . '

'It's not far, is it? I'm sure your gods will protect you.'

'Maybe they have sent you to do that?'

'Why on earth would they send me?'

Why indeed? Flora thought. She looked down the beach again. Mairi was right. It wasn't far. And these things took ages. She'd heard women complain of that time and again. If she went slowly she would do well enough, though an arm would be so good to lean on.

'Mairi, please . . . '

But the other woman was lost in her prayers once more and did not even turn around. Well, fine, Flora thought, if that was the way Christians behaved she was glad she wasn't one. Picking up her stool in one hand and grasping her poor, pulsing belly in the other, she turned her feet up the beach towards Bebba's burgh and her face up to Frigga, mother of the gods, to beg for mercy.

Frigga, however, was in a recalcitrant mood. The pains came quicker and lasted longer. Flora felt the dizziness close in and turned her face down to the sand. She found the footprints she and Mairi had left on their way out and followed them one after another after another. Still, though, the shelter of the old rock seemed far away. She cried out but the boats were long gone and the sands empty and the sea breeze snatched at her shouts of distress and carried them out across the waves where the seagulls flung them mockingly back at her.

'I'll get you there, baby,' she muttered. 'I'll get you there safe.'

But the sand seemed to be sucking at her feet and the sea to be laughing at her and the only thing she had to clutch to was the stool that grew heavier and heavier until, finally, she had to drop it. It fell with a thud and, with another, she fell after it.

*

'Flora! Oh, gods help us, Flora! I have you. Here, I have you safe.'

'The baby,' she gasped to whoever was leaning over her.

'Is it on its way? Don't worry. I'll get you home.'

Strong arms went around her and she felt herself being lifted up.

'I'm heavy.'

'And I'm strong. We can do this. Hold onto me.' She slid her arms around a thick neck and opened her eyes to see Lars looking down at her, his fine blond hair like an ethereal haze around his head. 'I saw you from the watchtower. I thought you were a seal at first. What are you doing out here alone?'

'Not alone. Mairi ... I was with Mairi. But she ... She had to pray.'

Another cramp came, the most intense yet, and she screamed against it but Lars held her tighter and kept on moving forward. She felt the motion of his walk change as he left the sand and hit the rock of the cliff path. She was nearly there, nearly home.

'The stool, Lars. I dropped the lovely stool.'

He laughed, a soft, reassuring sound.

'Never mind about the stool.'

'But I like it.'

'I'll fetch it.'

'Promise?'

'I promise. Let's get you safe first.'

Safe – such a wonderful word, especially spoken in his low, steady tone. When the next spasm came she bit down against it. Her back felt as if someone were stabbing hot needles into it and her whole body shook. She felt a pain between her legs and squeezed them together.

'I think it's coming, Lars.'

'Just a few moments more. Help!' he called over her head and she heard voices and, praise the gods, the creak of Bebba's burgh's gates and over the top of it all her mother's cry.

'Flora! Oh, my sweet Flora.'

She reached out for her.

'It's coming, Mama.'

'Good,' Bebba said, firm and sure. 'That's good. It will soon be over.'

Flora felt Lars set her down on furs and wondered where she was but there was no time to care because this baby might have been slow deciding to enter the world but, mind made up, it was in Loki's own hurry. She grabbed at the furs and looked into her mother's eyes and pushed down with all her might. She felt as if she were being ripped apart and had to battle to keep on pushing against the agony but then she felt it all give way and heard, like the rasp of a seagull only fifty times sweeter, the cry of her child.

'It's a girl,' Bebba said. 'It's a beautiful Princess of Denmark.'

She lifted the little creature into Flora's arms and all the pain and the fear and the struggle melted away on the instant. The gods had not sent Mairi to help her but they had sent her Lars and now she looked up to see Hamlet rushing in, beaming wonderingly at her, and knew herself to be blessed indeed.

Chapter Twenty-four

'You!'

Mairi squinted into the low sun and saw someone marching furiously towards her. Oh, no – it was that Ofelia woman, the she-warrior with her shaved head and her criss-cross bandages. Why did she have to seek her out now, when she was glowing from prayer? She watched the other woman strut her arrogant, wide-legged walk towards her and shivered. Damned pagans – all they cared about was war and sex and feasting. They'd even fooled themselves into thinking that's what they'd find in the afterlife.

Mairi allowed herself a soft laugh under her breath. Ofelia and her kind were going to have a long time to rue their ignorance when the hellfires licked at their over-indulged bodies – and it served them right. Not one of them had listened to her or, if they had, it had only been to ridicule and pick silly holes in her theology. Their minds must surely be smaller than Dal Riatan ones for they could not grasp the simple principle of the Holy Trinity. Even Flora, who had seemed at least vaguely intelligent, had just niggled at inconsequential details and failed to see the most important thing: the glory of God's love for man, made manifest in Christ's great sacrifice upon the Cross.

'You could have killed her!' Ofelia seemed to be screaming. 'You could have killed them both.'

She was waving her arms about and ranting like a mad thing but what on earth was she talking about? Killed who? Mairi wouldn't kill anyone; she was a Christian.

She looked around for escape, furious at having her peaceful walk disrupted in this way. She had communed with God in the dunes, truly felt Him blessing her for the first time since she'd come here, and then He had sent this beautiful sunset, soft with the pinks and oranges of the Holy Land and shot through with the scarlet of His blood, to bolster her on her walk back to the dark rock of Bebba's burgh. She had been walking more and more slowly, reluctant to return to Aethelfrith's raucous warriors' hall, but now it seemed one of his damned warriors had come to her.

'Good evening, Lady Ofelia,' she said stiffly as the woman – if woman she was – came stomping up to her.

'It is *not* a good evening. Or, at least, it nearly wasn't. And all thanks to you.'

Mairi looked to God's marvellous sky, fading now to the thinnest line of pink, and prayed for calm.

'I'm not sure of what you are speaking, Lady Ofelia. I've been out in the dunes for some considerable time and have done nothing.'

'Yes, nothing!' the madwoman spat and now she drove a sharp finger into Mairi's chest. 'That is exactly what you did – nothing! You wrapped yourself in your bloody selfish prayers and left poor Flora to walk home alone even though she told you that she had birthing pains. Who does that, Mairi? Who neglects another woman in that way?'

Mairi felt a nasty tug of guilt. She did remember Flora saying something about wanting help back to the royal estate but she had hardly been insistent.

'I didn't realise. I was . . . '

'Praying. Of course you were. You know, Mairi, if you turned your eyes away from your bloody heavens and onto your fellow humans for a moment, you might be a better person. I thought your Christ preached love and care? I thought he died to save mankind?

Was that so mankind could float around ignoring each other and looking only to him? Was it?'

'No! Is Flora well?'

'She is. No thanks to you. She is mother to a beautiful girl – a Princess of Denmark and Bernicia.'

'Praise God!'

'No, Mairi, praise Lars. He saw her on the beach, collapsed from exhaustion and in great pain, in the final stages of birthing. If it had not been for his sharp eyes and swift action she would have birthed that princess alone, on the dirty sand. She could have died. They *both* could have died. And it would have been your fault.'

'I'm sorry.'

'So you should be. Hamlet is furious. You neglected his wife – his true, loved wife, not his pretend virgin one – in the most callous possible way. You think your precious prayers are the most important thing in the world but they're not. They're as empty as that stupid piece of wood that clever trader tried to flog you earlier. Open your eyes, Mairi – your faith is a fake.'

'It is not!'

'It *is*. And, worse, it's blinding you to the really important things in life – friendship and decency and love.'

'Love?' Mairi looked at the ragged woman before her. Her cropped hair was growing back in spikes around her head and the bandages on her face had come loose in her fury and fallen away to reveal puckered, ugly skin. Who was she to lecture Mairi in this way? 'What would you know about love?' Ofelia froze and Mairi pressed home her advantage. 'If I am unnatural then you are even more so, dancing around in trews, brandishing your sword as if you're so clever – and for what? Because you're every bit as scared of getting close to people as I am. I've watched you, Lady Ofelia. You live on jokes and insults and showing off your physical prowess. Well, you don't have to have a sword to be strong, you know.'

'I know that.' Ofelia's hand went to her scabbard but thankfully she didn't draw it. 'But fighting is *my* strength and I see no reason not to make the most of it just because I have a womb.'

'A womb as empty as my own.'

'By my choice.'

'Are you sure?'

'I'm sure. And I don't need a sword to fight.'

She bunched her fists threateningly and Mairi shrugged.

'Fine. Fight me. Kill me if you wish. Perhaps I deserve it.'

'You do.'

'Go on then.' Ofelia glared at Mairi in the last glimmers of sunset and Mairi folded her arms. 'Don't you dare?'

'Oh, I dare all right!'

Suddenly Ofelia was upon her, slapping her and spitting at her. Caught out, Mairi stepped back and fell over Ofelia's carefully positioned foot, landing flat on her back. The breath was knocked out of her but there was little time to snatch it back before Ofelia was straddling her, grasping at her dress to yank her up, fist raised in readiness. Mairi closed her eyes.

'Hail Mary, Mother of God. Hail Mary . . . '

'I'll knock your bloody prayers right out of you, Princess Mairi. No, not princess. You are not a princess. You're scum. You . . . '

'Ofelia, let her go!'

Ofelia hesitated and Mairi seized the chance to yank herself free. She tried to roll away but she was still trapped between the she-warrior's powerful knees and could only cover her face with her arms and pray for God to save her. It was not God who pulled Ofelia away, however, but Hamlet.

'That's enough, Lia.'

'It's not, Hamlet,' Mairi heard Ofelia protest furiously. 'It's not enough. She's a nasty piece of work and she deserves a battering.'

'Maybe, but it is not your place to give it.'

Mairi's heart quailed. She'd thought herself saved but did Hamlet just want to take revenge on her himself? He, at least, had the right to beat her but that did not stop the fear of it searing through her. Christ endured crucifixion, she reminded herself, but it seemed small consolation.

It was almost dark now, just the sheen of the low moon across the water lighting up the silhouettes of Hamlet and Ofelia as they faced each other above her. If she crawled away they might not find her. She could hide in the dunes and then head north. It would be a hard journey. A penance. A pilgrimage even. If she walked far enough she would surely find a nunnery and could beg them to let her join their community. It was like a ray of hope in the night and she clutched at it and began, slowly, to creep across the sand.

'Not so fast, Mairi. I'm not done with you.' Hamlet was over her in an instant. She heard Ofelia trudge away but could focus on little but her husband's furious face, ice-pale in the moonlight. 'Stand up.'

She scrabbled to her feet.

'I'm sorry, Hamlet. I didn't realise Flora was so close to her time.'

'She told you she was.'

'Then I didn't hear.'

'You mean, you didn't *want* to hear.'

'No, I ...'

'Silence!' There was a knife-edge to his voice that Mairi had not heard before. 'You have offended me, Mairi, in so many ways. Yet I have been patient with you. More, I think, than many men would have been. Have I not? Have I not, Mairi?'

He grabbed her arm, twisting it behind her, and she cowered before him.

'You have ... truly you have, Hamlet.'

'And how have you repaid me? By refusing to talk to my people, by refusing to help with even the simplest tasks on the estate, and by locking yourself away with your precious three-way god as if we are nothing to you. Nothing! Do you think your father would be pleased? Do you think he would consider you to have done your duty by him? Upheld the alliance that is keeping him and his people safe from King Aethelfrith's might? Do you?'

Mairi shook her head.

'No. I have sinned. I . . . '

'Not sinned, Mairi. This isn't about religion. It is about simple humanity. You think we are "pagan", that we are ignorant, violent, cruel even but not one other person in all of Bebba's burgh would have left Flora to crawl along the beach alone. Not one.'

'I'm sorry. Truly. I was stupid.'

'You were cruel.'

She gasped.

'Not that. I'm not cruel. I didn't realise she needed me.'

'Which was cruel. You were too caught up in God to pay attention to man. This has gone too far.'

'What do you mean?'

'You are lost in the heavens and need to return to earth.'

'How?'

'Take off your dress.'

'No, Hamlet, I . . . '

'Take it off! I am your husband and I command you to take off your dress.'

'No. I don't want . . . '

'Enough, Mairi! It cannot always be about what you want. Your precious god put you in this world and you must fit into it. Take it off.' Mairi fumbled for her ties. Tears clouded her eyes and she felt giddy with fear. 'For Frig's sake!'

Hamlet drew a long knife from his belt and, yanking her arm behind her again, put the blade to her neck. Mairi felt the metal ice-cold against her skin before he twisted it and cut down, ripping the fabric apart. He let go and grabbed the dress instead, tearing it from her.

'I will put a baby inside you, Mairi, and then we will see if you "realise" what Flora went through.'

'No!'

'Yes! You are my wife in name and must be so in flesh if this is to work. Perhaps then you will try to be a part of my world – to help me as you should. As you *must*.'

Again the knife slashed and now her shift fell away and she was left naked before him.

'Hamlet, I'm sorry. Truly. Please don't do this to me. Not here, like a beast.'

'But you *are* like a beast, Mairi.' Hamlet's voice was icy. 'On your knees.'

'No, please.'

'On your knees, beast!' He pushed her to the ground and yanked her up by her waist so that she knelt before him. 'You are a woman, Mairi, not one of your damned angels. You are flesh.'

Mairi buried her face in the sand. The granules filled her mouth but she bit down gratefully on them. This was her scourge, her punishment. It was right. She deserved it. But, oh, dear Lord, could she bear it? She felt his hands thrust between her thighs, pushing them apart, and fear engulfed her.

'I'm sorry,' she babbled. 'Truly, Hamlet, I am sorry. I apologise, I do. Not to God, not to Christ but to you. To you and to Flora. Please, Hamlet, please let me apologise to Flora.'

'Oh, I will. Later. Afterwards.'

'Afterwards,' she repeated, more a moan than a word.

She swallowed and closed her eyes but nothing happened. There was a long silence then she heard Hamlet sigh.

'You're not worth it. Get up.'

'What?'

'Get up. Look at us. Look at *me*! I told you before, I'm no rapist and you nearly reduced me to one. Here.' He shoved her torn shift at her and she sat up and grabbed at it. Sand filled her mouth, her hair, her eyes. It ground against her skin and she welcomed the roughness. 'Come back to Bebba's burgh.'

'No. Leave me here. I'm not worth it, you said so yourself.'

'But you are still my wife, of sorts. I told you, Mairi, no one in this estate full of people you despise so much would abandon a woman in distress and I am no exception. Come.'

He pulled her to her feet and draped the ripped dress around her like a robe then nudged her towards the great rock.

'Tomorrow,' he said as she shuffled at his side, 'you will go and see Flora. You will apologise to her and do homage to our daughter. You will do it first thing, *before* you pray. Understand?'

She nodded.

'Speak, Mairi. You must not hide in silence any longer. It offends me.'

'I understand.'

'Good. And then you will pack. We sail to Denmark as soon as the tides favour us.'

'Yes, Hamlet.'

So this was it then, this was to be her fate. She was to sail into the pagan lands, shamed and hated. Christ was jeered when he rode into Jerusalem on a donkey, she reminded herself, but she was not Christ and was no longer sure He was walking with her on this terrible path down which she had turned. Hamlet had spared her again but it felt little like escape and she would gladly have taken her own shamed life this very night if suicide had not, Lord help her, been the greatest sin of all.

PART THREE

Chapter Twenty-five

The Northern Seas, September 603

Ofelia looked out across the great stretch of the Norwegian coastline and felt her whole being swell with the beauty of it. The breeze off the sea was coldly crisp but it flooded into her lungs, as heady as the finest wine. She drank in the sight of the myriad rocky islands and the quiet way the flat sea eased between them and knew that she was almost home at last. This was what she had missed.

Bernicia was a wonderful place, save that there was so very much land to it. Even at the coast great rocks like Bebba's burgh insisted on imposing themselves on the landscape as if bullying the sea into submission. In the Baltic lands of home, however, land and sea existed in perfect harmony, one giving way easily to the other. As Ofelia studied them with rising joy she knew that she had been far too long off the whale roads and felt herself coming truly alive once more. This was what she'd been saved for at the Battle of Degastan. This was why she'd fought her way back to health. She was going home to Denmark and she was going to take it and make it their own. Hers and Hamlet's, to rule as king and constable.

It didn't sound quite right somehow. Ofelia glanced back down the boat, reluctantly taking in charcoal-haired Mairi huddled in the stern and blonde Flora dead centre, seated with her baby below the mast on some sort of fancy chair that Ofelia was sure threw out the balance of the boat. Here were Hamlet's wives – his queens once she'd made him king – and it wasn't right having them on board. It made them all vulnerable. What if there was an attack? What use would they be then? They couldn't fight and, worse than that, would require valuable men to protect them.

Bloody Lars had sworn to Hamlet that he would be Flora's personal protector if she came with them, and Hamlet, the fool, had accepted. It made no sense. Why not leave the womenfolk safe in Bernicia until the warriors had secured Denmark and then call them over? But, oh, no! Hamlet had said there was no way he was leaving Mairi to 'mire herself deeper in Christian nonsense' and Flora had been determined to come too.

'You're only six days out of childbed,' Ofelia had told her. 'It's too early for you to sail. It will be a long journey and a hard one, with perils at the other end.'

'I can manage if you can,' Flora had said, looking pointedly at Ofelia's bandages.

'But think of the baby.' That at least had given Flora pause and Ofelia had tried to push home her advantage. 'It will be cold at sea and food will be limited.'

Flora had thought about it, peering down at her child with the sort of doe-eyed devotion that seemed obligatory in new mothers. Hamlet had watched her in much the same way and it had been all Ofelia could do not to vomit on the pair of them, and the baby besides.

'She won't be cold snuggled against me,' Flora had decided. 'And I will be feeding her so that will be fine too.'

'And if we are all massacred on arrival?'

'Ofelia! Is this conversation necessary?' Hamlet had demanded.

'I think it is. Flora needs to understand what might happen.

Obviously none of us wants to be brutally murdered but, you have to admit, it's a possibility.'

'We may be killed in battle, yes, but even Feng would not kill an innocent woman.'

'Or her royal baby?'

'*Girl* baby.'

'So? She still carries royal blood. Is not your own royalty, Hamlet, from your mother?'

He'd hesitated to reply but Flora had not.

'If you are all massacred, I would choose to be massacred with you.'

'Flora, that's madness.'

'Maybe but I want to come.'

She could be stubborn, that much was for sure, and so here she was with little Princess Bebba – named for Flora's mother because Hamlet had refused to give her his own treacherous mother's name – and both of them surviving the journey irritatingly well. Flora looked pale, yes, but it just made her blue eyes bigger and her fair skin more luminous, especially next to Ofelia's.

She had cast off her bandages the day they'd set sail. The skin beneath was no longer red but that was the best that could be said of it. A thin line ran from the edge of her eyebrow down to her now jagged jawline with a network of smaller lines leading off to either side, like the map of a river. In between, the skin was raised and puckered and although Flora's oil had perhaps done a little to soften it to the touch, it had done nothing to improve its appearance.

'It will keep it stretchy so that it continues to heal,' Flora had insisted but somehow Ofelia doubted it and had told her to keep the damned stuff for her belly. You couldn't go into battle smelling of lavender; it wouldn't be right.

She'd never felt more self-conscious than when she'd walked out of the barracks bare-faced for the first time since the horrors of Degastan and made for the boats. People had tried not to stare but had not really succeeded and it had been a relief when Eric had slapped her on the back and said, 'That should frighten Feng.'

'My thoughts exactly,' she'd agreed with a grateful smile.

'I think it suits you. You always looked deceptively nice before.'

'And now I look suitably hideous?'

He'd frowned at her.

'Not hideous, Ofelia. More sort of beautifully terrifying.'

She could almost have kissed him right there and then but had remembered herself in time and just given him a wink and set to checking the equipment. Now she looked around for him and saw him seated on the gunwales, polishing his sword. She moved closer.

'Good to be going home.'

'Very good,' Eric agreed. 'I can almost taste Denmark on the air.'

Ofelia nodded and sat by his side, leaning back to look down into the blue water as it rushed past the boat. The sea was thankfully flat but there was a fair wind to blow them down towards Zealand. So far, they'd stuck to the Norwegian coastline to avoid being seen by any Jutlanders on lookout. Both Hamlet and Ofelia hoped that their old countrymen would be loyal to them but with Wiglek at large there was no telling who had control anymore, or what spies might be about. Home was no longer home to them – or at least not yet. Now they would steer a course down the middle of the Kattegat Sea, hopefully out of sight of Jutland to the west and Skane to the east. If they got it right no one would spot them until they were less than a day from Helsingør on the far east coast of Zealand.

Feng would have little time to muster a decent defence and even if he did Hamlet and Ofelia had a plan. They'd sketched it out in the last evenings before departure. It had had to be once Flora was asleep and Hamlet was free of cooing-over-baby duties but all the same it had been the first time in ages that they'd been alone together and she'd treasured it.

'Are you sure you're up to this, Ofelia?' he'd asked over and over.

'I'm sure, Hamlet.'

'You were so sorely injured I thought you'd died, truly I did.

When I carried you back to Bebba's burgh it was only the burning of your poor fevered skin against mine that told me you were not yet gone but I expected it at any minute. I felt I was merely conveying you to Valhalla.'

'Or Hel.'

'Valhalla for sure. You fought like seven men, Ofelia.'

'How do you know? You were in another part of the field.'

'And never will be again. We should fight side by side. Always.'

That, Ofelia had thought, would be paradise indeed, especially if he fought on her uninjured side. Hamlet had said nothing about her face, just put his fingers to the scars, stroking them with a featherlight touch that had made them sing as if they were her most intimate parts.

'The marks of life,' he'd murmured.

'A constant reminder of battle.'

'A constant reminder of how nearly I lost you.'

That had made her stupid heart sing almost as much as the scar and she'd had to turn from him to hide it. She was his constable now, no more.

'About the fighting side by side idea,' she'd managed.

'What about it?'

'It might have to wait for one more battle.'

'Why?'

She'd explained her plan, though he'd resisted it at first.

'It's too dangerous, Ofelia.'

'It's our only chance,' she'd countered, and bit by bit as the fire burned low and others retired to bed around them he'd come to agree. Soon it would be time to put the scheme into action.

The boat was turning, pointing away from Norway and straight towards Zealand. If the wind stayed fair they would reach the little island of Anholt by morning and there they would part.

'Are you ready?' Hamlet asked now, coming to sit on her other side.

'Ready. Eric?'

Eric nodded.

'Ready and eager, constable. Let's kick some treacherous Feng arse!'

'That's the plan,' Ofelia agreed, grinning at Hamlet who gave a slow, sombre nod.

The problem, they both knew, was that landing even a skilled and well-equipped army on a beach was a precarious business. A relatively small landforce could wreak havoc on men trying to disembark and numbers of them might be lost before they could even form a shield wall to fight their way off the beach. If they did not secure a victory before Feng's reinforcements arrived all would most likely be lost. What they needed was the element of surprise and that was where Ofelia's plan came in.

She and Eric (it should have been Lars really but he was too insistent on his sworn role as bloody queen-protector) would take thirty men in the two lightest, fastest boats and sail from Anholt a few hours before Hamlet and the body of the fleet. Taking a Zealand-born pilot each, they would land unnoticed – or so they hoped – in one of the many private inlets along the north coast and make their way stealthily across land to Helsingør. When Feng's hastily mustered troops lined themselves up gleefully in the dunes to await Hamlet's attack, their arses would, if all went to plan, be quite literally there to be kicked. Or, rather, slashed. The enemy would be forced to turn and fight a rearguard action and Hamlet would be free to land and come swiftly to their aid.

It was, as Hamlet had said, dangerous. It was also, as Ofelia had said, their only chance. And besides, she had cheated death once and had no intention of letting it take her this time. With her feet on Denmark's dear soil at last she would be invincible. She was going to find Feng and she was going to kill him. No more princes – this time she wanted the king himself.

'You will be careful, Ofelia?' Hamlet asked her now.

'Of course. There are too many men relying on us for me to be anything else. Women too.'

Hamlet gave a dry laugh.

'If – *when* – this works, Ofelia, and I am king, I will grant you anything you desire.'

'Anything?'

She raised a suggestive eyebrow at him and he returned it with a look of dark longing that turned her insides upside down before she remembered she wasn't meant to be this way with him anymore. The problem was that her damned body didn't seem to be getting that message. Abstinence had heightened her hunger for something but for the first time ever she wasn't sure it was battle.

She looked guiltily over at Flora then caught herself. Guilt? That wasn't an emotion Ofelia had any time for. Mairi was the expert on guilt and at least now she had something to be guilty about. Ofelia hadn't spoken a word to the woman since she'd left her with Hamlet on the beach but she'd seen her creep back into Bebba's burgh, dishevelled and wretched, and hoped he had punished her appropriately. Flora might be soft and gentle and far too kind, but she was a good woman and Ofelia was determined to protect her. Not as determined as Lars was, mind you, and at least he wouldn't forget his duties in the heat of battle.

The loss of Earnfrith still haunted Ofelia at times, even though she knew it should not. She had not asked the boy to bring her water. He'd come onto the field of his own free will and she should not reproach herself. Guilt was pointless. It pulled you back into the past where nothing could be changed instead of setting you to the future where all was still to be won.

Determinedly, Ofelia stood up and went back to the prow, putting an arm around the figurehead dragon's carved neck and turning her face, with his, to the south and glory.

'Watch out, Feng,' she hissed across the waves. 'We're coming for you.'

Chapter Twenty-six

Helsingør, September 603

'Arses!' Eric whispered.

Ofelia jumped.

'What?'

'There – enemy arses. We've done it, Ofelia, we've found them. And look!'

He pointed out to sea where Hamlet's ships were hoving into view. The gods were on their side indeed for so far the plan had gone perfectly. Ofelia and Eric's pilots had steered them, unseen by any but a white-beard fisherman, into a small inlet less than a day's tramp from Helsingør. The small troop had unloaded and then, under the old man's astonished gaze, filled the boats with stones and sent them to the depths just above the tideline.

'Dig them up if you wish,' Ofelia had said to him as they'd hefted their packs and made for the dunes, 'but wait a few days, will you?' He'd nodded dumbly. 'The gods bless King Feng,' she'd said as an afterthought.

'And feast with King Otto,' had been the low and comforting reply.

The people had not, then, forgotten Feng's predecessor. If Odin willed it, they would hopefully welcome his son, and certainly when Eric had braved a small village to buy supplies that night he'd reported back to the others, hiding in the woods, that he'd heard grumblings about taxes and restrictions that had given them further hope. The people, it seemed, would be easily conquered, but first there was the battle to win.

Ofelia scanned the landscape from the old barrow grave she and Eric had climbed at the back of the low plain leading to the beach. Their men were still hiding in the woodlands behind but they'd wanted to check the lie of the land and it seemed they were in the perfect spot. Hamlet looked set to come ashore right in front of them and Feng's troops had all been led out of the safety of the royal estate and were hidden from the ships by tall grass. They were not, however, hidden from Ofelia's rearguard.

Odin wanted Feng gone, she knew; she could almost feel the power of Denmark's long-dead warrior masses pulsing from the grave beneath her. She stretched out her limbs, as she used to do, to absorb it into herself. She might not have joined the dead yet but they were welcome to join her if it meant victory over Feng.

'It's perfect,' she whispered to Eric, watching as the enemy soldiers pointed at the ships and nudged each other. Many drew their swords, eager to cut down the invaders though they would be some time landing yet.

This was the critical point. She and Eric must be patient and bide their time. Only when Hamlet's first warriors wet their feet in the shallow waves and Feng ordered his charge could they strike. Ofelia shifted in the grass. She hated waiting.

'Not long, Ofelia,' Eric murmured, putting a hand on her arm to still her. She nodded gratefully.

'You're a great warrior, Eric.'

'And a great lover?'

'That too.'

'Ofelia . . .' He shook himself. 'Oh, never mind. Let's get into the trees in case anyone thinks to look back.'

It was a long wait, far longer – or so it felt – than the whole day and night of creeping across country to get here. They dared not talk, nor eat, nor even polish their swords for fear of being caught at this critical point. But at last Ofelia crawled back up onto the barrow and saw Hamlet's ships so close that she could make out the lines of his dear face. He was looking up, right at the very spot where she lay. She longed to stand and wave, to let him know she would not fail him, but she dared not and could only pray he could sense her, here and ready.

She gave a low osprey's call to signal the men into position and felt them creep out from under the trees and fan out around her. Below them Feng's men were straining forward just as eagerly. Not one of them thought to look to their rear, so intent were they on the sweetly approaching shipfuls of vulnerable enemies. Perfect!

Was Feng there with them? She assumed Wiglek was in Jutland but the odds had to be reasonable that Feng was on Zealand and Ofelia eagerly scanned the lines for him. She could see no one in a crown or even a simple diadem but it would be just like him to hide amongst his men. Then again, he might be anywhere else in Denmark, miles from here and almost impossible to track down. They might be in for a long, slow war of attrition and Ofelia wasn't sure she could bear that.

Send me Feng, she prayed silently to Thor. *My sword itches for him; deserves him. It was my blade that changed Hamlet's wyrd to life and my blade that will bring death to his enemy.*

The sky seemed to darken, as if Thor had heard and was readying himself to help. The waves rose slightly and, with a crash, they threw the first of Hamlet's ships onto the shore. Flora and Mairi would be in the rear boat, kept safely out at sea until battle was won or they had to turn and flee. She assumed Lars was with them and was suddenly glad of it but there was Hamlet, leading the charge like a true king.

'Now!' someone screamed below them, shrill and twitching with anger. Ofelia was sure she recognised Feng's tone but there was no time to think about it.

'Now!' she echoed to her own men and, leaping up, she led the charge.

Feng's men were quick but they had sand beneath their feet where Ofelia's had grass, plus the slope to quicken their pace. Ofelia and Eric were upon the enemy before they were anywhere near Hamlet and their men had half of their opponents down before they even knew what had hit them. Those still standing hesitated and, caught between Ofelia's charge and Hamlet's swiftly arriving troops, many more were dispatched. Barely even the first boatful of Hamlet's men got a taste of the enemy before those of the king's men still left alive were throwing up their hands in surrender and falling to their knees amongst their lost comrades. Ofelia seized one by the collar.

'Where's Feng?' He stared at her, terrified. 'Where's King Feng?' she repeated. 'Where's the bloody king? Is he with you?'

The man nodded.

'He's here. Or he was. Who . . . who are you?'

She gave him a sideways leer through her scarred face and a slow wink.

'I'm Thor's pet witch.' He looked even more terrified. 'And I'm pleased with you – or I will be if you can sight me your cowardly king.'

The man, trembling visibly, cast around him and pointed suddenly back up the beach to where a thickset man in a plain tunic and simple leather jerkin was running for cover.

'Thor blesses you,' she threw at him and was gone after the king who hid as a peasant and ran as a coward.

'Ofelia!' she heard Hamlet call. 'Ofelia, we've won.' But they hadn't. Not yet.

She plunged into the dunes and saw the man darting sideways towards the woods in which she had herself hidden just a short time ago.

'Feng!' she called. 'King Feng . . . if king you are to flee the field.'

He turned, saw her lone figure coming towards him, and squared his shoulders defiantly.

'A king should live.'

'And a prince too.'

'What? Who are you?'

He took a step towards her, sword raised, and then, seeing her face, recoiled. Ofelia smiled.

'I am your wyrd, Feng – come and meet it!'

He fought well, she had to give him that, but she had Thor on her side and a sword fuelled by fury and a lust for vengeance and it was no contest. The door to the underworld felt well and truly open now but it was not Ofelia who would be stepping through it.

'Who are you?' he asked again as she stood over him, a foot on each broken hand and her sword raised for the final plunge.

She leaned down and looked straight into his terrified eyes.

'I am Ofelia, Feng. I am Lady Ofelia, come back to take Hamlet's crown for him – the one you are not even brave enough to wear before your men. Feast well in Hel, traitor!'

And with that, she pierced his neck and let his last breath gargle onto the sand in a crimson flood. She stood over him a moment, drawing her own breath and feeling the elation of victory start to well up inside her. No one would carry her from this battlefield! Then she stepped aside, cut Feng's head smoothly from his shoulders, and, lifting it by the hair, marched back onto the dunes.

'King Feng is dead,' she cried to the men on the beach. 'Long live King Hamlet!'

They turned, gasped, and then fell to their knees before Hamlet but he was already running – running to her.

'You are a marvel, Ofelia,' he cried, 'a marvel.' And at last it felt as if it might be true.

The moment they arrived at Helsingør it was as if they had never been away. Ofelia had always been scathing about the Zealanders before, scorning them for their many tiny differences from her own Jutish people, but now it felt glorious to simply be amongst true Danes once more. They marched on the estate with the captured warriors roped in a line behind them and Feng's head on a spear carried in front and the gates swung open immediately.

All were on their knees as they passed into the main compound, the servants in two lines to guide them to the great hall, and there in the doorway, also kneeling, was Hamlet's mother.

'Lady Gertrude,' he said coldly, stepping up so that he loomed over her.

'Hamlet, my son.'

'And king.'

'The gods be praised. I begged mighty Odin to keep you safe.'

'You might have been better begging your precious new husband – killer of your first.'

'Feng did not . . .'

'We all know what happened, my lady.'

He did not, Ofelia noticed, call her mother.

'It is in the past, Hamlet . . . my lord king. May I not be glad to welcome you now?'

'Certainly,' he said. 'You have little choice but to do so. Now, my men are hungry. My women too.'

'Ofelia is with you?'

'My constable, Lady Ofelia, is with me, yes.'

He looked around and Ofelia stepped forward, stubbly head held high and scarred cheek turned defiantly to Denmark's ex-queen.

'Welcome, my lady,' Gertrude managed, battling to hide her distaste. 'You fought bravely, I'm sure.'

'Ofelia killed Feng,' Hamlet said. 'I will be rewarding her with high honours.'

Ofelia held her head high as everyone stared curiously at this monster who was to help rule them but now Hamlet was ushering Flora forward with, in her shadow, Mairi, and the constable had to step aside.

'I present to you my wives, the new Queens of Denmark.'

'Wives?' Gertrude asked faintly.

'That's right. Won in alliance with powerful lands over the Northern Seas – alliances that will greatly benefit Denmark under my rule.'

Hamlet sounded every bit the king and Ofelia wondered how she could ever have doubted his desire for the throne. She watched as he led his queens forward and displayed them to the assembly.

'Princess Flora of Bernicia, my first wife. And our daughter, Princess Bebba.'

'A daughter?'

Gertrude leaned longingly forward but Hamlet pulled Mairi between her and her granddaughter.

'And Princess Mairi of Dal Riata in the Celtic lands.'

Mairi, Ofelia noticed, had unfurled a little in the sudden attention. She was standing tall for the first time since Bebba's terrible birthing and took her place at Hamlet's side with something like pride. How dared she? Ofelia thought bitterly. How dared she step up as Queen of Denmark after doing nothing but despise Hamlet and his people? How dared this interloper stand there in a place of honour before the Danes whilst she, Ofelia, was left to watch from the sidelines?

As if hearing her thoughts Hamlet beckoned her forward too but her place was behind the royals and, with Lars jostling to be near Flora, she was left at bloody Mairi's shoulder as Hamlet presented his tableau of power to the Danes. And so it went on. At dinner, a rough, awkward affair in which Hamlet held court over a strange group of servants and prisoners, Mairi and Flora sat either side of him and Ofelia was left at the end of the table with only the delights of tormenting Gertrude with her deformity to keep her amused throughout the interminable meal.

At least once the tables were pushed back Eric was there to make her laugh and a number of the prisoners came forward to say how glad they were to see her back and to have Hamlet restored to his rightful place as king. They would, of course, have to say that with their lives in his hands but they seemed sincere all the same, especially as more ale was sunk and rude, bitter stories about Feng's rule began to pour out. Even the mercenaries from Norway and Sweden, whose pockets had been lined with Feng's silver, seemed to have little good to say of him and were eager to swear fealty to Hamlet.

'The country is not won yet,' he said to Ofelia when he had time to seek her out a little later on. 'Wiglek is on Jutland with my stolen title and will not cede to us easily but we have the court and can make the rest follow, I am sure of it. I owe you a great debt, Ofelia.'

'You do,' she agreed solemnly.

'And will repay it. I will raise you to great honours, I promise. Your uncle Peder will be proud.'

'If he still lives.'

'I am told he does and we will find out for sure when we march on Jutland and secure it. We must go to all the islands, make certain of all the people. I will not be a king who hides away on his estates.'

Again Ofelia was struck by how he had grown into his role, as if the Danish soil had nourished him and let his royalty unfurl.

'You have thought about this a great deal?'

'Of course.'

Maybe, then, it was not Danish soil. Maybe Hamlet had been ready all along and it was she who was finally seeing it. Her body stirred and she had to fight it under control, forcing her back straight as a poker while she saluted him.

'It will be an honour to serve you, my lord king.'

He looked right into her eyes as if he could see everything she was feeling and was about to say so, but then Princess Bebba gave a high-pitched little gurgle and he turned her way instead. The baby had woken and Flora was feeding her right there with everyone looking on, apparently delighted by the pretty domesticity of the scene. Ofelia shivered.

'Go back to her, Hamlet. Go back to your queen. The first of your queens. The people should see you together.'

323

'But I'm talking to you.'

'We are done talking. Now, go!'

She gave him a little shove. He resisted at first but when she shoved him again, harder, he shrugged and turned away.

'If that's what you wish.'

It wasn't but she knew her place. It had been made abundantly clear to her at dinner and that was fine. It suited her. She didn't want to be at the centre of court life, having to look pretty and be nice to people all the time. She'd turned her back on all that when she'd refused, aged nine, ever to wear gowns again, and she'd been right to. Besides, she was tired. She'd killed a king today and she needed to sleep in a good, soft, gloriously Danish bed.

But somehow, when she finally tumbled into that bed, sleep would not come.

'Psst! Ofelia, wake up.'

'I wasn't asleep. Who's this?'

'Who do you think?'

She sat up and peered into the gloom of the barracks.

'Hamlet?'

Her body sang.

'I can't sleep.'

'Me either.'

'Come outside with me.'

She considered refusing but not for long. Slipping out of bed, she pulled on her trews and grabbed her sword belt.

'Shhh,' he cautioned as they slid between the other warriors' beds.

She giggled.

'You are king now, Hamlet, you don't need to sneak around. You can simply command.'

'I'm not used to that yet. And, besides, I like sneaking.'

His hand found hers and together they made it to the door and slipped out into the night. There were sentries either side but they bowed and turned their heads politely aside.

'Come on,' he urged.

'Where are we going?'

'Swimming.'

'What?'

'Swimming, Ofelia, in beautiful Danish waters.' He pulled her towards the main gates and waved them open. The guards rushed to obey. 'See, I *can* command.'

'And you choose to command *this*? You're mad, Hamlet.'

'I'm restless. I can't believe we've done it, Ofelia.'

They were beyond the estate now and wandering down the gentle slope towards the water. Ofelia thought of the steep cliff path at Bebba's burgh and couldn't quite believe it either.

'It was so easy,' he went on.

'It was so well planned.'

'That too. I am blessed in you, my warrior, my constable.'

'Your friend.'

'Friend,' he agreed, his voice husky.

He stopped suddenly and pulled her close against him. She felt his touch ripple through every tiny particle of her body and it was all she could do to stand stiff in his arms.

'Where's Flora, Hamlet?'

'She's asleep.'

'What if she wakes and finds you gone?'

'Then she'll understand. Besides, she has Bebba now. She's content.'

'Is a child so amazing?'

He looked out to sea for a moment and then said, 'It is, Ofelia. It truly is. It puts the world in place somehow. Perhaps because it gives you something more important than yourself to consider.'

'How can *that* be amazing?'

'Oh, Ofelia!' He broke the embrace to cup her face in his hands. It was her chance to step away but she could not find the will to do so. 'Maybe one day you will find out.'

She shook her head against his fingers.

'I'm not made for motherhood, Hamlet, as my own mother was not. I was never more important to Lady Sigrid than herself. Or, at least, than my father.'

'It was the action of a moment, Ofelia, a decision made on impulse and from grief.'

Ofelia shook her head again and put her hands to her ears to block out the scream that was forcing its way out of the land of the dead and heading straight for her heart.

'Oh, no, it was planned, I'm sure of it. She knew what she was going to do before they ever lit the pyre. She was fully prepared and she never . . .'

She heard her voice crack and clamped her lips shut on the scream that threatened to burst out of them. Hamlet leaned down and slow, softly, kissed them apart. She felt herself melt instantly at his touch. *You're just his constable,* she fought to remind herself, but it had been so long, so very long.

'Hamlet,' she moaned.

'She never what, Ofelia?'

'She never even said goodbye,' she choked out, and then he was kissing her harder, drawing her fiercely against him as if he would take her right into himself and she could resist no longer.

She kissed him back, gulping breath out of him as the scream receded. And as they fell to the sand she knew that now, at last, she was truly home.

Chapter Twenty-seven

Flora liked Denmark. She'd only been here three days but already she was impressed by the discipline and calm of the court. The kitchens were very well organised and the routines of the day were set out clearly and kept to with a strictness that was a balm to her orderly soul. The domestic staff had been keen to ask her opinions on their household management but they had everything in hand and she'd been pleased to tell them so.

Gertrude had retreated to her bower and it seemed everyone was happy to let Flora take her place so daily she toured the estate with Bebba on her hip and Mairi hovering behind like a nervous shadow. Then, once the sun had reached its height, they sat either side of Hamlet on a beautiful oak bench at the top of the great hall and received a steady parade of men and women keen to swear their loyalty to the new king and queens. It was very flattering and, as they all came with rich gifts to substantiate their words, exciting too. Flora had not felt she had lacked for jewels in her father's kingdom but in these first days in Denmark she had more than doubled her little treasury and had had to commission a casket in which to keep her new ornaments.

If she was honest with herself, as she tried always to be, Flora would have preferred not to have Mairi here, but the poor woman had been so apologetic about her conduct during Bebba's birthing, and was so clearly eager to make amends, that she hadn't the heart to shut her out and so they stood united in this country they now seemed to rule. Ofelia, of course, was disgusted with Flora's forbearance.

'How can you be so nice to that wretched woman?' she'd asked when they'd bumped into each other in the forge yesterday.

Ofelia had been commissioning a new dagger and Flora a fine roasting frame for the grand feast Hamlet was planning for his inauguration as king and they'd stood together over the fire as the smith had bowed and flushed with pleasure at his fine orders.

'She has said sorry, Ofelia,' Flora replied.

'And that makes all well, does it?'

'Not really but what more would you have her do? The past is determined and she cannot go back and change it. None of us can.'

'Don't I know it?' Ofelia had said darkly, staring deep into the heat of the fire, and Flora had taken her arm.

'If we forgive, Ofelia, we can move forward.'

'If we forgive, Flora, we expose ourselves to future hurt.'

Flora had shaken her head at her friend.

'Nonsense, Lia. We are always exposed to hurt but that doesn't mean we should go looking for it.'

'You are too gentle, Flora.'

'Or you are too harsh.'

Ofelia had laughed then.

'Or both. Perhaps it is as well. You can shape Hamlet's court and I can watch his back.'

'And Mairi?'

'She can pray. And, ideally, stay out of the way.'

Mairi, however, seemed to stick to Flora like a burr in a dog's fur. It was becoming increasingly annoying but when a dark-eyed man arrived in the hall, sending a shiver through the gathered courtiers, Flora was glad of her fellow queen's company on the exposed bench. She saw tension grip Hamlet's body as he strode to the front of the dais and looked down at the new arrival. The man dropped ostentatiously to the floor and crawled upon the bare boards on his hands and knees. At her side, Mairi gasped and clasped her thin hands together in something strangely like admiration. Flora pulled Bebba close against her chest and watched intently as the man drew closer.

'Lord Wiglek,' Hamlet said coldly and now she understood.

This was his uncle, the man who had stolen Hamlet's princedom from him, the man whose brother had killed King Otto. How dared he come here like this?

'King Hamlet,' Wiglek said from his prostrate position before them. 'It is glorious to see you here for we were told you were gone to Valhalla.'

'Told by whom?'

'Why, by all, my lord king. *All*. The messengers brought the news from across the sea and we lit solemn beacons across Denmark in your honourable memory.'

'I'm sure you did. And then, Wiglek, you took Jutland.'

'I did, my lord, as my royal duty, and I have kept it safe and prosperous for you.'

'You are too kind.'

Wiglek glanced up briefly, as if believing his nephew was thanking him, and then cowered once more. Flora, looking at the taut lines of her husband's frame, imagined the harshness of the stare the grovelling man had received and felt a flash of pity for him before reminding herself that he was their enemy and hardening her heart as best she could.

Hamlet leaped suddenly off the dais and landed before Wiglek with a crash of boots on board.

'You killed my father, Wiglek.'

'I did not! Truly. I had nothing to do with that – nothing, you must believe me. I knew Feng had been nursing grudges but not that he was plotting murder.'

'So you admit it was murder?'

Again, Wiglek half looked up and Flora saw him quiver with the effort of finding the right words.

'I know it now, my lord king, yes.'

'You knew it the moment Feng seized the throne.'

'It was too late then.'

'Not true.' Hamlet's voice lashed out like a whip and he made a visible effort to control himself. 'It was too late for my poor, royal father but not too late for justice to be done. If you knew Feng had ordered regicide, why did you not kill him?'

The answer took a little time to come and when it did it was in a voice that was soft, almost tearful: 'He was my brother.'

'As was Otto.'

'I did not kill Otto.'

'But Feng did.'

'It seems so. I didn't know, truly. I didn't know anything. I was as horrified as you, my lord.'

'And yet you stayed at his side.'

'He was my *brother*. My elder brother. I'd always served him; I didn't know what else to do.'

'You were weak.'

'Yes, my lord, I was. I was weak. *Am* weak.'

Hamlet snorted.

'Not so weak that you could not take Jutland. It seems to me, Wiglek, that you benefitted as much from Otto's death as Feng did. You were happy to share his fate then and therefore . . . ' Hamlet's voice rose and he stepped so close to the grovelling man that the toe of his boot pressed on his uncle's splayed fingers ' . . . you deserve to share it now.'

'No!' Wiglek clutched suddenly at Hamlet's leg. 'No, nephew, please. Show mercy. All good kings show mercy.'

'Feng did not.'

'He was not a good king.'

Bebba had woken at Wiglek's cry and now began batting her little head against Flora's chest. Flora jiggled her, whispering soothing words to try and keep her quiet. This was hardly the place to suckle but she could not bear to miss a moment of the confrontation.

'So you renounce your princedom then, Uncle?' Hamlet demanded.

Wiglek cringed and crawled back a little.

'Of course, if you so wish. Though you are king now, you know, and will need a strong prince to carry your rule to the west and . . .'

'I have a prince, thank you. I am naming Ofelia Prince of Jutland.'

A ripple of astonishment ran around the court and Flora heard Ofelia gasp. The she-warrior stood, clutching her hand to her mouth and staring at Hamlet in astonishment. This was not, then, a plan they had concocted together. Good.

'Ofelia?' Wiglek dared to protest. 'But Ofelia is . . . is . . .'

'My most trusted warrior. And a Jutlander born.'

He turned and beckoned her forward. Flora could see questions in Ofelia's eyes but she was a warrior to the bone and knew when to stand strong before an enemy. She stepped up to Hamlet's side with her slim shoulders squared and her scarred face held high as she looked down at her predecessor and Flora felt a rush of admiration for her spiky friend. Hamlet clapped her heartily on the back.

'She will rule wisely, do you not think, Wiglek?' The man had little choice but to agree. 'And she should start now. What, Prince, should be this man's fate?'

Flora glanced at Mairi and saw her eyes fixed upon Wiglek in open sympathy as he quivered before Ofelia.

'He surely deserves to die?' Flora whispered to her co-wife.

'He surely deserves a second chance,' Mairi whispered back. 'As the man said – a good king should show mercy.'

Flora looked back to Wiglek and then around the Danish court, all craning forward to hear the ruling. Mairi spoke true, she supposed, and what harm could the man do with his support all drained away? She looked back to Ofelia and could see the scarred profile of her face curling in disdain as she opened her mouth to pronounce judgement.

'Perhaps, Prince Ofelia,' Flora said clearly, 'you would like to withdraw to consider your judgement?' Ofelia looked back at her and frowned while Flora hurried on: 'No one minds waiting on a prince's decision.'

Hamlet glanced back too and nodded.

'Good idea. Let the supplicant wait.'

He nodded to his guards and two of them stepped forward to stand over Wiglek as Hamlet ushered Ofelia towards the small room at the rear of the hall and offered an arm each to Flora and Mairi. Together they swept away, a furious buzz of conversation rising in the hall the moment they were out of sight. Flora sank gratefully down onto a stool and put a now mewling Bebba to her breast. Ofelia rolled her eyes.

'Must you do that, Flora?'

'Yes, I must. You don't want her crying to disturb your deliberations, do you?'

Ofelia tossed her head.

'There are no deliberations to be made. I don't know what we're doing out here. Wiglek must die.'

'Why?' Mairi asked.

'Why? Because he was part of a plot to kill Hamlet's father.'

'Do we have proof of that?'

'I heard him myself. I heard him and Feng plotting. That is . . . I heard them complaining together about Otto.'

'But not actually planning murder?'

'Well, no, but even Feng and Wiglek wouldn't have been stupid enough to speak it out loud. The intent was clear.'

'From Wiglek?' Flora asked. Then, seeing Ofelia fight to remember, felt she had perhaps pressed her too far. Who was she, only four days in Denmark, to question a native? 'I'm sorry, Ofelia. It's not my place to interrogate you. I know nothing of what went before, save that you were both sorely used. I'm sure you are right in your judgment.'

'But is she?' Mairi demanded. 'It seems to me that it is not so much about what happened before as about what is happening now. If the man is penitent and swears loyalty, then should he not be given a chance to prove himself?'

'He did us grave wrong, Mairi,' Hamlet said.

'So, forgive him. Show him you are the better man. And, er, woman.' She glanced nervously at Ofelia and rightly so for the new prince looked furious.

'We'll be the better men once he's in his grave,' she growled.

'Or you might just give his followers a grievance against you,' Flora said.

Ofelia swung fierce eyes her way but it was clear she was thinking about all they had said.

'Forgiveness is weak,' she said, but the words lacked conviction.

Mairi intervened.

'You know, Ofelia, I remember my father once telling me that the reason he had embraced Christianity was for the power that forgiving men gave him.'

Flora saw Ofelia frown.

'He told me something like that too,' she admitted reluctantly. 'He told me that he ruled by collaboration, cooperation and coordination.' She looked momentarily confused and then shook herself. 'But he lost, Mairi. He lost to *us*, so why should we listen to him?'

'Because in this instance his advice may be right.'

Ofelia turned to Hamlet.

'What do you want to do?'

The new king paced between his three women, considering. Flora watched and wondered at this curious triangle they now seemed to form around him. He caught her eye and then looked down at Bebba's soft head as she suckled. He gave a small smile.

'I think perhaps, after our martial arrival, a gesture of mercy would be welcomed by the people.'

'You want to let him live?' Ofelia demanded.

'For now. Though with a very, very close watch kept on him.'

Ofelia gave a wolfish smile.

'Now that I can manage.' She threw her hands in the air. 'Very well. We will show mercy. Does that please you, Mairi?'

'It does.'

'Shame. But I suppose we can't have everything.'

And with that she swept back into the hall, Hamlet scrambling after her. Mairi looked to Flora.

'Were we right?' she asked.

Flora stared at her, surprised by her own sudden uncertainty.

'It felt right.'

'It did, didn't it? Yes ... yes, it did. Are you coming out?'

Flora checked Bebba but she was still guzzling hungrily.

'You go, Mairi. I'll listen from here.'

Mairi nodded and slipped through the curtained doorway, leaving Flora, for once, blissfully alone. She rested her head back against the wall, held Bebba a little tighter and closed her eyes as she heard Ofelia announcing Wiglek's pardon to the court, her voice taut with disdain for her own words. Hamlet swiftly took over.

'There has been enough bloodshed in Denmark,' he declared loudly. 'You are my kin, Lord Wiglek, and I embrace you as such.'

Flora was left to imagine the man being raised up but even through the heavy curtains she could hear him crying noisily and singing Hamlet's praises. She knew Mairi would be beaming at the fruits of forgiveness and Ofelia glowering suspiciously behind the others, but the courtiers were applauding now so it seemed they had made a popular decision. It was a strange triangular governance behind the king but if they kept it strong, it might just work.

Chapter Twenty-eight

Aarhus, Walpurgis (May Day) 604

Mairi stared through the flickering flames to the naked body of the man tied to the rough cross and felt an unexpected surge of awe. She had always thought of the pagan religion as confused and ugly but here was Odin tied to his tree, and the sight was beautiful. She felt light-headed from the nine-day fast the court had been observing (another thing she had not thought pagans capable of) and it was all so pleasingly hazy that if she squinted past the rapt Danes and blocked her ears to the skald's Norse words, this could almost be Christ on his Cross.

She wasn't sure if the similarities were a comfort or cause for disquiet but over the last winter in Denmark she'd learned to take the former wherever she could and so gladly embraced the ecstasy of the tableau. At that moment, however, the lights were extinguished and she gasped and clutched involuntarily at the person to her right.

'All is well, Mairi,' Flora whispered. 'The light will return with Odin's acquiring of knowledge.'

Mairi felt Flora's hand pat her own and squeezed it gratefully in return. She knew she'd followed her co-wife around like a lost lamb when they'd first arrived at the Danish court but despite the other girl being half her age she had seemed so much more assured in this strange, Danish court. Her mother was a Dane by birth so perhaps it was in her blood. Either that or her paganism had bound her to her new subjects but, bless her, she had included Mairi in governing decisions wherever she could. And with Hamlet's ferocious words about her being a part of his world still ringing in her smarting ears, Mairi had worked hard to fit in.

It had not come naturally to her. Speaking to God, she found, was far easier than to other people for other people insisted on speaking back, but she had hidden behind her ignorance of the Danish form of Norse and bit by bit had accustomed herself to being in society. She still prayed, of course, but only at sunrise and sunset. In between she had forced herself to the looms and had found surprising satisfaction in the steady creation of a fine cloth or even, as she'd progressed, a rich pattern. Her father, she had thought more than once, would have been pleased to see her being useful, but her father was in the past and it was the people here whose good opinion mattered now.

At Yule she had gifted Flora a wall-hanging all of her own creation showing the intertwined leaves of what she hoped looked like her beloved herbs, and had been rewarded with beaming smiles from her fellow wife and even one or two from Hamlet. He worked hard at his kingship, even she could see that. He ruled with studied care and earnest attention to detail, a marked and perhaps even welcome contrast to her father's more volatile style, and she was grateful to be a small part of it however out of place she sometimes felt.

She had not yet found the courage to spread the word of God to anyone, though Hamlet had at least let her set up little chapels on all the royal estates they had visited and a few days after Yule he had brought her a gift of her own – a fine silver cross, studded with jewels. She'd cried when she'd unwrapped it from the linen in which it was bound.

'You never had any wedding jewels,' he'd said awkwardly. 'A trader brought this to me the other day and as soon as I saw it, I thought of you.' She'd been touched beyond belief and even more so when he'd added, 'You are doing well here, Mairi.'

He'd taken her hand a moment and his touch had moved her almost as much as the gift. She wore it all the time now, not around her neck for all to see, but at her belt as a private talisman. Soon she must start telling people here of the true faith. It was her duty, she knew, the reason she had been brought to this strange land, and she cursed her own cowardice in staying silent with every day that passed. But at least when she felt nervous or shy her fingers could scrabble for the cross and its solid, heavy shape would give her strength.

She felt for it now but already the lights were flaring again and she saw, in the mirror pool below the stand-in god, a carved collection of runes. They were strange, primitive characters with none of the depth of meaning of Latin but they looked fascinating all tumbled together in the hearth light and Mairi determined to learn more of them. Hamlet had told her once that Ofelia had written his wyrd into the runes. She wasn't sure what he'd meant by that but she could see now that if she were to try and change the minds of any of these Danes she needed first to understand the way those minds were shaped.

'Odin be praised!' people were calling out all around her and lost in the moment she almost called out with them but caught herself and murmured a near-silent Hail Mary instead.

'Is it not awe-inspiring?' a voice asked at her other shoulder and she turned to see Lord Wiglek.

'It is,' she agreed cautiously for Ofelia was hovering near, her scar unusually livid in the low light. Hamlet had charged her to keep guard over his uncle and it was a duty she fulfilled with ferocious diligence. 'It reminds me of Christ's death on the Cross.'

'Christ is your god, Lady Mairi?'

'He is God's son.'

'I see.' Wiglek moved a little so that his broad back shielded her from Ofelia's dark scrutiny. 'And how does this remind you of his death?'

'Do you really want to know?'

'Of course. Why would I not?'

'He is not one of your gods.'

'There are, surely, many ways of considering the world, my lady. I do not feel certain that I have yet found the right one.'

Mairi felt a little glow inside, a spark of excitement. Was this a sign from God? Was this how her mission to the Danes might start?

'I can tell you of my faith, if you wish it?'

'I do,' he said, touching her arm gently. 'Truly I do. I have been in the darkness and I wish to come out of it.'

'That's wonderful.'

Mairi clasped his hands. She had been right to exhort forgiveness, for now Wiglek's soul could be saved.

'And people of our age can surely still find new truths?' he went on, smiling at her.

Mairi stared at him. *Our* age? She supposed she was nearer to his years than to Hamlet's. The thought was a little discomfiting but in truth it was good to talk to someone more mature and before she could think about this further he was asking more questions.

'So, Christ is which god's son?'

'The only God.'

His eyes opened wide and Mairi fumbled for the cross at her belt but then he put a gentle hand under her elbow to guide her to a bench and said, 'Tell me more.'

Mairi did her best to rein in her excitement for fear of boring him but Wiglek remained attentive, sitting with her throughout the very welcome meal that was served after the ceremony. She kept it simple, avoiding anything about Adam and Eve and telling Wiglek only of God creating the world and sending His son, Jesus Christ, to help men understand and reach Him. Wiglek asked all sorts of questions and before long she realised they were amongst only a few people left in the hall. She looked around.

'Where is everyone?'

'Gone into the bushes,' he told her.

'The bushes? Why?' He raised an eyebrow and she flushed. 'Oh. Oh, I see. Of course. How very ...'

'Pagan?'

'No! That is ...'

'If your Christ was made man, Lady Mairi, then he must surely understand the pleasures of the flesh?'

She stared at him. She'd not considered that before. Desperately she combed her mind for fragments of scripture but could come up with nothing stating clearly that Christ had been celibate. After all there'd been Mary Magdalene – had she not been close to Jesus? So close that the other disciples had been unhappy about it? Had she not washed His feet and wept at the Cross and been the first to see Him raised from the dead? Had she, then, been His wife? And how, in this land without monks or priests to help her, would Mairi ever know?

'I'm not sure,' she admitted eventually.

Wiglek smiled at her.

'Well, let's hope he did. The union between a man and a woman is a beautiful thing and if your god sent his son to earth, I hope he was kind enough to grant it to him.'

'Beautiful?'

'Of course.'

Confused, Mairi looked around the hall again and saw Hamlet sitting in his great chair talking earnestly to Ofelia and her uncle, a greybeard called Peder. The old man was shrivelled and lined and looked at Ofelia with dog-like devotion but he seemed a decent person. Mairi watched closely as they spoke, seeing the sharp lines of Hamlet's handsome face in the candlelight and the sparkle in his brown eyes as he listened intently to the old man as if he were the most important person in the world.

But now Peder was rising, resting heavily on his thin arms to lever himself off his stool. Hamlet stood up to help and his eyes met Mairi's. He smiled at her and she rose to her feet.

'I should go and talk to my husband,' she said to Wiglek.

He looked pleasingly disappointed but nodded and, grabbing her hand, dropped a light kiss onto it before bowing himself away. Mairi stared at the spot on her skin for a moment then shook herself and went over to Hamlet as Ofelia, thank God, slid off after Wiglek with nothing but a small snarl in Mairi's direction.

'Is all well, Mairi?' Hamlet asked, patting the bench at his side.

'Quite well thank you.' She sat down. 'I was talking to your uncle of Christianity.'

'You were?'

'He still seeks forgiveness, I think, and a new, purer way forward.'

'Then let's hope you can offer it to him.'

He smiled at her again and she felt warmth course through her body. God had indeed known what was best for her when He had sent Hamlet. She swallowed and looked up into his handsome face.

'Where is Flora?' she asked.

'She's gone to bed. She felt rather sick. We think – hope – she is with child again.'

'Truly? Oh, that would be wonderful. She's such a devoted mother. I love to see her with Bebba.'

'You do?'

Hamlet looked very surprised and she wondered what sort of monster he thought she was. The worst sort no doubt.

'I do. I know I was . . . neglectful at Bebba's birth.'

Hamlet reached for her hand.

'That is in the past, Mairi. Forgotten.'

She looked up at him and saw only sincerity in his eyes. He really had forgiven her. A weight lifted off her shoulders.

'Thank you. And I am truly glad that they survived for they are so lovely together.'

'They are.'

Hamlet looked towards the door to his wife's bower with a fond smile and Mairi battled to bring him back to her.

'I never knew my own mother. She died when I was just two years old, birthing my brother. He died too.'

'I'm so sorry.'

She shrugged.

'Father married Dorothea less than a year later and she was always like a mother to me. We were very close.'

'That's good,' Hamlet said and she nodded vigorously, though a tiny, uneasy part of her suddenly wondered if it was actually true.

She'd always been close to Dorothea, yes – as close as she could get. She'd sought her out whenever she could and seized at her stepmother's faith as a way to be bonded to her but had Dorothea actually welcomed that bond? Suddenly Mairi recalled the teasing fondness her stepmother had shared with her sons and looked back on her own, rather intense relationship with her with new unease. The others had been Christian too, of course, but they'd never clung to their faith as tightly as Mairi did. Had Dorothea thought her odd? Did she miss her now? Was she sorry to be kneeling alone in their little chapel or just relieved to be free from Mairi's ravening faith?

'Mairi? Are you sure you are well?' Hamlet asked.

She blinked and looked at him.

'Just learning to see myself through others' eyes.'

He frowned.

'That's hard to do. Don't assume the worst, will you?'

'Why do you think I would?'

'You seem attracted to punishment.'

'I do?' Mairi stared at him, aghast. 'I am trying not to be, Hamlet. I am trying to be part of your world.'

'I've noticed and I'm glad of it. You are happy in Denmark?'

'Happier than I thought I would be.' She swallowed. 'I am learning.'

'It is not too hard, I hope?'

'Happiness is not a feeling I am accustomed to.'

'Oh, Mairi!'

He laughed and pulled her into a hug. It startled her and she jerked against him but then she felt the warmth of his chest and the strength of his arms and gratefully gave in to the feeling of security they brought her. She must, after all, take comfort where she could. Wiglek's words about the union of man and woman returned to her and as she looked up at her husband of almost a year she made up her mind.

'I would like, Hamlet, to be a bigger part of your world.'

'In what way, Mairi?'

She swallowed. Could she say it? Dared she?

'I would like, please, if you think it fit, to . . . to . . .'

'To?'

'To be your true wife.'

The words rushed out of her like ale from a barrel. She flushed scarlet and tried to look down but his hand went to her chin and kept it high.

'You are sure?'

She nodded.

'I will never be a nun here in Denmark, will I? And at the moment I am not a wife either. I am a nothing.'

'That's not true.'

'It feels like it. Will you, Hamlet?' Still he looked at her. 'I . . . I would like to give you a child.'

That was true. She hadn't realised it before but it was so very true and, beyond that, she would like to give *herself* a child. Someone to love with the sort of open, uncomplicated devotion Flora so clearly felt for little Bebba.

'That would be good, Mairi,' he said. 'And I think – hope – you will find the act less unpleasant than you fear. It can be most . . . invigorating.'

'It can?'

'Very much so.'

His eyes had taken on a faraway look again. He must be thinking of Flora; Mairi had to do this and now, before she lost her nerve.

'Where shall we go?' she managed, fighting to keep her voice steady. 'To the bushes?'

His brow darkened.

'No, not the bushes. Two years ago to this very night I was in the bushes when my father was murdered.'

'I'm sorry. I didn't realise. With Flora?'

Even as Mairi asked she knew that couldn't be right.

'No, not with Flora. It matters little who I was with, Mairi. It is more a question of who I *should* have been with. I should have protected my father and I did not.'

'But you have avenged him now?'

He looked down at her and, to her great relief, smiled again.

'"Avenged", Mairi? Are we making a pagan of you?'

She flinched. They would never make a pagan of her. Quite the reverse; she would make Christians of them. And maybe she had made a start tonight. She glanced round for Wiglek but he was gone and that was probably for the best. They could talk another day. For now she had other duties to attend to.

'If vengeance it is important to you,' she said carefully, 'then it is important to me. As your wife.'

'As my wife,' he agreed, 'my true wife.' And then he took her hand and led her to her bower.

Chapter Twenty-nine

Viborg, August 604

'Are you sure you're all right doing that?' Flora asked Lars. 'It looks very hard work.'

Lars paused in his digging and leaned on his shovel. It was a hot day and Flora couldn't help noticing his sweat-damp shirt clinging to his muscular chest. Bebba was napping in the nursery and Flora should probably go and check on her but she was so enjoying seeing her new herbery take shape.

'It's good training,' Lars told her with a grin. 'And I need that. Ofelia says I'm getting tubby.'

'You are not!' Flora said indignantly.

'Thank you, Flora. I think it's maybe more that she's getting too thin.'

'I think you might be right,' Flora agreed. She'd noticed last night that the fiercely fit Ofelia had looked rather gaunt. 'Is she not eating enough?'

Lars considered.

'She's eating all right but now you mention it, she rushed off from training yesterday and I swear I heard her being sick in the bushes.'

'Sick?'

'Hmm. Unusual for her. Perhaps her stomach is upset.'

'Perhaps,' Flora agreed but her hand went thoughtfully to her own stomach. 'We should keep an eye on her.'

Lars laughed.

'She wouldn't like that. And, besides, she's right about one thing – I need exercise with no battles to keep me fit.'

Flora sighed.

'I'd rather you were all tubby if it meant no battles.'

Lars lifted the shovel again.

'Me too but I don't mind the digging all the same. It's good practice for when I get my farm. Now, what next?'

Flora strode around the patch of land Hamlet had given her for a herbery here in Viborg. He had grand plans to build a fine new hall, like the one his father had built at Odense, and was eager to add many modern outbuildings too. Flora's was to be the first. It was a fine, flat area and he'd commissioned carpenters to build her a sturdy hut, but while the wood was being cut and weathered she'd been keen to get on with digging the herb beds and last night at dinner Lars had volunteered to help out.

She suspected he'd had a little too much of the fine new ale the excellent brewers here in central Jutland had provided, but he'd arrived this morning, shovel at the ready, and had already turned over two of the four beds she wanted. Given that the sun was hot and the ground hard, he must be exhausted.

'Next, Lars, you need to rest and have a drink. I can fetch some ale from the brewery if you'd like.' He shook his head, confirming her suspicions, and she smiled. 'What about some fresh apple juice then?'

'Thank you.'

He sank gratefully onto a large stone he'd dug up from the middle of one of the beds and she went over to the brewery to fetch the juice. The brewers had been kind enough to give her a corner to herself and just this morning she'd tried out the apple press she'd found gathering cobwebs behind the mash tubs. It had reminded her of her press back in Bernicia and turning the handle had been momentarily like turning back time. Now she filled a tankard from the small keg and headed back outside. She spotted Lars immediately for the sun was shining straight down onto his mop of blond curls, tangling in each one like gold thread.

'You should be careful sitting there,' she called, 'or Mairi will think you are one of her angels.'

He reached up and felt at his back.

'No wings yet. I'll not find my way to Christian heaven, I'm afraid.'

Flora handed over the juice and looked up into the blue skies.

'What if she's right, Lars? What if there *is* a heaven?'

This was a question that had been niggling at her ever since her strange conversation with Mairi on the day of Bebba's birthing. Before she'd met the Celtic princess, it had never occurred to her to question the gods or their place in the world, but hearing a different set of ideas had disturbed her and every so often she asked Mairi more about her curious faith. It did not seem to Flora that the White Christ was the answer but his existence certainly raised questions. Might there be other truths out there she was yet to discover?

'If there is this place called heaven,' Lars said, 'I bet they drink your apple juice there. It's delicious, Flora.'

'Thank you. But, seriously, what if the Christians have got it right? How can we know?'

'We can't. The gods – *all* gods – are a capricious lot. All we can do, I think, is live the best lives we possibly can and then no one can reproach us.'

'But what if we die and find out there is only one god and he won't let us into this heaven?'

'Then he isn't much of a god, is he?' Lars looked at her more closely. 'Are you really worried, Flora?'

346

'I wonder, that's all, especially at night.'

'Then nudge Hamlet awake and get him to reassure you.'

She kicked at the newly turned earth.

'He isn't always there.'

'He isn't? He doesn't sleep with Mairi, does he?'

'I don't know. I haven't asked.' She closed her eyes as if doing so might block out the truth but she knew from experience that nothing did that and, anyway, she had never been one for lies. 'I don't think it's Mairi he goes to,' she admitted.

Lars groaned.

'Ofelia?'

'Maybe.'

She'd thought for a long time that Hamlet had stopped going to his funny female prince. He'd seemed stiff around Ofelia, determinedly treating her as he might one of his male followers, but once they'd got to Denmark something had changed. He was as loving as ever to Flora but she sensed a charge whenever Ofelia was around, like a summer storm waiting to break. And now the other woman felt sick . . . A sigh escaped her lips and Lars took her hands.

'Those two are complicated.'

'I know.' She squirmed in his hold; it felt far too nice. 'He told me all about it. About your mother and . . .'

'And her throwing herself onto my father's pyre as a glorious martyr instead of staying to look after us?'

He said it matter-of-factly. Flora stared at him.

'Does it upset you to talk of it?'

He drank the last of his juice and peered into the tankard as if hoping for more to materialise.

'Not really. I mean, I can see it is upsetting. And I know it upset Ofelia but I was only seven at the time. I don't remember it happening or, if I do, it's Ofelia's white face I can see, not mother's burning body. And after that, it's all Ofelia – sleeping next to her, running around with her, teasing her, loving her. She was all I had and all I needed.' He sighed. 'It was harder for her, I suppose.'

347

'I'm sure you were a support to her.'

'I tried to be but I'm just a simple man, Flora, with simple desires – food, warmth . . . '

'A farm?'

'A farm, yes. And a family.' He leaped up suddenly and thrust the tankard at her. 'Thank you for this. Better get on. We've still got two beds to dig.'

He yanked the shovel out of the ground and set to digging with new energy. Flora watched feeling useless but yesterday the midwife had confirmed that she was with child again and told her sternly not to strain herself in any way.

She wandered back over to the brewery to return the tankard, thinking of what Lars had said. Had Ofelia replaced his mother for him, or did her loss still hurt him somewhere deep inside even if he didn't realise it? Why, for example, had he not married if he was so keen for a wife and family? They'd been in Denmark nearly six months now, so it didn't make sense.

She thought of her own mother and felt a familiar ache. Bebba had come from Viborg where she stood now, and Flora often found herself picturing her here before Aethelfrith had arrived and carried her back to Bernicia – like Flora's own journey in reverse. Not that she wasn't happy in Denmark. The people had been very welcoming, Hamlet treated her well, and little Bebba grew bonnier and more entertaining with every day. It was just that Flora so wished her daughter's namesake could be here to share her.

She'd heard tell, just before Yule, that Queen Cathryn had given birth to a son and had imagined the stoic way Bebba would have borne the pain of it and wept for her mother as she'd known she would not do for herself. Hot on the heels of this had come the happier news that Udela was to be married to a prince of Strathclyde. Flora had wondered if this was her father finally choosing diplomacy over war and hoped so. She'd hoped, too, for her fretful sister's sake, that the prince in question was young and handsome and, above all else, kind. She'd been glad for Udela but even more worried for their mother if she was now to be left alone.

She'd sent messengers to ask Bebba to come and live with them back home in her native Denmark but the reply had come that her mother was grateful for her kindness and yearned to see her but must stay in her rightful place in Bebba's burgh with her husband and her people. Flora expected it but had been disappointed all the same. Maybe once Flora had her second child Bebba would change her mind, or at least come for a visit, but for now she could be with her only in her thoughts.

Flora put the tankard down, said thank you to the brewers and headed back out. She could see Lars digging away with furious concentration but another figure beyond him caught her eye: a tall, slim woman, watching intently. Something about the way she stood was so like Bebba that for one moment Flora actually thought she'd willed her mother here, but it must have been a trick of the light, or of her own imagination, for as she drew closer she saw that it was Lady Gertrude. Flora sidled uncertainly up to her.

'Good day, my lady.'

'Good day, my lady queen. What are you digging?'

'*I'm* digging nothing,' she said with a rueful smile. 'I'm not allowed.'

Gertrude's eyes filled with hope.

'Then you are with child?'

'I believe so.'

'Congratulations! I love children. Sadly, I was only blessed with one.'

'Hamlet.'

'Yes. And now he hates me.'

Flora shifted uncomfortably and looked around, wondering where Hamlet was. He would not, she knew, like her talking to his mother but Gertrude looked so sad that Flora was powerless to walk away.

'He struggles to understand how you could have married Feng,' she replied carefully.

Gertrude nodded and wrapped her arms around her slim form.

'I struggle to understand it too. I'm not proud, Flora. Would you tell him that? I was lost, confused. I shouldn't have been, I know. I look at what happened and I can see the evil Feng did but he was good to me. He was kind, charming.'

'At first?'

'No, always. Right up to his death. Increasingly, I saw him grow angry and greedy with others but never with me.'

Flora put out a tentative hand to her mother-by-marriage.

'Maybe he loved you?'

'Maybe he loved the fact that he'd seized me off Otto. I don't know. I was stupid but what else could I have done? He offered me protection, Flora, and I seized it with both hands. I took safety over justice, I know, but would I do it differently if it happened again? I'm not sure I would be strong enough.'

'I understand that,' Flora said, 'but what about Hamlet? If you loved him so much, why did you let Feng send him to his death?'

'His death?' Gertrude stared at her, aghast. 'What do you mean? Hamlet's not dead. He has thrived from his mission to the Angles' land.'

'Only because of Ofelia.' Gertrude looked genuinely shocked. 'Ask her about it.'

'I wouldn't dare. You tell me, Flora, please.'

She sighed.

'Very well. Ofelia found the runes Feng sent to my father by a messenger. They called for Hamlet's death.'

'No!' If Gertrude was acting she was doing it very convincingly for she was looking at Flora with pure horror on her face. 'Feng wouldn't have done that. He knew how much my son meant to me. You must be mistaken.'

'Ask Ofelia,' Flora repeated. 'Or Hamlet. He was there. The runes asked my father, King Aethelfrith, to see Hamlet dead.'

'So why didn't he?'

'Because Ofelia changed them to ask for his marriage instead.'

'To you?'

Flora spread her hands wide.

'To a bride of my father's choosing, yes. Hamlet has, I hope, thrived but that is no thanks to Feng. Your husband deserved to die, my lady.'

'And I deserve Hamlet's hatred. Thank you for telling me, Flora.'

Gertrude turned to leave but her eyes were so desperate, Flora couldn't bear to see it.

'Will you talk to him?' she asked.

'What's the point?'

'You can make him understand.'

Gertrude shook her head and dug her toes miserably into the fresh-turned earth. Then suddenly she looked up.

'Maybe you could speak to him with me?'

'Me?' Flora swallowed nervously.

'Yes, you. His queen. You are so kind, Flora, and so wise.'

Flora groaned. People were always telling her she was wise but she did not feel it and especially not when faced with this situation. Hamlet hated his own mother and with good reason; no amount of so-called wisdom could help her negotiate that. Gertrude stepped a little closer.

'Imagine if you fell out with your daughter,' she all but whispered. Flora started at the idea. 'You cannot imagine it, can you? You cannot picture a time when your lovely baby would fight against you, but all children grow up and learn to assert themselves. It is the way of the world.'

Flora shook her head.

'Hamlet did not simply "learn to assert himself", Lady Gertrude. It is more that you married the man who murdered his father.'

'I did.' Gertrude bowed her head and slowly turned away. 'You're right, my lady. It was unforgivable and I must accept that. I will go away, I think.'

'Where to?'

'Denmark has many islands small enough to shelter a lone

woman who wishes to live as a hermit. I will live out my days in seclusion.'

She began to move away and, watching her, Flora saw again the outline of her own mother. She could never imagine falling out with Bebba and it twisted her heart to think that Hamlet did not know that kind of maternal love. Surely, if they could forgive Wiglek, they could forgive Gertrude too?

'My lady, wait!' Gertrude looked back, a spark of hope in her pale eyes. 'Let me try and talk to him. I can promise nothing, but I can at least try.'

'Truly? Oh, Flora, it would mean so much to me. I would be so grateful.' Gertrude rushed back and Flora gave her a weak smile. 'Now?' she asked.

'Now? Oh, no, I don't think . . . '

'It's just that . . . '

Gertrude pointed past Flora and she looked over her shoulder to see Hamlet stepping up to Lars, slapping him on the back and clearly teasing him about his menial work. He hadn't seen her yet but any moment now he would. She sighed. Now, she supposed, was as good a time as any, though her heart wavered as Hamlet turned and saw her. He smiled at her but then, noticing Gertrude, his expression turned to stone.

'Lady Gertrude,' he said stiffly.

Flora swallowed.

'Hamlet,' she said, 'your mother would like to speak to you.'

'I have no mother.'

He glared at Gertrude and Flora had no idea what to try next but to her astonishment Lars stepped in.

'No, Hamlet,' he said quietly, '*I* have no mother. Ofelia has no mother. Flora has no mother here in Denmark. You, at least, have a chance of knowing your mother.'

Everyone stared at him. He gave a sheepish shrug and grabbed his shovel, digging furiously to cover his confusion. Hamlet watched him for what felt like forever and then slowly turned back to Gertrude.

'What, then, would you like to say to me, Lady Gertrude?'

She looked terrified but she was a queen at heart, born of a royal bloodline, and as Flora watched, her mother-by-marriage drew herself up tall and looked straight at her son.

'I would like to say that I am sorry, Hamlet. I would like to say that I was weak and scared and foolish. I would like to say that I did not – at least, at first – believe that Feng had killed Otto and that I never, until Flora told me just now, knew he had ordered your death. I would not have allowed that, Hamlet. I would have died myself, ten times over, rather than let you die for you are the most precious thing in the world to me and always have been.' She stopped, twitched at her skirts and then stilled herself again. 'That is all, Hamlet, son, king. Judge me as you wish.'

Hamlet looked at her. Flora watched him struggle with himself and longed to fold her arms around him and comfort him but he had to do this alone. He glanced her way and she gave him a pleading look. He was a father now; surely that must help him to understand what Gertrude was saying. She put a hand to her belly and saw something, at last, flicker in his eyes.

'A king should be merciful,' he managed to say.

'And a son?' Gertrude dared to ask.

'A son should ...' His voice cracked a little. 'A son should be loving.' Gertrude took an eager step towards him but he put up a hand to stop her. 'It will not be easy, Mother. I'm sorry but it will not. But we shall spend time together perhaps?'

Her spine stiffened again.

'I'd like that. And, Hamlet, may I spend time with little Bebba too? She is so very dear to me and I can help her and Flora. I can teach them both about Denmark: its history, places, customs.'

'What do you think, Flora?' Hamlet asked, not quite looking at her.

'That would be of benefit to me,' she said carefully.

'Then, yes. Good idea. And now, let me see these herb beds of yours.'

Gertrude took her cue and, with a stately bow, excused herself. Flora moved over to Lars who gave her a small smile behind Hamlet's stiff back. She returned it gratefully but with her husband's expression still stony it seemed Gertrude's harmony with Hamlet might have been won at the expense of Flora's own.

Chapter Thirty

'Ofelia? Ofelia, I need to talk to you. Now.'

Ofelia looked up from honing her sword blade to see Lars storming down the barracks looking sweaty and cross and most unlike his usual self. She sighed. She'd been feeling nauseous since that ridiculously fatty bacon at breakfast and had been hoping for some peace and quiet this morning, but she'd never to admit to physical weakness so she forced a smile onto her face.

'I'm always happy to talk to you, Titch.'

'Don't call me that.'

She jumped.

'Lars? What's wrong? What's bothering you?'

'*You* are.'

'Fair enough. In what way?'

Lars looked around at the handful of men lounging in the barracks and grabbed Ofelia's arm.

'Let's go outside.'

'Fine. We will. You can let go of me, Lars. I'm not resisting.'

'Right. Good. Sorry.' For a moment he looked more like his usual calm self but then he turned on his heel and snapped, 'Come on then.'

She still felt queasy but worry outstripped her stomach problems and she threw down her sword and ran after him.

'Is it Peder, Lars? Is he . . . ?'

'It's not Peder.'

'Oh. Good. Then . . . ?'

But still Lars was marching off and not until he'd reached a quiet spot behind the pigsties did he stop. The pigs looked up but seeing nothing to interest them went back to rootling hopefully in their trough.

'So?' Ofelia demanded. 'What's so secret that only the piggies can hear it?'

'It's you, Ofelia. You and Hamlet.'

'What about us?'

'Are you rutting with him?'

'Lars . . . '

'Are you? Come on. I'm not your bloody little brother now. I'm a man, Ofelia, and I see things.'

'Clever you.'

'So? Are you?'

'What business is it of yours?'

'You're my sister, Ofelia. We're family – all the family we've got bar Peder and he's enough on his platter just keeping himself alive. We need to look out for each other.'

'And that's what you're doing here? "Looking out" for me?'

'Yes. For you and for your reputation.'

'My *reputation*! Gods, Lars, I don't give a damn about my reputation, save that people think I fight well. I am not, as you might have noticed by now, some courtly lady with her virginity to protect from all comers.'

'You're certainly not! Very well then, I care about *Hamlet's* reputation. He is King of Denmark, Ofelia, and he has a queen.'

'Two queens.'

'So he doesn't need you as well.'

'Maybe he needs me more than ever.'

'As a warrior, yes, but not as a woman.'

She bit her lip.

'I can be both.'

'Can you? I'm not so sure.'

'You can be a warrior and a man.'

He raked his hands awkwardly through his curls.

'I know. It's unfair but that is the usual way so it's easier for me. You are treading a rare path, Ofelia, and perhaps therefore it has its own rules.'

'Rules?'

She felt bile rising in her stomach, mixing very unpleasantly with the bacon and put her hand down to settle it.

'Are you sick Ofelia?'

'Sick?' She whipped her hand away. 'No. Of course not.'

'Then there is no excuse.'

Ofelia glowered at him. Since when had her brother become so sanctimonious?

'What do I care for rules?' she snapped. 'And why does it matter what Hamlet and I do or don't do?'

'It hurts Flora.'

'Ah!' She paused, looking him up and down. 'And that hurts you, Lars?'

He glared at her.

'A woman like Flora should not have to share her husband.'

'But she does, with Mairi.'

'That cannot be helped. Flora is at least the primary queen and she is to bear him another heir.'

'Is she indeed? Clever girl.'

Lars' eyes narrowed.

'Show more respect, Ofelia. Flora deserves to stand at the king's side and *you* should stick to fighting at it. Hamlet asked you to be his wife; you refused. Why must you, then, insist on having him anyway? It's greedy, Ofelia – greedy and selfish.'

Ofelia stared at her brother, stunned by the bitterness in his voice. It curdled her poor stomach and she rubbed surreptitiously at it as he eyeballed her, feet planted wide, shoulders broader than ever.

'You need to stop, Ofelia. Stick to Eric. He loves you.'

Ofelia jumped.

'Eric! Rubbish, Lars. Eric and I just scratch each other's itches.'

'You really believe that?' He shook his head almost pityingly at her. 'Are you blind, Ofelia, as well as greedy? He loves you.'

She put her hands to her ears.

'That's rubbish, Lars. Rubbish! What's got into you, banging on about love all of a sudden? It's love that gets people into trouble if you ask me. That's why I've always stayed well away from it.' He looked at her, his blue eyes mocking her and she hated it. 'I don't do love, Lars,' she insisted.

'That's not true.'

'It *is* true. Why will no one believe me?'

He stepped closer to her.

'This is me, Ofelia, your brother. I know you can do love because I've lain at your side, night after lonely night, and I've felt that love.'

Ofelia felt her stomach churn; she really was going to vomit soon. Why was he insisting on dragging up that dark time? She didn't need it held over her like a weapon. She felt instinctively for her sword but she'd left it in the barracks so she faced Lars with her fists balled instead.

'No, Titch,' she said carefully. 'You're wrong. What you felt there was not me loving you, but you loving me.'

He gasped and for a moment looked seven years old again, lost and confused, then his eyes hardened into purest steel.

'I see,' he said. 'How stupid of me. Thank you for the correction.'

And then he was gone, striding away, every line of his body taut with hurt, and she was left to sink down against the sty and wish the whole damned conversation had never been forced upon her. She shouldn't have said that to him but, then, he shouldn't have meddled. What business was it of his what she did or with whom?

She looked to the pigs, snuffling for food, and felt reassured by them. Why couldn't humans be more like pigs? Why couldn't they just attend to their basic needs and get on with life? But then a piglet came out of the sty, blinking itself awake and almost falling over its own stubby legs to get to its mother, and the sow looked up and gave a funny little snort of delight as it bundled into her.

Ofelia sighed and closed her eyes. She didn't understand it. For two long years in the Angles' land she'd battled to return to Denmark and now they were here, triumphant, it all felt as flat as her homeland's pathetic landscape. Her stomach churned again and she kicked crossly at the pigsty wall. This was no use. She would find Hamlet and she would do some hard training and perhaps that would snap her out of this ridiculous self-pity. There was surely nothing like dancing with death to remind you of the joys of being alive.

'Gods, Ofelia, enough!'

Hamlet stepped away from her, holding up his shield and sword to ward her off.

'Tired already, Hamlet?'

'I certainly am. What's got into you today?'

Reluctantly Ofelia let her sword drop. She pulled off her helmet and wiped sweat from her forehead with her tunic sleeve. No doubt she stank but at least the churning in her damned stomach had ceased. Mind you, now she'd stopped, she did feel a little dizzy. She leaned quickly back against the barracks wall before she made a fool of herself but Hamlet was looking at her with concern and she didn't like to see it.

'Women's problems,' she shot at him.

'I doubt that.'

'Why? Do you not think of me as a woman?'

He sighed and put down his weapon next to hers.

'You know I do, Ofelia. What's wrong?'

'I'm not sure,' she admitted. 'I'm just out of sorts, that's all. I was so desperate to make you King of Denmark and now we've done it, it all feels a bit ... dull.'

'Dull?' He laughed. 'There's no pleasing you, is there? You're a prince now, Ofelia.'

'I know and I'm very glad of it, truly, but what do princes actually do?'

'Govern their princedoms. Ride around and meet the people, hear their grievances, pass judgement.'

Ofelia shook her head.

'I don't think I'm the right person to be passing judgement on anyone.'

Hamlet grabbed her by the arms.

'Nonsense. Odin's balls, Ofelia, you've been passing judgement on people since you were tiny!'

'Well, maybe I was wrong to.'

Now he looked really confused.

'Has someone been saying something to you?'

She kicked at the dirt beneath her feet.

'Lars says I should leave you alone and settle for Eric,' she admitted.

Hamlet laughed again.

'He's probably right.' That teasing voice – so easy, so familiar – seemed to work into the knots Lars had tied into her joints and loosen her off. 'Will you?'

She looked at him.

'I'm not sure. You've got two wives to please already.'

His brow darkened.

'Not in that way. Flora only seems interested in making me talk to my mother.'

'Gertrude? Why?!'

'Reconciliation. Forgiveness.'

'Forgiveness?' Ofelia spat into the dust. 'I'm sick of forgiveness. It's a stupid Christian concept and as far as I can see it only creates trouble. We'd be far better off without Wiglek still hanging around the court. And without your treacherous mother too.' Hamlet flinched and she feared she'd gone too far. She put out a hand to him. 'Flora is a kind girl and that's very commendable but does it help you to rule?'

'I'm not sure,' he admitted.

'And as for Mairi . . . she'd have everyone chained to the White Christ if she could and that would make every one of us as weak and pathetic as her. What use is she to you, Hamlet? The only thing she gets on her knees for is to pray!' Hamlet coloured and she gasped and peered at him more closely. 'Doesn't she? Oh, my dancing sword, Hamlet, are you ploughing your second wife at last?'

He bristled and stepped back, brushing invisible dirt off his tunic.

'Nothing so vulgar, thank you, Ofelia. But I am showing her the joys of marriage, yes.'

'Gross! Rather you than me.'

'And I'm sure she'd rather me than you too.'

Ofelia forced a laugh, though the thought of Hamlet bedding Mairi was curiously disturbing. Why should she care if he'd taken the stupid little Christian's virginity? It was about time after all. She pushed herself off the wall, willing her head not to spin.

'You definitely don't need me then,' she threw at him, making for the barracks door.

He caught at her arm, yanking her back.

'I always need you, Lia. You know I do.'

'Well, you shouldn't.'

'That's beside the point. I'll prove it to you if you'd like.'

He ran his spare hand up under her tunic and stroked his fingers across her hot skin. It flared deliciously across her body and she squirmed.

'Hamlet!'

'Don't you like it?'

She did; far too much. She pulled away.

'A little stroke like that? No, thank you. Save your fancy tickles for your pretty wives.'

She turned her back and heard him sigh behind her. She should go. She was doing no one any good in this mood. But before she could take a single step he spoke again.

'I didn't choose to marry them, Ofelia.' His voice was so soft that she had to lean back a little to hear him. She placed a hand on the wall to steady herself and felt him creep closer. 'I married Flora because *you* carved her into my runes.'

'To save your life.'

'I know it and I thank you. And I thank you for Flora too because she is a wonderful woman.'

Now it was Ofelia who sighed.

'So stay with her and leave me alone.'

'I wish I could but it seems you are bound into my wyrd.'

'Are you going to blame me for your marrying Mairi too?'

'I am for I was so stricken with worry about your wounds that I was not alert enough to avoid all the politicking around the match.'

'That's as pathetic as she is.'

'I know! That's what I'm telling you. You are as much a part of me, Ofelia, as my own bones. When you are strong, I am strong; when you are hurting, I hurt too. It is not a choice, simply how it is. I love ...'

'Don't!'

'Very well.' After that he was silent for so long that Ofelia thought he had left but suddenly he said, 'Meet me tonight.'

'Where?'

'The barrow.'

That caught her attention and she turned to face him at last.

'Which barrow?'

'The one on the moors. The one with the ...'

'Gap at the entrance?'

'Yes.'

'Why?'

'Because maybe it's time, Ofelia. Maybe it's time you opened it up and faced the dead at last.'

'You don't want to do that, Hamlet.'

'But *you* do. You've done so much for me, Lia – let me do this for you.'

'Tonight?'

He nodded and she felt something thrill through her – the joy of an adventure perhaps, or the prospect of a challenge, or just a sense of herself as Ofelia, rather than as a part of a lopsided triangle around the king. Forget Lars and his stupid, simplistic rules. She and Hamlet were different; they had their own rules. And, besides, Hamlet was the king now so if he ordered her to do something she was duty bound to obey.

'Tonight,' she agreed, and when he smiled, the gods help her, she wished it were already dark.

As she watched Hamlet head back to the hall she felt the final vestiges of her damned sickness drop away at last. Now all she needed was someone to help her while the hours of daylight away and she thought she could see just the person. Her eyes narrowed mischievously and, bouncing lightly on her toes, she headed into the heart of the compound.

Chapter Thirty-one

Mairi came out of the weaving shed and leaned on the doorframe, drawing in breaths of fresh air. She had been working with an especially fine wool today and little wisps of it had got into her eyes and throat until she'd felt she was almost becoming part of the fabric. She sucked in a few more breaths and placed a tentative hand to her belly. Was she feeling sick? She thought perhaps she was but feared it was more from the wool than a baby planted inside her.

The act of marriage had turned out to be something of a revelation. It had been uncomfortable the first time, painful even, but the pain had been mixed up with all sorts of other sensations that had made it seem somehow unimportant and the gasps of pleasure Hamlet had made at the critical point had truly moved her. And then, afterwards, as he'd held her, she'd felt so at peace.

The union between a man and woman was, as Wiglek had said, a beautiful thing and already it was hard to remember what had scared her so. She'd been frightened, she thought, of giving herself but hadn't realised she would receive as well. A baby would make it even more wonderful. She yearned to hold an infant in her arms and to see Hamlet look at it and at her with the same pride with which he looked at Flora and Bebba, and she prayed every day for this sign of God's favour on her mission to Denmark.

Now she stretched out her back and closed her eyes to better enjoy the feel of His newly warm sun on her face.

'Feeling stiff, Lady Mairi?'

Her eyes flew open to see Ofelia standing before her, helmet clutched under one arm and her hair dark with sweat around her scarred face. Mairi cringed.

'No. I'm very well, thank you.'

Ofelia stepped closer.

'It's probably all that bed play. It can be hard work, especially at your age.'

'I beg your pardon ...'

'You should try a few different positions perhaps. Use different muscles.' She leaned in so close that Mairi could smell the musk of the woman's body and feel her damp hair blowing against her own cheek. 'You should go on top.'

Mairi jerked away and caught her elbow against the weaving-shed wall. Pain lanced through her, though not nearly as sharp as the implication behind Ofelia's words.

'My marriage is none of your business.'

Ofelia grinned and put up her hands.

'True. I'm just offering a bit of friendly advice, woman to woman.' She winked lewdly and Mairi shivered.

'You're not a proper woman,' she snapped, feeling for the doorframe behind her, desperate to get away.

'Oh, I am. Ask Hamlet.'

'What?'

'Ask Hamlet when you see him. Not tonight though – tonight he'll be at the old barrow. With me.'

Ofelia winked again and then stepped forward suddenly, grabbed Mairi's face in both her rough hands, and planted a hard kiss upon her lips.

'Get off me,' Mairi protested, but the she-warrior was already swaggering away, laughter trailing behind her like poison ivy.

Mairi sank down to the ground and scrubbed at her lips, trying to brush off the lingering taste of the wretched woman, but it felt bitterly imprinted upon her. What had Ofelia been saying? What had she meant? Her head spun and she scrubbed harder at her tainted lips.

'Lady Mairi, are you well?'

She looked slowly up into the steady gaze of Lord Wiglek.

'Quite well, thank you.'

She dropped her hand to her side but her lips stung still and she could not stop herself from rubbing at them once more. He leaned solicitously over.

'Has someone hurt you?' She shook her head. 'Because I would hate to see anyone hurt you.'

'You would?'

His eyes were full of concern and it touched her. Slowly she put out a hand to be helped up and Wiglek grasped it instantly, his grip firm and strong.

'Can I fetch you some ale perhaps?'

'No, thank you.'

'Some water then? Something to eat?'

She smiled.

'Truly, my lord, I am well.'

'A blackberry perhaps?'

'A blackberry?'

He smiled and gestured to a lavish bramble curling up the perimeter fence behind the weaving sheds.

'They are ripening and the first ones are always the sweetest. See.'

He moved over to the plant and, drawn by the simple joy of the harvest, she followed. Sure enough the white flowers were giving way to green berries and although most were still small and hard, a few were plump and purple with juice. Wiglek reached up, plucked one from the top and held it out to her.

'Try it, my lady.'

He lifted it to her lips and she tasted the sweetness cutting through the bitter gall of Ofelia's sweat-stained kiss. Despite herself she smiled and he slid the fruit gently into her mouth, his eyes upon her so intently that she felt herself flush almost as dark as the berry.

'Good?' She nodded dumbly and he turned to look for more. 'Was that the Lady Ofelia I saw with you?' he asked from among the leaves.

'It was.'

'She's trouble, that one. Always has been.'

'Really?'

'Oh, yes.' He turned to face her. 'She was wild as a child. Ran around with the boys like an untrained hound. Lord Peder was supposedly in charge of her but he never looked up from his tally sticks long enough to care, so she and Lars did what they wanted.'

'Lars does not seem so wild.'

'No. Lars is a decent man. Perhaps, then, it is Ofelia's inherent nature that is the problem.'

'Perhaps she was born with the devil inside her?'

'The devil?'

'Satan,' Mairi explained. 'He was one of God's angels but became jealous of God's power and rose up against Him. He was cast out into the darkness where he works night and day to turn men against God.'

'Or women.'

'Exactly.' Mairi let Wiglek feed her another berry as she thought about it. 'Ofelia is always vile to me.'

'You should not allow that,' he said. 'You are queen.'

'I am, aren't I? Perhaps I should talk to Hamlet.'

'Perhaps.'

'You do not think it a good idea?'

Wiglek put up his hands, stained from the berries.

'He is your husband, Mairi. You know him better than I. All I will say is that Ofelia is a bad influence on him. She controls him to her own ends.'

Mairi nodded. That much she had seen for herself. Ofelia was always dragging Hamlet to training in the yard or knucklebones in the barracks.

'It's as if,' she said, 'despite having fought for it, she doesn't actually like him being on the throne.'

'Exactly.' Wiglek looked at her with something like awe. 'That's exactly it, my lady. You're very astute.'

'Oh, I don't know about that. I . . . '

'You *are*. Ofelia insists on her role as protector to the king but really she just wants to play warriors with him. That and . . . '

He stopped.

'And what?' Mairi demanded but he shook his head.

'Nothing, my lady. It's nothing. I merely counsel you to keep an eye on her, that's all.'

Mairi nodded thoughtfully.

'She said something strange just now.'

'She did? What about?'

'About an old barrow. What does she mean by that? What old barrow?'

Wiglek frowned.

'There's a barrow grave just up the hill from here. It was dug by the Ancients to house their dead. I seem to remember Ofelia was always fascinated by it.' He came a little closer. 'What else did she say?'

'That she was going to do something there later. Something with Hamlet. What did she mean, do you think?'

He looked around and then leaned in to speak in a low voice.

'Some sort of rite perhaps? We have many of them, you know, and not all of them fit for an onlooker's gaze.'

Mairi looked at him, horrified.

'A sacrifice?'

He looked over his shoulder to be sure they were not overheard.

'I hope not, my lady. We are surely more civilised than that these days. And yet . . . '

'And yet?'

'You can never be sure with Ofelia. Do you know how her mother died?' Mairi shook her head. 'Threw herself onto her husband's funeral pyre. Burned alive.' Mairi put her hands to her mouth and he curbed himself. 'I'm sorry, my lady. A gentlewoman like yourself should not have to hear of such things but it happened all the same, so who knows what Ofelia plans?'

Mairi felt a momentary flash of hope that Ofelia would follow her mother's example in seeking an early death and then felt ashamed; the damned she-warrior turned her into a terrible version of herself.

'I don't know about Ofelia but I'm sure Hamlet wouldn't do anything like that,' she said hastily.

'No. No, of course not. All the same, I should perhaps keep an eye on him, to be sure he's safe.'

'Really? Oh, that would be very kind of you.'

Wiglek looked abashed.

'He is my nephew, Mairi, and, of course, my king. He has forgiven my past and in return it is my duty and my joy to care for him now.'

Wiglek looked so intent on his plan that Mairi wasn't sure where to put herself. She glanced awkwardly up to the sky and noted with some relief that the sun was heading for the trees.

'I should go,' she said. 'I must pray before dinner is called.'

'Of course.' Wiglek bowed low, then coughed awkwardly. 'Only ...'

'Is something wrong?'

'Not wrong. Oh, no, my lady, nothing is wrong. I just wondered ... might I, perhaps, come with you to prayer?' Mairi stared at him, unable to believe what she was hearing. He flushed. 'No matter. It was just an idea. A foolish one. I don't want to interrupt your time with your god.'

'He is not *my* god, Wiglek. He is *the* God. And I would be delighted if you came.'

'Truly?'

'Truly.'

'I would be so very grateful. My brother Feng once told me that I did not plan carefully enough for my future. In that – if in nothing else, of course – he was right. Perhaps you, Queen Mairi, can help me make that plan?'

She felt a thrill run through her at his trust and slipped her arm under his.

'With God's help, I'm sure I can,' she said, and led him towards her little chapel with a new and very welcome sense of power.

Chapter Thirty-two

'I wasn't taking her side.'

'I know that.' Hamlet gave Flora a tight smile and belted up his best tunic. All over the compound people were heading to dinner and they should be in the hall already but were both lingering in their bower. 'Besides, it is your job as queen to keep the courtiers at peace with one another.'

'Is it?'

Flora considered. Certainly, her own mother had always smoothed over arguments and done her best to keep the mood of the court sweet. Flora remembered the dignity with which Bebba had received Cathryn into Aethelfrith's household and felt a painful pang of longing for her.

'I suppose so,' she said. 'But, Hamlet, it is more than that. Mothers are special to their children.'

'Which is why,' he shot back, 'they should be especially careful not to hurt them.'

'True.'

Hamlet was pacing their little bower like a wary animal and Flora felt strangely timid before him. Usually he was an easy man to read but when it came to Gertrude his emotions were as tangled as the runes in Odin's mirror.

'It is, of course, up to you how you deal with her,' she offered nervously.

'I know that.' He stopped in his pacing to glare at her then suddenly softened and crossed the floor to clasp her to him. 'I know that,' he said again, more softly. 'I just don't know *how* to deal with her. But that is not your fault, Flora. You are being your usual kind, reasoned, w—'

'Don't say wise.'

'Why not?'

'Because I'm not, not yet at least, and especially not here in Denmark where there is still so much for me to learn.'

'For me too,' he said. 'I sometimes think that I've spent so much time chasing my throne that I no longer know how to settle on it.' He lifted his royal diadem off the hook and squinted down at it. 'I fear maybe I was better at firing burning arrows at rebel armies than presiding over a court.'

He looked at her then, his eyes so full of confusion that she could not bear to see it. She went to him and placed a hand on his cheek.

'That is not *you*, you speak of Hamlet, but Ofelia.'

He gave her a sideways smile.

'You may be right,' he agreed, dropping a kiss on her forehead, but his eyes had moved to the door and she knew, perhaps more clearly than he did himself, that Ofelia *was* Hamlet and that if she was restless, so was he. In that, Flora was powerless to intervene and she could only hope they would somehow sort it out for themselves.

'Is Ofelia ill, Hamlet?'

'Ill?' He frowned. 'I don't know. She does seem a bit out of sorts. Why?'

Flora shook away her suspicion. She didn't want to face it, so if no one else was going to that suited her fine.

'No reason. Shall we go to dinner?'

He nodded slowly then clamped the diadem on his head and offered her his arm.

'Come, Flora, my queen, we shall go to dinner and I shall do my best to talk to my mother.'

'Only if you wish to.'

'Only if I am able.' He squeezed her hand. 'You know, don't you, little one, that you are a very good wife?'

'Too good,' she tried to joke.

But he squeezed her hand tighter and said sombrely, 'Too good for me,' then dived out into the night, tugging her with him.

They were spotted immediately and people flitted towards them, eager to grab a moment with the king. Flora saw Hamlet straighten his shoulders and twitch his cloak into place as if physically assuming the mantle of kingship. He smiled graciously and listened solicitously and, watching him, Flora knew he was a natural ruler and wondered what had happened to make him doubt himself. Was it just the talk with his mother? She hoped so for surely time and care would heal that breach.

The door to the hall stood open to the spring air and light spilled out across the compound, noise tumbling after it. Flora heard cheers and laughter and hurried gratefully forward to see a crowd had gathered inside, forming a circle. At the centre of it stood Ofelia, dancing lightly on her toes with her sword held aloft to slice away pieces of the fruit that people were tossing into her little arena. Flora watched, mesmerised, as the she-warrior hopped and spun, halving apples and plums and even tiny sloes as they rained down upon her. It was an impressive act, though the fruit was being crushed into the boards beneath her dancing feet and Flora thought pityingly of the poor serving girls and boys who would have to scrub away the stains tomorrow. Not that Ofelia would care about that.

In truth she was relieved to see the other woman looking so fit but the fruit was running out and, as someone reached for a ham hock one of the servers was trying to carry to the tables, she stepped hastily forward, clapping loudly. Instinctively those around her joined in and then, spotting Hamlet, drew hastily back and the circle opened up to let him move forward.

'Fine tricks, my Prince of Jutland,' he said loudly.

'It is as well to keep sharp,' Ofelia responded, 'for you never know when enemies may strike.'

'True,' Hamlet agreed solemnly. 'I will sleep easier in my bed for knowing I am now protected from rogue plums.'

Everyone laughed and he ushered Ofelia towards the top table, turning to offer Flora his arm so that she might accompany them, but she waved him on and stepped aside to tell the stewards to have the fruit picked up before it was trampled further.

'Ridiculous display,' someone said in her ear and she turned to see Mairi glaring at Ofelia as she took a seat at Hamlet's side.

'The people liked it.'

'The people are foolish.'

'Mairi! That's not true.'

Mairi grimaced.

'Very well then, the people are too easily pleased.'

'Is that possible?'

'Sorry?'

'Is it possible to be too easily pleased? It seems to me that it is a gift to find amusement where you can for there is little enough of it in the world.'

Mairi frowned.

'That is not so, Flora. If you are amused by trivialities you will not look past them for the greater truths and beauties.'

'And yet you will be amused all the same.'

Mairi tossed her head.

'You don't understand. It must be a pagan thing, I think, to be so easily dazzled by surface show. By ritual, not substance.'

She put a strange, hard inflection on the word "ritual" and when Flora looked closer she saw a pale, almost manic sheen in her co-wife's eyes.

'Have you been at prayer, Mairi?' she asked.

'I have, yes. And not, for once, alone. Others, it seems, are starting to see the value of a thoughtful, considered, true religion.'

'Which others?'

'Lord Wiglek for one. He seeks a new way forward.'

'New?'

'More righteous.'

Flora felt a rare flash of temper rising and fought hard to control it.

'I do not see myself as unrighteous, Mairi.'

'You are a kind girl,' she allowed, 'but you could be so much more if you embraced Christianity as Wiglek is doing.'

Again Flora's temper flared but there was something wild in the air tonight and she refused to add to it.

'I'm glad to hear you have a convert,' she managed. 'Now, shall we eat?'

Mairi looked cross at being robbed of a confrontation but then suddenly beamed and pushed past her, and Flora turned to see Lord Wiglek offering his arm to her companion. She watched uneasily as they made a stately progress up the hall together then suddenly realised that hers was the only empty place at the top table and had to hurry forward. Even Gertrude was seated, smiling shyly as Hamlet leaned over to say something to her. Flora knew she should feel pleased to see that but it was suddenly hard to summon the energy for pleasure.

She stared up at her place, feeling indescribably weary. Already Ofelia and Lars, sitting either side of the gap, were leaning in to talk to one another and if she just slid away now they would easily close it. She felt a yearning to go to the nursery, scoop up Bebba and crawl into bed with her, but she was a queen now and as such all the people in this hall were her children. Reminding herself how her mother would act in such a situation, she set her head high and stepped onto the dais.

Instantly Lars spotted her and leaped up to hand her into her place in the line of Denmark's governance. She smiled gratefully at him but even before she could sit down, Ofelia pounced.

'What think you of ghosts?' she demanded.

'Ghosts, Ofelia? I suppose I try not to think of them at all.'

'But do you believe in them? Are the dead still with us?'

'I hope not.'

'Why?' Energy was bubbling from the she-warrior like a spring from the ground though Lars was right that she'd got horribly thin. 'Why, Flora? Why do you hope that? Would you not like to talk to your brother again?'

Flora shivered.

'No, Ofelia, I would not. That is, I miss Earnfrith greatly and I would very much like to talk to him if he were still alive, but what would be the point in communicating with the dead when we cannot actually live with them?'

'What indeed?' Lars said but there was no deflecting Ofelia.

'Do you not have questions for him?'

'No.'

Ofelia rolled her eyes.

'You are so incurious, Flora.'

That stung.

'I am not. I am hugely curious about everything in this world and in particular about what we can do to make it better, but I see no point in wasting that curiosity on the dead.'

'Quite right,' Lars said. Then, 'Leave it, Ofelia.'

Ofelia, however, simply looked the other way up the table.

'Mairi likes ghosts, don't you, Mairi? She has her own ghost, a "holy" ghost. Does he talk to you, Mairi, your ghost?'

Mairi looked down the line and gave Ofelia a haughty stare.

'He is not a ghost but a spirit.'

Ofelia roared with laughter.

'Are they not the same?'

'No. The Holy Ghost is not a tangible figure but a presence within one's soul.'

'Soul?' Ofelia queried.

'Don't worry about it,' Mairi threw back, unusually defiant. 'You don't have one.'

'And I don't want one if this ghost of yours is floating about in it!'

'He is not ...'

Mairi stopped herself and Flora noticed Lord Wiglek's hand on her arm and saw him whisper something into her ear. Whatever it was, it seemed to calm the spiky Dal Riatan and Flora supposed she should be glad of that but already she weary of this meal.

'Tell you what, Ofelia,' she said, 'you chase the dead and if they say anything worthwhile let me know.'

Ofelia looked at her so long and hard that Flora began to feel uncomfortable, then suddenly the she-warrior flung an arm around her.

'I will, Flora, I will. You are right – you should stick to the living for you are good at dealing with them. Better than I am, certainly.'

'That's not ...'

'When are you due?'

She nodded pointedly to Flora's belly and Flora looked down in surprise. They had not, surely, announced her pregnancy yet.

'Hamlet told you?' she asked tightly.

She shook her head.

'Lars did.'

'Lars?'

Flora tried to look to her other side but Ofelia grabbed hold of her chin.

'When will you announce it?'

Flora squirmed away.

'Not yet. I want to be absolutely sure. And, besides,' she added, striving for a little levity, 'I can't face another dawn trip to the rings. Do you do that here in Denmark?'

Ofelia frowned.

'I don't know. It's a woman's thing.'

'And you are a woman, Ofelia.'

'Not a proper one!'

She pulled a comical face and Flora had to laugh. Ofelia was maddening, infuriating and confounding, but she was fun too. She was also wrong.

'I gather you've been feeling sick, Ofelia ...' she started, but just then the servers leaned over with big platters of fish and the conversation was lost in the ceremony of serving it up.

Flora picked at hers as best she could but her appetite was small and it disappeared completely when she noticed Ofelia barely touching her own. She happily handed her food to Lars when his was all gone.

'Are you well, Flora?' he asked.

'Quite well, thank you. A little weary. I think I may retire.'

'Already?'

'If Hamlet will allow it. He has a second queen here after all and his Prince of Jutland besides. I'm sure he can spare me.'

'Not if he has any sense,' Lars muttered, but rose to hold back her chair all the same and she went to Hamlet.

'If you will excuse me, my lord, I am very tired tonight.'

He stood.

'Of course, if you wish it.'

Did she? Not really but she hadn't the energy for court ceremony and it was with relief that she let herself out of the noisy hall and made for the peace of her bower. She needed sleep, that was all. Everything would feel better with sleep.

But sleep would not come. Flora lay listening to the sounds of the hall as they rose and then slowly died away. She waited for Hamlet to come to their bower but he did not. He wouldn't want to disturb her, she told herself, but she could not stop wondering where he was – in the hall still, in the barracks, with Mairi perhaps? She knew, though, that it would be none of those and eventually, sick of chasing her own mind round in loops, she got up and went outside in the hope that the night would still her restlessness.

She could hear a murmur of conversation from the hall and the odd voice or snore from the buildings around. A clatter of dice suggested that a few men were still awake in the barracks but most of the court must now be abed. As she should be. Flora glanced to the nursery, straining for the sound of Bebba crying, but there was nothing.

378

And then, on the far side of the compound, she saw the big gates shift. A guard stood forward with a torch then saluted and faded back to his post, though not before the flame lit up a diadem and she knew that it was Hamlet sliding through the gates with a lithe, slender woman at his side. Ofelia. Of course.

Flora leaned back against her bower and watched the pair disappear through the gates and then reappear moments later in the low moonlight, climbing the slight rise that passed for a hill here in Denmark. Where were they off to? And why?

Flora shook her head at herself. Surely she knew why? With a heavy sigh she pushed herself up to go back to bed but then the gate creaked again and she turned back in time to see the guard saluting once more as a second pair of figures left the compound. The first of them turned to offer an arm to his lady in the glow of the guard's light and, to her astonishment, Flora saw that it was Lord Wiglek and that the lady with him was Mairi.

The gate closed behind them and then they, too, headed up the hill, a little slower than Hamlet and Ofelia but with the same steady purpose. Flora stood stock still, watching as the four people disappeared onto the moors. She should go to bed and forget it all. The king was there and one of his queens besides so he did not need the other. And yet, there was something about the composition of that ill-assorted group that she did not like. She looked to the stars for guidance but they winked blankly back at her; she would have to make up her own mind. Before she could hesitate further, she made for the hall in search of help and, seeing the man she sought, ran thankfully inside.

'Lars!'

Ofelia's brother turned and leaped up from the fire.

'What is it?'

'It's Ofelia,' she told him. 'She's gone up the hill with Hamlet, and Wiglek and Mairi have gone after them.'

Lars' eyes narrowed.

'Wiglek? What does he want with them?'

He looked to his burly companion, who had also risen to his feet.

'I don't know,' Eric said, 'but I doubt it's anything good. They could be in danger, Lars. Ofelia could be in danger.' Horror glittered bright in his eyes and he reached for his sword. 'Where have they gone?' he demanded of Flora.

'I don't know, truly.'

But Lars did.

'The barrow,' he said. 'They'll have gone to the bloody barrow! We must follow them, Eric.'

But Eric was already gone.

Chapter Thirty-three

'Are you ready to do this, Ofelia?'

'I am.' Ofelia put a hand to the big stone standing across the barrow entrance. It was shaking. Damn. She looked back at Hamlet. 'What's going to be in there anyway?'

'A barrow ghost?'

'I doubt it. There's been a gap at the top for ages so surely a ghost would have slipped out long ago?'

'I don't know. Maybe. I've never seen one, Lia. And neither do I want to.'

Now she was here, Ofelia wasn't so sure she wanted to either. She felt a little nauseous again but she'd said she'd do this and she couldn't back out now or she'd be haunted by her own cowardice – a more determined ghost, she was sure, than any long-dead ancestor.

'There's no ghost,' she said, with far more conviction than she felt, and then, before she could think about it any further, set herself against the stone and pushed.

She'd expected resistance, expected the weight of it to confound her, or at the very least for the tendrils of moss and ivy hugging the stone to the barrow to create a tension, but with that first big thrust the great stone gave a soft creak, almost a moan of relief, lifted up from the ground and then tilted towards her. Ofelia just had time to spring back, tugging Hamlet with her, before it crashed to the ground and there, gaping darkly, was the entrance to the barrow.

They both stood, stunned, but the lure of the tunnel was too great for Ofelia.

'No turning back now,' she said, grabbing Hamlet's hand and stepping onto the stone. He drew his sword and she gave a low laugh. 'What good will that do you against sprites and spirits?'

'I know not but I feel better with it to hand.'

There was no arguing with that but right now they needed a torch more than a blade. Ofelia took her pack off her back and drew out a rush-candle and a flint. It was hard to see in the low moonlight but finally she managed to strike a light and set it to the wick. The little flame guttered, then caught and she headed quickly into the barrow before the wind could blow it out. It took a moment for her eyes to adjust but when they did, the fear drained out of her to be replaced by fascination.

'Hamlet, look!'

She pulled him after her and felt him relax a little as he, too, took in their curious surroundings in the flickering torchlight. They were in a neatly built, almost perfectly straight corridor made of carefully aligned stones. Ofelia put a hand against them and felt the wall, cool and strong. She remembered a similar wall up on the great bell hill at Aet Gefrin, another marker from those long-gone.

'Why don't *we* build with stone?' she asked Hamlet.

'I don't know. It takes too long, I suppose.'

'But look how secure these walls are. No enemy would get through. And no fire arrows either.'

She looked at him across the candle and they shared a smile at the memory of King Aedan's war shelters burning in the valleys of the Angles' land. It seemed a long time ago. Hamlet's route to the kingship had been a circuitous one but now they were here, Ofelia regretted not a minute of it. Not even his marriage to Flora. Mairi she could have done without but that hadn't been her fault. One little wound had kept her from Hamlet's side for a few days and he'd got himself saddled with a Christian! She smiled and pulled him further on.

The tunnel was maybe twenty paces long and cut into the walls in sharp lines were little alcoves, like deep shelves. In each one lay a skeleton, seeming to leap into white relief when she turned the candle their way but all lying serenely, staring up through sightless eye sockets to the stone ceiling above.

'Not ghosts,' she murmured, 'just men.'

'Or women,' Hamlet said at her side.

Ofelia put out her hand and gently touched the nearest arm bone.

'It's impossible to tell.' She looked back at him. 'Do you see that, Hamlet – underneath, it's impossible to tell. We are the same in all that is essential.' She stroked the arm. It wasn't as cold as she'd have expected and was pleasingly soft to the touch. 'Who do you think they are?' she asked.

'I don't know. Local rulers? They must, surely, have been important people to have been enshrined with such care. Perhaps rulers of Denmark before us.' He, too, reached out and touched the arm. 'This one might have been my great-great-great-great-grandfather. Or yours.'

'It is comforting, is it not, that they are laid here in state?' Ofelia thought of the charred remains of her parents' bones, undignified little lumps in the ashes of the boat the next morning. 'Perhaps we should be buried like this?'

'Perhaps. But I'm not ready to be buried yet, thank you very much. There's too much life still to be lived.'

'There is.'

Ofelia lifted the candle higher to see if there were any runes or marks to speak to them of the dead but she could see nothing. She heard Hamlet draw a sharp breath and turned to him.

'All well?'

He nodded.

'It's just ... you look beautiful standing there.'

'I do?' Inexplicably her eyes filled with tears and she hoped the light did not catch in them. 'Must be barrow magic.'

'Must be,' he agreed, his voice husky, and Ofelia felt her loins stir. 'Beautiful Ofelia,' he murmured, and suddenly it was as if they were back in that very first time when they had still been young and unscarred by life. He stepped closer, taking the candle out of her hand and placing it on the nearest ledge before laying his sword alongside it and pinning her, suddenly, against the stones.

'Here, Hamlet?'

The thought sent a shudder of excitement through her.

'Well, it seems there are no ghosts and these poor fellows have not seen life for a long time. We should perhaps show it to them again in all its glory.'

'*All* its glory?'

'Yes,' he agreed firmly.

He pulled her sharply against him but her sword tangled in his legs, keeping them apart. He reached down and unbuckled the belt, laying it carefully on the floor.

'I might need protection,' she protested, but he kissed her words away and ran his hands up under her now loose tunic, making her gasp with pleasure.

'Not now,' he murmured. 'You have faced the dead, Ofelia, and they are no threat to us. No threat at all. It is time, my love, to think of the living.'

He lifted her suddenly, setting her on the nearest ledge, and if one or two bones were bumped, she didn't think they'd mind. And then, as his lips moved lower, she didn't think at all, just lost herself in him as she always had.

Outside, Mairi paused to draw breath. This little slope was nothing like the great crags and mountains of home but it seemed she had grown used to the flat land of Denmark all too quickly and her lungs were starved of air after even this brief climb. She looked around her as she recovered, horribly aware of strange shapes and lines in the darkness.

They'd heard a crash a little while back, a loud thud that had seemed to shake the ground beneath them, and she'd feared the worst but could see no cause for alarm now and was determined to stay calm. Wiglek had not wanted her to come with him after Hamlet and Ofelia but if they were preparing some sort of hideous sacrifice then she needed to know. It was her duty as a Christian and as a queen.

'Where can they have they gone?' she asked him now.

Hamlet and Ofelia had been moving quickly but up here the land flattened out into moorland and they could see a long way in the bright moonlight. The pair had definitely not been going fast enough to have made it out of sight and there were no woods or bushes to screen them from view, just a few twisted trees standing like broken warriors against the sky.

'The barrow,' Wiglek said softly, pointing to their right.

Mairi looked curiously at the small, bulbous hill, noting a strange shape on its near side. No, not a shape but a hole. How could that be?

'Be careful, my lady.'

Wiglek took her arm and together they crept closer and saw a huge stone lying on the ground in front of it, crushing the heather flat and revealing a cave beyond. Mairi crossed herself and looked to the skies. Dear God, this was a sign, a miracle! She was like Mary Magdalene come to the tomb to find the stone rolled away and Christ risen from the dead. With trembling fingers, she untied Hamlet's cross from her belt and clutched it before her.

'Hail Mary, Mother of God. Hail Mary . . . '

She edged closer. It could not be Christ's tomb, she told herself. The blessed Lord had died six hundred years ago and in Jerusalem, not on a Danish moor. And yet, by the silver light of the moon the cave seemed to suck her towards it, and it was hard not to believe she was there, a part of the glorious Resurrection. Was this why

God had led her to Denmark? Would this be the focus for her mission to the pagan lands?

'Hail Mary, Mother of God.'

She stepped onto the stone and tried to peer inside the barrow but it was dark, save for a mysterious flicker of light halfway down what seemed to be a tunnel. She felt a tremor of fear and told herself not to be ridiculous. If Hamlet and Ofelia were conducting some pagan ritual it was to gods who did not exist and could not harm her. Clutching the cross in front of her, she moved towards the entrance but a strange sound made her stop once more – a low moan, like a creature in pain.

'What do you think they're doing?' she whispered to Wiglek.

He stared past her and his eyes, for a moment, seemed to glint with something like excitement, but it must have been the moonlight reflected in them for when he turned to her, he seemed reticent, scared even.

'I'm not sure. Perhaps we should leave them to it.'

'After we've come all this way?'

'It might be . . . private.'

'It might be *wrong*.'

'But he is king, Mairi, and I a mere lord. I'm not sure I should presume to interrupt him.'

Mairi drew herself up straight-backed. There were more noises now and the flame was flickering wildly. What if they had some poor innocent held in there? Or if Ofelia were hurting Hamlet? The woman was Prince of Jutland now and might want more and Mairi could not just stand outside and let evil happen. That would be almost as bad as committing it herself.

'*Let those who love the Lord hate evil*,' she murmured, '*for He guards the lives of His faithful ones, and delivers them from the hand of the wicked.*'

'What's that?' Wiglek asked.

'It's a psalm.'

'It's beautiful.'

'And true. Hamlet may be king, Wiglek, but I am queen and I am going to stop this now – in the Lord's name.'

Wiglek grabbed her hands and kissed them.

'You are a noble woman indeed.'

Mairi flushed. Feeling discomfited, she looked back to the barrow entrance. It was dark and forbidding and the flames were moving as if Satan's own hand was wafting them, but Wiglek was watching her with something like awe and she could not disappoint him. Holding the cross even higher, she picked up her skirts in her other hand, stepped determinedly into the barrow, and froze.

This was not at all what she had expected. This was no pagan ritual, no dark sacrifice, but something far, far worse. Hamlet *was* in there. And Hamlet *was* moaning – but not in pain. He was halfway down the tunnel, lit up by a small rush light as if God above were revealing the horrific truth to Mairi, and he was with Ofelia but certainly not being hurt by her. He had the damned she-warrior held tight against him, her legs high around his back, and was driving into her with such fierce, abandoned desire that the whole cave of the dead was rocking with it.

Mairi put her hand to her mouth and felt the cross – the cross *he* had given her – cold against her lips. She was betrayed, forsaken. She tried to mumble a prayer of thanks for this enlightenment but could find no gratitude, or sense of mercy or justice or right, only dark, bitter, searing pain. The cross fell from her hand and bounced on the earth floor but still Hamlet did not notice her and, with a sob, she turned and fled.

She stumbled blindly out onto the stone, tripping off its edge and going sprawling face first in the heather. She scrabbled at the rough little stems for purchase and forced herself up. She had to get away from here, had to escape.

'Mairi? Oh, dear, Mairi, what's wrong? Is it evil? Are you hurt?'

Wiglek came rushing to her but she could say nothing. She looked back into the cave and now the sounds from within seemed so obviously, so mockingly, those of passion that they pierced her like the deepest knife stroke.

'Whore!' she spat out.

She hated such language but not as much as she hated Ofelia. Hamlet being with Flora she could understand. She had been Hamlet's wife first; he had a duty to her, as he had to Mairi. But Ofelia . . . ? How could he do that? How could he desecrate his flesh by burying it in that vicious, scarred, she-devil of a woman?

'Whore?' Wiglek asked and then sucked in a breath. 'Ah. I see. They are . . . ' He rested his hands gently on Mairi's arms. 'That's terrible, truly. A wonderful woman like you does not deserve such treachery.'

'Wonderful?' she stuttered.

'Wonderful,' he repeated firmly. 'This youth, king or not, has insulted your honour, Mairi, and I will talk to him about it. Now.'

'But . . . '

'But what? I will interrupt him? Good. So I should. Fret not, Mairi, for I am his uncle and he will listen to me. Stay here and I will see you avenged.'

'Not avenged, Wiglek,' she said, trying to stop him though only half-heartedly.

He went bounding inside and Mairi sank back, fighting not to drown in her own sorrow. But now, incredibly, someone else came labouring over the rise of the hill – a big man, sweating and rasping for breath. He did not even glance Mairi's way but made straight for the barrow, reaching it just after Wiglek and plunging inside without a moment's hesitation. What on earth was going on? Had he come to rut with the whore too? How many men did she entertain up here in this dead men's cave? Denmark was truly a land of wickedness.

Mairi forced herself to her knees in the heather and looked desperately to God's skies, trying to fight away the awful image of Hamlet in his treachery.

'Hail Mary . . . ' she started but could get no further before tears drowned her words and she could only bury her face and give way to them.

Ofelia buried her face in Hamlet's neck and nipped at his skin as his pace built. She felt her own body responding to it and let the waves of pleasure begin to rise. What a shame Lady Mairi had gone; perhaps if she'd stayed she'd have seen what passion should look like.

Hamlet hadn't seen his second wife, thankfully, or he might have insisted on stopping. Loki knew what the woman was doing up here but she certainly hadn't been expecting to see this. Ofelia smiled wickedly at the memory of her pasty, Celtic face going as white as the skeletons rattling excitedly behind them and clamped her legs tighter around Hamlet and rocked with him as, with a cry, he exploded within her.

'Don't stop,' she panted, feeling her own pleasure mount.

She arched back to let him deeper in and saw a shape fill the doorway again. So Mairi was back. Good. Let her watch. She looked towards the intruder, her vision blurred by the glorious sensations running up through her body, but they receded instantly as her eyes fixed on the figure. Those shoulders were too wide for Mairi, the tread as it came towards them too heavy.

'Hamlet!'

'Ofelia, my love . . .'

'No, Hamlet. Beware!'

She pushed him aside and reached for her weapon but it was somewhere on the dark floor. She saw the intruder lift his blade and heard Hamlet roar and dive towards him. She scrabbled on the shelf for his sword but found only bones – and now a fourth person was entering and all was confusion. She had nothing, it seemed, to fear from the dead, but the living might drive her to the otherworld if she didn't move fast. Ofelia snatched up a leg bone, hoping, at least, to use it as a club – but now Hamlet's roar had turned to a shrill, desperate wail of pain.

'Hamlet,' she cried, reaching for him, but he fell at her feet.

She had no idea if he were dead or simply wounded and had no time to look for the blade was coming for her. She lifted the bone but the man sliced it in two and came on. He stepped over Hamlet's crumpled body and across the tiny candle. Ofelia looked for a face but saw only the flash of iron as the sword came slashing down towards her. She put up her hands to shield herself and then heard the unexpected ring of steel on steel before she was roughly pushed aside. Her head hit the stone walls she'd so admired, pain seared across her skull and then she was lost to the darkness.

Chapter Thirty-four

The first thing Flora saw was Mairi, lying in the heather like a peasant girl, weeping into her hands. She rushed up to her.

'Mairi, what's wrong? Are you hurt?'

Mairi peered up at her through tears and snot and tangles of hair.

'I am, Flora. I am mortally hurt.'

'Where?'

'My heart.' She grabbed Flora's dress, pulling her down. 'He has betrayed us.'

'Who has?' Flora glanced uncertainly back to Lars who stood to one side. He had refused to rush ahead with Eric, instead gallantly escorting her up the hill, but now he paced around them as Mairi wept loudly. 'Mairi, what is it?'

'Hamlet! He has betrayed us both ... and with *her*. Ofelia. Whore!'

Flora jumped to hear the ugly word come from Mairi's prim mouth. She glanced towards the barrow.

'They are in there?'

'Yes. Together. He was, was ...'

Flora sighed and crouched down in the heather.

'I know.'

'You know?!'

'I know, yes. Hamlet confessed it all to me. They have been through a lot together.'

'So? We are his wives.'

'But he is a man, Mairi, and a king besides.'

'That does not excuse it.'

'I do not think he seeks excuses.' Flora looked at her and something clicked in her brain. 'Have you and he . . . ?'

'Yes!' It was a wail, thin and desperate. 'Yes. Just a brief time ago. I . . . I thought it best. But it wasn't, was it? He didn't want me, did he? He wanted *her*!'

'It's less a want, Mairi, than a need. Like eating or breathing.'

'But *I* want to be that to him.'

Flora closed her eyes.

'So do I,' she murmured, but it was not to be, she knew that. She cleared her throat. 'Better to have a part than none at all,' she said. Then she heard a strange, hoarse cry from Lars and spun around to see him staring in horror at the entrance to the barrow.

Slowly, reluctantly, she turned her eyes that way and the horror seeped straight into her own bones. For there, standing in the dark doorway, was Lord Wiglek and in his arms, limp and lifeless, the body of the king.

'Hamlet!'

Flora wrenched herself free from Mairi's grasp and ran. Lars ran too and they came together before Wiglek.

'I was too late,' he cried, tears streaming down his face. 'I tried to save him but I was too late.'

'Who killed him?'

'Ofelia . . .'

'No,' Lars said. 'Not Ofelia. She would never do that.'

'Wait,' Wiglek said. 'Ofelia tried to save him too but it seems her sword was out of reach.'

'Then . . . ?'

'He was jealous, I fear. He was like an animal enraged. I was too late to save them, though I ran him through for vengeance.'

'Who?' Flora demanded.

'Eric?' Lars whispered.

'He wouldn't,' Flora said. 'Not Eric. Eric was gentle.'

'Eric was a warrior, Lady Flora,' Wiglek said. 'And his blood was up. That does strange things to a man.'

'Not this strange,' Flora insisted, but already she was doubting herself and now Mairi was creeping over to join them.

'I saw him,' she said. 'I saw him come running up the hill. A big man, yes?' Flora nodded. 'I saw him,' Mairi repeated. 'He went into the cave, sword raised. He killed Hamlet! He killed the king!'

She began wailing as Wiglek laid Hamlet's body tenderly across the stone. Flora stared down at it. How had this happened? She watched, stunned, as Lars sidled past and went into the barrow. She heard him sob and wanted to go and comfort him but her legs did not seem to be working so she stood there, uselessly, while Mairi wept at her feet and Wiglek wept at her side and Lars wept inside the barrow.

And then a voice said, 'Shut up crying and help me, will you?' And all – or at least part – seemed to come to life again.

'Ofelia?' Flora stumbled forward as Lars came out, one arm around his sister who was pale and staggering but whole. 'You're alive!'

'Of course I am. I . . . oh!' She stopped before Hamlet. 'The gods help us! Is he dead? He cannot be.' She fell to her knees and threw herself across the king, grasping at his neck, his wrists, his chest, desperately seeking out the beat of life within him. 'He cannot be,' she said again. 'He cannot, he cannot, he cannot!'

Her cries echoed across the moors and no one dared try and stop them.

'It is a sad, sad night for Denmark,' Wiglek said eventually.

Ofelia looked up at him. Slowly, she pushed her hair away from her scarred face and rose to face him.

'Is it?'

He looked a little startled but stood his ground.

'It is, my lady.'

'Prince.'

'My lady prince.' Was his tone mocking? Flora could not tell. She could tell little save that Hamlet was dead. 'He was killed for love of you.'

'No.'

'I'm afraid so. Poor Lord Eric was driven mad with passion.'

'That cannot be.'

'Did he not love you?'

'No. That is ...'

'Did you not share a bed with him?'

'No. I mean, sometimes, but he knew, he understood.'

'It seems not. You and the king made a ... a startling sight in there. Poor Queen Mairi was most distressed by it.'

Ofelia looked to Mairi, still huddled in the heather.

'You,' she said accusingly, advancing on Mairi, but Wiglek grabbed at Ofelia's arm, holding her back.

'Do not hurt the queen,' he snarled.

'She's not the queen, not anymore. Hamlet is dead. Dead!'

The realisation of it seemed to sweep over Ofelia anew and all the fight went out of her. Flora watched, horrified, as every line of her strong body seemed to collapse in on itself and she fell across the king's body once more.

'Hamlet is dead,' Wiglek confirmed solemnly over the woeful chorus. 'The king is dead.' Then he looked around, lifted the crown to his own head, and added, 'Long live the king.'

Flora looked to Lars, who looked to Ofelia, but she was still prostrate over Hamlet, as if she might cling to the ankles of his spirit as it went to the gods, and up here in the darkness, with only the stars as witnesses to the dark events of this sorry night, there was nothing for anyone else to do but fall to their knees.

Chapter Thirty-five

Aarhus, October 604

Ofelia clutched her arms around herself and watched as the druids circled Hamlet's poor, dead body, lying in state high up in the centre of the ship. She felt sick again and sore and shaky and utterly, utterly lost. Why, why, why had she gone into the wretched barrow? Why had she dragged Hamlet in with her? And why had she let him unbuckle her sword? She had wanted to be a woman for him, had wanted to cast off her role as warrior and give herself to him wholeheartedly, and it had been a dreadful mistake. This was all her fault. She'd shot up that hill, chasing the dead, and had brought death to them all. Lars was right – she was greedy and selfish and now she was punished and all of Denmark with her.

King Wiglek was presiding over the ceremony, doing his best to look sombre though his glee was shining so bright that Ofelia was stunned no one else seemed to see it. He had sung the song of Eric's treachery so loudly and so convincingly that all had been taken in and plenty, to her amazement, had testified to Eric's devotion to herself.

'And to Hamlet,' she had insisted, over and over, but no one had wanted to listen to that.

Eric should have been with Hamlet now, lying in state at his feet as his faithful servant to the last, but Wiglek had ordered him a traitor's death. The cowardly court had obediently cast his body into the woods, to be devoured by beasts, but Ofelia and Lars had crept out under a cloud-covered moon and honoured him with a funeral fire. It had not been a grand pyre like this one but the gods would see it all the same and would know, as Ofelia was sure she knew, that Eric had been there to save his king, not to kill him, and had paid the ultimate price for his loyalty.

Her senses might have been knocked from her in the barrow but she did not need her eyes to know what had happened there. Wiglek had stolen Hamlet's life for his throne, just as Feng had stolen Otto's, and this time there would be no coming back. She should never have forgiven him, never. He had been plotting from the start and had needed nothing more than bloody Mairi's gullibility to find a way in.

She looked bitterly at the Dal Riatan woman now, standing at Wiglek's side, her eyes all wet with pious tears. He had promised her churches everywhere and little arse-headed monks and she had bought it as easily as she would have bought that fake piece of the "True Cross" back on the beach at Bebba's burgh. She had sold Hamlet for Christ and it was a poor, poor exchange.

Ofelia felt tears sting her own eyes and looked furiously back to Hamlet. Any moment now they would light the fire beneath him for she could see the men with the brands, just waiting for the signal to cast them into the ship. It was coated with lard to ensure it flared easily, just as Ofelia's arrows had been back in Bernicia, and it would take only a little time for the flames to engulf the dead king. She couldn't bear it.

While Hamlet's body was still there she could almost believe he would yet leap up, hold his hand high and laugh at having teased them. But that was a nonsense, for he had an ugly, jagged line across his neck and his blood was emptied from him. She'd felt that blood pulse around him so many times in the past. She'd felt its warmth in his fingers when they'd held hers, seen it animate him when he'd fought at her side, and known it pulse furiously as they'd moved together, chest to chest – heart to heart – locked together in love.

She closed her eyes against the image but now, as the druids' prayers reached fever pitch, she recalled Geir's burning three years ago. That had been the night Otto had made Hamlet heir to Denmark and the night Hamlet had made her his own. His very own. The ever-threatening tears spilled at last from her eyes and she put her fingers wonderingly to them, feeling the strange moisture like a balm against her skin.

'With you it is everything,' he'd told her the first time they'd lain together, and she'd shhh-ed him and told him it was just scratching an itch.

What a fool! It had been so simple to Hamlet and to Otto too: 'It is unusual,' he had said, 'for a prince to wed his constable but you are an unusual woman, Ofelia.' Otto had believed that their union was written in the stars and maybe it had been. Maybe, all along, she had been wrong.

The tears flowed faster and Ofelia let them, not caring who saw. She could feel Lars hovering behind her, Flora too, but both knew to leave her to her grief and she was grateful for it. She had trodden life's path alone from the moment her mother had gone and saw no reason to stop.

But now there was that other pyre in her mind's eye – that first one. There was her father's body where Hamlet's lay now and there was her mother before her, all in white, watching as Ofelia watched now and waiting for the flames. And yet? *Had* Sigrid planned it, Ofelia suddenly wondered as the men with the brands stepped forward, or had grief simply consumed her as the flames consumed the ship?

The tendrils of memory that had taunted her before suddenly

swirled, reforming at last into something solid: that morning, before the funeral – her mother dressing her with care, stroking her hair, holding her close and promising her honey-nuts in bed later. Later! Why would she have said that if she had not intended to be there to feed her them? No one else had brought the nuts. It had been Sigrid's plan so had she not, then, intended to die? Was that the reason she'd never said goodbye?

Her scream echoed down the years, as it had so often, but now Ofelia heard something new in it: terror and fear and desperation. Why had Ofelia lost these parts of that dread day? The flames, it seemed, had taken them, as they had taken so much.

She stretched out her hands, fumbling after her mother – not the fevered figure bounding from her into the flames but the one who'd held her earlier that day, the one who'd promised her treats. It had not been planned after all. Sigrid had not wanted to leave them. She'd been sucked, screaming, into the flames by grief and despair and love.

Love.

Ofelia didn't do love. That's what she'd told Lars. What she'd told Hamlet. Gods, why had she told Hamlet that? Why had she let him live – and die – thinking that she did not love him, when the naked truth was that she was nothing *but* love for Hamlet?

'No,' she wept as, in a graceful arc, the five brands curved into the sky and landed in the ship, snatching at the lard and then the wood, devouring it and growing before their eyes as they snaked towards Hamlet's body. 'No!'

She had not told him in life but she would tell him now. She would go with him now.

'Hamlet!'

She lifted her feet and ran. She had become her mother and at last she understood. The pain of the fire would be nothing to the pain of living on without him. It would be a bliss to throw herself onto his chest one last time and be consumed with him as he had consumed her.

She heard gasps, cries. She cared not. She was done with what other people thought. She was done with being the strange one, the woman in man's clothes, the scarred warrior, the lone wolf. She was done with all of it. She saw only the flames and there, in their heart, Hamlet.

She was so close now, so very close. She bent her knees to leap but someone had hold of her tunic hem. Someone had hold of it so tight that she could not leave the ground.

'Let me go, Lars!'

She spun furiously back but it was not Lars. It was Flora.

'No, Ofelia.'

'I love him!'

She roared it loud, up over the merciless crackle of the flames so his spirit might hear it and know she was coming.

'I know you do. And he knew it too.'

'He didn't. I never told him. I refused to tell him.'

'He knew all the same. You two were as one.'

'Which is why I must die with him.'

'Or why you must live for him.'

'No,' she said again. 'It doesn't work that way, Flora. I am too weak for that.'

'Then live for his child.'

'What?'

Ofelia stared at Flora and she smiled.

'You carry it, do you not?' Ofelia frowned; had Flora gone mad? 'Your sickness . . . ?'

Behind her the flames spat and she looked back to see they had reached Hamlet and were biting into him. She had to go to him. Now. And yet . . . She put a hand to her stomach. Was Flora right? Was this the root of her upset stomach? When had she last bled? She had always been irregular but she could not even remember the last time. She'd long since stopped using her potions, thinking the gods had seen that she would be terrible as a mother and made her barren, but maybe that was not true.

'I believe I might be,' she murmured, still hardly crediting it.

'Thought so,' Flora said, far more certainly. 'So live for your child, Ofelia, as your mother did not live for you.'

'She died from grief.'

'She died from lack of friends to hold her back. I can hold you, Ofelia. Lars too. You are not alone.'

'But I do not have *him*.'

'No.' Flora let go of her tunic. 'No, you do not have him.'

She stepped back a little but her eyes stayed fixed on Ofelia, as if begging her to make the right choice. Ofelia looked to the flames. They had reached Hamlet's chest now, his heart. She stared up into the swirling smoke and saw his dear, dear face within it.

You are so good at living, Ofelia, he said in the tendrils of her memory, but was she? Could she be?

'It's too hard,' she cried out to him.

Nothing is too hard for you, Ofelia.

That was true. At least, that was how she had always lived her life and now it was how she must go on living it. For him. For them.

She put out her hand tentatively. Instantly, she felt Flora grasp it and tug her gently away as, behind her, the boat caved in on itself and Hamlet was gone to the land of the dead, taking with him the scream that had haunted Ofelia for so very, very long.

Epilogue

Limfjord, September 606

Far up on the shores of the Limfjord, in the very north of Jutland where the solid mass of the great moors splinters into island after hidden island, a small child wakes, sits up his bed and, with an impish smile, shakes his mother awake. She groans and, looking in through the curtain, Flora sees Ofelia grab the little boy and roll him, giggling madly, beneath the woollen blankets.

She smiles to see it. The blankets were a gift from the new Queen Mairi, sent to them secretly via a humble trader with no message save the inherent promise of warmth and protection. Mairi married Wiglek soon after his treacherous assumption of the throne and is apparently trying to bring the court round to Christianity. It won't work of course; Danes aren't that stupid. Flora supposes Wiglek's newfound Christian charity might keep him from pursuing them but it seems safter to stay far from his reach. Besides, they are happier that way; they are all done with kings.

'Do you remember,' she asked Lars back when they were all still raw with grief for Hamlet, 'how you told me once that you would have been too kind to your enemy if you released him and then he turned and stabbed you? Well, you were right.'

But he shook his head vehemently, his eyes red-rimmed but certain.

'No, Flora. You said that in that case your enemy had not been kind enough, and *you* were right. Kindness is better than cruelty every time.'

It is, perhaps, a creed Mairi would approve of but they are done with religion too. They give thanks every day for the blessings of nature but offer no prayers to any particular god. Whatever is to come after death can wait, for heaven is to be found here in their own little farm. As Flora turns back towards the hearth to watch Lars cutting bread for himself and his two young workers, she smiles. He cares for his men well. He might have just two for now but he values them as much as a battalion of warriors and, in return, they love and serve him loyally.

The farm is thriving. They have twenty cattle and more sheep. The corn is ripening for a second year in the hard-dug fields and Lars has recently bought a healthy brood of piglets that the girls adore. If three-year-old Bebba is ever missing she can be found amongst them, scratching their backs and straightening their tails, watching with glee as they ping back into a curl.

Flora notices Lars cutting extra ham and gives a little cough. Her husband looks up guiltily and gives her a sheepish grin.

'It's nippy out this morning. The lads need food in their bellies to keep them warm.'

'You're right,' she agrees, moving forward.

'And you do too,' he says, sliding an arm around her waist and feeding her a slice.

'I have enough in my belly to keep me warm.'

She curves her hands around its swell and he kisses her.

'I know it and I thank the gods every day for our blessings.'

Flora kisses him back. She thanks the gods too. She thought Hamlet a gift as a husband but always knew herself second-best behind Ofelia, or perhaps third-best with Denmark also jostling for his attention. With Lars she stands first and she realised, when finally he approached her for her hand, that she always had. She told Hamlet once that hearts were rarely given to the deserving but when she gave hers to Lars it was as if everything finally slotted into place and she has never once regretted staying in Denmark to become a humble farmer's wife instead of fleeing for Bernicia.

Her father still thrives over the Northern Seas. Aethelfrith's borders expand all the time and his young wife's belly too for Cathryn seems to produce a new child for him with every year that passes. Udela has also had several children over in Strathclyde but more astonishing than all this is that Bebba, at forty years of age, has borne another son and Flora prays that he brings her mother comfort. He will, at least, be heir to the thriving estate all now know as Bebba's burgh.

'Are the girls still abed?' Lars asks, pulling Flora back into her own land.

'No,' says an indignant voice and there is Bebba in the doorway, tugging along little Gertrude, named for Hamlet's mother who died just days after her son, her heart irreparably broken. Both of their nightdresses are covered in mud. 'We've been in with the pigs.'

'Of course you have!' Lars snatches them up, one in each strong arm. 'Your poor mother is forever washing your clothes.'

'She doesn't mind,' Bebba retorts. 'She says ...' she screws up her little face, remembering ' ...that "life is for living, not for keeping clean".'

'Does she indeed?' Lars grins at Flora. 'Then she has only herself to blame. Ah, good afternoon, sister.'

Ofelia, emerging from her bed with her son on her hip, sticks out her tongue at him.

'Hamlet needed his rest.'

Little Hamlet rattles the beads on Ofelia's plaits in seeming agreement. For some time she kept her dark-blond hair loose but one day after her son's birth she told Flora she was fed up of it getting in her way and demanded her old hairstyle. Flora felt it something of a shame to have the more austere look back in place, but apt too. This way Ofelia can get on with things, which is how she likes it best.

'I thought I might start Hamlet riding today,' she says now.

'Ofelia,' Flora protests. 'He's not yet two.'

'So? He's strong and he has good balance and he's . . . '

'Restless?' Flora supplies.

Ofelia gives a little shrug.

'I guess so. But look, Lars, don't you think that funny little pony you insisted on rescuing on the moors will be perfect for him? For them all. Bebba, Gertrude, fancy taking a turn on the pony's back?'

'Yes!' Bebba roars and Gertrude is quick to follow.

'Good,' Ofelia says. 'That's good. And if you're lucky, your father will be watching and will smile with the gods to see you all at play.'

The children go tumbling out of the door, shouting excitedly, and Flora looks to Ofelia and sees a soft smile play across her scarred lips as she watches them go.

'Beautiful Ofelia,' she says and, though Ofelia tosses her head so that her beads clack against one another, she does not, at last, contradict her.

Acknowledgments

Writing acknowledgments is both a privilege and a fear. I love having the chance to thank the many people who help me to complete my novels but am always terrified that I'm going to miss someone important out. So, to pre-empt that, thank you to ALL my dear friends and family for being there as I go through the slightly mad process of researching and writing about events way, way before our own lifetimes. You all give me a wonderful present to keep me happy and grounded whilst writing about the past that fascinates me so much and, dearly as I'd love to be able to travel through time, I'd always choose to come back home to all of you. Thank you.

Special thanks, as always, to Stuart, Hannah and Alec who have to live with me day in, day out and put up with my constant 'Did you know that in 600 AD . . .' contributions to every conversation. Stuart, in particular, deserves a medal for his patience in the face of endless doubt, worry and boring droning on about my precious work. Thank you.

And on that note, I'd like to thank my 'writing friends', the fabulous Julie Houston and Tracy Bloom, with whom I have been lucky enough to share many a 'writerly' walk (much like normal walks but with a lot of talk of publishers and agents and novel plots) and indeed, many a 'writerly' drink besides (also much like normal glasses of wine but with even more talk of publishers and agents and novel plots!). Writing can be a lonely business and it's wonderful to have people with whom to share the experience. Both Julie and Tracy are always full of wise advice so thank you for all your support.

Much gratitude is due to my editor, the fabulous Anna Boatman, who is such a wonderful source of advice, encouragement and, perhaps most importantly of all, wine! She's truly championed me and my work and hasn't been put off as I've headed further and further back into the mists of the past, for which I am hugely grateful. She, Ellie, and the whole team at Piatkus are marvellous and I thank Ofelia's gods that I have such lovely publishers.

I couldn't finish without thanking the brilliant Kate Shaw, partly because it's always a good idea to keep your agent on your side, but mainly because she just *is* brilliant. I'm very excited that she is now going it alone with The Shaw Agency, which will be a huge success, and am delighted to be a part of her illustrious stable. Thank you, Kate.

Last but by no means least, I must thank you, my readers, as the whole exercise of writing my novels would be utterly pointless without you. My absolute favourite bit of this job is hearing from people who have enjoyed my stories so do please feel free to get in touch via Twitter – @joannacourtney1, Facebook – @joannacourtneyauthor or my website – www.joannacourtney.com.

Historical notes

All my previous novels have been set in the pre-1066 period, so for this one I really enjoyed delving a little further back in time to 600 AD. What fascinated me most was to set my novel in Denmark, a country which had not yet been touched by Christianity, and to explore the fabulously rich Norse culture. Northumbria was also still pagan but when I looked into the Celtic world, I found an area which already had well established Christian communities and studying the clash of the established Norse religion and the new Christian one intrigued me – most especially the astonishing similarities between so many of the festivals, practices and even actual legends. There is some discussion of that below, but first a little about the sources for this 'real' story of Hamlet and how they compare to Shakespeare's immortal play.

Reality vs Story

Real Names

As in all my other novels, I have chosen, where appropriate, to alter the real names of some of the characters to sound smoother to the modern ear and so, hopefully, not interrupt the flow of the story.

There are, however, only a few in this book:

Hamlet	*Amleth*
Otto	*Orvendil*
Cathryn	*Acha*

Records do not condescend to note Aethelfrith's daughters in any detail so I chose Flora and Udela as names of the time. It is the same with Mairi, who was almost certainly called something else – unrecorded – at birth, but may well have taken that iconic name at her confirmation as was often the practice.

It is not clear from records which children Aethelfrith had by Bebba and which by Cathryn (Acha) or, indeed, in what order he married them. It seems to me most likely, however, that he married Danish Bebba after his early period of exile in Denmark and Deiran Cathryn to cement his later conquest of that region, as I show in the novel. It certainly seems highly credible that they were his wives at the same time, as bigamy was far from uncommon in this period.

Acha gave Aethelfrith many sons, several of whom reigned after him but it has been convincingly argued that at least one ruler, most likely Oswiu, must have been Bebba's son to have kept the name Bebba's burgh alive for the fortress. With no evidence to the contrary, I like to think that Oswiu was a late blessing for Aethelfrith's Danish wife.

Evidence for the real Hamlet

Needless to say, records from 600 AD are sparse and unreliable but there is clear evidence of the rule of King Rorik, Hamlet's grandfather. The Skioldungs (petty princes/kings) of Denmark are listed in *Scandinavia Ancient and Modern*, written by Andrew Crichton and Henry Wheaton in 1843 and probably taken from the Yngling Saga, written by Snorri Sturulson in the early thirteenth century.

In this, Rorik Slyngebaud is identified as king in 588. It is unlikely that some of the kings, Rorik included, ruled for as long as the list makes out (Olaf the Mild, for example, apparently ruled for 80 years – highly unlikely in a period when the average life expectancy was only about 40) so some are certainly missing. And to find them, we have to turn to Saxo Grammaticus – a celebrated 'historian' writing in Iceland in the twelfth century from oral traditions and earlier works now lost, and the first to record Hamlet's existence. An imaginative man, fond of dramatic effects and witty trickery, Saxo's story of Amleth, the grandson of Rorik, is long and rather winding but if you are interested, it can be easily bought in modern versions and is well worth a read.

It includes the details that Hamlet's father was murdered by his uncle who then married his widow, and that Hamlet then feigned madness to save his own life. There are various bits of trickery involved in this, including them testing him with the temptation of a woman (the early incarnation of Ofelia) which he escapes thanks to his foster-brother, and hiding a man beneath the straw whilst Hamlet speaks to his mother.

Also in Saxo's story, Hamlet is sent to England with secret orders for his death which he discovers and alters to ensure the deaths of his minders instead, securing for himself the hand of the king's daughter. And in this 'original' he then returns to Denmark to retake his throne before going back to Britain to fetch his wife. Whilst there he is sent to woo the Scottish queen Hermentrude on the king's behalf. A man-slayer who has had every previous lover murdered, she luckily – or not – falls for Hamlet, and he for her, so they marry. Sadly, once he takes her back to Denmark she turns on him and plots with Wiglek, leading eventually to Hamlet's death and her marriage to Wiglek and assumption of the sole queenship. And with that, as Saxo succinctly puts it, 'So ended Amleth'.

Shakespeare's Play

It is easy to see some of the features of Shakespeare's famous play in Saxo's early version of the story:

- Rosencrantz and Guildenstern were born out of the retainers with the letter asking for Hamlet's death and, indeed, still carry it in the play.
- Shakespeare's Hamlet feigns madness and kills Polonius when he hides behind the arras in his mother's room.
- Hamlet travels to England, although in the play he is attacked by pirates who handily bring him back to Denmark so he never actually makes it to English, or indeed Scottish, shores.
- We see him being tempted by Ofelia as an 'updated' version of the temptress figure, though sadly the bard chose to make her a rather weak, girlie and ultimately mad figure – something I saw fit to correct in *Fire Queen*!
- It is also possible to see Hamlet's good friend Horatio in the foster-brother who warns him of temptation.

What Shakespeare has essentially retained are all the dramatic tropes and trickery of Saxo's story but placed squarely in an Elizabethan context and perhaps the only surprise is that he did not include the marvellously evil Hermentrude. It is, mind you, far from certain that Shakespeare read Saxo Grammaticus himself. The story of Amleth was recorded on manuscript in the thirteenth century but found popularity later when it was printed in a French version by Francois de Belleforest as part of his 1570 collection of tragic legends, *Histoires Tragiques*.

The first recorded English translation of this, *The Hystorie of Hamblet*, appeared in 1608 but Shakespeare's play seems to have been first performed in 1602. There is no evidence that Shakespeare could speak French so either copies, now lost, were around before this or he used another source.

This was most probably a play written in the 1580s of which, sadly, no copy or even record of the title have survived. There are accounts of performances at Burbage's Shoreditch Playhouse but all that we know of the play is that it had a character named Hamlet and a ghost who cried 'Hamlet, revenge!' It is usually attributed to

Thomas Kyd but it is, of course, possible that it was actually written by Shakespeare as an early prototype of the play he perfected and released into the world in 1602.

I should state now that we do not know as recorded fact that Hamlet made it to the Bernician court of King Aethelfrith, or came up against the Dal Riatan King Aedan, though Saxo tells us that he married both an Angle and a Celtic princess and the most prominent petty kings in the relevant areas at the time were these two men.

Female warriors

There is no actual historical record of Ofelia in Hamlet's court so I have shamelessly created her as a female warrior because the idea of this fascinates me and because there truly is evidence of such figures.

Perhaps most thrilling is the recent discovery that the body of an honoured warrior, found buried in Birka, Sweden, in 1889, and long held up as an example of a fierce chieftain or professional soldier, is actually female. Some have raised questions about whether there was a second body, now lost, or whether the role was more symbolic than actual but to me far and away the most exciting – and simplest – solution is that this was, indeed, a female warrior and probably a female war leader. I hope further research will be done into this and eagerly await its conclusions.

Whatever the realities of the Birka warrior, there is no doubt that Norse legends offer us plenty of female fighters, such as *Brynhildr* in the *Vǫlsunga saga* and *Hervor* in *Hervarar saga ok Heiðrek*, and whilst these are clearly fiction, they must have been based on fact to be accepted by the audiences of the day.

There are also historical accounts. Saxo Grammaticus reported that shield-maidens fought on the side of the Danes at the Battle of Brávellir in the year 750. Then the eleventh century Byzantine historian John Skylitzes, recorded that when Sviatoslav I of Kiev was defeated by Emperor John in the Siege of Dorostolon in

971, the victors were stunned at discovering armed women among the fallen warriors.

Neither of these writers were known for their servitude to absolute truth (not considered a vital element of 'history' in the period). Their elaborations, however, tended to be more in the mythical additions to their tales than in fabricating roles for people. They both speak as if they are telling the truth about female fighters and I think we would be wrong to dismiss the idea as some sort of collective fantasy.

What's more, we know that there were female war-leaders among the Celts – Boudicca being the most famous example – and that occasionally female warriors crop up in much later history. Robert Guiscard, the Norman Duke of Apulia, who conquered much of Italy, married a local aristocrat called Sichelgaita, celebrated as a woman of great stature who fought like a man and frequently led troops into battle. Joan of Arc was a celebrated war-leader and, if we put aside issues of her saintliness, there is no doubt that she was able to command troops even as late as the misogynistic fifteenth century so for me there can be little doubt that whilst female warriors were not a normal part of life, there were enough to make the successful ones an accepted part of society.

The World in 600 AD

The Norse Cosmos

The Norse people largely believed that the cosmos was crafted around *Yggdrasil*, the giant Tree of Life, in whose branches nestled nine worlds. At the centre was *Midgard*, the land of men, and at the top was *Asgard*, the land of the gods, with the two connected by *Bifrost* – the rainbow bridge. There was also a second land of the gods, *Vanaheim* – home to the Vanir tribe of gods (as opposed to the leading Aesir tribe in *Asgard*). The other lands were both population-specific, such as *Alfheim*, land of the elves, *Jotunheim*, land of the giants, and *Svartalfheim*, land of the dwarves, and condition-specific, like *Nilfheim*, land of ice, and *Muspelheim*, land of fire. Beneath the roots sat *Hel*, or *Helheim*, the land of the dead (or at least of those dead not granted entry into the feasting hall of *Valhalla* in *Asgard*). *Yggdrasil*'s roots were nourished by *The Well of Urd* which was looked after by the *Norns* – a trio of women with the power to see into the future of men and even to influence it. The moon and the sun were pulled around the skies above the tree in chariots driven by the brother and sister gods, *Mani* and *Sol*, and the whole tree was encircled by the threatening sea-serpent/dragon, *Jormungand*.

There have been many attempts to draw this cosmos but this is a little disingenuous as the people of the time seem to have felt no need to pin it pictorially. The view of the world as a tree that needs nourishing is an appealing and even logical one, but for those that believed in it, it was a world that was in constant flux. They looked to the regular turning of the seasons, marked by great festivals (see below), to reassure themselves that it was still stable enough to sustain life.

Norse gods

The Norse gods can be quite hard to pin down to specific characteristics and beliefs as any number of different stories circulated about them and more were added daily, so that it was less a set-in-stone pantheon than a well of legends from which individuals could draw whatever they wished. The gods were believed to be the ancestors of men and to have a continued, and in many ways fairly human ongoing life, so they were marvellously fluid figures. Nonetheless there seem, by 600 AD, to have been some fairly accepted truths about some of the core gods:

Odin, otherwise known as the *Allfather*, was the chief of gods in *Asgard*. He ruled the Aesir tribe and presided over *Valhalla*, the great hall where dead warriors went to hunt all day and feast all night in glorious perpetuity. He was a god of war but also of poetry and, although he was supposedly a great figure, he also features in many human stories in which he ventures far from *Asgard* on sole quests and adventures. He was far from infallible, sometimes playing tricks and getting himself into trouble and that seems to have been acceptable to his people who did not expect their gods to be immutable figures. Perhaps most known for his quest for knowledge, *Odin* is believed to have died momentarily in return for eternal wisdom, as represented by runes.

Thor was believed to be *Odin*'s oldest son by his wife, *Frigga*, and grew to prominence in the later Viking age as the god of war, known for his strength, courage and sense of duty, and it is to him that Ofelia turns when she is bored in Bernicia and desperate for combat. His weapon of choice was his hammer *Mjollnir* (lightning) and thunder was the noise of it being wielded in the defence of the land of the gods and, indeed, of men.

Freya, Ofelia's favourite goddess, is the 'party girl' of the gods. Known for her fondness of love, fertility, beauty and fine material possessions, she is accused in one of the Eddic poems of having slept with all of the gods and elves, including her brother, *Frey*, and she doesn't refute this. She is also, however, associated with magic and control of the souls of the dead and is a knowledgeable and powerful figure, worthy of Ofelia's devotion.

Loki is the god that Ofelia calls upon in the 'night of the arrows' as he was renowned for his sense of mischief. His place in the Norse pantheon is the most uncertain of all as stories about both his parentage and offspring abound and often contradict each other. He is, however, usually held to be the father of the dubious trio of *Hel*, goddess of the underworld, *Jormungand*, the fearsome sea-serpent/dragon and the giant wolf *Fenrir*. Known as a shapeshifter, he features regularly in stories as a troublemaker for both men and gods.

The Norse Calendar

For ease of understanding I have chosen to stick with our months to denote the passing of time in this novel but they are not names that the people of the time would have recognised. The core pattern was the same – the year being divided into twelve moon phases, with an additional thirteenth one inserted every few years to keep the 'months' in line with the solstices and, therefore, the seasons.

The darkest period was called *Skammdegí*, meaning the Dark Days and the brightest period *Nóttleysa*, which pretty much means insomnia, showing how short the nights often were (and are) in Scandinavia. The winter months were, as far as we can tell from sparse records: *Gormánuður, Ýlir, Mörsugur, Þorri, Goa* and *Einmánuður*. And the summer months were: *Harpa, Skerpla, Sólmánuður, Heyannir, Tvímánuður* and *Haustmánuður*.

Norse Festivals

Jul (or Yule) took place across the twelve nights at the end of our December and was the most important of all Norse holidays, marking the birth of the new sun.

Disting took place around our February 2nd and was a celebration of the arrival of Spring.

Eostre was marked around our March 20th as a celebration of the Spring Goddess of the same name and was a festival of renewal, rejoicing and fertility.

Walpurgis was celebrated around our May 1st and many of its traditions live on in May Day. If *Eostre* ramped the joy of *Disting* up a notch, then *Walpurgis* really took it to new levels. This was a night of joy and lust, although also one of darkness as it marked *Odin's* self-sacrifice upon *Yggdrasil* and the dead were believed to have full sway upon the earth on this last night of the *Wild Hunt*.

Midsummer was celebrated then (as now) around June 21st on the solstice, or longest night, when the power of the Sun was at its height.

Lithasblot was the name given to the harvest festival, held at the start of our August to give thanks to *Ertha,* goddess of the Earth, for her bounty and to ask for blessing on the year to come.

Winternights was at the end of our October to mark the beginning of the winter season. It had its roots in the Celtic festival of *Samhain* and remains important today as Halloween.

The Wild Hunt. The Norse believed that the winter weather of storms, darkness and general disturbance, was created by the *Wild Hunt* riding across the skies. This was the gods chasing down the dead who had been released through the winter, led by the evil wolf *Skoll* who wished to catch *Sol,* the sun, and kill her before she gave birth to her daughter – the new sun. *Odin* led the charge on his eight-legged horse *Sleipnir,* and *Frey,* brother of *Freya,* rode out on his boar *Gullipnir* at the darkest point of the year to defeat the wolf and ensure continued light in the world.

Influence on Christianity

I hope that readers of this book will have noticed (as Mairi does) a huge number of similarities between several of the Norse festivals and later Christian ones and I find this fascinating. Before researching this book, I already knew that the Christian church was incredibly clever at 'adapting' existing festival dates for their own calendar to make people more likely to accept them but I didn't realise quite how many of the actual features of the festivals and, indeed, the stories behind them, were also retained:

The death of Odin: As discussed in the section on *Walpurgis* above, *Odin* was held to have had himself tied/nailed to *Yggdrasil*, the World Tree, for nine days of suffering in order to understand the will of the gods through the runes. He died – albeit only for moments – in order that the rest of the world could have the light of understanding, a tradition quite clearly echoed in the story of Christ's sacrifice upon the cross.

Hel: *Hel* was the goddess of the underworld, living in *Hel* or *Helheim*, the dark realm beneath the earth where those not honoured with entry into *Valhalla* in the land of the gods (because they had the foolishness to die of illness rather than battle wounds) were condemned to go. The word seems to have been lifted direct into Christian tradition and as *Hel*'s brother was the sea-serpent *Jormungand*, it is easy to see how together they formed an early prototype of the fork-tailed *Satan*.

Fasting at Walpurgis: The Christian church was far from the first to invent the idea of fasting to honour the gods and the nine days leading up to *Walpurgis* and *Odin's* death could be said to be the precursor to Christian lent when Christ wandered in the desert before his own sacrifice.

Eostre: So many of the inherent traditions of today's Easter celebrations come directly from pagan times, including gifts of coloured eggs for prosperity and fecundity for the coming season, and the use of the hare or rabbit as the symbol of this festival for its reproductive ability. Even the name Easter comes not from Christian teachings but from the name of the Norse goddess of Spring and I enjoyed exploring the clash (or, indeed, meeting) of the two cultures in the scene of poor, devout Mairi's nightmarish wedding.

All Hallows: Much like Easter, many of the traditions (these days more secular than religious) of Halloween come straight from *Samhain/Winternights*. The leaders of the early Christian church were clever enough to appropriate the idea of the dead walking the earth, marking All Saints Day on November 1st and shifting the pagan sense of awe for one's lost ancestors into a fear of the dead to ensure that people turned to the saints – and therefore the church – for protection.

Jul: As with *Walpurgis* foreshadowing Christ's death, *Jul* or Yule (a word we still use today) set up many of our traditions surrounding his birth. That holly and ivy come from pagan notions is quite well known but perhaps less so is that Father Christmas has his roots in *Odin*, and Rudolf in *Odin's* eight-legged horse *Sleipnir*. Even the tradition of leaving out shoes/stockings for gifts comes from Norse tradition, with them offering gifts of hay and honey-balls for the tired horse, much as we now leave out carrots and sherry! Similarly, the idea of the twelve days of Christmas can first be found in pagan times when they were seen as the critical days when the new sun was carefully nursed into life.

Valisblot: (or *Vali's* feast, *Vali* being *Odin's* youngest son) is one other festival that, although I don't actually explore it in the novel, is worth a mention here as it fell on February 14th and was later smoothly transmogrified into Saint Valentine's day.

Places in the novel

Denmark

I had to totally re-learn my idea of Denmark when I started researching its geography to write this book. I confess I had always thought that what I now know to be the peninsular of Jutland *was* Denmark but although Jutland is a large land mass, Denmark is actually made up of over four hundred islands of varying sizes, of which the key central pair are Zealand and Fynn. Indeed, at the risk of massively over-simplifying, it could be said that Zealand is a little like the south of England with its perceived riches, power and slightly better climate, whilst Jutland, with its hardier, more remote peoples, could be said to be like the North. Certainly Ofelia and Hamlet, true Jutlanders, see it that way.

The picture is further complicated when we look at Denmark in 600 AD, as at this time – and for many centuries after – it also included the province of Skaane, which is now the southerly tip of Sweden. Looked at in this way (see the map at the start of the book) Zealand is very much central to Denmark with Jutland and Skaane protecting it, like giant parentheses, either side.

It is to be expected, therefore, that the High King would normally base himself on Zealand. Those familiar with Shakespeare's *Hamlet* might have expected to find him ruling from Elsinor or Helsinor, on the westerly coast of that island, but although it does seem to have been a recognised place at the time – and is where Ofelia and Hamlet choose to attack when they return to Denmark – central government seems to have been predominantly from Roskilde, sheltered at the bottom of the huge Roskilde Fjord. Helsinor was most likely a guard/communication post between the central island of Zealand and the corresponding Helsingborg just across the narrow Ore Sound in Skaane.

Bernicia and Deira

I had to work hard to resist calling Aethelfrith's kingdom Northumbria as it was not known by that name until sometime later, though I did foreshadow it by showing him yearning to create a kingdom of North Angles to rival those in the East and the South, areas we more readily know as 'Saxon'. Bernicia was the northerly half of the north-west coast of what is now England, around Bebba's burgh (Bamburgh – see below) and Deira was the southerly half around what would later become Durham and York. There had long been skirmishing between the rulers of these two areas but Aethelfrith was the first to truly unite them and subsequent leaders from both sides (Aethelfrith was eventually defeated by Cathryn's exiled brother Edwin who ruled after him before his own son retook the throne) worked to keep the larger kingdom intact.

Bebba's burgh is now known as Bamburgh and is still a beautiful and striking fortress, though the current lovely building is a culmination of centuries of building and rebuilding from the Normans onwards. There is strong evidence that it was originally called Dinguardi and that its modern name came from Aethelfrith's Danish wife, Bebba who held it as her own. Bede in his *Ecclesiastical History of the English People*, completed around 731, tells us that: *Eadfered Flesaurs (Aethelfrith the Flexer) reigned twelve years in Bernicia, and twelve others in Deira, and gave to his wife Bebba, the town of* Dynguoaroy, *which from her is called Bebbanburg.* We do not know if Aethelfrith gifted it to her when he married his second Deiran wife, as I show in the novel, but it certainly seems to have become known as Bebba's burgh around this period.

Aet Gefrin is now known as Yeavering and it is still possible to take an open path up Yeavering Bell and see the remains of the ancient hillfort on the top. I would strongly recommend visiting it if you get a chance as it is a striking place and, although there are no remains of Aethelfrith's wooden halls there any more, the smaller, flat-topped hill on which it was built can still be clearly seen.

Dal Riata

Dunadd was a great fortress at the heart of the numerous peninsulas and islands of western Scotland in what is now Argyll. It was set on a dramatic single hill within a large area of flat, marshy ground so stood both secure and easy to see from miles around.

Occupied from at least 2000 years ago as a hillfort, and marked by ancient ringed fortifications, visitors to Dunadd can still see ancient rock carvings, including the 'ring marks' that are found all over Britain and that Flora's women so gleefully use to invoke fertility in Bernicia. Dunadd rose to prominence in 500-800 AD as the centre of Dal Riata with Aedan as one of the key figures in its importance.

Dal Riata was the home of the Scots tribe, originally based in Ireland but by 600 AD also firmly occupying the watery mainland of western Scotland (as it was to be known later). Aedan was king of that mainland area and was a longstanding and influential ruler. He worked for years with Columba – later Saint Columba – to set up the famous monastery on Iona from which to spread the word of Christ and it is thanks to Adomnan, one of Columba's success-ors who wrote a biography of him towards the end of the seventh century, that we have much of our information about the area and its activities.

I hope that these notes explain some of the history behind *Fire Queen*. It perhaps tells you that Ofelia was harder to unearth from history than Lady Macbeth in *Blood Queen* but, although the actual characters were tricky to trace in any detail, the geographical, cul-tural and political contexts are all as accurate as I could possibly make them, ensuring that although we will never be able to prove this is the way the events unfolded, it is very possible that they did so. It has been a joy for me to release Ofelia from the shackles of Shakespeare's rather wet interpretation of her character and to let her into the world as a strong, vibrant and exciting woman and I hope you enjoyed this version of her story.

The myth of Lady Macbeth looms large.

Discover her story ...

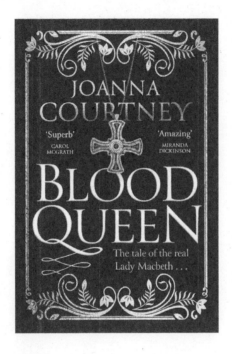

Available now from

piatkus